An unrepentant rogue discovers danger and unexpected passion when he finally meets the fragile lady he could have wed in this second Distinguished Rogues romance.

"Do you know what I think, Giles?" Lilly's low voice teased him, her fingers brushing his sleeve.

"What is that, oh frightening ghost?"

She laughed and danced away a few steps. "I believe you want to kiss me again. Your face is quite stern."

"That could be an accurate assumption, Miss Winter." At her giggle, he added, "It is altogether possible for me to assume, in turn, that you wish to kiss me as well." He raised an eyebrow and then lunged for her.

BESTSELLING AUTHOR

BROKEN

Distinguished Rogues

DISTINGUISHED ROGUES SERIES

The characters and events portrayed in this book are fictitious. Any similarity to real persons, living or dead, is purely coincidental and not intended by the author.

Dedication

———◆———

To NaNoWriMo ~ for prompting me to finish a
first draft in under 30 days.

Prologue

———— ◆ ————

London, 1811

It was a rare day when a disturbance could interfere with Giles Wexham's pursuit of pleasure, but the presence of a ghost hovering at the door of Huntley House's guest bedchamber proved a real distraction for the Earl of Daventry.

The delicate specter shimmered at the edge of the room, neither writhing nor moaning, but watching with an intensity that would disturb if she were made of flesh and bone.

Until now, Giles had never seen a ghost. He had always supposed these visions were the product of a bored mind, but he had to admit that being the subject of a ghost's attention was not as frightening as he'd always heard. In fact, Giles found it downright arousing.

The little wraith seemed to float, and he wondered if a strong puff of air would dismiss her. A halo of wispy, white-blonde hair hung around her pale face and cascaded over her shoulders to her waist, disordered, as if just raised from sleep or the grave.

Delicate lips formed an O as her gaze dropped low to the woman on her knees before him. He grew harder, if that was possible.

Unaware of their audience, Sabine, his lover for the night, continued to bob on his length. Giles bit back a moan of intense pleasure as the dual attention stirred every sense he possessed.

Thin, ghostly fingers twisted into the folds of her rumpled white shroud as if nervous, though what a ghost could be nervous about escaped him.

Although he would have liked to prolong the moment, his lover's efforts were producing pleasurable results. Sabine had her hand cupped around his stones, so Giles gave up on the soulless ghost in favor of the warmth of mouth and fingers.

He curled his hand around his lover's neck and closed his eyes to focus, enjoying the wet lips encircling him. Pleasure clutched his spine and he thrust his hips forward, impatient for sweet oblivion to claim him. After four good strokes of hand and tongue, his whole body pulsed and shivers raced down his legs at the force of his much-needed release.

Yet when he raised his lids to view the room, disappointment stung. The ghost had vanished into the night as if she'd never been.

Chapter One

———◆———

Summer, 1813

Giles forced a smile to his lips to welcome Lord Winter to his country estate in Northamptonshire. "Winter," Giles called. "Welcome back to Cottingstone."

The newcomer shook his head. At least the old baron could pretend to look pleased that Giles had broken his rule about receiving a guest at Cottingstone Manor. But no, Lord Winter's face wore a perpetual frown, just like every other time their paths had crossed in London.

"Daventry." The older man's quavering voice, pitched somewhat lower than Giles', betrayed exhaustion. "The place hasn't changed."

Giles held out his hand. "You must be weary. Dinner won't be served for an hour, but I have some excellent whiskey to soothe you while we wait."

The baron crushed Giles' fist. "Brandy would be preferable in its place—especially today. But first..." Winter returned to the carriage.

Giles took a step back toward his butler. "Dithers?"

"I shall switch the decanters when I return to the house, milord," he promised.

"Do that, and ask Cook if dinner can be brought forward,"

Giles murmured. "Lord Winter doesn't appear in good health."

"I don't believe *his* health is the problem, milord," Dithers replied.

Without another word of explanation, the butler stepped back, leaving Giles to ponder to whose health he had referred. The baron traveled alone and often. His servants all looked a disciplined, healthy bunch. But they moved carefully on the carriage and didn't speak overloud. The horses were settled swiftly, too. Calm, efficient, eerie.

As Giles stepped out of the way of a burdened footman, a bloodcurdling howl erupted from beyond the house. Every man stopped and stared, not in the direction of the sound, but at the dark carriage they were unloading.

The steady pounding of paws heralded the arrival of Giles' ancient wolfhound, Atticus. Judging by the dog's speed and his whining agitation, something was seriously amiss with him. In fact, this level of energy from the hound was more than a little surprising. He had spent most of Giles' visit lying under his feet snoring.

Atticus skidded to a stop beside the closed door of the carriage. If the door had been open, Giles was sure the hound would have barged his way in. He ignored the restless horses and stunned attendants to haul his beast out of the way. The dog was heavy and determined to stay exactly where he was, but Giles managed to pull him aside.

Lord Winter stared at the dog, nodded, and then stepped into the carriage. When he emerged a few moments later, he held a body in his arms.

Atticus, generally so docile, whined and whimpered, straining against Giles in such a fashion as to cause alarm. Lord Winter adjusted the black-cloaked figure, and the bundle moaned.

Every hair on the back of Giles' neck rose. That was a woman's moan—one in great pain. He renewed his grip on the restless dog.

Lord Winter moved slowly toward the house, keeping his movements smooth. The grim set of his features showed just how much effort he expended not to jostle his burden. There was agony on that rugged face, too much grief for one man to bear alone.

With a hitched brow, Giles glanced at his butler, but Dithers revealed nothing. The butler scurried ahead to push the main doors wide and gestured Lord Winter inside. Giles followed, imitating the baron's quiet steps and keeping Lord Winter in sight.

Just inside the doorway, the baron stopped and bent his head to the bundle in his arms.

"Atticus." A voice carried to Giles' ears, eerily soft and pain-filled.

Giles only just managed to stop the dog from flinging himself at the woman.

"Atticus, come." Again, that voice called his hound, and a pale arm slipped from beneath the black travel cloak to hang down limply.

Atticus whined, pulling Giles forward unwillingly. The dog reached the woman's hand, rasping his wet tongue against it. At first, she jerked back, but returned to rub the dog. Since Giles held the beast, he couldn't miss the shudder that vibrated through Atticus. Giles was stunned by the sensation.

"Atticus, heel." The woman spoke again, and Giles tensed as the voice tickled his memory.

The wolfhound calmed instantly, pulled free of Giles' slackened grip, and moved along with Lord Winter. Troubled, Giles followed them upstairs.

Once at the chamber, a nurse, who Giles only now noticed, pulled the drapes closed, ushering Dithers out with agitated flicks of her hands. Lord Winter lowered his burden to the high bed, removed the dark cloak, and pulled the blankets tightly around her.

From his position at the doorway, Giles noticed no more details of the woman, but her identity intrigued him. She knew his dog's name? What was Lord Winter doing driving across England with an ill woman in tow? Surely, he could have arranged some other care, rather than dragging her on what appeared to be a painful journey.

To his surprise, Atticus padded across the room and stepped onto the dais. Once on the bed, the hound nosed in close to the woman's hand. Surely Lord Winter would shoo him away.

But the woman clutched at the dog's shaggy coat, pulling him against her side with a soft sigh.

His guest said nothing as he joined Giles at the door, so Giles stepped aside to allow the baron room to pass. Winter looked over his shoulder once before closing the door on the woman, dog, and nurse.

"What the devil is going on?" he demanded.

"Not now, lad," Winter begged and turned away.

Giles stared after his guest in shock at his lack of manners then hurried to catch up. He rarely entertained guests for a reason. Giles liked privacy and peace at Cottingstone.

"I trust you had an uneventful journey," he asked.

Winter grunted and strode for Dithers who was holding a glass of brandy.

An hour later, not even spirits and a pleasant meal had sweetened his mood or made him more forthcoming. The food had been more than satisfactory, braised duck with plum sauce, followed by truffles and plum pudding.

The company at the table, on the other hand, had been poor.

Giles was fast losing his patience with the baron. Unease knotted his shoulders. The woman's voice nagged at the edge of his memory. She was a puzzle he couldn't solve. The man opposite offered nothing by way of explanation for her presence but stoically downed glass after glass of Giles' best brandy as if determined to forget.

The baron had aged in the last few years. Iron-gray hair graced the sides of his head and candlelight reflected off the top. The once proud Corinthian dressed with supremely dull taste, but, given his habit of constant travel, perhaps that was more a matter of practicality than choice.

"Never thought she'd survive this long," the baron began suddenly, staring into his glass as he swirled the contents around. "Been years more than I thought she'd have. Dragged her from one end of the country to the other in the hope of a cure, but it has all been for nothing. Quacks and charlatans. Every one of them useless."

Lord Winter poured another large drink with unsteady hands. "She was such a bright little thing, always ready with a smile. Full of life. A perfect angel." He shook his head as if frustrated by his own words. "I just could not bear to leave her behind. You have to be so careful with her."

Giles didn't respond, but he inched closer, intrigued by Winter's words to be sure he caught them all.

"Too many accidents. Too many mistakes. Her reaction to your hound was the first real response I've witnessed in years. I'd stopped believing she was there. It has gotten my hopes up again, but nothing good can come to her now. It's too late."

"I'm sure you're doing the best you can," Giles said, not knowing if he spoke the truth, but positive he should say something rallying.

"I wish I could believe that. No man should live longer than his child."

It took only a moment for Giles to review the Winter family tree in his mind. He reared back. "That's *Lilly?*" Giles jerked at his cravat, suddenly hot at the thought of her.

"Who else did you imagine it might be?" Winter's composed veneer blurred away fast under the influence of brandy. He sat forward, eyes alight with anger.

Giles had no answer other than the truth. "I was told your daughter died years ago, sir."

Lord Winter's face turned an ugly shade of red. "And who told you such a blatant falsehood?"

As a rule, Giles preferred to speak the truth, but in this case, he hesitated. He did not like to meddle between a man and his wife, but if Lady Winter had spread lies, the baron had a right to know. "I'm afraid your wife informed me, sir."

Lord Winter slumped in his chair, rubbing a hand over his face. When he looked up, the baron's face held pain. "What is a man supposed to do when the mother of his child would rather her be dead?" Lord Winter sobbed on the last word, rusty grief shattering the peace of the room.

In his entire life, Giles had never been in the presence of a crying man. Drunk, vomiting, or fucking, yes. Occasionally all three on the same night, but never crying. Where was one supposed to look?

Lord Winter cried like a man who had held back years of anguish. Giles sat silently, waiting uncomfortably for the storm to pass. Lord Winter shifted in the chair, finally turning his face away. The man surely had to be embarrassed.

Perhaps he should pretend he hadn't heard the sorrow. Giles rose from his chair, poured Winter another drink, and then moved to the window to look out into the stormy night. But his body screamed for flight.

Years ago, Winter's daughter had fallen from Cottingstone Bridge into the stream that ran, flood full, through the property. She'd only been a young girl at the time, and her injuries were so serious that their betrothal had been severed soon after. When Giles had crossed paths with Lady Winter wearing mourning black in London, she had spoken of her lost daughter with credible grief. But why would Lady Winter wish people to believe her daughter was dead?

He glanced at Lord Winter as several odd things about his behavior fell into place. Lilly remained unwell after all this time. Had Lady Winter given up home and rejected the burden Lilly's care would impose on her?

Behind him, Lord Winter blew his nose, then clinked glass against teeth as he took another drink. "I know my search for a cure cannot continue. I have to accept that, but I cannot take her home. Living at Dumas would certainly speed her death."

The baron paused to clear his throat, as if his words had suddenly stuck. Giles was half-afraid Winter would suggest he still marry Lilly. Surely, God wouldn't torture them both with such an ill-advised union.

"I have heard there is a place in Wales that might take her, a home of sorts. I have made plans to see it soon, but I do not believe Lillian can handle the journey yet. With your agreement, I would like to leave her here while I inspect the situation and make arrangements. She will be no trouble. It's why I pressed for the invitation to visit. You see, Cottingstone is on the way. If it is acceptable, I will return and take her there as soon as she can travel again."

Giles swallowed a sigh of relief, but panic still threatened. Giles had a well-deserved reputation as a rake and Lord Winter was so upset that he was not thinking properly. "You cannot mean to leave her in a bachelor household?"

"I know it is beyond the pale to impose on an old association. I would not consider it normally, but you see how she is. Travel is very hard on her; she can barely stand an hour in the carriage. If

Lillian can rest here for a time, she will be stronger for the next stage of the journey. The nurse is capable of taking care of her. You need do nothing to entertain her. I hadn't initially intended to tell her where we are, but she recognized the dog and remembers this place, it seems. She said to thank you for inviting her to stay."

Giles caught his open-mouthed reflection in the night-dark glass and swiftly closed his mouth. Thank God his back was to Lord Winter. Giles hadn't expected her to remember him; he hadn't spoken to her since she was a child.

Try as he might, he couldn't think of an excuse that would have them both gone tomorrow but the obvious one he'd already brought up. Lord Winter had to know of his reputation. His presence could ruin any innocent woman's good name just by breathing the same air she did, no matter her physical state.

The baron must be barking mad to consider leaving his daughter without an army of stiff-backed chaperones between them. It was the grief talking, Giles thought. Come morning, the baron would see reason and change his mind.

Giles made a noncommittal sound, turned to the sideboard, and poured himself a very large brandy. God, he was going to need it. When Lord Winter eventually bade him good night, Giles took his brandy decanter to bed with him.

The ghost haunted his dreams that night.

In brandy-infused visions, the white-clad girl glided round and round him as he lay back on his soft bed. He yearned for her touch, but she remained elusive, just out of arm's reach. Her soft whisper spoke to him of earthly delights she could no longer share.

Giles dared her to come closer, to spread her tattered soul over him, to ease the ache they both shared. A cold touch slid along his straining leg muscles. He breathed raggedly, begging her to come near, to keep her hands on him. Ghostly fingers brushed against his thigh and he groaned, kicking the remaining sheet off his body, overwhelmed by need.

Lightning cracked outside the manor and he woke with a start. He was alone, as if the ghost had never been. Flashes of light danced on the walls as he blinked away the remnants of sleep and sat up against the headboard of his large empty bed, breathing hard.

The memory of the ghost had plagued him the last two years, disturbing his dreams, invading his waking moments too sometimes. The little sprite had the instincts of a bloodhound and found him every time he dabbled in pleasure within the walls of Huntley House in London.

Tonight's dream was different. The sense of being together was strong, more like the moments she appeared in his waking hours. Present but apart from him. Her watchfulness added to his arousal, but she usually kept a distance. Only he dreamed of further intimacies.

Giles' laugh echoed in the empty, dark room as thunder boomed outside.

What folly. He lusted after a ghost—a dead woman.

———— ✦ ————

Bartholomew Barrette clenched his fists to keep from strangling the blacksmith. Worthless, empty intelligence was all the imbecile could sprout. Instead of doing as he pleased, watching the blacksmith's eyes bulge as he crushed his throat, Bartholomew barked an order for his groom to give the dirt-encrusted behemoth something for his trouble. Then he'd wait in the taproom for his carriage to be ready.

Voices stopped as he stepped through the low doorway. He paused to get his bearings. Farmers with sun-branded faces turned to watch his arrival, no doubt stunned by his fine appearance. It wouldn't be every day that a man of his distinction graced this hovel, a village too insignificant to be recorded on any map. No doubt his presence would be the highlight of their puny, miserable lives.

He let them look their fill.

Satisfied with the awed silence his presence evoked, Bartholomew peered through the swirling pipe smoke and attempted to find a pleasing location suitable for a man of his station to sit. The inn was grimy and poorly arrayed, so he raised an eyebrow at the nearest mud-splattered farmer, choosing a window spot out of all the occupied chairs.

At the innkeeper's prompting, the slow-witted farmer vacated the space. "A right busy afternoon we're havin', sir. Can I get you sommat to drink?"

Placated by the man's attention, Bartholomew graced him with a look and gingerly lowered himself to the chair. "Ale, and be quick about it."

The greasy innkeeper hurried to do his bidding, pausing to offer a stubby-toothed smile to a cow-faced piece of fancy before disappearing from sight. Bartholomew clenched his teeth, patience wearing thin at the innkeeper's easy distraction.

The man could flirt when he'd done his duty and served a paying customer. How much he'd get would depend on how quick about it he chose to be. Given the state of Bartholomew's temper, the man would be lucky to see a farthing.

Conversation resumed around him at a low rumble.

The blacksmith had claimed no black carriage had passed through the village today or yesterday. He'd heard the same news from every stop thus far as he retraced his steps. The old man couldn't vanish from the world, no matter how hard he tried. Winter always relied on friends to provide him houseroom, for him and that greedy brat he carted about.

The barkeep scurried through the tables and pushed a tankard across the battered wood. Bartholomew didn't thank him. He tossed a coin to the table with careless grace. The man took it and his rank stench away.

How to find them quickly?

The old man had never evaded him before. It was unusually slippery of him to depart in the dark of night without saying where he was headed. The nurse he'd bribed to report to him hadn't managed to send him word about the last minute trip either.

He would have to backtrack, find where his uncle's carriage had parted ways with his expected heading, and then use all possible speed to catch up with them before Lilly was buried.

He needed to see her body.

Given he was Lord Winter's only male heir, he had a devilishly tricky need to avoid accusation of any involvement in Lilly's murder. He couldn't risk losing his inheritance.

Bartholomew swallowed a mouthful of ale then grimaced at

the taste. The coaching house served pigswill instead of ale. He'd never been served a fouler drop. He pushed the tankard away in disgust.

The innkeeper hurried over. "Can I get you sommat else, sir?"

Bartholomew didn't bother to reply. His mind burned with anger as yet another simple wish failed to eventuate. He curled his fingers into a fist, but a movement at the door diverted him from the innkeeper. "Carriage is ready, Mr. Barrette."

At last.

As he strode out the door, he made a vow not to let the old man and that pathetic bitch forget him. A man with Winter blood pulsing through his veins could not tolerate a snub from his own flesh and blood. He would not.

The stable hands held his horses and carriage at the ready. He flung himself into the dim recesses, thumping the wall in anger to signal his wish to be off with haste.

The hard lurch fed his rage, and he cursed the limits of his purse. When he had Dumas, and rescued Lilly's dowry from limbo, things would change. He would have the respect he deserved, and the money to pay for the best of everything.

As the village fell behind and the thought of ruling over Dumas turned his mind from anger, he smiled. The title would gain him his rightful position, the death of his cousin would ensure his coffers were never depleted to dangerous levels, he could afford to marry whomever he chose, and he would have the current Lady Winter at his mercy.

He'd had enough of the haughty bitch too.

Chapter Two

———◆———

Lord Winter didn't present himself for breakfast the next morning. Most likely, the baron's aching head would be painful but tiny in comparison to his embarrassment over the outpouring of emotion the night before. With any luck, the older man would spend all afternoon with his daughter and change his mind about leaving her at Cottingstone.

"Lord Winter has requested a breakfast tray in his chamber, milord."

Giles glanced at his butler. "Did he give any indication of when he might put in an appearance, Dithers?"

"No, sir. His valet was particularly close-mouthed about his employer's habits," Dithers remarked sounding very pleased. "A lot of loyalty there."

As the butler fussed with the breakfast dishes, Giles studied his servant. Tall, lean, impeccable in his dark tailored suit, Giles had no idea why he was lucky enough to retain Dithers' services. Despite his experience as a superior butler, the man had accepted the country position without complaint, allowing another to rule over the London townhouse upon Giles' accession to the title. But even after five years buried in the country, Dithers still looked out of place.

"Hmm. Well, nothing to be done until the baron is free. Then I'll work on changing his mind."

Dithers made another of those disapproving noises he favored, but Giles chose to ignore it. The longer the man worked for him, the poorer his adherence to the strictures of the master-servant roles. Given Dithers' exceptional performance in all other areas, Giles chose not to chastise him for his slips. Avoidance made for comfortable living, after all.

He took another swallow of coffee and nearly spit it out. There was no greater ill than cold coffee. He pushed it aside. "Have you seen Atticus this morning?"

"I saw his tail and not much else," Dithers replied. "He is with Miss Winter."

Giles could understand if Atticus behaved this way because of another dog, but from what he could gather, Lillian Winter was barely conscious. Despite Giles' considerable unease over her presence, he wondered what she was like.

He set aside his napkin. "What about the rest?"

"The rest of what, milord?"

Giles glanced at his butler. The man had to know curiosity over the woman he might have married if circumstances had been different was killing him. Did he have to spell it out? "What are the servants saying about Lord Winter and his daughter?"

"They're happy with Lord Winter's decision to leave her here."

Giles' breakfast flipped in his stomach. "Why?" Were they all mad?

Dithers' face hinted at a smile. "They are relieved Miss Winter will remain behind in comfort when her father departs. They have no fear for her safety."

Giles scowled. "Servants can be an overly opinionated nuisance."

"Of course, milord, we can surely be a trial." Dithers grinned. "Can I fetch you fresh coffee?"

Giles glanced into the half-empty cup. "Yes. But I'll take it in my study."

He left the smug butler behind and strolled along the hall, thinking about his uncomfortable situation. He did not want the awkwardness of having the woman who could have become his wife under his roof. It was embarrassing.

"Did ya see the nurse's reaction to Atticus licking Miss Winter's hand, Daisy?"

Giles stilled beside the staircase, listening to a maid gossiping on the upper floor.

"Thought she'd keel right over on the spot. And that nurse! What a foolish woman to climb onto the windowsill when Atticus came back. I wouldn't count on her for comfort if I was feeling poorly."

"Well, the dog did growl when we straightened the bedding, but Miss Winter don't notice a thing. She lay so still I was sure she was a corpse until her papa picked her up and she moaned."

"Hush, Maisie, you'll get us into trouble gossipin' about the quality."

The maids moved away and Giles considered the nurse Lord Winter had brought with him. He hoped the woman was as competent as described and that she could do her job without supervision.

As he pushed open his study door, he tried to guess Lilly's age. The accident had happened when she was perhaps fourteen. Just below the age of becoming a woman. She would be about twenty now, he supposed.

Six years of pain and suffering had passed when she should have been dancing, giggling, and marrying. And having babies to hold. He shuddered. If all had gone according to plan, they'd have been married for the last two years.

"Is anything the matter?"

Giles spun to find his butler gazing at him in amusement. Dithers knew full well what bothered him. He would be saddled with an unwanted responsibility. Female, no less, and not one he could associate with without that shackle reattaching to his leg. His servant could show a sliver of compassion. "Nothing that concerns you."

"Of course. Your coffee, milord." An innocuous statement, but laced with the tremor of barely suppressed humor in his tone.

Damn all butlers to hell.

Giles took the cup, his mind still occupied by the woman upstairs. In age, Lillian Winter was a woman. But in her mind, would she still be a young girl? Giles had no interest in girls. He liked his women intelligent, initiated into love play by someone else, and independent. He did not have the patience to deal with emotional, needy women.

"Do you require anything else, milord?"

Yes, an experienced woman to take his mind off his current nightmare. "No, go about your usual duties and stop bothering me."

The sooner he returned to London the better. Giles smiled. Perhaps Lady Huntley would hold another ball at Huntley House, the location of all his encounters with his little ghost. Given his eagerness to attend all her functions, he thanked God Lady Huntley had no daughters still unwed.

He had seen the ghost six times in total, each occasion quite memorable. The little sprite seemed unshakable, except perhaps once. Giles had shocked her then. The tryst had not been particularly decadent, but her reaction to the presence of two women cuddling up to him had spoken of disappointment and hurt. Her reaction puzzled him.

Giles sipped the strong coffee while he glanced out the window, noticing the wild gardens leading toward the southern boundary for the first time. He drew back. When had the gardens reached such a state?

The terrace doors refused to open to a light touch, so he shoved against them, wincing as they groaned in protest. Stepping outside, he stalked toward flowerbeds grown wild with nature. Weeds twined amongst the roses and delphiniums that had once been the pride of his mother's gardens. He followed the path to the ornate pond at its center and found it clogged with weeds.

Looking back at the house, he could see the beginning signs of neglect. Vines clung to the walls where they had once feared to go. The spire on the southern turret looked bent. Had it been struck by lightning?

He soaked his boots as he followed the garden path grown thick with long weeds pushing between flagstones. He grimaced. His valet would shriek at their state when he returned, but given Giles' usual care of his wardrobe, the man could bear the rare inconvenience.

Despite the wild, unkempt state, the grounds were still peaceful, but he should deal with the garden and the house soon. Turning, he saw the manor clearly for the first time in years: a grand old house bowing under the weight of neglect. His.

Giles liked to live his life with no responsibilities, but he did want the luxury of being able to retreat to this place for a long time to come. It may only be for his pleasure, but since he took pleasure very seriously, the house needed repair to restore it to its former glory.

Determined to correct his neglect, he walked around the old house and grounds, inspecting every detail from the disused stables to the twisting creek that flowed through the estate.

The stone bridge was still solid, built by his grandfather years earlier, its stout footings and sides impervious to the rushing water. Giles rested his elbows on the stones, watching the dark water slide beneath.

Lillian Winter had almost died in this very spot. They said she fell. He leaned forward on the high, smooth stones. It might be possible if the girl liked climbing. Despite Lord Winter's assurances she was an angel, perhaps Lilly had hidden an adventurous nature. He only remembered her vaguely. She'd had an impeccable lineage that met his parent's requirements for his bride and had been receiving instruction on managing a household for a number of years.

That was all he'd cared about at the time too.

He crossed the bridge and followed the river along the bank until the water flowed smoothly, less agitated by the rocks that she must have struck. Giles winced at the image, glancing back to the bridge and large boulders littering the stream.

What must it have been like for Lilly? The drop from the bridge, the insistent tug of floodwater and fabric as the heavy weight pulled her below the surface. Giles shuddered and looked about him. This was where Atticus had saved her.

He should have guessed Atticus would only respond to someone he felt protective of. When Giles had heard what his dog had attempted to do, pulling at the chit until her head remained above water long enough to be rescued, he'd been so proud. Until the moment they confessed Lilly would likely die anyway, at least. He'd feared the bites Atticus had inflicted pulling her toward the bank had speeded her demise.

But she had not died after all. She was tougher than he'd been led to believe. Yet all he knew of her were the tales told in hushed whispers and private thoughts penned carefully into a small journal he had found years after her supposed death. He still had that journal at the manor somewhere. He should at least unearth it and return it to its rightful owner.

Giles pulled a weed from the ground and twirled the stem between his fingers. From here, he could see the window of Lilly's bedchamber. What inner devil had prompted his butler to put the woman in a room facing the scene of her accident? Lord Winter, if he ever opened the drapes and looked out, would think them cruel.

Perhaps it would be all right. Lilly would only be here a short time, and then she would go to Wales. The thought saddened him. A life without any form of pleasure—that is what Lillian Winter lived. He did not know how anyone could survive such a boring existence.

He ambled back to the manor, pausing often to consider the extent of work required. Judging by what he saw, he would need some extra hands to bring the estate up to scratch. Perhaps he should have listened to his friends more over the years, but he had never aspired to make Cottingstone a great estate. All he needed was to keep the manor in good order and receive the rents, both here and from his London properties, to live a comfortable bachelor's existence.

A glance at Lilly's window reminded him to find the journal, but he wondered where he had put it. In his current rooms? Or perhaps packed with his childhood mementos packed away in the attic?

Attaining the upper floors by way of the servants' stairs was a moment's work. At a hall window, he spied a female figure walking about the garden's perimeter. Her gait was unfamiliar. It must be poor Lilly's nurse, which meant Lord Winter would be visiting with his daughter now. It was the perfect time to renew his acquaintance with Lilly. Her father could act as chaperone.

Instantly, Giles quashed that idea. He had a vast dislike for conversing with chaperones hovering and dissecting his every word. And there was also the very real worry that Lord Winter might view any request for a meeting as a cause for hope for marriage between them.

When he'd learned of her supposed death, Giles had taken out Lilly's journal and read it. At fourteen, Lilly hadn't been completely enamored of marrying. Neither had he been, for that matter. But the arrangement was a long-standing contract from his ninth year. As he grew older, he grew less pleased with the notion of an arranged marriage, but he'd known his duty and fallen silent on his parents' choice. Aside from the lure of her dowry and lineage, they'd promised Lilly would be no trouble to manage.

Giles pushed on the attic door. The hinges creaked, ending the silence. He shook his head again. That would never do. Another repair to see to.

Boxes of disused toys and oddments littered the walls and he scratched his head. Where might the little book be? Oh, yes. He remembered now. He had left it with the butterfly collection he'd abandoned years go, and the case still resided in the nursery one floor below. He tugged the protesting door closed, turned, and stalked to his former quarters.

He felt immediately out of place, far too large compared to the furniture in the room. His aborted butterfly collection lay on a high shelf, so he lowered it down carefully, and blew dust from the hazy glass. There it was, nestled between the dead forms of a Painted Lady and a Peacock butterfly. He had left her journal among other dead things.

Cringing, Giles opened the case, lifted out the small book, and returned the case to the shelf. He flipped the cover. Pages of childish words, moments of pleasure amidst a lifetime of loneliness. He remembered feeling rather sad by the end of reading it.

He slipped the journal into his inner pocket. Maybe Lilly wouldn't like her father to know of her lonely musings. She had hidden the journal, after all. Perhaps it would be best if he returned them to her after the baron departed and see if she wanted it back.

"Ah, there you are, lad," Lord Winter exclaimed, hovering in the doorway. "I thought I heard someone thumping around in here. Not exactly where I imagined I'd find you on such a pleasant day."

Since the baron's chamber was on the floor below, the older man had no reason to venture into the nursery either. Unless…

Giles stifled a groan. This was the last room Lillian had stayed in before her accident. Had Winter thought to wallow in memories of his daughter when she'd been in perfect health? Giles edged toward the door. He didn't want to witness this.

"I was just reminding myself what the old house looked like," Giles said. "I haven't been in this chamber in years." And didn't plan to return. Children were not in his future.

"No need to imagine…" Lord Winter's voice trailed off, hands clenching tightly on a slate. It still held childish writing. Lord Winter's hand shook and the slate broke apart, smashing to pieces on the bare hardwood floor.

Alarmed, Giles approached the baron. Blood had leached from his face, but aside from that he was unharmed. "Don't worry about the mess. I'll send a servant to deal with it. Let's go enjoy what's left of the day."

Giles guided the unresponsive man toward the door and shut it behind them. Poor man. The writing on the slate had been childish and repetitive: "I will be good."

It wasn't his sister's handwriting, nor his. It matched the writing in Lilly's journal.

By the time they reached the drawing room, Lord Winter's color had returned to normal, but he reached for the brandy as soon as it came into view.

Giles left him to get foxed again, and turned to his letters to avoid participating in another uncomfortable conversation.

The first few he had were invitations. But a note from a friend caught his eye and he broke the seal.

Dear Daventry,

My sister has agreed to marry a crushing bore. The date is set for a month away and I'm under siege about my own wedding. I'm begging for an invitation to Cottingstone to get away from my mother and her obsession with planning the perfect wedding breakfast. Please. Help.

Yours most sincerely,

Viscount Carrington

Giles choked off a laugh, glancing at his companion to see if Lord Winter was paying any attention. He didn't imagine Lilly's father would appreciate levity, even if his friend's situation was damned funny.

Poor Carrington—stuck in London with just the women of his family. They would be in an absolute frenzy of activity. Giles supposed he could save the lad from his mother's unsubtle attempts at arranging a double wedding.

He cringed when he thought of Carrington's intended bride. She was a dragon in the making, far too controlling for Giles' taste. Why the viscount had agreed to the match was beyond his understanding. Especially since Carrington's heart was engaged elsewhere.

But Giles refused to interfere.

He had meddled once, at great risk to a friendship he valued above all others. Even though that situation had turned out well, it could very easily have gone the other way. Still, he'd be more than happy to help Carrington avoid the parson's clutches a mite longer.

Grinning, he reached for a sheet of paper. Carrington could come and, as an afterthought, Giles asked him to bring more brandy. At the rate Lord Winter was imbibing, there would be very little left in the decanter by the end of the week. He would need a lot more for when the baron returned from Wales. He had no doubt Winter would require considerable fortification to complete his plans to exile his daughter.

He returned to his stack of correspondence, picked up one, but was overwhelmed by the scent of lilac. He flipped it over and was surprised to find it bearing the address of a recent lover.

My dear Lord Daventry,
These weeks without you have been too dreadful to relate. London is so dull and lifeless. Come back soon. I miss your touch.
Very truly yours,
Lady M.

Giles shuddered. A love note? Lady Montgomery knew exactly when he was returning to London. He had been very specific. He didn't like that she'd attempted to entice him back. Their affair was a casual fulfillment of basic bodily needs—nothing further.

If she was that starved for attention, she should find someone to take away the ache. He wouldn't care. Hell, Sabine should rejoice in his lack of possessiveness. Apparently, though, his lover had the idea their affair had progressed beyond the simple pleasure he meant it to be.

He didn't think a letter was the appropriate way to remind her of his indifference to permanent relationships, so he slid her letter to the side and reached for the next. Sabine's note would feed the flames as soon as he got to his feet. Perhaps by ignoring her demands, he'd communicate the affair was well and truly run its course.

Chapter Three

———◆———

Lord Winter's parting the next day took some time. While Giles watched on, horses and carriages drew up in front of the house, swarming with servants as they prepared for departure. Much to Giles' discomfort, the baron planned to take most of his staff with him. Only the nurse would remain behind to care for Lilly.

Giles found that thought vastly unsettling. He did not like that Lilly was solely reliant on the services of one person. When the baron had also requested his silence regarding his destination, alarm bells pealed.

He thought it was obvious that he wouldn't say a word about Lillian Winter's presence. Why would he tell the world that he had a single, unmarried woman staying in his country house without a proper chaperone? But, while Giles waited for the man to depart, he had to wonder why it was so important he keep the baron's destination secret too.

"I believe the carriage is ready, milord," Dithers informed Giles unnecessarily.

"Yes, it appears so."

"I'm certain the baron will be back before you've realized he's gone."

"Hmph, I will remember you said that, Dithers. I wish he wasn't doing this to me."

"You sound frightened, milord." Dithers sighed. "She's just a woman."

Giles scowled. He'd used his best arguments last night to try to dissuade the baron, short of threatening to ruin the chit, from going. Lord Winter had not shared Giles' reservations. "Shut up, Dithers."

Giles wasn't truly irritated with the butler, but he had to take his annoyance out on someone. There was no female here he could take to bed to redirect his frustrations. Servants, despite their giggling suggestions, were off limits. Maybe the butler had a point. How much trouble could one ill woman be?

He turned from his perusal of the servants, climbed the steps toward Lilly's bedchamber, and struggled not to hurry. He told himself quite firmly that he was keen to have Lord Winter on his way quickly so he might return with similar speed. It had absolutely nothing to do with his curious need to catch a glimpse of the woman who might have been his wife.

A virgin. Giles shuddered. What on earth was wrong with him?

He was in the country to rest until the next round of amorous diversions. He did not allow complications or virgins, to dominate his thoughts at Cottingstone. He was here to replenish his enthusiasm and relax.

He turned toward Lilly's bedchamber and saw a flash of dark skirts hurrying away. The nurse, he supposed. What a timid, scurrying creature.

"Do you have to leave, Papa?" Lilly's voice reached his ears and he paused outside the open door, unwilling to interrupt their farewells. He leaned against the wall, waiting and conveniently able to eavesdrop.

"I am sure you will be comfortable here, daughter."

"Yes, Papa, I'm sure Giles will look after me very well." Her voice sounded different, stronger, but Giles was surprised she referred to him by his first name. What exactly did Lillian Winter think she was to him? He hoped she knew her father had ended their betrothal.

Giles eased closer to the door, but he could see nothing except darkness within. He had no right to eavesdrop, but he had learned a great many things by that very poor habit.

"You must take particular care while I am gone, Lillian. Do not allow yourself to give in too frequently. We do not want to impose on Lord Daventry too greatly. He has been very good about you being here."

Sheets rustled and when Lilly answered, her voice sounded muffled. "I know, Papa. I will do my best and rest a great deal. I am sure everything will be just fine. Do not worry. Have a good trip, but hurry back. I'll miss you."

There was a lengthy pause before he heard sheets rustle again and then the heavy tread of Lord Winter approaching the door. Giles moved back with every stealthy skill that he possessed to hide the fact he'd been listening, but Lord Winter seemed unsurprised by his presence.

"Your carriage is ready, sir," Giles informed him.

Did Lilly know of her father's plans for her future? Judging by Lord Winter's face when he raised his chin, she did not. The man was as distraught as he had been the first night of his arrival.

Tears streamed down the older man's face and he mopped them up hurriedly with a square of clean linen. Lord Winter obviously loved his daughter. Leaving her behind for this errand must be tearing him in two.

Atticus chose that moment to return to the house. He moved purposefully to Lord Winter, nuzzling into the older man's hand for affection. The baron scratched behind the hound's ears, earned a contented whine for his efforts, and then Winter leaned down to whisper into them. Atticus' ears flattened, and then he turned, ignoring Giles to reenter Lilly's room.

"You have a good hound there, Daventry. I did not credit that he would remember Lillian as he does. I am sorry if my daughter has deprived you of your companion, but I am grateful for the dog's devotion. Atticus distracts her from her pain. I feel happier knowing he stands guard over her."

Giles stopped the baron with a hand on his arm, holding him back when he would have left. Hints and innuendo be damned. "Stands guard over her? Is there something you are not telling me?"

Lord Winter glanced around to judge the position of his daughter's bedchamber, then encouraged Giles farther along the hall. "I did not want to trouble you, but strange things happen around Lillian. Odd accidents. I do my best to always be nearby. You have seen Atticus' behavior. He will stand in for me as best he can. You need not worry yourself over her."

Giles was not satisfied with that response, but it appeared all he would get. Lord Winter shrugged from his grip and headed out of the manor at a sprightly pace. Giles jogged to keep up.

"The faster I am away, the faster I can return. You will be here until I get back, won't you?"

Giles groaned. He would be lucky if he made the next Huntley ball to see his ghost again. After such vague hints, Giles doubted he possessed enough resolve to leave Lilly here alone.

Lord Winter vaulted into the conveyance and, together with the more usual level of noise, the carriage departed.

Giles watched the drifting dust settle with quiet resignation. Years spent building a sterling reputation as a rake and reduced to a nursemaid by a few well-chosen words. At least he could expect Lord Carrington's company soon.

Giles stopped cold. Damn. How the hell was he going to keep Lillian Winter's presence from the viscount? Giles shook his head. He could not stop the viscount's visit now, but at least Carrington knew how to keep his mouth shut. His friend hated gossip as much as Giles did. Yet, in a strange way, Giles was pleased to think that someone else would learn of Lilly's existence.

He glanced up the staircase as he trudged inside again. Lord Winter hadn't extended him the courtesy of an introduction, just the pleasure of providing a roof over Lilly's head. Perhaps later he could work out an excuse to check on her personally. He had a journal to return, after all.

He'd have to arrange it before Carrington arrived. Maybe tomorrow, or the day after, but certainly before the viscount charmed her into falling half in love with him, as every other female in London was prone to do.

Feeling somewhat better, he looked around his home but shuddered. There was a lot of work needed around the old place. The sooner he got his staff to work, the better. He would hire extra hands from the village and have them start straight away. At least his extended stay would not be a complete waste of time. The broad front steps needed scrubbing too.

He headed to the servants' quarters, where he was sure to find Dithers and Mrs. Osprey at this time of day. They stood in surprise when he entered the housekeeper's sitting room, but he waved them back to their places.

Glancing about him, he noticed how cozy the two of them appeared. He settled into a sturdy-looking armchair and told them what he wanted done. They both nodded, but it was not until he was near the end of his orders that he noticed the strange gleam in his housekeeper's eyes.

"Do you have concerns, Osprey?"

"No, my lord, everything can be done as you requested, quicker with the extra hands from the village. Was there any particular completion date for the work? Any important event in the near future we must plan for?"

Giles peered at her then scoffed. Her tightly clasped hands gave her away. "No, Mrs. Matchmaker. I am not getting married." The housekeeper slumped. "Much to your obvious disappointment."

"I'm sorry, my lord. It's just that the house is so quiet these days, and I cannot help remembering that your father was a father of two by your age."

"Hmm, my parents married young. Much good that did them."

"They were happy," Dithers and Mrs. Osprey murmured in unison.

"Yes, until my father broke his neck. Enough. Just because I have been cajoled into playing nursemaid doesn't mean I have changed my opinion of women and the position in my life they occupy."

The pair exchanged discontented expressions, and then Mrs. Osprey sat forward. "About the young miss? Do you have any idea how long your intended will be staying with us?"

Giles looked at Mrs. Osprey hard. "The betrothal ended at their request years ago, Osprey. You would do well to remember that and not cause discomfort to Miss Winter. The baron wants us to conceal her presence at Cottingstone and I quite agree with him."

Mrs. Osprey frowned, unconsciously rubbing her hands over the chair arms. Had she forgotten that, too? After a moment of fierce contemplation, she blushed. It appeared she *had* forgotten.

Dithers leaned toward the housekeeper. "You should

concentrate on your duties, Ossie, and not let the nurse's talk of the past confuse you. Something isn't right with that one. She's sticking her nose where it oughtn't to be."

"Well, you're just annoyed because your charms don't work on her," she snapped.

A vein pulsed in the butler's temple. "I beg your pardon," Dithers ground out through clenched teeth.

As the spat developed between his servants, Giles considered his butler's earlier words instead. The man was not a high stickler, but he was particularly observant. If Dithers had concerns about the nurse, Giles would do well to heed them. Lord Winter's passing words, *strange things happen around Lilly*, troubled him even more now. "I have not spoken to the nurse, but Miss Winter is the daughter of a baron and deserves to be shown proper respect during her stay. Watch what you say around her. I would not like her made uncomfortable by references to the past."

Mrs. Osprey held the butler's glare a moment longer and then her face blanked of all emotion. She turned to Giles, and it was as if that disagreement had never started.

"Of course, my lord. I never considered that she would understand us."

Giles clenched the arms of his seat. "Where the hell did you hear that she won't understand you, and from whom?" He had heard Lilly's soft words and believed her mind sound. Such a statement was clearly ridiculous.

"Why, the nurse herself, my lord," Mrs. Osprey confided. "She told me not to fret because Miss Winter won't ever understand what's going on around her. She said she'd take care of everything."

Giles' estimation of Mrs. Osprey's intelligence sank. "Mrs. Osprey, I am sure you have something to do. Go. Do it somewhere else. I want to have a word with Dithers about the south border."

Mrs. Osprey fussed her way out the door, never noticing the pained glance Dithers cast at Giles.

The butler sighed, long and loud. "She grows worse each year. It sneaks up on me at times like this."

Giles wiped a hand over his face as he contemplated his housekeeper's unhappy future. "You're certain her mind is failing?"

"Yes, milord." Dithers slumped in the chair, regret creasing his features. "She forgets the strangest things at times. I spend half my day discreetly following her about."

"She does not have family nearby, does she?"

"No. She has lived at Cottingstone all her adult life. Her parents died long ago and her remaining family sailed for Australia a few years back. She's heard nothing of them since. Ossie knows nothing except the manor."

Judging by the butler's face, Giles guessed he expected him to turn her out. His housekeeper was losing her mind, a little bit each day, more noticeable to Giles because of his longer absences. He was not a monster but, in time, something would have to be done for the woman. She would not be able to manage such a large role on her own.

Dithers fidgeted with his cuff nervously, clearly agitated by the situation too. Giles decided to contemplate the dilemma another day. "Perhaps you should have married her, Dithers. Then she would have had an appropriate surname."

His blush caused Giles to chuckle out loud. Dithers, a confirmed bachelor, was a rogue of the servant class. At forty, he still cut a fine figure, but no longer chased the ladies. A fact that confused the hell out of Giles. He had gotten his first lessons in seduction listening to the man spouting his conquests to the head groom when he was a lad. Blushing did not suit him.

"Keep an eye on the nurse, Dithers, and try not to antagonize my housekeeper."

Chapter Four

———————◆———————

This house was familiar.

Lilly remembered hurrying down the long halls through rooms filled with warmth and light. But she couldn't run any longer, and she missed the caress of summer sun over her skin.

It was dark now, cold. Her bare feet trod upon timber floors as she made her way through the manor, moving silently from room to room, searching for someone, anyone awake in this dark place.

"Dum, dee, dum, dee, dumpty dum," Lilly hummed.

She missed laughter the most, and especially smiles. No one smiled at her now—not happy smiles, anyway. They were always just a bit lacking, brittle and fake. Her papa never smiled anymore. But Lilly remembered a day when he had spun her round and round so fast that her feet left the ground. She had shrieked at him to stop, or not stop, laughing so hard her sides had ached.

Laughter was just a memory that tormented Lilly's restless nights.

"Oh, that's right. Humpty Dumpty sat on a wall," Lilly sang, pleased to dredge the line of a childhood favorite from her imperfect memory. The words echoed in the empty hall and she grew afraid of the strange echo.

Unsure of many things, she leaned against the wall to rest and looked up. The nursery where she had stayed during her last visit was on the upper level, far away from any of the guest rooms so she couldn't bother anyone. Getting there required too much energy, and her heart fluttered in her chest already. She pushed her weary body away from the wall and peered at the portrait opposite.

The lady in it seemed familiar, but it took Lilly a while to place who she was. Giles' mother. Lady Daventry had given her a pretty pink parasol for her birthday and kissed her cheek, promising they would be great friends when she grew up. Lilly had carried it with her every day until it broke. She couldn't remember why it broke, only that she'd been angry about the loss and had cried into the countess' gentle embrace after discovering it in pieces.

"Humpty Dumpty had a great fall."

Lilly knew all she wanted to know about falling and turned away from the portrait, dragging her heavy limbs onward. She leaned against a solid door at the end of the hall, pushed until it opened, and smiled at whom she found.

Giles. His heavy breathing filled the room.

While she longed for companionship, she dared not wake the earl, a man who was meant to be her husband when she grew old enough to marry him. She moved past a bureau, snagged a ruby cravat pin as she went, and stood at the foot of the massive bed to observe him in silence. Papa had warned her not to impose.

Firelight licked over his sprawled golden form, and nothing else in the room had the power to capture her attention. Only the man.

The twisted linen hinted he was naked under the sheet and she stifled a giggle.

The absence of Giles' clothes did not shock her. They were often missing. Sometimes pushed down around his ankles, or gone completely. He looked peaceful in sleep; the laugh lines of his face relaxed as he breathed, even and deep.

Smiling that his ginger hair was as tousled as always, she traced her fingers over his sheet, enjoying the slippery linen against her skin.

His foot was close and she touched him, brushing the tuft of ginger hair on his big toe with her fingertips. His leg twitched away and she raised her eyes along the lean length of him. So much skin exposed.

In London, she'd never viewed him all at once like this, or from so close a distance. Despite his habit of making love to every woman he seemed to meet, Lilly thought him perfect. Sleek like the caged jungle cats her papa mentioned were in London, but intent on giving nothing but pleasure.

He kicked the sheet the rest of the way off and her breath caught.

He was beautiful. Whole and unmarked.

Unlike Lilly who had hard lumps of skin on her arms and back.

She let her eyes rest at the junction of his thighs and his body changed as she watched. He grew and lengthened so much he surprised her. Lilly swayed forward, curious to get a better look, but he moved and touched himself, a ragged breath hissing from between his parted lips.

An aroused Giles was a comfortable sight to Lilly. It was just something he did, as commonplace as flicking his hair from his eyes or brushing a speck of dust from his coat sleeve.

Dragging her eyes away from Giles' changing form, she looked around the room. In the firelight she noticed pale walls, dark timber, and pillows on every chair. She liked his bedchamber best of all the strange places she'd been taken to. The banked fire created a dreamy warmth that made her want to curl up and sleep. She glanced back at the naked earl.

Giles must be hot. The sheets bunched at the foot of his bed, but he touched and pulled on his length, rolling over onto his front to rub himself into the sheet.

Eyes locked on his flexing hips, Lilly twirled the ruby pin between her fingers, marking time until his breath hitched. She did not even need to see his face to know he enjoyed his pleasure. She crossed the room, but glanced back as she opened the door, smiling at the familiar low groans that rang through the chamber.

He made that exact same sound every time he played with other ladies. Lilly wrinkled her nose. She did not like the other women very much. They could do things with him she couldn't. They could dance and walk about in his company all night if they wanted. Lilly could never gad about in society. Her injuries were too severe.

She tugged on the heavy door and stepped into the dark

hallway. Nails clicked on bare timber and she reached for Atticus. He licked her hand urgently, but through the fog of her dulled senses, she could not raise enough concern for his distress and continued her wandering.

The other rooms were empty and cold. No one else slept on this floor. Lilly wondered where her papa was and lurched toward the stairs to go below. Descending the stairs took a long time and she leaned heavily on the railing for support. Atticus was not a great deal of help as he clutched a mouthful of nightgown with his teeth, tugging in the opposite direction. Lilly continued down.

Still, ignoring Atticus was hard, but she reached the bottom step anyway and turned to look about. She could see nothing except darkness outside the open front door. Papa would not be outside. He did not like the dark, and neither did she. No one good would be out there in all that blackness.

Moving from memory, Lilly shuffled to the open drawing room doors, but knocked over a small table that never used to be there. Unfortunately, she couldn't right it, so she left it where it fell.

Atticus tugged on her gown and an unmistakable rip broke the silence. Too weary to scold, she turned, laid a hand on his shaggy coat, and patted him clumsily.

Skirting the fallen table, she moved forward, her feet dragging on the thick wool carpet. She enjoyed the sensations tickling her toes, but the drawing room was as empty of life as everywhere else.

She returned to the doorway, retraced her steps to the main staircase, and looked up. She knew where she could see a familiar face. Giles was upstairs, but it was such a long way back to him.

Maybe Papa was in Giles' study. When she found the room, it was warmer than she expected, scented with cigar smoke but deserted.

Lilly swayed, exhaustion tugging her limbs. Atticus whined. She gripped his coat to reassure him, but overbalanced and fell partly against the hound, slumping to the floor in an untidy heap. Her companion whined again.

"Quiet now. I'm unharmed," Lilly whispered.

A thick sheepskin rug cushioned her body and tickled her

cheek. She pushed up with her arms, but could not raise herself even to her knees. Atticus barked and nosed her cheek. She used what little strength she had left to wrap her arms around him.

"Atticus, be still."

Atticus wriggled, perhaps trying to help, but Lilly's arms were heavy and weak all at once. She could not hold on. She landed heavily on the floor, hurting her head when she fell beyond the soft sheepskin.

Lilly sprawled in a long spill of moonlight thrown from the high, un-shuttered windows, waiting for dizziness to pass. She could not get up, so she curled into a ball and clutched her useless hands.

The room spun out of focus. Faces came and went. Serious men and women, dressed in wigs and jewels, smiling benignly upon her. A clock ticked, chiming once, twice, three times.

"All the king's horses…"

Warmth pressed against her back as Atticus lay his full length against her. If she could remember the word, he would bark for her. It was simple. Just one word and he would wake Giles. She was sure the earl would come, pick her up, and take her somewhere warm if she asked nicely.

But the nursery rhyme was all she could remember. She opened her mouth to speak, but retched instead, forgetting all about seeking help as waves of nausea shook her.

"Couldn't put humpty together again."

———◆———

Giles woke late, tired and worn out. He had again dreamed of the ghost with white hair. His sheets had not been this sullied by his solitary sleeping since he was an untried boy. He raised his head and looked about the room. Last night he'd imagined singing, for God's sake.

His door stood ajar, so he pulled the top sheet from the bed and wrapped it around his waist just in case one of the housemaids walked past. He was not going to be the subject of conversation between that pair of bird-witted chits.

For the first time, he had dreamed of the ghost touching his possessions. Giles had woken, rolled over, and flexed his hips against the mattress, completely caught up in the fantasy that she was beneath him. Pleasuring himself with the friction of the sheet and the scent he imagined she might wear. Lemons. It had only taken a moment before he had groaned into his pillow.

He rang for his valet, dressed, and ate a hearty breakfast, ignoring the frowning expression Worth wore as he poked through his bureau drawer and jewel box. He was reviewing his plans for the day when Dithers knocked on his door, and came in without waiting for permission.

That was certainly not like him. Dithers hovered on the threshold, spotted him, then barreled across the room, agitation clear in every step. The world slowed as he drew closer. There was obviously not going to be good news in the greeting.

"The nurse has run off, milord." Dithers sounded incensed by such a dereliction of duty.

Giles closed his eyes. He should have seen this coming.

"Maisie went to fetch the woman because Miss Winter's breakfast was growing cold, but we have not been able to locate her."

Giles reached for his jacket and tugged it on, pausing only long enough for Worth to thread a jade pin into his cravat. "Right. Of course." He pinched the bridge of his nose as the valet fussed with the fit of his sleeves. This was not going to be an easy day. If the nurse had abandoned her post altogether, where did one find another?

Dithers hovered at the edge of his vision. When Giles looked at the white-faced man, unease rippled through him as he sensed there were more bad tidings to come.

"Miss Winter is missing from her bedchamber. We went to check her room for the nurse and when we did not see her there, we also realized the young miss had left her bed."

Dithers finished his speech to Giles' back.

Giles ran the short distance to Lilly's room and skidded into the doorframe. He stopped in shock. The drapes were open wide and a frigid wind blew in through the window. A chair stood in front of it. Surely, the pain was not so great that Lilly would take her own life? Not here. Not now.

Giles crossed the room with a sinking heart, forcing his feet to the open window. He looked down. There was no body below on the pavers. He slumped in relief, but then turned to look about him.

The bedding, turned back untidily, looked as if Lilly had slept there for at least a little while, but the hearth was cold. A dark cloak lay over the chair back and Giles recognized it from Lilly's arrival at Cottingstone. Was she dressed in just a nightgown? Last night had not been particularly warm. To be dressed so lightly could not be good for her health.

"The main door was wide open this morning too, milord." Dithers finished his bad tidings from the doorway.

"Were we robbed, Dithers?"

"Not that I could detect, so far. I was busy checking the silver when Maisie reported the nurse missing. I thought we should search for Miss Winter first."

"Yes, do that." Giles looked around the room, puzzled.

Where was Atticus? Why had the dog not made an appearance yet? It was not at all like him. Giles strode out, checking all the rooms near this one, but found no sign of Lilly. He dispatched his staff to search the upper rooms.

Giles cursed the fact that he had so few staff. At a moment like this, he could do with a few more. Had the nurse abducted Lilly? He should probably have the servants search for a ransom note, too.

The library door was closed and he found the room unoccupied. He slammed the door behind him, frustrated by the woman's disappearance. Giles thought he heard a faint noise but couldn't determine where the sound came from. He crossed the hall to check the drawing room and found a small table on its side—the same one he always tripped over when deep in his cups. He righted it and eyed the room. Had she sought escape? A quick check behind the curtains and furniture produced nothing. All the windows were secure, as expected.

Giles retraced his steps to the main staircase and looked up. Dithers and his staff darted in and out of the upper rooms, but none looked hopeful. He glanced at the front door again, pondering what benefit could be found in abducting a woman so grievously ill.

A whine echoed down the hall.

"*Atticus!*"

The dog whined again. Giles headed for his study. Someone must have locked Atticus inside. That would explain his silence up until now. Perhaps the dog could search for the girl. He had never trained him to do so, but perhaps, given his pet's devotion, he could find Lilly.

But the door to his study was already open—which begged the question: why would the dog not come out?

Giles rushed to reach the threshold.

Atticus looked at him with a mournful expression, and then lay his large head back down over the still white form slumped in front of the cold hearth.

Lilly. A tangle of pale hair lay over her features and the floor. He hurried across the chamber, avoided her sickness to kneel next to the woman, and reached for her hand. A ruby cravat pin fell from her nerveless fingers.

Ignoring the expensive trinket, he rubbed her hand. She was freezing cold.

Atticus stopped Dithers and Mrs. Osprey at the door with his warning growl.

"You found her, milord! What a relief."

"Dithers, get her room warm again. Hurry. Her skin is like ice."

Giles chafed her thin hands and considered how best to lift her. He remembered Lord Winter's agonizing slowness and gentle hold, but he hadn't seen the man lift her. What if he made her pain worse?

Atticus watched intently, as if he understood Giles' dilemma. But there was no help for it. Although he did not know anything about the extent of her injuries, Lilly could not possibly remain on the cold floor.

"Lillian? Lilly, wake up. I need to move you, sweetheart." He received no response and, alarmed, he checked for a pulse at her wrist. It was hard to find and very faint. He cursed and then eased his hands under her thinly clad form.

Giles lifted her easily into a sitting position then raised them both, pulling her tightly against his chest. She was light. Too light. He held nothing but air. Beneath the stench of sickness, he detected the faint scent of lemon in her hair.

He swayed a moment on his feet then carefully made his way out of the room, up the long steps, and along to her bedchamber. Atticus moved ahead of him and barked once. By the time Giles got Lilly to her bedchamber, Dithers had the window closed again and the fire relit.

The sheets were cold. Atticus settled himself along one side of the bed, seemingly content that Giles was in charge, but kept a distance. He possibly did not care for Lilly's new aroma, but at least she was alive.

As Giles nestled her in the bed, he touched the cold glass of a bottle and removed it to read the label.

Laudanum, and all of it gone.

Giles' heart thumped. His mother had used the same poison to follow his father into the family burial plot.

"Get some hot water, Mrs. Osprey. Quickly, woman," he snapped, thrusting the empty bottle at her.

The housekeeper looked at the bottle and blanched, stuffing it into her pocket, and out of his sight.

Giles fussed in confusion, tugging the dirty strands of hair clear of the pillow so they lay to wait for the warm water. He would rinse them out and they could dry over a towel, but that wouldn't make her better. He reached for the blankets and cocooned them around her body loosely, wishing this had not happened. Cataloguing tasks helped keep his panic at bay, but he wanted her father back. Now.

He reached for her small white hands and rubbed, hoping to warm them using friction. Combined body heat could warm her swiftly, but he would not consider joining her in bed until he grew desperate about her condition.

Mrs. Osprey arrived with the dish of water and Giles took it from her. He cleaned Lilly's hair carefully himself, washing all traces of sickness away, and toweled it dry. When Mrs. Osprey handed him a comb, he tugged it through the damp ends slowly. Beautiful hair—silver-white, thickly curled around her face, neck, and torso. He laid the strands over another towel and finally raised his gaze to her face.

Lilly's eyes were closed, he could see that much. Her pale lashes lay heavy against the swells of her cheekbones. A sting of emotion rippled through him, and he struggled to understand his reaction.

Lilly was a tiny woman. Pale like moonlight. He moved her hair further back from her face.

And forgot to breathe.

Hollow rushing filled his ears and the world around him darkened, focused on this one place. The sparkles floating in front of his eyes were blinding, until he simply had to draw in a breath of lemon-scented air to keep seeing the vision lying in the bed before him. The drapes were still open, and it was still day.

Lillian Winter was his ghost.

Chapter Five

———◆———

Giles staggered back from the bed in horror. His hands rose, as if to ward away evil.

All this time. His mind blanked for a moment, and then he knew the truth.

He was going to fry in hell.

His soul would be eternally damned for the stupidity he had wallowed in for the past years. He closed his eyes and counted to twenty. It was just not possible. Lilly could not be his ghost.

Reopening them did not change his situation. Perhaps a good stoning would.

"God save me," Giles whispered.

"Beg pardon, my lord. Is something the matter?" Mrs. Osprey asked.

Giles could not answer. His thoughts swam around in circles. He walked toward the window but glanced back at the bed. "Oh, fuck."

Mrs. Osprey gasped, but he did not care if he offended her delicate sensibilities. He was already in a great deal of trouble. Far more than he thought he would be in when he'd been saddled with Lillian Winter as a guest. Offending his housekeeper with his poor choice of words was the least of his troubles. God was punishing him for his wicked ways, and the torment was going to continue for a long time to come. For all of eternity, perhaps. He swore again.

"Milord, please," Dithers begged.

"Of all the stupid, idiotic, insane lapses of judgment, I think this one is possibly the finest in the known world." Giles couldn't stop the flow of words. "Just couldn't keep it in my bloody trousers, could I? No, no, just wave it about and display myself for the world to see. Fuck, you arrogant bloody beef-witted fool. Goddamn it."

He looked at the bed and swore some more, probably shocking poor Mrs. Osprey into palpitations, because Dithers removed the woman from the room. He was alone with Lillian once more.

Another breach of etiquette, but who was counting, right?

"God damn me."

If her father found out what Lilly had seen him doing… Giles shuddered.

Pistols or swords?

Would he have a choice? He doubted there would be even one witness. A shallow grave and a rumor he'd gone abroad. Giles had never professed an interest in the sea, so he hoped that someone, someday, would look for his body, if only to give his uptight sister the chance to say she had seen it coming. He might just deserve what was coming, too.

He walked back to the bed and stared down at the face on the white pillow. Lilly hadn't moved. Pale and perfect, one thin hand draped at her side, and not a hint of color showing. Was she truly alive? He hesitated to touch her again, but he had to be sure.

With trembling fingers, he touched the back of her pale hand and flinched, awareness of her existence thrumming through him in an unwelcome rush.

Atticus whimpered, looking at him over her prone body, tail thumping the bed in anticipation. The dog was waiting on a miracle, was he? Giles touched her hand again, rubbing his fingers in small circles, upwards to her wrist. She was cold. Her pulse, when he found it, was still slow.

Dithers reentered the chamber, and Giles stepped away from Lilly, guilt and self-disgust whirling in his brain.

"How is the young miss, milord? Is there a change? Anything I can get for her?"

Yes, a pistol or a great big blunderbuss would do nicely, so

Lilly could shoot him. He deserved a ball between his eyes. He would even hand her the weapon and cheer her on as she pulled the trigger. If she ever recovered from whatever had happened to her last night, that was.

Giles struggled for an appropriate response, but could only manage two words. "Hot bricks."

Dithers departed, leaving him alone with his self-recriminations.

He strode to the fire and threw in another log. The blaze scalded his face and he was glad for it. Perhaps it could cleanse away the darkness he left behind in his wake. Behind him was an example of his darkness. He turned to look long and hard at the lump under the bedding. He had imagined what his ghost had been like when alive too—now he would get to find out.

Perhaps.

He wanted to laugh at the situation, but feared he might leap over into madness. He had played many a wicked game in front of this innocent woman, dreamed of doing unending, unearthly feats of passion in her cold embrace. Never once had the possibility entered his lust-filled brain that she might have been real.

Alive.

Or that she would be the woman once intended for his bride. What the hell had she been doing in London, gadding about Huntley House in a nightdress?

He brushed his fingers across her palm, an intimate gesture usually shared between lovers.

Startled at his unconscious relocation to Lilly's side again, he clasped his hands behind his back. Lapses like that would only turn up the fires of his guilt. He was seared on both sides and his bollocks were shrinking in retreat. He had better start keeping his trousers on, and his hands firmly to himself, if he wanted to enjoy what was left of his life.

He sank into a chair on the far side of the room and dropped his head into his hands. His behavior put him well beyond the pale. He knew it very well, indeed.

He looked up as Dithers returned, handling the cloth-wrapped bricks carefully. Giles looked at him blankly.

The butler waited patiently, but after a moment he quirked his head to the side. "We will need to get the bricks in around her soon, milord. Shall I lift the covers, or will you do the honors?"

Giles bristled at the thought of any man near Lilly. He stalked to the bed, placed himself between his servant and the unconscious woman, and lifted the covers.

"She isn't much bigger than when the accident happened," Dithers mused.

"You've met her?"

"I was here temporarily for the house party. I remember them bringing her back to the manor."

An irrational irritation grated on Giles' nerves. He'd deliberately absented himself from the house party, had been away at the time of the accident, to avoid the girl. He hadn't lain eyes on Lilly since she was little. If he hadn't avoided doing his duty and entertaining his mother's guests, he might have recognized her as the ghost and behaved far differently. He might have spoke to her, made love to her instead.

That thought shocked him to his boots.

He was attracted to the ghost. No, not the ghost. He was attracted to Lilly, the woman who was supposed to be his wife. A woman whom he'd thought dead.

Dear God, what the hell was he supposed to do with her now?

The butler moved to insert the bricks, but Giles took them from him and placed them around her feet carefully. When his hand brushed over her toes, he found them ice cold.

"See if you can find some stockings or such," Giles said as he rubbed her tiny feet, trying to stimulate some warmth.

Dithers rattled drawers open and closed, finally returning to thrust a pair of thick, white stockings at him. Giles was completely unfamiliar with the style, but loathed them on sight.

The butler chuckled at his reaction. "Not many garments in those draws to choose between," Dithers commented. "I would venture that she does not get about much. I did find this. It's a fair likeness."

Giles stared at the palm-sized portrait of himself, made years ago. To Giles' mind, it didn't look anything like him. "Put the trinket back where you found it."

Giles slipped the ugly stockings up to her knees under the nightgown, being careful not to peek, but the more he touched, the more he wanted to touch. Disgusted with himself, he pulled the covers up, picking up her hand, meaning to tuck it under, too. He noticed a scar and turned her arm. In the raw light of day, the bite marks his dog had inflicted were hideous.

"The scarring could have been worse, but they've healed over nicely and I never heard she developed an infection from them," the butler remarked. "Without Atticus, she would have drowned. That was a deep hole he pulled her from."

Dithers' informality made it easier to forget the problems Giles would face when Lilly was conscious again. He tucked her arm under the blankets, pulled them up over her chest and to her chin. Her face was cold too. His knuckles grazed her jaw and he fought the urge to cradle her face in his hands. What was wrong with him? And what on earth was it about Lillian Winter that attracted him?

She wasn't even conscious. Usually his amorous inclinations tended to die without some form of reciprocation.

Giles stood back to study her. What should he do next?

"Shall I have Daisy sent up to sit with her?" Dithers asked, breaking the silence.

Since he had a sneaking suspicion that he shouldn't trust himself where Lillian Winter was concerned, that was probably best. "Yes, do that. I will stay until she is warm again. Fetch me the folio from my study, as well. I may as well get some work done."

"I am sure she will recover, milord."

"You cannot know that," Giles snapped, then took a deep breath, letting it escape slowly to calm himself.

"She isn't as frail as your mother was, milord. Miss Winter has clung to life this long, hasn't she?"

Giles didn't answer. Lilly may not be as frail as his mother, yet the existence of laudanum in the house brought the pain of her loss rushing back, turning his thoughts to chaos. He took another deep breath. Calmer, he glanced at Dithers, who was on the point of leaving the room. "Has the nurse been located?"

"In all the excitement, I did forget about her, milord. Do you want her pursued?"

His suggestion was ridiculous, given the number of staff they had here. Too few for an attempted recapture. "No, but inform me immediately if she returns to the manor. I will not know how to deal with her absence until Lilly wakes, in any case."

Giles stared at the still form in the bed, but heard the unmistakable snort that passed his butler's mouth. Was it because he'd slipped and used Lilly's first name? Giles ignored him and Dithers left without another word, though he did not take Giles' worries with him.

Lilly could still die. Giles didn't want another death at Cottingstone to haunt him. Another failure to torment his restless moments.

When the maid came to relieve him, he chose to remain too.

Hours later, he turned his head to watch his sleeping ghost. Night had fallen and she still hadn't moved. Somehow, he'd grown accustomed to the panicked beat of his heart. He stood, stretched out the kinks from sitting so long, and ran his fingers along the coverlet-covered arm. She twitched, but other than that small movement, she did nothing more encouraging.

After glancing over to check if the maid was still napping, he captured a limp strand of hair and rubbed it between his fingers. Giles loved the color, the texture. He sighed. He should not be alone with Lillian Winter. Given the way his mind was working, he would be extremely bad for her reputation. Lilly would soon go away for the rest of her life and never see the world again.

Giles finally understood his mother's depression over his father's sudden absence from her life. Seeing Lilly, knowing she was destined for a reclusive existence, unsettled his stomach. Incarceration was as bad as death.

Mrs. Osprey slipped into the room and sent the maid away. "Are you recovered from the shock, my lord?"

"As much as I will ever be. My apologies. My earlier outburst was unforgivable," he muttered.

"I imagine she's something of a surprise—so pretty and fine boned. An angel."

"You've met her before, too?" It was clear from her tone that she was fond of Lilly.

"Yes. Before her accident, I was assigned to serve her at first."

"You were to watch over her?" He snapped out in surprise. "I can see you did a fine job of it."

Mrs. Osprey flinched and fussed with her tray of food. "Lady

Winter dismissed me from my duties the day before the accident." Regret clouded Mrs. Osprey's features, draining Giles' anger as swiftly as it had come.

"Why did she do that?"

"She said I was a bad influence on her daughter. She urged your mama to dismiss me." Mrs. Osprey's chin firmed. "It was only a plate of sweets I took to her. I didn't know the baroness had issued an order that she be denied."

"Denied what?"

"Denied food, my lord, as punishment."

"What reason could there be for that?"

"I never did hear, but I did learn that this particular form of punishment was often used by Lady Winter. The poor thing was starving." Mrs. Osprey's voice broke to a wail on the last word.

Giles ran his fingers through his hair. "You gave her more than just sweets, didn't you?"

Mrs. Osprey fidgeted. "Yes."

Giles thought about the risk Mrs. Osprey had taken to feed Lilly as a child. She could have been dismissed for disobeying. "Well done, Mrs. Osprey."

Mrs. Osprey gave a half smile, but tears threatened to fall. "You should eat before your dinner becomes cold, my lord."

Giles ate quickly while Mrs. Osprey fussed about the room. She should be a Dithers, he thought, wondering why she had never married. She had always been a pretty woman to his way of thinking. Surely the men of her class were not as blind as all that. There was that small problem of her mind slipping, but it should only be a small consideration. Only he and Dithers had noticed it so far.

"I have some soup for Miss Winter too. Will you assist me, my lord?"

Giles pressed the napkin to his mouth and stood. "Of course. I can finish my dessert later."

He approached the bed, tugged back the covers, and reached for Lilly's shoulders to raise her upper body. She did not resist him. She was as soft as a rag doll. Giles sat behind her, letting her body rest against his chest while one of his hands cradled her face. Mrs. Osprey leaned in close with the spoon and pressed it to Lilly's lips.

At first, nothing appeared to happen—but then Lilly moved, lashing out with her arms, knocking the spoon from his housekeeper's hands.

Mrs. Osprey's reaction was comical. Her hands flew into the air and she rocked like ninepins. They were fortunate Lilly had not hit the bowl of soup.

"Now, now, Miss Winter, none of that nonsense. Just got a nice bit of chicken broth to strengthen you. Here now, try again."

Mrs. Osprey once again pushed the spoon at Lilly's mouth, and again she avoided it.

While Mrs. Osprey dithered, Giles stroked the side of Lilly's face. "You must eat, Lilly. Your father will be vexed with me if you do not. If he returns and finds you ailing again, he will no doubt take me to task over the matter. Do not fight poor Mrs. Osprey. She is a good, kind woman who wants to see you well again. Eat her chicken broth and save me from dining on it for breakfast tomorrow."

The bundle resting against his chest struggled, but he held her firm, splaying his fingers across her ribs. Lilly stilled.

Mrs. Osprey held out the spoon again. The housekeeper beamed when the spoon was received and drained to her satisfaction. Lilly managed five more mouthfuls before she turned her head away, snuggling farther into Giles' chest.

She had not consumed enough to feed a sparrow, let alone a grown woman, but at least she had taken something. Mrs. Osprey gathered up her things and departed the room, leaving Giles sitting on the bed with Lilly still cradled in his arms.

Giles' experiences with women in his arms were limited to the times he had held them during sex. He liked the tactile contact of a partially clothed or naked body against his, but he was unsure of what he was doing still holding Lillian Winter. He found he liked it very much.

God help him if he ever had her naked.

He swallowed an oath even as he traced the curve of her face, trailed along her jaw and upper neck, unable to resist touching her translucent skin. She was so soft and delicate.

"Giles?"

His cock throbbed from hearing her speak his name. When he didn't answer immediately, she wriggled as if preparing to move.

"I have you safe, Lilly."

His words calmed her. Lilly slumped and fell silent. In a short time, Giles realized she had fallen asleep against him. He eased out from behind her back and laid her gently against the pillows. She didn't stir. Her eyes were closed and her breath sounded even and deep. He covered her again, wishing he might have seen Mrs. Osprey's view. He wished he had caught a glimpse of her eyes.

Chapter Six

———•———

The first things Lilly noticed were the brightness of her room and the fact that there was no nurse snoring by the hearth. That last was unusual. She had never been truly alone since her accident. There was always an efficient and upright woman in drab muslin waiting to spoon a hefty dose of laudanum into her often-unwilling mouth.

Sometimes the pain was bad enough that she was glad to drink it. But not always.

Because of the laudanum, time passed in a blur. She could not always tell one day from another. If she were honest—one year from the next. The world was moving faster than Lilly could comprehend, and the seemingly sudden changes frightened her.

Her nurses did not always talk. The current one did not. Lilly only learned of things from her papa as he gently reminded her what day it was, where they were, and read parts of the newssheet to her until she fell asleep again.

Lilly frowned, momentarily swamped by confusion until she remembered she was at Cottingstone Manor. She breathed easy—she'd loved this place as a child. While her parents had dined and chatted the day away, she had slipped out to enjoy what little freedom she could find.

As the only child in residence, she had spent hours alone in the nursery, playing with the boy's toys she'd found and writing secrets in her journal. Not that she had many secrets, but she had pretended her journal was a friend. She'd always wished for one. Wolfhounds did not count.

A yip gained her attention. There was Atticus again, his long muzzle shot through with gray, feet twitching in sleep. He'd grown bigger than she'd ever imagined he would become. She smiled, but became immediately aware that she ached all over.

Pain was a familiar sensation she expected but tried her best to ignore. No matter how the doctors had prodded and poked, nothing took the pain away except for laudanum. But the potion also took the world away.

Another memory rose. A spoon placed gently against her lips. A flurry of anxious words. Usually the nurses were very grim about her consumption of the stuff, but the voice she remembered held kindness.

Papa had left her alone.

Lilly's heart stilled. He had not once left her side for more than a few hours since the accident. He'd said he would be gone for days, maybe longer. She gingerly removed her arm from the blankets and reached for the dog, twisting her fingers into his shaggy coat and securing them over his ear.

She would not cry, but she was suddenly very afraid at a memory that rose up to fill her with dread, shattering the little bit of peace she had that day. It was a memory she had long wanted to forget.

Her mama had whispered, "If you cannot get better, then you may as well be dead. You are nothing I can take any pride in."

Pain had blinded her then. She couldn't breathe or see. The next things Lilly remembered were her parents screaming at each other across her bed, and shooting pain arcing down her spine and into her skull as she struggled for each new breath.

That was the last time she had seen her home or her mother. Papa had never taken her back.

A wet tongue dragged across her wrist, breaking her thoughts. Atticus had woken and was inching toward her, sad eyes searching her face. She moved her wrist away from his tongue, tugging him tightly to her side. Blinding pain gripped her so she closed her eyes, breathing through her mouth to survive it. When the spasms had passed and she could open her eyes again, the dog's nose was inches from her own.

Lilly pushed his muzzle away until he settled beside her. Needing his comforting presence, she laid her arm around him and squeezed as much as she could without causing more pain.

It was wonderful to touch another warm being. It happened so rarely. Papa was so careful not to aggravate her injuries that he only ever skimmed her brow to check for fever.

She squinted at what she could see without moving. A pretty rose-pink room surrounded her, perhaps one of the guest rooms on the first floor. Lilly liked the room very much, but wished it were darker.

Her pulse throbbed behind her eyes and she fought to ignore the warning sign of an impending headache. It was not often that she could appreciate the places she stayed, but the room was lovely.

Chicken broth.

She remembered sipping chicken broth from a blue-edged bowl and suddenly wished for some more. Her tongue rasped dry over her lips at the memory. The warm liquid had slipped down easily, but she had become full so soon, and tired too.

Atticus had been beside her, but farther away from her than normal. She remembered the sharp, sweet smell of sickness, but the memory lurched and merged with others. She remembered old faces, Lady Daventry's portrait, and carpet under her cheek. She shrugged away the memory, fearing it might never make sense.

Lilly moved a little, trying to ease the uncomfortable pressing of her full bladder. There was no help for it; she would have to call the nurse. But what was her name? Lilly racked her brain. Dibbs. Yes, that's right.

She took a quick breath and turned herself toward the direction she thought the chamber pot might be. While sharp knives of pain sliced through her head, she remembered another arm around her, strong like Papa, but different.

A man had held her. His scent had soothed her nerves, his deep voice had rumbled through her ribs. But she had been unable to see the body that owned the voice. He had used her name, too. He'd begged her to eat the soup so he did not have to. That warm body had cradled hers as she sipped the broth, his breath fanning over her cheek, keeping the chill of night at bay.

A firm hand had held her head gently against a hard chest, soothing the skin of her cheek and jaw. Those same fingers had stroked her neck, too, taking away her dizziness and replacing it with peace. Papa never did that. He would never think to rub her feet or slip stockings over her cold toes.

Cold...she remembered being cold. She shook her head suddenly, but the action pulled a whimper from her throat. After all this time, she should know better. Little movements were all she could manage.

When she opened her eyes, she faced the foot of the bed on the other side, but there was still no sign of the nurse. Turning her head the remaining distance, she took in the rest of the room and gasped.

There was no nurse in the room. Instead, sprawled out on a chair close to the bed was a ginger-haired Adonis, the most beautiful man Lilly had ever seen—and she had seen a fair bit of this one.

Giles Wexham slept beside her bed, between her and the bare window. For a moment, she was distracted by the unusual sight of the early morning sunrise, but she quickly returned to Giles.

In sleep, the lines around his eyes were softer, the ginger stubble on his jaw longer than she had ever seen it. His hair was disordered, his clothes rumpled, but that was not an unusual appearance for him. She gazed at him in speechless wonder. What was he doing here?

Startlingly blue eyes opened, and she pulled her arm away from Atticus to watch Giles waking from sleep. He was a very beautiful man, but so very wicked. He regarded her in silence, his eyes never leaving hers for the longest time.

Lilly understood why she did not speak. Giles' presence always rendered her mute, but she knew he liked to talk, especially to women. She had observed Giles, while remaining hidden from society, watching him charm and conquer other women with the ease of one sure of his appeal.

Giles moved slowly, a sleek predator even by day. He drew close to her side, and she had to adjust the angle of her head to keep him in view. Pain lanced through her skull.

When her vision cleared, she found Giles leaning over her, enveloping her in warmth and the scent of clean male. Oh, he was wonderful. Whatever it was he bathed in helped her relax into the mattress once more.

It was a little unnerving to have him so close, though. She was not used to gentlemen, but a buzz of pleasure fizzled through her at his undivided attention. His face slowly creased into a smile so unlike what she was used to seeing. He looked pleased to see her, and she smiled in return.

Lilly saw his eyes dip down to her mouth. Surprise held her still until she wondered how long it had been since she'd scratched at her teeth. She pressed her lips together.

"Hello, Lilly." Giles spoke her name softly and warmth spread over her limbs.

"Hello, Giles," she mumbled.

His even, white teeth were as blinding as the light. "It is good to see you awake. I was beginning to worry. Your dreams must have been wonderful to sleep for so long."

"I don't remember dreaming."

He straightened, but didn't leave her line of sight. "I appear to have lost my dog to you. What sorcery have you over the beast, fair maiden? Atticus has barely left your side in days."

She did not dare turn her head for fear of causing more pain. "He is a very good dog, Giles. He was kind to me when I was here last."

"Yes, I heard about that. I apologize for the damage he caused your limbs."

"He was kind to a child left alone for much of the house party. We had a great deal of fun together. It was my last great adventure." Lilly slowly reached to touch the dog, sweat breaking out across her face at the effort of keeping silent. "Call the nurse, Giles. I have need of her."

Giles frowned, erasing the friendly face she had just started to get used to. "I am afraid you are looking at your temporary nurse. The blasted woman up and left your employ in the dead of night. She abandoned you."

Lilly's mind whirled. She needed to get out of bed and relieve herself. Giles could not be her nurse. "Call for a maid, or the housekeeper."

"I cannot do that either. They are busy elsewhere."

"Oh, no," Lilly sobbed, struggling to free herself from the

heavy blankets, hissing as pain and the ever-present nausea swamped her.

"What the devil are you doing?" Giles gripped her shoulders. She winced as the pressure twisted her body to a position it did not like.

"I need privacy." Lilly pulled the covers back, but could not suppress a groan as spears of pain stabbed down her limbs.

"Privacy for what, for God's sake?"

"Just have to…" She could not say it aloud—not to him.

"Oh, for heaven's sake." Strong arms scooped her up, holding her close to that calming scent. Lilly closed her eyes over her tears. "Where is it you need to go?"

"The chamber pot," she whispered, humiliation heating her cheeks.

She had just asked the most handsome man she had ever laid eyes on to help with such a personal matter. Could her circumstances sink any lower?

His movements jarred her body. His loud steps assaulted her mind. He eased her downward, but just before touching down, the fabric of her nightgown slid out from beneath her bottom.

If pain hadn't robbed her of sight already, she wouldn't be able to look at him. Thankfully, his loud steps hinted that he'd moved far away.

When she was comfortable again, she gathered her strength to stand, but Giles returned. He swept her up without a word, took her back to bed, and tucked her in with more care than any nursemaid ever had.

"What can I get you, Lilly?"

He pushed her sweat-damp hair from her face then patted soft linen against her skin. Unwilling to see the pity in his gaze, she kept her eyes closed. She was such a failure as a woman.

As the pain settled down again, bare fingertips brushed her temple. More tears gathered and these fell down her cheeks. Giles kindly brushed them away without a word.

"I am thirsty."

His fingers wriggled into Lilly's hair, supporting her head as she rose. Cool, slippery glass pressed to her lips and she took a few hasty sips with her eyes still closed. Lilly lay back, gasping for air. The pain had obliterated her ability to hide how bad she felt.

Again, Giles brushed her face with a touch as gentle as a feather. "Will you eat now?"

"In a little while, perhaps."

Something strange brushed against her temple. She opened her eyes. Giles' lips were an inch from her skin. Warm breath beat against her cheek as his head settled to touch hers. She snapped her eyes shut.

"You need to eat, Lilly. I will have the housekeeper bring up a tray for you, but do not ever hesitate to ask me to help you. I have a great deal to make up for."

Giles made a small, indistinct sound, and then he withdrew from the bed. When she reopened her eyes, he was truly gone from the room and she was all alone. Only Atticus stayed.

However would she be able to forget what had just passed?

Lilly lay still as the pain receded to a dull ache, attempting to alter the memory so it wasn't a chamber pot he carried her to but a cushioned chaise, complete with champagne and cherries to nibble on. That memory would be much easier to contemplate if it were true.

When Giles returned, she found she could look at him without blushing. He brought servants with him, one for the fire and one for the chamber pot. Her little fantasy crumbled as the contents flew out the window.

"Good morning, Miss Winter." A plain, round-faced woman carrying a well-laden tray hurried toward her. "I'm Mrs. Osprey, his lordship's housekeeper. Do you remember me?"

Lilly searched her mind, but shook her head the tiniest amount. "I'm sorry. My memory is not what it should be. It's nice to meet you again, Mrs. Osprey. What have you there?"

"Scrambled eggs, ham, fresh buttered bread, and a saucer of hot chocolate. A breakfast fit for a lady." The housekeeper beamed, set the tray down on the bed, then shooed the dog away when he took too much interest in it.

Lilly gulped back sudden nausea at the thought of eating all that food. She closed her eyes tightly.

Giles covered her wrist with a light pressure that sent shivers down her spine. "What is it?"

"Too much," Lilly whispered, blinded by the urge to cast up her accounts. Not that there would be much to come out, but dry retching was horrid and always made her headaches worse.

She breathed her way through the sensation and eventually opened her eyes. Mrs. Osprey and the breakfast tray were gone.

"My apologies. We did not consider that your stomach might be delicate. Mrs. Osprey will fetch something plainer," Giles murmured, brushing a handkerchief across her clammy brow. "Are you all right now?"

He refolded the cloth but Lilly was puzzled by his attendance. "Yes, the nausea has passed. I would eat it if I could. Please apologize to Cook for the inconvenience."

"Don't worry about Cook. She will enjoy the challenge," Giles assured her, brushing her hair away from her face.

He glanced at his hand then laughed heartily at something only he found funny. He didn't explain. Unfortunately, his movements shook the bed.

Lilly could not help but groan aloud. "Can you measure me a portion of laudanum, please?"

"I am afraid not." Giles squeezed her hand gently in his larger one and held it tightly. "On my order, we do not keep that mixture at Cottingstone. Mrs. Osprey checked through your baggage and could not find further bottles anywhere. You will have to survive without."

Giles waited for her reply, but she didn't know what to say. She had never had to deal with the pain without the medicine before. Surely, she could manage until Papa returned.

Giles rubbed the back of her hand, soothing her worries away for all of a minute. "Can I do anything else for you?"

Her eyes fluttered shut. Although the dark frightened her, she couldn't tolerate the bright light any longer. Her pulse beat a fast tempo behind her eyes, sending sharp pain to the top of her skull. "The light is too bright. Would you mind closing the drapes?"

"Of course. Mrs. Osprey, place the tray next to me, and see to it," Giles directed then shifted closer. "Lilly, have a bite of this."

"What is it?" Even her own words hurt.

"Just bread."

Something soft brushed Lilly's lips and she opened her mouth to take a small bite. Could the day get any worse? Now he was feeding her. She managed three bites before clamping her lips closed.

"You need to eat more than that, Lilly. It's not enough to feed a sparrow," Giles grumbled, and Lilly had to wonder why he should care so much. No one else ever did. She opened her eyes to find him regarding her somewhat quizzically, as if she was a puzzle to solve. "Try to eat more later, all right? I don't want you wasting away."

"I will try."

"I have your word?"

Lilly frowned. What did it matter to him whether she ate or not? But he appeared to be waiting on her answer. "Yes, you have my word."

That seemed to appease him; his shoulders relaxed, and he stood. "Good. I will check on you later, but Mrs. Osprey will stay and keep you company. Get some rest."

It was good he was leaving. Her head had begun to throb in earnest now. But her tightening throat choked off her farewell as he disappeared from view. He was better off without her company.

He was perfect.

Chapter Seven

———◆———

"Milord, Mrs. Osprey believes Miss Winter has developed a slight fever," Dithers informed him after dinner. "She has some concerns and wishes for your opinion."

Giles cursed. He had spent the day thinking Lilly's health somewhat improved, but he should have known it was too good to be true. Of course, the other reason he had stayed away was that he did not trust himself in Lilly's company. He had developed an annoying habit of touching her and he had no right to do that.

Yes, well all right, this morning he had attempted to kiss her brow, too.

To distract himself from temptation he had gone over his plans for the restoration of Cottingstone Manor. He'd hired laborers from the village and they would start tomorrow. Ten additional men would be about the house and grounds for the next two weeks—bringing order where chaos now reigned.

The little business he had brought with him from London was complete by late afternoon, and he sat alone in his study, glass of port in hand, doing what he usually did at the manor: recuperating.

The life he led in London, a life spent in the pursuit of pleasure, actually required a great deal of energy to maintain. There were places to go, women to chase, possessiveness to avoid.

Yes, a very exhausting life.

Except that tonight he could not settle comfortably. His mind kept turning to the problem he housed upstairs. "You are certain she has a fever?"

"No, milord. I said that Mrs. Osprey thinks she has one. We do not always agree, but I have not tested her wisdom on the young miss. You told me not to annoy your housekeeper, and I am hesitant to place my hands on Miss Winter to check her diagnosis."

"You could lose a hand that way," Giles growled, but the shock of uttering such a territorial statement aloud rocked him.

"That is what I thought, milord. Hence my coming to you." Dithers glanced around the chamber with the appearance of idle inspection, but his clenched jaw hinted he was trying very hard to keep his face blank of expression.

Giles held back another growl. Dithers' amusement was the least of his problems. Lilly needed him and he wanted to assist her. After the things he'd done before her innocent eyes, he had a lot to make up for.

"I will be there directly."

Dropping his drink to the desk, Giles stood, tugged down his waistcoat, adjusted his sleeves, and controlled his footsteps out of the study. It would not do to appear in too much of a hurry— even if his heart pounded in anticipation of seeing her.

Dithers had said that the fever was slight, but the man rushed ahead to open her bedchamber door as if she were bound for the afterlife at any moment.

The first things Giles noticed were that Atticus was not in the room, and the edges of the chamber were as dark as Hades. Giles could barely pick out Mrs. Osprey sitting in the chair by the bed, wringing her hands in obvious agitation.

His feet propelled him all the way to the edge of the bed without pause. *May as well be controlled by strings and a master puppeteer, you idiot.* He touched Lilly without conscious thought. Too hot. Her skin seemed tight with heat.

Giles did not know what to do. He had no knowledge of healing whatsoever.

Haunting gray eyes flickered open and struggled to focus on him. He shifted closer so she didn't have to move her head to see him, but her eyes were dull, reflecting vast pain. "Lilly, where do you hurt?"

"Aside from the usual places?" Lilly's rasping voice pained him, and she swallowed and grimaced to prove her discomfort. He nodded, brushing her hair back from burning-hot cheeks, enjoying the touch of his fingertips on her skin even if she was suffering. Her eyes closed again. "My throat hurts, and I have a headache."

Giles continued to stroke her skin and listened as her breathing settled in time to his strokes. Christ, he could play this woman like a lute if she was well enough. She seemed unusually responsive to him. "Where are the usual places you have pain, Lilly?"

He was curious about her injuries. Hell, he was curious about everything related to her. He stroked her skin until she answered. "Neck, back, arms, and legs. The places that bounced off the rocks the hardest."

He touched her scarred wrist. "Do these pain you?" He rubbed his fingertips over the rough bite marks.

"They never have that I can remember. Everything else hurt worse."

A throat cleared, reminding Giles that he had an audience and that he shouldn't be touching Lilly more than was strictly necessary. Giles truly wished he could stop himself. "What can you recommend, Mrs. Osprey?"

Mrs. Osprey's eyes fell to Lilly, nodding as she thought over a treatment. "Honeyed tea to soothe her tender throat, cold cloths applied to reduce the fever during the night, and a broth to give strength. If Miss Winter could manage to eat more it would be a blessing," Mrs. Osprey mused.

"Very proper, Mrs. Osprey. See to it."

Mrs. Osprey fluttered from the room.

"Dithers have more firewood brought up and another jug of cold water." Dithers remained. "What is it now man?"

The butler leaned close enough to whisper. "I hope you know what you're doing with her, milord. You are the last Wexham, if you remember."

"Yes, obviously," Giles scowled.

"Don't get too caught up in playing nursemaid. We do wish to keep you in good health," Dithers pointed out as he trailed after Mrs. Osprey.

"Dithers has turned into a mother hen," Lilly murmured behind him. "Instead of the scallywag I expected."

Giles turned. "You remember my butler?"

"Bits and pieces. The maids were all enamored of his smiles when he was only a footman."

"You would never guess it to look at him now. Nothing but stern glares for everyone."

"Even you?"

Giles chuckled. "Especially me. He had a well-earned reputation for breaking hearts as a younger man. More than one lass fell in love with him, but he kept his dignity and never married. I cannot understand why he does not trust me," Giles confessed, trying to act wounded.

"He does have a point. Under normal circumstances, you would be a dangerous man, indeed. But he quite forgets that it is impossible to seduce someone as ill as I am," Lilly whispered, voice breaking over some of the words. "I'm not worth the effort."

Giles arched a brow. Her lack of affectation was refreshing. "And what do you know of seductions, Lilly?"

"More than I care to, Lord Daventry." She said no more, and closed her eyes again.

Giles watched her closely, fascinated by her sharp breathing and the rise and fall of her breasts.

Ashamed that he thrummed with lust, he hurried to the basin on the dresser and poured tepid water onto a cloth. Lilly needed his care, not his wayward imaginings. At least she had no idea of the thoughts swirling through his head.

He squeezed out most of the water and crossed back to her side, lowering himself to the mattress. As the bed bowed under his weight, he noticed Lilly biting her lip and realized *any* movement disturbed her comfort.

He dared not move again, and he pressed the wet cloth to her face. Her exhaled breath on the inside of his damp wrist sent a shudder rolling through him.

After the cloth became too warm to provide any comfort, he faced a dilemma. He needed to re-wet it. But when he stood he would certainly disturb her again. He did not want to give her more pain. He glanced over at the door, listening in the hope of approaching assistance.

"I am sorry," Lilly whispered.

Perplexed, Giles looked down. "Sorry for what?"

"This is not how you usually spend your time, is it, Lord Daventry? I am apologizing for disturbing your peace." She kept her eyes downcast and Giles was bothered by her retreat into formality. He had grown to like the way she said his name.

"Giles," he reminded her. "No, you are correct. I have not tended many bedsides. However, I am more than happy to be beside yours. Usually when I am here, I keep to my own company and rarely speak to anyone. Do you perceive the improvement in my circumstances? I have the opportunity to talk to a very pretty girl and rise before noon."

He enjoyed caring for her very much, a surprise that left him a little giddy. Despite, or perhaps because of, her injuries, she was very easy to be near. He didn't have to be anything but himself— a very rare experience. He leaned close to whisper into her ear. "The servants want to call a doctor to attend *me*."

When Giles leaned back, she stared at him. He smiled a slow, seductive smile, one that had worked on many a pretty woman. Lilly did not smile back.

"That was poorly done of you, my lord." Lilly's voice wavered as she spoke. She turned her head away abruptly, only to gasp in pain.

Giles ran back over his words, puzzled. He had not said anything that should have upset her. He rose to refresh the cloth, looking out the crack in the drapes as he thought. Calling a doctor because the servants thought him mad was a joke. Had someone tried to commit her to Bedlam at some point?

He looked back to where she lay, doing her best to ignore him, and could not credit it. Her mind was too well formed for madness. No, it must have been something else.

The only other thing he had said had been a compliment. She was pretty. She mesmerized him. Lilly had done so since the first night he saw her. If she thought she was unattractive then someone must have said as much. Giles wanted to shake the person who had dared make her think so poorly of herself.

He walked back over and stood a moment gazing down at the

face he could not get enough of seeing. "Lilly, look at me."

Her eyes flickered and opened. He leaned over so she would not have to turn. "I do not lie, Lilly. You are very pretty. Trust me on this."

She blinked tears and Giles wiped her face, taking the evidence away. He waited for the tears to stop. She finally glanced at him and smiled hesitantly. He reached out and rubbed the damp cloth across the tip of her nose, then went to fetch the bowl so he would not have to leave her side again.

Lilly stayed silent while Giles cooled her, and he had time to wonder if her family had dampened her spirit before, or after, the accident. Lady Winter was a vain woman, in his opinion, and he could credit her with attempting to quash the confidence of her daughter so she had all of the attention. Lilly was prettier, after all, and would one day outrank her. Perhaps it was done out of jealousy.

Mrs. Osprey went to bed when Lilly's fever abated, but Giles stayed. He could tell that she was in pain from her old injuries now, and it seemed more than she could bear in silence. He had Dithers fetch a bottle of brandy from his study, and a single glass for the fiery spirit, then dismissed him.

As the house fell silent, Giles reached for the amber liquid. He poured a deep glass, holding it to her lips so she could drink. She gagged on the unfamiliar taste, but he had nothing better to offer.

When she had drunk down a full glass, she began talking with a slight slur to her words. "Of course, what I notice most of all is that no one touches me anymore. Only Papa." She shook her head. Apparently the brandy was quick to numb her pain. "Oh, and you do. Your hands are so warm and soothing. I wish that you could keep doing that."

"What was that, Lilly?"

"Oh, you called me Lilly again. I thought I had imagined it. You smell so good, too. Not like him. His breath smells like rotting fish. Eww. I hope he does not come here."

As Giles touched her face and his thumb stroked her lower pouting lip, he wondered whom she meant. Perhaps a doctor? But Lord Winter sounded as if he had given up on doctors, so he could have promised no one would come near Lilly again.

Her breath puffed over his thumb and Giles, struggling not to become aroused, set the glass down on the floor. She was far too trusting, never protesting as he slid his hand to her shoulder to rub across muscles grown stiff with tension.

Lilly shifted sensuously beneath the covers and an idea came to him. One of his greatest gifts was his ability to use his hands to give pleasure. He wondered if Lilly would let him try it out on her.

Many a woman had crumbled under his skilled fingers, and offered him everything if he would just keep rubbing her back. Would it work on Lilly's injuries and give her some relief?

When Giles rubbed just a bit harder, Lilly took in a shuddering breath and her muscles relaxed. That gave him hope. "Lilly, would you trust me?"

No sane woman would ever say yes to this question if she had plans to keep her skirts down, but he wondered what Lilly's response would be anyway. He continued to stroke over taut muscles. She breathed deeply on each stroke.

Her breath caught. "Yes, I trust you, Giles. I probably shouldn't, should I?"

"You are right to doubt me, but I want to try something. I want to roll you over and rub the muscles on your back and legs to see if that gives you some relief from the pain. Do you think you could bear it?" Giles gulped before he confessed the last part of his plan. "I would have to remove your nightdress to do so."

That wasn't strictly true, but she would enjoy the experience better without the linen rasping over her delicate skin. Lilly studied his face for quite some time before she pulled the ribbon at the neckline of her nightgown undone, and rolled away from him. She moved slowly and Giles was able to wriggle the material down. When her back was exposed to her hips, he gasped out loud.

Lord, she was thin.

Giles could easily see all the bones of her ribs and back, sharp under pale, thin skin. He gulped at the scars she bore. White, jagged lines spread over her upper back and one hip. Lilly panted loudly and so did he, but his frantic breath was not from pain.

Giles hurried to the door. It would be just his luck to have Dithers return right now.

When the door locked, he raced back to the bed, knowing he had a short amount of time to experiment on her injuries. He crawled onto the bed over her very carefully, rubbing from the base of her spine up to her shoulders in one gentle sweep. Lilly whimpered.

"Did that hurt?"

"No, Giles."

Using both hands, he set to work without speaking again, straddling her hips to begin with, but careful not to place any weight on her body. She moaned against his pressure, and he grew more certain with each pass of his hands that her moans were not of pain, but relief.

He rubbed over her spine and shoulder blades, out along her arms. Giles returned to her neck and worked softly there for some time, then returned to her back and bumped along her bony rib cage, down to where her nightgown stopped him. He reversed himself and drew the material up her body, baring her legs and her backside.

His mouth grew dry. He could not have spoken if his life depended on it. There were more scars on her legs. He rubbed his hands up and down, noting the tightness of the skin and muscle, then rubbed her tiny feet, too, and spent considerable time softening them.

He worked back up and over her whole body again and again, enjoying having his hands occupied on bare skin, and getting no suggestion from Lilly to stop at any point. Aside from the occasional deep moan, she rarely made a sound.

When he did stop, he stared at her soft skin and swallowed hard. The scars did not detract from her body. She was beautifully formed—small waist that could do with some extra padding, along with her ribs, generous hips that flared out to perfect globes that made his mouth water. Given his position and the angle of her legs, he could just make out a thatch of white hair between her legs. He groaned, tempted to bury his head and taste her.

A loud snore stopped him cold. Then another sounded, and he snorted. He was painfully aroused by his good-intentioned actions, but she was asleep.

Giles scooted off the bed and adjusted her nightgown so she

was decent again, then carefully rolled her over to her back, never even glimpsing her breasts under the thick material. He pulled the blankets up to her chin, just to make sure that view was definitely barred to him.

When the bed looked as if Lilly had not had company, he crossed to the door and unlocked it. Quietly, he re-crossed the chamber and took his place beside the bed, stretching out to imitate sleep in case Dithers thought to check on his activities.

Giles tried to subdue his raging erection, and took some time doing it. Dithers peeked in just as he had won that war. He brought with him a light supper and wished Giles good night, glancing at him with a strange gleam in his eyes.

If Giles didn't know better, he would bet that Dithers had lowered his standards and stuck his eye into the keyhole earlier to peek through.

"They've not passed through here, Mr. Barrette."

Bartholomew looked up at the hovering groom and scowled, none too pleased with the news. Another day wasted, another day lost scouring the countryside for Baron Winter's coach. He had been so certain the old man would have headed toward familiar haunts, but this time he'd gone to ground good and proper.

He glanced at his dust-covered servant, Brown, through the gathering gloom of the taproom. "We'll spend the night here. Be ready to depart at first light." The man tugged his forelock and scurried out of the taproom.

Curse that bitch to hell and back.

At least this tavern served better swill, and he could safely drink his fill tonight. It also offered a better class of tart. A comely wench swung her hip close to his arm so her skirts brushed. She apologized, but then did it twice more. She leaned forward to take his empty tankard away, giving him an unimpeded view of her breasts.

Strumpet.

But at least she was blonde.

He ordered another ale, noticing the innkeeper's gaze on the woman too. A wife, or a daughter, Bartholomew didn't give a damn. She'd be after coin for her troubles either way.

He kept track of her movements. When the innkeeper grew distracted by another patron, the woman slipped out the back, glancing over her shoulder to see if he had noticed. After a moment or two, Bartholomew climbed to his feet and followed.

Moonlight made the shabby kitchen garden pleasing, and he found the woman waiting by a garden wall. Without a word, she drew him near, clutching at his arse like a woman possessed by passion. If he didn't know just what she was after, and what she'd actually get, he might have been amused.

"You'd best be quick. My husband's got a terrible temper, but I've a mind for a pretty dress."

He turned the little woman against the wall, slammed her head against the rough stone and hitched her skirts high. "You should be more afraid of me than your husband. No one knows you're with me."

The tart whimpered.

"And they never will. I'll pay you well, but shut your stupid mouth, or this will only get rougher."

Her head nodded marginally. He freed himself from the tight confines of his breeches, spread her thighs, and took her with one hard thrust.

She cried out, but Barrette was too consumed by hatred to do more than tighten his grip on her hips. He forced her legs wider, slamming into her with every frustration he'd carried on his shoulders for the past days.

He wished this was Lillian. The perfect daughter would make a perfectly good fuck if he could ever catch her alone. He'd bend her to his will – force her to do things with him and no other. He would make her father regret his decision not to accept his suit. Lilly's dowry should stay with him and Dumas.

He finished with a grunt, straightened his clothing, and dumped a generous handful of coins on the ground. She gasped for breath, but made no move to straighten herself. He walked away, but after a few steps he turned back to offer advice. "Buy any color dress you like, but not lemon. Only a walking corpse wears lemon."

Chapter Eight

———◆———

Giles woke late the next day, which was surprising, considering that he was sleeping upright in a wingchair in Lilly's bedchamber. His back ached from the strange position, and he groaned as his knotted muscles protested.

Blinking rapidly, he noticed the room was as bright as the partially closed drapes would allow. But he could clearly see that the fire had gone out long ago. He'd slept right through the night without stirring, and he hoped Lilly had done the same. When he turned toward the bed, he found her watching him with her lips slightly parted. He smiled at her, happy to see her awake already.

Her hair was mussed quite badly, her nightgown parted at her throat where he'd failed to tie it securely, but her gray eyes held his calmly. He wasn't sure what kind of reception he'd find this morning, but then Lilly smiled, and Giles was grateful for the chair beneath him. "Good morning," she said.

When she smiled, she was not just pretty, but so beautiful she defied description. He was leaning over the bed, his hands beside her arms, staring down into her face before he knew what he was doing. Clear gray eyes looked back at him. He could see no clouds of pain masking her view.

His smile widened. "You're feeling better?"

"I feel so much better this morning. Thank you, Giles. Last night was a wonderful idea. However did you learn to do such things?"

Giles considered telling her the truth, then changed his mind. It was best not to lower Lilly's opinion of him any further so early in the day. "Just something I picked up somewhere."

Lilly's eyes dropped away in apparent modesty, and he admired the soft sweep of her lashes fanned against her cheeks. Without her direct scrutiny, he could let himself imagine her skin against his tongue and lips. How she might appear in the throes of passion.

It was wicked and wrong of him to consider an invalid in that light, but she stirred in him a beast that longed to pleasure as much as protect. Lilly's eyes shifted behind her lids. The way her body stilled gave him an idea. He could swear she was assessing his form.

A quick glance down reminded him that his mode of dress was improper. He had removed his cravat and opened his shirt collar when he had settled down to sleep.

Giles hoped he had not shocked her. His throat was exposed. She would probably be able to see all the way down inside his shirtfront. Did virgins scream at the sight of chest hair? He stayed still and, to his amusement, her eyes dipped.

This morning he was blessed with a fortuitous lack of erection. At this distance, she would not have been able to pretend not to see one. Thank God she had fallen asleep last night when his trousers had been uncomfortably tight.

Her gaze flickered up again, and he noticed a light blush had spread across her cheeks. The color suited her much better than the sickly pallor of yesterday. When gray eyes lifted to his, the blush turned bright pink.

Giles decided to be kind and moved his body back a bit. If Lilly was discomfited by his proximity, he would do his best to behave. Still, he caught her wrist lightly and traced soothing circles on her arm.

Lilly didn't pull away, but she did lick her lips. That pink tongue caused more mischief than she knew. He had to imagine the nude figure of the corpulent Lady Barrow to control his desires.

In the still chamber, the sound of her rapid breath rang loud in his ears. He affected her, and the thought made him smile. At least he was not completely alone, the only one unable to retain complete control over their behavior.

"Are you hungry?" he asked, breaking the silence that had thickened around them.

"Yes, a bit." She faltered, looking down to where her toes would be.

"Shall I send for your breakfast now?"

It occurred to him that it should be an uncomfortable morning for both of them. While he had been aware of Lilly's effect since he had first lain eyes on her, this was the beginning for her. Attractions had a way of rendering one speechless, and given he'd had his hands all over her bare skin last night, he should have expected some awkwardness between them.

She licked her lips again and Giles' groin throbbed at the dart of her tongue. "Not yet."

She didn't say any more, and with a start he realized she would never make demands on him. She wasn't being coy, or trying to wheedle his attention. She simply thought him too busy to bother. "What is it you need, Lilly?"

Lilly's sigh stirred the air beside his ear. "I need the chamber pot again."

He didn't care that she needed him for such a personal matter. He could not say whether he would do the same for any other woman though, but for Lilly, it appeared he would do anything to make amends.

"Here, let me help you." He helped her sit, but she swung her own legs over the side unassisted, showing a great deal of white leg in the process. Lilly never noticed or covered up. She perched on the edge and then slid off the side onto the floor.

Giles glimpsed a great deal more of her body. He could not prevent the surge of blood to his groin, but he did manage not to groan aloud. That, in itself, was quite an achievement.

Lilly had lovely legs. When he glanced at her face, she had closed her eyes and an odd smile played about her mouth. He wondered what she was thinking.

"No pain," Lilly whispered, as if reading his mind.

Startled, he gripped her arm tighter as elation roared through him. Surely, he was not that skilled. "None at all?"

"None yet."

Not willing to risk dampening her mood, he held out his arm and guided her across the room. One hand curled around her back, the other holding her hand. The posture was so reminiscent of dancing that he thought he heard music. He nearly laughed at the absurdity.

He did not promenade with women; he just fucked them a lot. The closest thing he had to female friends was the Marchioness of Ettington, wife of his friend Jack, and Jack's twin sister, Virginia. Both of them accepted that he would not change. They were very tolerant women.

Giles left Lilly at the screened corner and re-crossed the room to the door. He did not want to leave her side, but lingering would make her uncomfortable. The doorway was as far away as he was prepared to go, though. There was always a chance she'd need him for the return to bed. He did not want to undo the good he had achieved last night.

He had men coming today to begin work, and he hoped that Dithers had already set them to some of the tasks. It was not a good day to have slept so late. There was so much to do and oversee.

"Giles, help."

He spun to find Lilly hanging on to the screen with both hands. He dashed across the room and caught her against his body.

Lilly's fingers scraped his skin as she clutched at the linen of his shirt, but he could not savor the sensation. Giles scooped her up into his arms and held her tightly, peering down at her pale, damp face. "What happened?"

Giles' stomach had fallen to his toes.

She clutched at him, panic evident in her every gesture. "The room is spinning."

He tucked Lilly tightly to his chest and stood still, waiting for her dizziness to pass. When she relaxed her grip on his shirt, he moved carefully toward the bed. "Hmm, perhaps you need to eat something more substantial today."

Lilly gulped and he decided not to mention food again for a little while. Her breath fanned across his skin, stirring his chest hair and turning his nipples to hard points. Heaven help him he was out of control around Lilly. She tightened her grip on his shirt again and the scrape of fabric across the points increased his arousal.

"Christ, you're good," he whispered, struggling not to crush her against him.

"Good?"

He hadn't realized he'd said those words out loud. It was clear he needed to regain his mind and put her down but, to his horror, his arms were reluctant.

"Good at being so reasonable. Any other young miss would be screeching at me about compromising her."

Lilly let out a large sigh. "No one would believe me."

Giles looked down at the tiny bundle in his arms. "You shouldn't be so certain."

He would believe it. An innocent girl had turned him into a throbbing mess of need. She hadn't even had to resort to batting her eyelashes at him to do it, either.

Giles lowered Lilly to a sitting position and reached for the pillows to stack behind her. He gently eased her back, gathering up her long hair and pushing the tangled mass behind her shoulders. He fussed until he was satisfied she was comfortable, and then slid the blankets up to her chest.

He stood back to survey his handiwork. Lilly's hair needed washing and a thorough comb. It hung limply around her face. How had they managed to care for her with all the pain she had endured before?

In fact, he found himself wondering about everything that had happened to Lilly in her short life. Giles had never been this curious about another person before and constantly surprised himself by his unasked questions. What the devil was wrong with him this week?

"You are quite thin, you know. All the bones of your ribs show through your skin." As he'd hoped, flaming color returned to Lilly's cheeks at his words. "It is quite understandable. Rome was not built in a day, after all. Do you think you could bear to eat soon?"

"If you think I should."

Giles nodded. "I do. Perhaps that will prevent the dizziness from returning."

He tugged the bell hard. The quicker he could get the servants in here, the faster he could protect her virtue.

Dithers arrived and smiled when he saw Lilly awake. She returned his smile shyly and quickly dropped her eyes.

"Breakfast for Miss Winter, Dithers."

"Just toast, thank you," Lilly added.

"Not just toast. Bring hot chocolate, a plate of scrambled eggs, fresh buttered bread, and be quick about it."

Lilly looked at him for the first time with something other than good feeling, and he just shook his head at her and laughed.

"I never knew you were domineering."

Giles smiled. "Do you think you know everything about me, then?"

"I was told what to expect."

Giles blinked. "Did my mother instruct you?" He sank down onto the edge of the bed and clasped her hand in his. Finally, they might discuss their aborted union, and then the subject could be put away forever.

"She sent me lists of your favorite things to memorize. I have to say, you have a remarkable sweet tooth."

"I've always thought that the best of life is saved till late at night. Sweet pleasures can be better appreciated and savored by candlelight."

Lilly scowled. "You are no longer talking about desserts, are you?"

Giles chuckled that she saw through him already. "What else could I possibly mean?"

She didn't answer. He let go of her hand and crossed to the drapes, prepared to part them. He shouldn't have teased Lilly, but she had the advantage over him; he only had his slick silver tongue to tease her with. She apparently had an arsenal of parental confidences.

Remembering Lilly's aversion to light, he only opened half— just enough to illuminate the room for the servants' duties, but not enough to blind her by accident.

Lilly was blinking rapidly when he turned, but she appeared to become used to the increase in light.

"You should eat as much as you can at every meal," he said. "You do want to get up out of that bed at some point, don't you?"

Truth be told, Giles had no idea what Lilly felt about her

confinement. Given their success of last night, he was busy plotting her future outside of this chamber, and it certainly did not involve one-way travel to Wales.

The life her father planned for her was unacceptable.

Lilly rose up. "Of course I want to get out of this bed. Do you think I like being dependent on everyone?"

Giles crossed his arms over his chest. "I know that I would not. I just do not know if you are the kind of woman who enjoys being waited upon."

It was a deliberate goad. Lilly bristled, but held back a smile. Oh, yes, Lilly had fire. Now that the potions were clear of her system, he intended to keep her this way. He did not contemplate how he could achieve such a feat when she left the manor, but he would do all that he was able while she remained under his roof.

"Your mother should have added tyrant to the list."

He took his leave with an exaggerated bow and stalked from the room, suddenly troubled with her situation. He didn't want her to be unhappy, but he was fairly certain that she would be if Lord Winter had his way.

In his chambers, he ordered a bath and then ate a hearty breakfast before heading out of the house to check on the work of the day. He was still outside when Dithers found him a few hours later and informed him that Lilly had eaten well but was resting again. That did not surprise him. She was terribly weak. Regaining her strength would take time.

Dithers tugged on his dark waistcoat and looked about him with pride. "What you did last night, milord. It was the right choice to make. She looks so much better for it. How did you know what to do?"

Giles sighed. He should have known his butler was watching his every move. "Her muscles were as stiff as one of Cook's cutting boards. I merely softened her a bit."

"You may have to do it again. I didn't think she was quite so comfortable the last time I took in firewood. She might be in pain again." Dithers clearly enjoyed making inappropriate plans for Giles' evening.

"Yes, it is more than possible. She probably will not say a word about it, though." Giles glanced up at Lilly's window, wishing to catch a glimpse of her. "Will you arrange for a bath for her this afternoon after she wakes? Have all the maids attend her. She will need assistance with her hair, I should think."

"Are you sure that is wise, milord? The girls are not particularly strong. What if they need assistance lifting her? Do you want me to go in, or send one of the Davis boys?"

Giles growled at the thought of one of his male servants anywhere near a naked Lilly, but what Dithers suggested was outrageous. Giles should not be in the same room as a naked and wet Lilly. Did they want him married faster than he could blink?

The answer, of course, was yes. Both his butler and housekeeper had dropped enough hints that he shouldn't be surprised by their intentions. Heaven spare him from matchmaking servants.

He tried to think of another way of accomplishing the task and failed. Now that he thought about it, she might need his support.

Hell.

What would she think of being naked in his presence with servants around her to see?

Giles caved. "Tell Mrs. Osprey that I will assist her. Make sure there are plenty of sheets available, will you? Oh, and a blindfold will be necessary."

"Are you sure about the blindfold, milord?" Dithers asked. "What if you should trip and drop her?" His butler struggled not to laugh, and had calculated his questions simply to annoy the hell out of him.

"I will not. Get on with your work and stop pestering me."

———— ◆ ————

Giles stepped into a room heavy with lemon-scented bathwater and wanted to turn back. A rogue such as he should not be in this room.

Domestic matters were best left to married men or nurses, and since he was a confirmed bachelor, he was positive Lord Winter would have him drawn and quartered for what he planned to do if he ever learned of it.

He crossed the room to the bed, but this time managed to

keep his hands to himself. He could tell that Lilly lay naked under the sheet that Mrs. Osprey had loosely draped over her. He would have to pick her up and lower her into the tub wearing that sheet, and step back before the water made it transparent.

He breathed slowly through his nose and tried to stay calm. Lilly seemed to be avoiding his eyes, too. That was probably for the best. He removed his jacket and rolled up the sleeves of his shirt, aware that Lilly's eyes had risen and were watching his arms become exposed.

"Mrs. Osprey, the blindfold."

Giles ducked down so the little housekeeper could tie the cloth, but a problem soon became apparent. It was the Wexham nose, of course. He could still see.

As a child, he had cheated shamelessly at blind mans bluff because the shape of his face provided a useful gap under his eyes. He could see Lilly's hand resting on the bed and when he stepped closer, he would see a lot more.

Mrs. Osprey guided him forward, and his hands shook as he lifted Lilly from the bed. He probably should confess to his view, but he held his tongue, carried her across the room, and lowered her into the nicely warmed water. He tried not to let his vision linger on the rapidly dampening sheet.

Lilly's breath caught as he brushed the cage of her ribs and the plumper muscle of her thigh with his fingertips as he released her. He stood, grabbed a towel blindly and backed away until he couldn't see. Giles liked the feel of Lilly in water.

As he dried his arms then waited, he tried to ignore the splashing and the soft conversation. Dear God, he hoped he could conquer his impulses before he had to return and lift her out.

"Lord Daventry, when you are ready."

Giles stifled a groan and paced back to do the housekeeper's bidding. Continuing the charade that he couldn't see, he veered into a chair. Mrs. Osprey caught his arm and edged him closer. He supposed he could blame his gasp his sore shin, but that wasn't what had elicited it. Lilly's silver eyes caught his and he knew that she knew he could see everything.

He could not help it. He was lost. Unstoppable lust raged through him as he bent toward Lilly.

The generous swell of her full breasts under the water damped sheet and pink, peaked nipples stood at attention.

Her breasts were such a shock. He'd assumed her flatter in the bust than she actually was, but Lilly's breasts were heavy and would fit into the palm of his hand perfectly. Dear God, he was more than aroused now; he was in agony.

If Mrs. Osprey had not been in the room, he would have taken them in his mouth and suckled until her fingers had threaded through his hair. He loved Lilly's breasts.

Mrs. Osprey squeezed out the extra water from Lilly's hair while he remained crouched beside the tub, straining for a body he craved as much as he needed air. Luckily, the housekeeper appeared not to notice his distraction.

He waited, his eyes devouring a perfectly proportioned body even with the sight of sharp ribs and silver scars. "Any time you like, my lord."

It took time to get his body to obey. Giles lifted her but held Lilly against his chest a long moment, inhaling the scent of clean, damp skin and enjoying every moment of it. Why he had ever denied himself the pleasure of watching a woman bathe was beyond him. Even blindfolded, it was the most erotic thing he had ever witnessed.

Lilly squirmed a little in his arms, forcing him to remember that he needed to move. He moved to the bed and laid her down gently. But his traitorous body followed. His lips grazed her temple before he could stop himself.

Shock pulsed through her tiny body. Giles pulled back and found her watching him warily, hands rapidly scrambling for the covers.

"I thought you were angry with me," she said.

Giles reached up and removed the blindfold, drinking in the sight of her damp shoulders. "No, not angry with you." She relaxed a bit, but to his way of thinking, her body appeared stiff. "Are you in pain?"

She bit her lip.

Giles nudged her shoulder, testing to see if she would try to hide her discomfort from him. She nodded with a slight movement of her head.

"Shall I come to you after dinner?"

This time, Lilly had to make a choice with a much clearer head than before. She knew exactly what he was capable of, but Giles would not impose himself on her if she did not wish for him to soothe her.

The things they had been doing could have dire consequences, not to mention the painful distraction of arousing him. He always liked to have his women willing.

"Yes, please come."

Giles nodded once, incapable of speech. Yes, please come. Such innocent words, but he knew exactly where he wished to come—anywhere she let him.

Chapter Nine

—◆—

Thursday progressed clear and bright while Lilly wallowed in her bed, longing to get out of it. She had not been truly out of doors in years. Traveling from carriage to house hardly counted. But, she could not do it. She could not go outside.

When Mrs. Osprey had opened her clothing drawers, Lilly noticed that there were no outdoor garments inside. When Lilly gave the matter some thought, it seemed as though she could not remember the last time she'd worn a proper gown, or even been fitted for one.

Oh, yes, she remembered the day of the accident. Lilly had been wearing her favorite lemon muslin with tiny embroidered flowers on the hem. A dress she thought pretty and delicate, a gown to make acquaintances envious.

Atticus had behaved himself admirably and had not put muddy paws on the fine material or dragged her into the wild grasses about the property. His obedience had made her so proud.

With a little coaching and outright bribery, Lilly had trained him the way her papa trained his hunting dogs. The wolfhound had responded eagerly. He sat on command, waited when she told him to, and walked beside her calmly as instructed. Yes, he had been very good that day.

She trailed her fingertips over the bedding. It was getting late. Giles had slept in his own room last night, and she had spent her first night alone since the accident. Lilly was not used to being alone at all and had found it difficult to stay asleep. Even her treatment last night had not relaxed her completely. It had stirred her in ways she did not understand.

Giles had been polite but firm with her body. He had kneaded deep into her shoulders and back, easing out kinks she was not aware she could possibly have had. He had been gentle with her neck and head, and she shivered again as she remembered his fingertips sliding into her hair and combing through the long strands.

The nurse's attentions to her hair had never felt like that. She'd shivered all over, but not with illness. The onset was too swift to raise concern. And the sensation had passed, changing to make her breath hitch when Giles kneaded the muscles of her bottom. She blushed at the memory of his warm hands, how long he had lingered, and how loud his breath had sounded in the still night.

But when his hands had swept down her legs, her face had grown hotter and she thought her reactions were embarrassment, not illness. His hands had run down the length of each leg repeatedly, pressed into the arch of her foot to send chills over the length of her body.

A tremor ran though her now. He had not spoken much last night, but she had been unable to hold back her moans of pleasure and relief.

Giles Wexham had very talented hands.

When he finished, he redressed her, tucked the blankets high, blew out the candle, and whispered good night before he left her alone.

Gentle, considerate and, above all else, affectionate.

She no longer knew what to think of him. This was not how he behaved around women in London. Even while in the laudanum-induced haze, she understood exactly what drove Giles Wexham. He craved excitement and pleasure.

Acting as her nursemaid must bore him to tears.

He was a rogue and spent his nights in the arms of any willing woman. She wondered how he did it. Was it hard to make love to a different woman every time?

Lilly could not understand how he could be happy wasting his time in her company. It was not as if she had any great wit or fascinating stories to tell him. He should be more than bored, but he was always polite and always returned. She was so grateful for the care he gave her that she couldn't bear to tell him not to visit. It had been a long time since she'd had such good companionship.

Her appetite had returned too. Breakfast this morning was larger than yesterday's. Lilly had eaten up every bite she could and had still looked forward to lunch. She wondered what Giles was doing. He had not come to see her this morning and she missed his face. It was probably not a good idea to rely on the rogue, but she enjoyed smiling with him. Giles had such a nice smile.

Lilly slipped her feet over the bed's side and stood, holding on to the mattress while she gained her balance. The window was a good distance away, yet she wanted to see the view outside.

She could only vaguely remember what the property looked like, and since it was such a beautiful day, the grounds would be beautiful too.

Lilly started across the chamber, disconcerted at first by the way the floor shifted beneath her feet. She made it halfway before the door opened behind her back. She turned, perhaps a little too quickly, to see who entered. Giles dashed across the room to catch her up in his arms.

Dizziness and a rush of heat scalded her cheeks, so she clung to him until the sensation passed.

"Off exploring again, I see. And where is Miss Winter headed this fine, sunny day?" His voice sounded pained and she wondered why.

"The window. I wanted to look outside."

Lilly lifted her chin, gazing at Giles' serious face, and noticed the shadow of new beard on his chin. She wished she could touch his face to see whether the stubble was as soft as it appeared. But that was no way for a lady to behave. She wasn't one of his women.

Resentment bubbled through her composure and, hoping to hide her thoughts, she dropped her eyes to his shoulder. Giles could have anyone he cared to claim, but he'd never claim *her*. She was too weak, too ill to be more than a passing interest to him. An object of pity to be humored.

Reminding herself for the hundredth time that her former intended could do as he pleased with any number of women, she raised her eyes to his. They shone with devilment.

The large hands on her back held her close against his warmth and she blushed anew, confounded by his touch, a caress without the purpose of providing comfort. His hands moved, sliding over her nightgown, and one cupped her bottom, thumb strumming over her skin in a way that was not soothing. All her nerves clamored in a disjointed frenzy.

"Lilly."

Lilly shook her head, unable to stand being so close to him. He let her go, and the cold of her own rebuttal chilled her. She reached for the support of his arm and moved toward the window once more.

At the window, she leaned on the stone ledge and glanced outside, trying to get her thoughts in order. She focused on the greenery shining in the afternoon sunlight, a fairy landscape where life was wonderful. When she turned her head, her breath caught in her throat.

"I apologize. I should have moved you to another room sooner." Giles fussed at her side. "I didn't mean for you to see the bridge again."

That awful place haunted her dreams. Yet in daylight, the spot seemed idyllic.

"No, it is all right, Giles. You don't need to move me. I would have to see it again one day. I would have made myself." Lilly smiled to reassure him, but she did find the view disconcerting. "Can you open the window?"

Giles leaned around her and pushed the window up, then settled his hands on her upper arms. Cocooned as she was, she barely noticed the bite of cool breeze that brushed across her front. Giles' heat, standing so close behind, warmed her and brought a blush to her cheeks greater than any breeze could conquer.

Lilly leaned out the window, hands sliding into the sunshine's rays, marveling at the warmth on her fingertips. Giles clutched at her body, one arm curling possessively about her waist, the other crossing her chest, palm flat to her skin.

Ignoring the burst of heat as his arm pressed between her

breasts, she turned her hands over, noticing the scars on her wrists and how the veins beneath her flesh stood out so clearly. The sight appalled her.

Giles leaned forward and covered the worst of the scars. "Don't fret on it."

"How can I not? They are so ugly. I'm ugly."

"No you are not. The alternative to bearing the scars is too horrible to contemplate. I am grateful you survived. The scars are simply a reminder that every day of one's life is precious." Giles hugged her a little tighter. "Besides, the rest of your perfect proportions make up for the slight flaw."

Lilly grinned and blushed to match. "Has anyone ever told you that you are a terrible flirt?"

He laughed, his breath stirring over her neck and sending her heart racing. "I do believe that has been brought to my attention before. Should I stop?"

Lilly thought about it for at least a moment. "I imagine after all this time that the habit might be impossible to break."

"Very likely." His lips brushed her neck. "I might find it quite a struggle to follow that request while you are near. You seem to bring out the worst of my behavior."

Giles' lips nipped at her skin. Pulsing shocks of pleasure curled her toes and she gasped, slipping her hand to cover his.

Giles chuckled, pressing his forehead to her hair and breathing deep. "Forgive me. I seem to have no sense of propriety today."

And she shouldn't allow him to hold her like this, but she had a desirable man heaping compliments on her head, turning her body so far away from pain that it was hard to remember who she was. She dared any lady to keep a right mind about her under such attentions.

He held her against him, a gentle rock to his hold keeping her conscious of his presence. She skimmed her hand back and forth along his arm, running her fingers over the back of his hand until he captured her digits with his. Shocked at the genuine affection, breath churning anew, Lilly searched the world outside for distraction.

Cottingstone Manor hadn't changed much during her illness. It still looked as though the grounds didn't belong in the real world, and the peace of the place washed over her. She sagged a little, letting the fresh scents fill her lungs and cleanse her soul.

"Can I go outside, Giles?"

"Not dressed as you are, that's for sure," he replied very firmly. "I have workmen on the other side of the house at this very minute, and, as much as I might admire the view, I am not keen to share your current attire with a bunch of sweaty laborers."

His fingers trailed down her chest and she looked down, noticing for the first time that her nipples were visible through the thin material. Startled, she watched Giles' fingers skim around the plump curve of one breast and then settle, fingers wide, on her belly.

Lilly wrapped her arms tightly around her chest and huddled against the window ledge. Her state of undress did explain Giles' forward behavior, however.

His hands skimmed her back, lightly kneading away her tension. Despite the impropriety and the transparency of her nightgown, she was still comfortable with Giles. But she must remember to wrap a blanket about her when she left the bed in future.

Lilly had no dresses to change into. It could take weeks for dresses to be delivered, but by that time the perfect day would be gone and she could never get to enjoy it.

Giles rubbed his hands up and down her arms. It was one thing she liked most about him; he always seemed to be touching her. Little kindnesses she shouldn't become used to.

Lilly stumbled toward the bed, dejected and fully prepared to burrow under the covers, pretending that it was snowing outside and miserable.

He curled his fingers around her arm, stopping her progress. "I have an idea," he said, urging her toward the bedchamber door.

Intrigued by his strange excitement, she didn't resist.

Giles poked his head out into the corridor then turned and scooped her up, curling her tightly against his chest. He walked directly across the hall, turned the handle to another room and darted inside.

It took a moment for her eyes to adjust to the gloom. Trinkets and personal items filled every surface. Lilly did not know whose room it was, but it was cold and had an unlived-in air to it, despite the lack of dust or dustcovers. Giles deposited Lilly in a wingchair by the window, and opened the blue drapes wide.

"Welcome to my sister's room. Consider this a shopping expedition, of sorts. Let me see what goodies dear sister has left behind."

Giles smacked his hands together with apparent glee and opened the nearest draw. He found stockings and threw a pair at her that was so fine and delicate, she could not believe they wouldn't tear the minute they were worn.

Next, a silk chemise settled over her legs. Lilly held it up to the light, and then her cheek to feel its softness. "Won't she care that you are rummaging through her possessions?"

"Katarina will never know. She only comes once a year, and that is usually for the spring clean."

Giles' sister seemed to have a veritable hoard of things tucked into all the corners of the room. When Giles produced shoes, he measured one against her foot. While they were not a perfect match in length, she could wear them without fear of tripping.

When Giles opened a tall mahogany wardrobe, he pulled out dress after dress in all colors and styles. Her mind spun from the excitement. The bed piled high with ball gowns, day dresses, riding gowns, and even a formal presentation gown that looked to be new. He chose a light muslin gown in pale yellow and dug around to find a shawl to slip over her shoulders.

"My sister insists on having a permanent wardrobe here, and we shall take advantage of it. Come, up on your feet, we have a dressing to attend to," Giles said.

Suddenly afraid of him, Lilly rose on shaking legs. He seemed determined to dress her himself, but that would mean he would have to undress her first. It was true that he had touched her entire body while he gave her relief, but she was always sure to keep clear in her mind the difference. Dressing her seemed far too personal and dangerous. "Giles, stop. You forget who I am."

———◆———

Panic settled over Lilly's features and Giles could have kicked himself. He had gotten carried away. He had no right to be alone with Lilly or consider dressing her, but she had seemed so sad at the prospect of not going out that he had quite forgotten his place in her life. He had none.

Giles watched her fidget and then walked to the bell. "You are right, forgive me. I will wait outside. Mrs. Osprey will be here directly to fuss over you."

Giles strode out of the room, irritated by the necessary delay. Damn it all, he had forgotten himself in the thrill of rampaging through his sister's wardrobe and making Lilly happy. He had picked the finest silk stockings because he had wanted to touch Lilly's skin as he pulled them up her slim legs. The chemise would have been near transparent and should have afforded him a fantastic view to enliven his fantasies.

Fantasies that threatened to become a daily relief.

Last night had been more difficult than he could have imagined. He had found himself unable to sleep and had crept down the hall to check on Lilly once. It was strange to feel displaced in his own room after just a few nights in Lilly's company.

Giles paced the hall while waiting for Mrs. Osprey to answer the summons. He did not have to wait long. Mrs. Osprey came twittering up the servants' stairs with Dithers in tow and ran the length of the hall to him.

"The lady requires dressing." He gestured to Katerina's room. "See to it, Mrs. Osprey."

Mrs. Osprey glanced at him in confusion, but crossed the threshold when Dithers nudged her.

Giles pulled the door closed and stood looking at it, considering. He would plan more than a mere moment in the sunshine. He would do his best to surprise Lilly. Gathering Dithers with him, they descended the staircase and headed for the terrace.

"It's a little sunny here. Are you sure this is the right spot, milord?"

"It's exactly perfect. Now, go find a few pillows and a blanket, and have Cook arrange a tray of delicacies. Be sure to bring it out as quickly as you can."

"Are you feeling all right, milord? You are going to a fair bit of trouble for Miss Winter."

"Dithers, I always thought you understood women? This is perfect." Actually, it reminded him of his mother. She used to sit out here, in this very spot, sipping tea and admiring her gardens. Lilly should love it.

Chapter Ten

————— ✦ —————

Lilly blushed as Mrs. Osprey crossed the room, eyeing the disaster Giles had created about her feet. "I take it the master was searching after something in particular."

"He wanted to dress me," Lilly blurted, still confused by Giles' abrupt departure.

The housekeeper's eyebrows shot up, and then she smoothed her expression to show nothing but mild interest. "Well, let's see what he has laid out for you."

Lilly stood and handed the shift and stockings to the housekeeper. With Mrs. Osprey's help, Lilly donned the unfamiliar clothing, skin itching as the layers covered her body.

When the last button slipped closed, Mrs. Osprey let her look at her reflection in a tall mirror. A tiny woman gazed back, hair a tangled mess about her face. While she bit her lip, Mrs. Osprey gathered her hair and smoothed the strands back behind her head in a tight knot.

"I look like my mother."

No sooner had the words passed her lips than Lilly wanted to call them back. She resembled her mother very closely, and the tight hairstyle only heightened the similarities.

Mrs. Osprey let her hair fall. "I think a softer style would suit you better, and be more comfortable. Come sit at the dresser and let me see what I can do."

Lilly sat gingerly on the low stool but couldn't watch Mrs. Osprey. While the housekeeper tugged and pinned, Lilly thought of Giles. Would he still be pleased to see her if she resembled her mother?

Lady Winter was very beautiful, starkly elegant and a sought-after companion. She also boasted a loyal band of male admirers who enjoyed her tart tongue as she flailed at the less-admired ladies of the *ton*.

Laughing at some poor creature's expense had never appealed to Lilly. But her mother managed to get away with her slights, and all because of her beauty. Lilly didn't ever want to be like her.

Mrs. Osprey placed a hand upon her shoulder. "There now. The master couldn't help but be pleased."

Lilly looked up at a stylish young woman, wispy hair allowed to escape the twisted knot on the back of her head and softening the sharp ridges of cheek and chin. Lilly smiled. Mrs. Osprey had managed to mute her resemblance to her mother, giving her softness where her mother had none.

Just to be sure that she wasn't imagining her improved appearance, Lilly pinched her own skin. "I…"

Lilly couldn't find the words to express her gratitude at first and the housekeeper turned away, collecting Lilly's nightgown until she might have a chance to control her emotions. "Thank you, Mrs. Osprey. I don't believe I've ever looked so well."

Mrs. Osprey beamed. "Nonsense. You were a very pretty girl. Your mama just never let anyone see you."

Lilly smiled, but then a flash of a memory burst into her mind. A younger Mrs. Osprey, twining ribbons through her hair, chuckling at Lilly's insistence she be her personal maid. The image contained the sharp pain of emotion.

Lilly had been as happy then as she was now. The young girl had been excited to be at her future home, whereas Lilly, at her present age, looked forward to nothing, because that future would never be.

———•———

Women always seemed to take some time dressing, so Giles was not surprised that, after all he had done outside, he still had to wait a few minutes more for Lilly. The time gave him a chance to consider if he had been at all excessive in his dealings with the woman.

He did not want her to think he was courting her, but was unable to bear seeing her unhappy, disappointed face. An altogether startling revelation, and one he would take great pains to hide.

Giles dragged his mind away from Lilly, toying with the idea of adding another garden to the north of the house, until the door opened behind his back.

Lilly was stunning. Lemon muslin suited her perfectly. The dress was just a little long and trailed on the ground at her feet, but the bodice molded over her breasts like a glove. If he could just have his hands inside those gloves, he would be a perfectly happy man for the rest of his life.

She smiled shyly at him and Giles walked forward to better view Mrs. Osprey's handiwork. Disappointment flashed through him as he saw that her hair had been pinned and pulled back into an elegant knot, with dark tortoiseshell combs attempting to hold back most of the stray wisps.

He let his gaze dip to the creamy expanse of shoulder and chest that was now exposed to his gaze and could not hold back the devilish thoughts that occurred to him. It was a shame that those same thoughts must have flowed straight across his face.

Mrs. Osprey scowled at him and slipped a soft shawl around Lilly's shoulders that reduced, but did not completely hide, his view. He was glad he had not chosen a sturdier, and consequently more prudish, gown. The view was spectacular. His sister would never look as well in it.

Giles held out his arm, quite prepared to escort Lilly anywhere. After a moment's hesitation, she placed her hand on him.

A muffled sob escaped Mrs. Osprey. When Giles flicked his eyes in her direction, he found the housekeeper's face tear-stained but smiling. Happy tears were the one thing about women he had never completely understood. Why cry when something nice happens?

He led Lilly to the top of the stairs, swept her up into his arms, and carried her down, feeling her skirts tangle between his legs in an innocent provocation.

He was hardening by the time he reached the bottom step. To hide his reaction from any gawking servants, Giles carried Lilly through the drawing room and exited out into the sunshine.

Just as he had arranged, the chaise lounge was well-stocked with pillows for Lilly's comfort and a tea tray, filled to overflowing, had been set beside it.

He lowered Lilly, shifted pillows behind her back, and handed her a plate of food. Then he poured a cup of tea and sat himself in an adjacent chair, sprawling out to relax and enjoy the view with her. This was more like it—peace, contentment, and a pretty woman by his side.

A few minutes later, Giles heard a muffled sniff and he lazily turned his eyes to Lilly. Tears flowed down her cheeks unchecked.

Lilly's teacup rattled and he quickly took it from her fingers. He reached into his inner jacket pocket for a handkerchief and brushed her tears away. The way she gazed at him with such profound trust made his heartbeat quicken.

Giles cleared his throat. "You look beautiful sitting there like that. If I could paint, I don't believe I could capture just how radiant you look today, Lilly. I doubt that anyone could."

"Thank you, you are very kind to say such outrageous things."

"Nonsense, merely stating the truth you were denied your whole life."

Once she seemed calmer, he returned her tea. With his hands braced on his knees, he let his gaze trail over her shining silver-white hair, over blushing cheeks. Even teary-eyed, she was a vision of soft, feminine beauty and, to his considerable alarm, he wanted to keep her all to himself.

Friends would laugh him all the way out of London if word ever leaked out how he was behaving. But honestly, he couldn't seem to help himself. Giles had never met a woman who intruded on his thoughts the way Lilly did. Her smile was addictive which meant he'd have to do something about her soon.

On the desk in his study, a large bundle of correspondence awaited his reply. Invitations to parties, letters of information on investment opportunities, and a growing pile of heavily scented letters from past and hopeful lovers. They all clamored for his attention, but he hadn't the slightest desire to answer any of them.

What he wanted, more than anything was to bask in this strange private world where he and Lilly could be friends and companions. With no rules or expectations.

Dithers hurried out onto the patio with a silver salver and a single letter on the top. Giles glanced at it and recognized Lord Ettington's personal seal. As he tore it open, he noticed that Lilly basked in the sun's light, her face turned up and a gentle smile playing over her enticingly kissable lips.

Giles shifted in his chair to make room in his trousers, and then scanned the note. "The Marquess of Ettington and his wife are expecting a child, Lilly. Jack is beside himself, and is holding a house party at his estate over Christmas. According to this, I'm to attend without argument. Anyone would think Ettington was the first man to find himself in this position. I wonder how Pixie bears him."

An unconscious shudder shook him at the domesticated tone of Jack's letter. Marriage had changed the coldest man in London into nothing more than a lap dog.

"Pixie? Oh, do you mean Lady Ettington? She's a tiny, dark-haired woman, isn't she?" At Giles' nod, Lilly smiled. "I believe I saw her in London. Lord Ettington was hardly able to keep his eyes away from her. I could see him watching from across the ballroom floor. He seemed very intense."

Lilly might have limited experience in society, but she clearly had been about on the most important evenings. And he enjoyed hearing her talk. "When was this?"

Lilly's face scrunched as she concentrated, but after a moment, she shook her head. "I can't remember, exactly. You were there, I think, beside Lady Ettington. Some memories are very confused."

She looked away suddenly, her face blushing furiously. The unspoken sentiment behind the blush hinted that some memories weren't quite so forgettable. Instead of being ashamed, he was glad she remembered him so clearly.

"Was Lady Ettington on my arm?"

Lilly nodded. The past was a tricky business to discuss between them. In all of the times that Lilly had seen him, he had been wrapped around a woman. How exactly did a woman of Lilly's inexperience deal with that kind of memory?

"That might have been the occasion when I tricked my stuffy friend into acting with a bit of uncharacteristic wickedness. And my first attempt at matchmaking, by the way. Given that everyone else paired them together, it was inevitable the marriage had happened so quickly. The announcement the night after they married was the most enjoyment I have had in Town for quite some time."

"Surely not the most enjoyment, Giles?" she retorted, and then clamped her hand over her mouth.

He would guess that Lilly had just attempted to tease him about his habit of public dalliance. He laughed. "No, not the most enjoyment, naturally. There were all the times I was able to see *you*."

Giles watched her skin blush fiery red, and called a halt to their flirting. It would not do to tire her too greatly, and he was truly trying very hard to remain her friend. Discussing his behavior in London was bound to touch on his wicked behavior here. He didn't need the slightest encouragement. Despite spending considerable time on the subject, he hadn't managed to come up with a valid excuse for ignoring every rule of society. "Why have you been wandering the upper halls of Lord Huntley's home all alone?"

Lilly shrugged and a shy smile tugged her lips. "I couldn't sleep and I was lonely. That night I had no pain at all and I knew you had accepted their invitation so..." She shrugged. "I wanted to see you but of course papa would never allow me to go."

He frowned. "Did your maids not try to stop you?"

She blushed again. "I sent them away to watch the dancing. It is very dull work watching me sleep."

"Not from where I've been sitting," Giles protested, and then grinned. "I find it quite fascinating that you make almost no sound."

"While you snore?" Her eyes danced with mirth.

He winked. "Keep that one to yourself. Along with everything else you know about me."

Once the tea had grown too cold to be pleasant, he picked Lilly up, blanket and all. Tucked securely against his chest, arms wrapped tightly around his neck, Lilly sighed, and he had to stop himself from backing her into the nearest wall and stealing a kiss.

Kissing would be very bad because one kiss always led to another.

Chapter Eleven

---◆---

After glancing up at the ceiling for the fourth time in as many minutes, Giles made a startling self-discovery. He did not enjoy being alone. After years of solitary living, he craved conversation.

The thought surprised him. Dining alone had never bothered him before. Before Lilly came to stay, that was, and turned his ability to think rationally completely upside down.

He dropped his feet to the floor in disgust and stalked to the window. Lilly was taking her afternoon rest and he didn't know what to do with himself. *Ridiculous.*

The quiet of Cottingstone had always comforted, but Giles found himself enjoying the long moments he spent in Lilly's company. He found her a curious little creature, and she had begun asking him questions about society. Not one inquiry was shockingly improper, but in their society, one poorly worded comment would reveal her ignorance and set her up for embarrassment.

Imagining Lilly in London, dressed and spinning about a ballroom, set his teeth on edge. He shuddered at what the ton tabbies would do to such a delicate, uninformed creature. Society would chew her up and spit her out in minutes.

They would give Lilly little concession for failing to live up to their expectations, despite having spent the last six years in agony. They would drive her back into her room if she were not prepared.

And Giles would be damned if he would let Lord Winter return, find her health improved, and then still pack her off to some remote estate. She deserved a better life than moldering in Wales.

Giles looked down at his clenched fists. He made his hands relax, but the unease stirred over Lilly remained. She deserved a full life after all she'd endured.

Making a quick decision, Giles sat at his desk to pen an invitation, asking Lilly to join him for dinner at seven. That would give Mrs. Osprey time to attend to her other duties, without rushing Lilly's toilette. He also gave her leave to avail herself to anything she might require from his sister's bedchamber.

Katarina would be incensed when she eventually learned, but she was not here to complain right now. Besides, this was Giles' home. He considered everything in it his.

Sealing the missive with festive red wax, he rang for Dithers. "See that this is delivered as soon as Miss Winter wakes."

Lilly would probably enjoy the experience of receiving mail on the little silver tray. He was not sure if she received letters, or even wrote them herself. She had received none during her stay.

"I believe she is awake now, milord." Dithers picked up the missive, but Giles couldn't miss the half smile that played at the corner of his servant's mouth.

"Well, see that she receives it, and that she has suitable materials to write a reply. I believe there is a writing box in my sister's chamber."

"Of course, milord. I should have thought of it sooner. Is there anything else you would like delivered?"

Giles shook his head. Dithers was becoming entirely too transparent in his liking for Lilly. The grin Dithers wore was far too telling, but the man turned on his heel and left Giles alone without another word.

Giles forced himself to read his mail while he waited, struggling with a strange impatience until Dithers returned with her acceptance, and then he went in search of Cook.

As he was speaking to Cook, Lilly's reply drew his attention. He looked at the note in his hand. Why the devil was he still holding the darn thing? He tucked it into his inner jacket pocket, close to his heart. Giles rolled his eyes at his own thoughts.

Cook readily agreed to his requirements: an intimate dinner for two and a sumptuous feast including all his favorite dishes. They settled on hare soup, roast duck with onion sauce, and vegetables. Dessert would be lemon syllabub.

He hoped she liked his choices. He had kept the menu simple since she still ate like a sparrow. He did not have any idea what her preference for food might be, but he was on a mission to smooth out her sharp curves. Curves that tormented him the moment he left her side.

Mrs. Osprey informed him with a mysterious smile that Lilly was waiting for him in the drawing room not long after. His lady was early.

Shock at his own thoughts spurred him out the door. Lilly was not his lady, and he was a fool to think so. He was simply her temporary protector—nothing more.

Lilly strolled the drawing room, fingertips running over the ornaments cluttering up the space. Tonight, she wore a gold evening gown with her hair curled into a loose knot at the back of her head. Stunning. Long ringlets cascaded over her shoulders, and a thin gold chain hung about her neck, falling into the valley between her breasts.

He gulped back an appreciative comment on her attributes that would shock her, and sternly reminded himself to behave like a gentleman. "My dear, you take my breath away."

"Thank you for the compliment, my lord, and the gracious invitation."

Giles bowed formally over her hand. When he raised his eyes to hers, he found her holding back a grin. He held out his arm and they proceeded into dinner at a stately pace, but Giles wished he could settle his arm around her waist instead.

Lilly's eyes lit up at the candlelit chamber. "Oh, you've gone to so much trouble."

"It's no trouble. I dine like this all the time."

But that was a lie. He might dine elegantly in London, but not here at Cottingstone. His staff had exceeded his requirements. Along the walls, his servants were dressed formally for the occasion. Davis Senior pulled back Lilly's chair, but Giles waved him away and seated her himself, admiring the curve of her neck and the trail of blonde locks down Lilly's back. Moving away proved difficult.

When the servants ladled out the first course, Lilly's hands twisted in her lap. She stared at the silverware before her. Giles suddenly had the insight that she had not sat down to dine formally as an adult often, if ever. Another near blunder on his part, but one he could help correct.

As the servants stepped back, Giles tapped absently at the correct implement. "I think the workmen should be finished soon, and then we will have peace here again."

Lilly's eyes flickered downward to his tapping finger, and then back at his face. "I hadn't noticed they were particularly distracting."

Giles picked up his spoon, twisting it in his fingers, fully aware that Lilly watched his actions closely. He spooned up a lady-sized portion and tasted slowly in the manner preferred by those of society.

"It's been frightfully disturbing to have so much noise about the place. I can hardly get my rest."

Lilly spooned up her first taste, and Giles watched her tongue swipe her top lip with interest. "Do you have much to recover from?"

"The season has been a touch wearing."

By example, Giles helped her through the various courses of the meal without a word spoken on the subject. When the dessert course arrived, Lilly appeared more relaxed at the table and asked questions about the current events in London. It was surprising, but she knew of a great number of the highest members of London society already.

"Papa has always tried to keep me aware of the important members of the ton, even if I have not had the opportunity to meet them. He could hardly invite them to take tea in my sick room, after all." She took a mouthful of the syllabub and closed her eyes in apparent pleasure. Giles tried not to laugh at her expression.

A flick of his hand dismissed the servants. "How has he managed to keep you undetected for so long? I assume you have been prowling about in nothing but your nightgown and cloak, given the state of your wardrobe."

Lilly grinned. "If a ball was held in the home we were staying in, he would bring me to a secluded spot to watch people and pointed out those I needed to know."

"I still don't understand how you were never spoken of. London is full of gossips and I never heard a word about your presence there."

"Perhaps the people who saw me don't gossip."

Giles had to include his own self in that number. He hadn't told a soul that he was seeing what he believed at the time to be a ghost. They might have thought him mad. But wonders would never cease—a secret could actually be kept in London.

"What of your mother?" he asked carefully. "What does she think of your travels over the country?"

He remembered what Lord Winter had said, but it had to be hard on the girl. She must miss loving feminine companionship.

Lilly set her spoon down. "I don't know my mother, Giles. I have not seen her since the accident. But that is no great change from when I was growing up. She did not feature heavily in my childhood," Lilly assured him. "I would rather not alert her to my improvement, if possible. She is not overly fond of me. Please don't write to her."

Giles tensed at her request. Somehow, Lilly was aware of her mother's preference that she not live after the accident. An appalling spike of rage thundered through him. No wonder Lord Winter had kept them apart.

Her light touch ghosted over his clenched fist, and he made an effort to calm himself. Giles turned to look at the innocent creature at his side and tried to smile, though he knew it would be a forced effort and not completely believable.

Giles' mouth trembled with the need to reassure her that, here at Cottingstone Manor, no one would wish her ill. For goodness sake, his entire staff had been standing on their heads to secure her comfort and happiness. Just consider his overdressed servants, for instance. Giles knew they hated those uniforms and he hadn't asked them to wear them. Nevertheless, he was sure they had done it solely for Lilly's benefit.

Lilly squeezed the back of his hand. "It is all right, Giles. I have had a few years to get used to the notion. I hardly think of her anymore."

"That still does not make it right though, does it?"

Lilly pried his fingers apart and took a firm grip on his hand. Giles' heart pounded in response.

"Of course it is not right, but it is what I have to deal with. None of us gets to choose our family, do we?"

Giles shook his head as he thought of the easy life he had led. His sister possessed the disposition of a screeching harpy, but she was as much trouble as an insect bite in comparison to the Winters. "Only one time," he muttered unwisely, as an appalling thought slammed into his head.

Luckily, Lilly didn't ask what he meant. There was one occasion when it was possible to choose your family. All Giles' inner barriers slammed into place and hid behind years of entrenched opinion, hiding like mice from a hungry cat. Giles loosened his hold on Lilly's hand and finished his glass of wine.

Marriage was the only opportunity Lilly would have to choose a new family.

Mother had claimed Lilly would have made a fine Wexham.

Lilly stood to leave the table and, instead of letting her go alone, they adjourned to the quiet of the library. Attended by two footmen and the silly maids, Giles regained his sense of humor. Servant chaperones, how quaint and ineffective. If he had wanted to sin, he had ample opportunities to run his hands into Lilly's hills and valleys each night as he massaged her.

At night, Giles could smell her scent quite clearly as his hands pressed into her derriere to relieve the day's built-up tension. Lilly for her part seemed to lap up every scrap of his attention.

Giles snapped up a deck of cards as a distraction from his wicked thoughts and taught Lilly the rudiments of vingt-et-un. As he had gathered, she had only limited experience with a deck, and they spoke about the other games popular in London. He considered playing a hand, but then Lilly covered her mouth and yawned.

"You should have mentioned you were tired, Lilly. We can play tomorrow if you wish. Let's get you up to bed before you fall asleep here."

"It is a nice room," she murmured as he drew her to her feet. The lemon scent tugged at his senses and inflamed his body. He hoped she didn't notice he walked with an odd hitch to his step.

At the bottom of the stairs, he swung her into his arms despite her protests. "Shh. Let me take care of you."

Lilly held his gaze a moment then twined her arm around his neck. Giles' cravat grew tight. Her fingertips brushed into the bottom of his hair and excitement raced down his spine. Those fingertips of Lilly's had a lot of seductive power for such an innocent.

He glanced at her snuggled in his arms and fought for breath. Her mouth curved upwards in a contented smile, and Giles was mesmerized by the lush curve of her lower lip. His heart beat double time as her eyes blinked up at him, and he glimpsed what he feared might be desire curling in their gray depths.

If Giles wanted to, he could take her to his bed tonight. A virgin. The horror of that thought didn't diminish his desire. But sharing a bed with a virgin had never been a responsibility he wanted.

Lowering Lilly to her feet at her doorway, he took her pale hand in his. Tiny and delicate. Giles pressed his lips to her knuckles without breaking eye contact. Lilly's lips parted on a sigh.

He stopped himself from continuing the kiss with an inward snarl. He might be one of London's wickedest rogues, but he did not debauch virgins. He would not ruin Lilly's life by hurting her when the affair ended.

———◆———

The night was still and the only sounds were the creak of the bed ropes and the brush of harsh breath against Lilly's skin. She was in absolute bliss. Giles' magic hands kneaded into her neck and scalp, giving her gooseflesh. He rubbed into her shoulders and she had to fight back a moan. When his hands settled in to knead her bottom and thighs, a quiver raced between her legs.

Lilly did not understand why she enjoyed Giles' touch the way she did, but she didn't want it to end. Giles Wexham was the most caring person she knew. She could never get enough of his touch or his attention. When his hands found her toes and tickled, Lilly pulled her foot out of his grip.

The next thing Lilly heard was a ragged groan before the door to her room opened and crashed shut. When she raised her head, Giles had gone.

Lilly sat up against the headboard, wondering what she had done. It was clearly something Giles did not like. She bit her lip and waited, hoping he would come back and explain his sudden departure.

After hearing nothing beyond her room, no sign of Giles' return, she struggled into her nightgown then blew out the candle. Wrapping a shawl about her shoulders, she curled onto the bed, eager to rid herself of a new discomfort. She ached, but not in any place she expected. What had she done?

The darkness held no answers. Lilly rubbed her neck where Giles' hands had been minutes before. She liked his touch far too much. Lilly had not been so muddleheaded that she could mistake the sound Giles made just before he left her. He groaned when he had sex. She wished she knew what to do.

Fucking. She thought that was what people called it. Someone had once whispered shocking words into her ear in the early years of her illness. Glad, coarse words, rejoicing at her invalid state. At the time, she had not understood what the sneering voice had suggested, that she would never be woman enough for a man, that she would never become Giles' wife. That voice was right.

Lilly ran her hand down her chest and brushed her fingertips over her nipples. They were painfully hard and she gasped at the sensation. But that was not the only place that pulsed. Her hand slid down her belly, parting her knees, and brushed over the curls at the junction of her thighs. The pain was lower.

Hesitantly, Lilly slid her fingers between her legs and her body quaked at the sensation. Her nightgown dampened between her fingers and her skin. She snatched her hand back.

Lilly wished she had someone to confide in, but she'd never had a close friendship and the housekeeper appeared too scatterbrained to risk asking awkward questions.

The only person she could turn to was Giles, but he was the entire problem. Before she had met him properly, she had never had these feelings. Her body had only given her pain. This was painful too, but the difference was distinct. Was there something Lilly could do to ease the yearning her body shook with every time Giles touched her?

These strange feelings were only growing, gathering strength the longer she knew him. Lilly wrapped her arms tightly about her chest to ward off the chill that threatened to reach her heart. He deserved better.

Giles was the first person to befriend her. He was kind and caring. These massages at night had finally brought her relief from the pain of her injuries that countless doctors could not. She was so grateful for his attentions, but they couldn't continue this way for much longer.

She could now see a future unfolding ahead of her, but how it played out was hazy. Her life, as ever, would depend on her father's decree. Despite his promises, he might decide to take her back to Dumas. Lilly shuddered and wondered if it was possible to fall asleep while in the same house as her mother ever again.

She had her doubts.

Chapter Twelve

———◆———

The day spent apart from Lilly had dragged. Giles discreetly watched her reclining on the chaise lounge, drinking in the sunshine of a lovely day, but knew he could not avoid her any longer. The time for truth had come.

From his position just inside the doorway, he let his eyes skim over the creamy expanse of her skin above the blue day gown that twisted about her body.

He liked her body too well. When he ran his hands over her legs at night, he yearned for her fine skin wrapped around his bare hips. He longed to take that fatal step and become her first lover.

Yet when her legs had parted wider last night— an innocent response to his tickling— his breath had lodged in his throat. He barely caught himself in time as he leaned forward to inhale the scent of her arousal, halting his intention to spread her legs wide and taste her.

Now in the cold light of day, he berated himself for his lack of control and his stupidity in spending too much time in her company outside the hour needed to soothe her pain away. Today, he needed to explain a few simple truths about how young women had to behave in society, what society expected of them, and the care she must take around him.

Giles had to make her understand and put some distance between them. Well, perhaps not understand the whole of it. He would not tell her exactly how well her body excited his, for instance. That would only complicate matters.

Once his hands touched her skin, Giles lost the ability to think and his world narrowed to the flesh under his fingertips. Lilly appeared to be his ultimate temptation and a direct path into the warmest corner of hell.

He would explain matters then leave, just as soon as her father returned from Wales. She didn't deserve to have an unrepentant hedonist like him lusting after her. He would return to London and quench the thirst that raged through him with as many willing women as he could find. Anything to remove innocent Lilly from his mind.

Resolved, Giles stepped through the doorway and Lilly turned her face in his direction. Although he'd like to believe the sun triggered the response, he could swear that his heart stopped beating for a full minute.

Giles paused at her side and his fingers closed over her shoulder. He squeezed. The soft silk of her skin burned his fingers and he itched to steal his hand down into the bodice of her gown to touch those full orbs. He had not meant to touch her at all, but as usual he could not seem to help himself.

"Good afternoon, Giles."

"Good afternoon, Miss Winter. I hope you have had a pleasant day," he replied formally, as well as he may have done with any young lady in London.

He needed to change every mode of address given to her. After this conversation, Giles would watch his words more carefully and do more to behave like a real gentleman. Once his friends heard about this, if he could bear to confess his part in the situation, they would howl with laughter.

"Yes, thank you." Lilly's smile faltered. "Mrs. Osprey has been very good company, but I fear I have taken up far too much of your servant's time. She must have other duties to attend to."

"Her time is better served by being a companion to you."

"I am used to being alone, Giles. I do not need to be entertained as a child might," Lilly reminded him.

"No, you are not a child, and I do realize that far too well." Giles had the opening he needed, but for the first time today, he feared he lacked the resolve to do this. "And that is why I want you to listen carefully to what I have to say."

Lilly's smile faded at his announcement, but she nodded for him to continue. Perhaps this would be more awkward than he had first thought. He slid into the adjacent chair and prayed he had not made too great an impact on her affections.

"Up until your arrival here last week, I was under the impression that you had died from the injuries of your accident." He paused a moment to gauge her reactions, but he could see no shock. "Do you understand me? All those times our paths crossed in London, I assumed I was seeing a ghost."

"I guessed as much."

"You never spoke a word aloud, and no one ever saw you but me. You have to believe me when I tell you that if I had known you were real, I would not have let you remain to see the activities I was engaged in."

Lilly's head dropped so low he could not decide what her reaction was. He leaned forward in his chair and she pulled back. Well, at least he had a reaction of sorts.

"As you know, I lead a less than conventional life, and enjoy every minute of it. Seeing you as you were and allowing you to see me in those embraces was a gross failure on my part. Your father, if and when he learns, would be well within his rights to call me out or shoot me immediately. I wouldn't blame him. You should not have been roaming around the halls alone in your nightgown."

Lilly squirmed. "I knew you wouldn't hurt me."

"Miss Winter, gently bred young women should never be alone with men such as me. You do realize that, don't you?" He waited for her to nod, but she never moved and he was forced to go on.

"You cannot be alone with me again. I am not to be trusted. If you had even the smallest inkling of the thoughts swirling through my head on most occasions, you would run screaming. Do not trust me or ever consider me safe. I don't have women as friends, Miss Winter. I enjoy them until they scream. You would do well to distance yourself from me." Giles stated it harshly, perhaps cruelly, but she needed to understand him clearly, once and for all.

"I know what you do with women, Giles. I have seen evidence

enough of that, haven't I?" She turned her face away.

"As I said, that was a grave mistake on my part."

Lilly tucked a lock of hair behind her ear and her hand trembled. His heart squeezed at the pain he inflicted, but he had no choice. Lilly had to be protected from him.

"I thought you had made an exception and decided to befriend me, but in truth I could not even raise your interest in that. Despite what you intended, I thought I was your friend. You were mine," she returned, steel lacing her tone.

Lilly stood, then laid a hand on his shoulder. She squeezed, just as he had done to her moments ago. Her scent wrapped around him, clogging his reasoning and threatening to unman him. He wanted nothing more than to wrap his arms around her legs and pull her body into his. His decision to give up his association with Lilly troubled him, and he desperately wanted to take the cold words back.

But it was best for Lilly.

When she walked away without another word or backward glance, Giles' chest grew tight. He wanted to call out to her, and tell her they would always be friends. But then what? Giles didn't know what to do with a woman other than to lay her flat on her back and give her pleasure. Lilly was better off without his kind of friendship.

Giles ordered himself to believe that and prayed he could make the lie true.

———◆———

Lilly returned to her room in dejection, letting the door slam shut behind her. The heavy thud was a death knell for the small hopes she hadn't realized she'd nurtured. She locked the door, too, determined to hide from the bleakness of life beyond the pretty walls. But the room's sunny aspect cut through her control like a hot knife through butter.

She was not a woman. Not really. Giles had no real interest in her and could not even be bothered to pretend about it any longer. Moving to the foot of the bed, Lilly gripped the bedpost and held on as a painful sob escaped her. She couldn't breathe;

her chest tightened tremendously.

Those mocking voices had been right all along. She was no good for anything at all in this life. Not even the most pleasure-obsessed rogue could be bothered to befriend her.

Without him explaining in so many words, Lilly knew deep down how it would go. The little woman, Mrs. Osprey, would become her only company until her papa returned.

And then what?

Would Papa drag her away to yet another house and perhaps leave her there, too? Perhaps he planned to see Lilly compromise herself and finally be free of his responsibility. He might have thought that Giles, a rogue with the wickedest reputation, would be keen enough for the dubious honor.

Lilly would like to think well of her papa, but he had left her alone with one of London's foremost pleasure-seekers. A man who would whisk away a beautiful woman if she so much as arched a brow at him.

She sat down, not on the bed but on the window seat, and gazed out at the small figures scurrying around the garden. At least they had friends, family, someone to turn to when they were sad.

Now she had no one. Another sob burst free. Furiously, Lilly wiped the tears away, tucked her heels up beneath her, and wrapped her arms around her knees to stop her shaking. When she laid her cheek on top, hot tears poured free beyond her power to control them.

Giles' rejection hurt so much.

A week ago, Lilly could not have sat as she did now. A week ago, she had excruciating pain. Giles had taken it away. Today, he had given it back tenfold. A week ago, Lilly had not fooled herself into longing for something more than what life had given her.

She looked around the room and grimaced at the memories the space evoked. She couldn't stay. She wanted to leave Cottingstone. And that thought was enough to begin a hopeless deluge of tears and sobs that racked her whole body, curling her into a tight ball of misery to grieve over the loss of an illusion.

A long time later, scratching at her door intruded on her misery and she stood to let Atticus into the room. Lilly was halfway there when she heard the sound of Giles' distinctive footsteps in the hall. She froze.

She couldn't see him again so soon. He shouldn't know how badly he'd hurt her heart. He would try to explain, offering useless words that would give her no comfort.

Giles believed that putting distance between them was for her own good, for her reputation. But Lilly knew he would be happier the minute she took herself away.

Atticus whined. Ignoring the dog was difficult, but she stayed where she was, three steps from the door, and hoped the wolfhound would go.

As Giles spoke to the dog, Atticus began scratching at the door in earnest. Lilly did not want to upset the dog, but she could not unlock the door to let him in. She might see his master.

Giles was not succeeding at calming the beast, and his heavy knock shook the door. When she bit her lip to keep from answering, he tried the knob. "Lilly, open the door."

She would not.

The door rattled in its frame as Giles pounded on the wood and Lilly jumped back, startled by his vehemence. She just wanted him to go away. She did not want to face anyone who had the power to hurt her so easily or without regret.

Lilly crept to the door and dropped down near the keyhole. Atticus whined as his sensitive ears picked up her movements. In a low voice, pitched directly to the dog, she commanded him to leave. A yelp assured her that he obeyed and the sound of scratching stopped.

Lilly turned away from the door. There, she was free of the man and his hound. The master could now forget she existed.

"That was cruel, Lilly. Unlock the door."

Giles' angry voice on the other side stopped her cold. Why did he care how she treated the dog?

Lilly refused to talk to him. He was not her friend. She was alone, and only had herself and Papa to please. A lonely, dark future instead of the bright one she might have had.

On the mantel was a bottle of Giles' brandy, a remnant of her first night of temporary relief. She wrapped one hand around the bottleneck while the other hand reached for the tumbler. Brandy, as with laudanum, would take the hurt away.

She set both down on the small writing desk, ignoring Giles' pounding at the door. Crystal clinked against the side of the tumbler as she poured a generous amount. Tonight, she would still be able to sleep no matter what racket he kicked up outside.

"Lilly, what was that? What are you doing? Come out of there," Giles ordered, but she was sipping her drink and the burn in her throat would not allow her to answer, even if she'd cared to.

When she'd consumed the first glass, she grimly kept drinking. The laudanum had kept her blissfully numb, and she longed for that peace once again. Strong emotions were too much to handle alone.

The door rattled in the frame again, but then thumping footsteps confirmed he'd gone away.

Lilly tried to be pleased by that fact, but was saddened by his quick withdrawal. Was she truly worth so little effort? Barty had always said so.

She paused with her glass pressed against her lips and tried to remember who Barty was.

The brandy did not aid her memory in any helpful way, but she drank it down and refilled her glass again. In the warmth of the window seat, a light draft stirred the dust motes and she found them more fascinating to study than trying to remember details of an old memory.

When the decanter level dropped low, Lilly frowned at it and wondered how she might acquire more. If her memory could be relied upon, and that was always doubtful, there might be a bottle in the drawing room, dining room, or even Giles' bedchamber.

Lilly dragged herself upright and weaved her way around the table. Getting there unfortunately seemed to require more effort that she currently possessed. The room dipped and swayed beneath her feet. She smiled, happier to dance among the dust motes instead.

Dancing was thirsty work, so Lilly attempted to pour the last of the brandy, but the dashed glass kept moving and she spilled most of it on the tabletop.

The door behind her crashed open and footsteps rushed toward her. Her sudden turn made the room rock alarmingly, but strong arms caught her before she landed on the floor.

"Ah, Lord Wicked, come to finish me off have you? Perhaps a quick dive off the bridge would save you from my company. Barty said I should have learned to swim."

Lilly giggled as the dust motes swirled around the earl's head like a divine halo. How absurd.

Even so, she let her heavy head fall against his shoulder.

"My God, how did you get this drunk so fast?"

She struggled to pull herself away from him. "What do you care? I'm none of your concern."

"Lilly, please try to understand."

Giles did not want her friendship. He didn't want to know her anymore. She shoved against him as hard as she could, but he was always going to be stronger.

The sudden movement was not a good idea, however. Her stomach roiled. Since Giles held her still, Lilly had no choice but to heave up the contents of her stomach—mostly brandy—all over him.

A long moment of silence reigned after her vulgar display and she spun away from the earl. At last, he was quiet. No more hurtful words passed his lips. Somehow, she found the bed and dragged herself across it.

———◆———

A proper lady should never overindulge in stronger spirits. That one would be his first lesson for Lillian Winter, and his cautionary tale for his fellow man. Giles pulled the last of his soiled clothing from his body by the time Dithers answered his hastily rung summons.

Unfortunately, the butler inhaled sharply at the scent of the chamber then started gagging. Had Giles understood why Lilly fought against him, he might not have behaved like a complete barbarian. Nevertheless, he still would not have let her go.

Dumping his soiled clothes on top of the ruined carpet, Giles surveyed the consequences of their conversation. Lilly had not taken the discussion well, after all. He'd been a fool to think that his way was best.

Clearly, Lilly hadn't agreed. As Giles gazed at her, slumped crookedly over the bed and oblivious to the world around her, he cursed his poor judgment yet again. He'd caused her more pain, but he especially didn't like that she had tried to drown her sorrows in hard spirits.

Flicking her hair from her cheek, his heart ached at the sight of Lilly's beautiful face splotched red from crying. He'd done that to her. Bastard that he was.

And the woman would have more misery to come from the aftereffects of the brandy later. She would ache like the very devil if she stayed in that position too. He rolled her so she lay straight on her back, tugging her gown to her ankles for modesty.

Dithers regained his composure and crossed to open the window, but gasped as he realized that the master of the house was naked. He hurried back to shut the bedchamber door. "Milord?"

"Don't say it, Dithers. I know how bad this looks." He pointed to the rug. "Grab that end, will you?"

Together they rolled the ruined carpet and clothes up into a log. Despite Dithers' scowling assistance, they dumped the whole lot out the window, removing the majority of the smell in the process. Still naked, Giles crossed to the dressing table to search for Lilly's perfume. He sprayed some into the air.

He could feel Dithers' scowl lancing his bare backside. "Dithers, go fetch me a pair of fresh trousers, a robe, and arrange to burn that carpet and everything with it, will you? I think they are beyond repair."

At the washbasin, Giles rinsed his hands and then dampened a cloth, prepared to cross back to Lilly. Dithers' expression was hostile. "*Now*, Dithers. Unless you want to wait for an innocent girl to wake and start screaming from the very sight of me."

"For Miss Winter, milord." Red-faced, the butler did as requested.

Giles looked down at the sleeping beauty and shook his head. Now he had two problems to deal with: Lilly's father, and an angry servant with the ability to make his life difficult. The cloth in his hand dripped water on his foot and reminded him to stop staring. He wiped over Lilly's face and lips, reached for her hands and wiped them too, then set the cloth aside.

He loosened her gown and eased it off her shoulders and

down her body gently. There were a few splatter marks along the hem that needed cleaning, he reasoned. He wasn't stripping her for any nefarious purpose. As Giles slipped her silk stockings down her legs, she moaned, and he found himself rising without the annoying restriction of clothes.

The red splotches faded from her skin, but her mouth hung open and, to his amusement, Lilly began snoring like a baby bear. His erection remained. So did her chemise.

Giles could not credit his physical reactions at such a time. He juggled the loose-limbed girl under the covers and tucked her into the clean, fresh linens, dragging the blankets up to Lilly's chin as he always did.

When he was done, he brushed his knuckle beneath Lilly's jaw, ending her snoring. Her lips pouted, brow scrunching unhappily at his caress. He chuckled, unable to fathom how such a quiet woman's emotions captivated him so very thoroughly.

He nuzzled her cheek and pressed light kisses to her skin. "Foolish girl, now I have another thing to feel guilty about. Your head will ache like the devil tomorrow."

Lilly turned her head until her skin touched his lips. He kissed her cheek again, and continued kissing until he reached the corner of her lips. He paused there and searched for the resolve to pull away, but he'd lost it.

Sometime after breaking her heart, he'd lost his own.

Lilly owned him.

Chapter Thirteen

———◆———

A scratch and shuffle of papers woke Lilly from a confusing sleep. Her eyes refused to open easily, and she lay in her bed wondering why her stomach ached so badly. Her mouth tasted of ashes.

Lilly cracked her eyes open a slit and groaned as bright light pierced her brain. Moving gingerly in the bed, she grew aware that her head throbbed in time with her blood. She wished she could remember why she felt so horrible. She'd gotten used to feeling good again.

Yesterday.

Yesterday, Giles had spurned her simple friendship and destroyed her fragile world. Yes, she remembered that too well. Her chest ached, competing with the pounding in her skull, and she was not sure which one was the winner. Giles had pushed her away, and she had come back to her room to hide her heartbreak.

She was always alone—it was nothing new—but she had become used to hearing Giles' voice and the touch of his hands upon her. Now both would be gone, and the sense of loss was overwhelming. Lilly raised a hand to her face to prevent the tears in her eyes from spilling, but her limb was as heavy as lead. Pressing her fingers against her eyes, she struggled to control her emotions.

At least her sense of smell hadn't deserted her. Lemon scent bathed the room in a comforting balm, subtle and soothing, a counterpoint to the pain in her head. She breathed deep and dragged her hand away from her face, rubbing over her aching chest. She was foolish to allow Giles' rejection to hurt her so badly. She curled up on her side to study the bedpost and the distant door.

She'd locked her bedchamber door last night. The first time she'd ever thought to take such a step. Locked out the pain that waited beyond, and had even sent Atticus away. Poor dog. But if his master didn't want her then she shouldn't monopolize his company.

Running her fingers over the stitching on the sheet with one finger, Lilly contemplated the mess her life had become. Nothing was ever allowed to be truly wonderful for long. She should be used to the disappointment, but as a child she'd had far different dreams than this. All she had wanted was a home and to marry someone who would be nice to her. It hadn't seemed too much to ask.

Lilly heard that faint sound again and realized someone else was in the room. It was probably just Mrs. Osprey. She must be reading or doing something equally involved, because she made scarcely a sound. The housekeeper must have used the spare key to slip into the room while she slept. Lilly hoped Mrs. Osprey had relocked it again. Not that Giles would seek her out anymore.

Not in the mood for company, Lilly lay still, as though she were asleep. She would prefer to pretend a while longer that yesterday had not happened, and that she had never become better acquainted with Giles Wexham.

Without Atticus in the room, she could pretend that this was just another bedchamber in a long line of anonymous guest rooms across England, an unknown location seen through a brief moment of clarity. Just at this moment, she would give anything to have the fog of laudanum settle over her and blur the world away.

But china clinked behind her, reminded her she was being rude. In fact, she was quite amazed at the silence the housekeeper had managed to maintain. Mrs. Osprey was a jittery sort of woman and stayed still for only very short lengths of time. Lilly supposed she should turn around so as not to appear impolite. It wasn't right to take her disappointment out on Giles' housekeeper.

With a sigh, Lilly turned over and faced the direction of the sound, blinking her eyes as if waking from sleep, but Mrs. Osprey was not there at all.

Giles sat at her writing table, pen poised beside his teacup with papers scattered before him. He was also looking steadily over his shoulder at her.

Lilly threw the covers over her head and scurried underneath, not wanting to face his rejection again.

However, the sudden movement made her head ache with fresh pain, and she couldn't hold back her gasp. She cursed herself for showing weakness in front of him, and pulled the covers tighter to her head.

The chair creaked and loud footfalls came closer, tapping against the wood like an army come to make war. Lilly buried herself deeper. Could the man not take the hint that she didn't want to see him?

She did wish Giles would not stomp across her chamber like that, either. He could at least walk on the carpet. Surely they could hear his footfalls all the way to India.

The bed dipped as Giles' weight settled on the edge, and Lilly tried to squirm away. Strong arms caged her in place, then bright daylight pierced her eyelids as he pulled the covers back. She put her hands up to cover her face.

Giles sat still, waiting her out it seemed, but she was not going to look at him no matter how long he stayed there.

"How bad is your head today, Lilly?" Giles asked quietly, but far too loud for her throbbing head to appreciate.

She stayed silent and wished him a thousand miles away. How dare Giles sound like he cared about her, today of all days? She tried to roll over, but he did not let her. His big hands pressed high on her chest and pushed her flat on her back, then grasped her wrists and pulled them away from her face.

Lilly truly did try to fight him, but she was nowhere near strong enough to hope to win. "Go away, Lord Daventry."

"No."

Lilly whipped her hands into fists, prepared to do something with them, but he chuckled softly and pressed her hands to the mattress beside her head, permitting her no movement at all.

She opened her eyes to glare at him, but the effect was ruined by the way the light made her flinch. Giles' gaze was sad when she could finally meet his eyes. Her head throbbed, so she stayed just where she was and did not fight him. It would not matter. He would go away soon enough.

Giles remained silent. She found herself hypnotized by his blue-eyed stare and the motion of his thumbs over her clenched fists. She relaxed her hands in defeat and attempted to pull them back, but Giles twined his fingers through hers and held tight.

She did not understand him. Surely, this was no way to keep his distance.

"Now, I believe I asked how you were feeling this morning, and I am still waiting on an answer."

"What does it matter? Please just go, my lord. I don't want you here. You don't want to be here, either. Stop pretending and leave."

"Giles," he reminded her. "What I wanted yesterday, and what I want today, have no bearing on the question. I need to know how you feel. You did drink a lot of brandy last night. Your head probably feels as if one hundred angry drummers are pounding away in there."

Giles released one hand and brushed her hair back from her eyes. Lilly froze at the look on his face. That expression was one she did not recognize. No one had ever looked at her in such a way before and she was tongue-tied.

He continued to straighten the strands and stroked the longer lengths through to the tips. No one ever played with her hair, either, yet he seemed fascinated by it.

"I drank brandy? I don't remember."

"That's probably just as well. It was not one of your finer moments." Giles' fingers brushed her ears and she squirmed away from the tickle. "Here, let me help you sit up. You have slept the day away."

His big hands eased under her shoulders and Lilly gingerly moved into an upright position. While Giles settled more pillows behind her back, Lilly breathed deep, savoring his scent and wrapping it around her like a well-loved blanket.

When she was comfortable, he sank down on the mattress edge again and just stared at her. A glance at the window confirmed that the sun was indeed setting.

When her gaze returned to Giles, he was no longer watching her face. His bright eyes were cast somewhat lower. Startled, she looked down. Why had she worn the fine silk chemise to bed? She breathed in to ask, but her indrawn breath displayed what held Giles' attention.

Stunned, embarrassed, and fascinated by Giles, she watched his hands grasp the edge of the blanket and drag it up her chest to cover her exposed breasts. Ragged breathing caressed her cheek and when Lilly turned, his blue eyes hid behind ginger-lashed lids mere inches from her own.

Up close, the man was breathtaking. Giles drew his hands back slowly, stroking the side of her body boldly. When he stopped touching her, Lilly could breathe freely again.

His blue eyes flared open and they were as bright as she had ever seen. "Are you going to help me out here or do I have to become a tyrant? Are you thirsty? Can you eat something? Is the light too bright? Do you need to go somewhere you would rather not name? Talk to me, Lilly. I only want to take care of you."

She licked her lips to speak. Her mouth was as dry as parchment. Giles' eyes followed her tongue. Lilly hastily croaked out a request for water and he fetched it. She was not hungry, but Giles returned with a plate wrapped in linen and uncovered a hunk of plain bread. He broke off a piece and handed it to her.

Lilly nibbled at it. Why had Giles returned to her again? He appeared in no hurry to leave, either. Nevertheless, it would come, she was sure of that. He was only delaying the inevitable.

In a flash of vision, she remembered fighting against him and frowned, unsure of when that had happened. She dropped her eyes and turned her head to look at the floor. The boards were bare. She glanced at Giles, but he had seen the direction of her gaze.

"It was not one of my favorite rugs." Giles brushed another strand of hair back from her face. "No matter, another carpet will be found in the attics today."

Lilly struggled with her hazy memory, then remembered that she had been sick—and all over him, too. Beyond embarrassed, she buried her head in her hands.

Giles leaned close, running his hand up and down her spine. "It does not matter, Lilly. It really does not."

The unmistakable sensation of Giles kissing her hair snapped her out of her misery, but sank her further into confusion. Giles kissed lovers. She moved her head away, catching a glimpse of that odd expression on his face again. He should not tease; that was just too cruel.

With a sigh, he brushed her hair back and placed the plate in her lap. "Eat something more and then rest. You will be better for it." He squeezed her arm, then walked to the writing desk again with stiff movements and returned to his papers.

———◆———

A short time later, Lilly stirred. Giles heard her feet hit the floor with a thud. Instead of turning immediately, he hesitated. He knew what he would see.

Everything he wanted. More than she should give to a man like him. He didn't want to turn around and catch another glimpse of her breasts through the thin silk, but he also couldn't stand not to watch over her.

Desperately Giles wished he had found a robe in his sister's wardrobe before today, but he had never remembered to locate one. He would send Mrs. Osprey to hunt for one today or, if he could bear to leave Lilly alone again, he would find one himself.

Bracing himself, Giles turned. Lilly was still holding on to the bed and exposed a great length of leg to his hungry eyes. Fighting the urge to hurry, Giles stood slowly and went to her, threading his arm around Lilly's waist as naturally as if he had done it a hundred times before.

She resisted initially, but soon gave up when his viselike grip on her waist refused to yield. It was either that or allow his hand to roam where it wanted.

Without a word, Giles led her across the room to the screened corner, and then stepped out into the hall, giving her privacy and him time to control his rampant erection. He flung open the door to his sister's overstuffed bedchamber and searched for a robe. He found one in the third drawer and snatched it up, hurrying to return to Lilly.

At the doorway, Giles swayed back. That chemise was too damn thin. The light streaming in behind Lilly had turned it transparent. His breathing hitched as he made out the swell of her breasts beneath the silk, the curve of her tiny waist, the flare of her hips, and the near-invisible pale curls between her legs. His body's response, which had not died away, roared out of his control and tented the front of his trousers in a very obvious way.

Giles drew the robe in front of his groin.

Teeth gritted, he crossed to Lilly's side, moving his traitorous body behind her and out of her line of sight. He'd always heard virgins were devilishly prickly about the sight of an erection at close range. He did not want to do anything else to lower her opinion of him.

Sliding the pink silk around Lilly's shoulders, he waited while her arms found the sleeves. Then he gathered the sides to cross them over her body before tying the sash and flattened his hands over her belly.

Lilly stiffened as he pulled her into his embrace, letting her touch arouse him further. His cock ached as he brushed against her tiny body. He couldn't hide his desire.

Standing this close together, he could rest his chin on the top of her head, but instead angled it so he could press his lips against her hair. He swayed, drawing Lilly with him, unwilling to ignore the curious sensation of winding himself around her without either one of them moving.

They stayed like that a while and Giles wondered what she thought of him holding her. Lilly had not said a word and he was loath to be the first to pull back. He loved this too much, her warmth, her smell, her trust in him.

A touch as light as the wind brushed against his fingers and let him know that she was not appalled at his behavior. "This is like dancing, isn't it?" Her voice wavered as she snuggled into him, tempting his desire higher than he wished.

"Yes, almost," he returned, but that was another lie. He'd never suffered an erection while dancing with any lady of the *ton*. Not in all his years of wicked decadence.

"I used to like to dance, but it has been so long I've probably forgotten all the steps. The waltz looks divine. Do you know how to dance it?"

"I have tried it a time or two, yes," he assured her, moving his hips against her bottom without meaning to.

"Would you teach me someday, Giles?" Lilly shook her head, brushing her blonde hair against his skin. "I'm sorry. Forget I asked that."

Her head dipped away and she looked down at the floor. Her fingers burrowed under his, trying to get free, but Giles was having none of that. Yesterday had been a mistake, and he fully intended to make it up to Lilly as quickly as he could.

He lowered his mouth to her ear. "I will teach you now. How about that?"

Despite his self-recriminations that he was moving too fast, he brushed his erection against her backside one last time and stepped back. Erection still outstanding, he turned Lilly to face him and she looked up. Her eyes were bright with confusion and pleasure, each warring for dominance.

Giles took her hands, placed one against his shoulder and took the other in his. He wrapped his arm around her back so it rested high between her shoulder blades and away from the temptation of her rear.

"This is the correct posture for dancing the waltz. The proper distance must be maintained at all times, or the woman will be censured by her peers and the man applauded by his fellows. Be sure to be the one to maintain the distance and do not rely on the man to do so, all right?"

Giles started them moving, slowly at first until Lilly got the hang of the steps. He knew the exact moment Lilly acknowledge his aroused state. Her hand flexed in his, gripping tightly, but she still watched downward. He tried not to become more aroused than he was.

A foolish wish.

He twirled her around slowly, conscious that too much spinning would not be good for her head but determined not to disappoint her. Giles persistently drew her closer, making Lilly enforce the distance between them until he gave up trying and just enjoyed dancing with her.

A knock on the door separated them. Giles gave Lilly a

moment to scamper back into bed before he acknowledged the knock. Dithers opened the door, peering at him and Lilly, then opened the door wide.

A maid entered, Maisie or Daisy—he could never tell them apart—bearing linen, and then the rest of his staff followed, carrying tableware and a dinner designed to please two.

Chapter Fourteen

———————•———————

Lilly let out a soft sigh as the last servant departed. Although she'd never given the matter serious thought before today, she preferred for only Giles to see her informally dressed. Now that they had gone, she could stop clutching her robe closed. "What do you like most about London, Giles?"

"Oh, there are so many things." Giles took a sip of wine.

He rolled the taste around his mouth in appreciation and the way he drank wine made Lilly want to giggle. "Do you go to the theater?"

"Yes, quite often."

"What is it like?" Lilly smoothed out the creases in the silk robe, admiring the smooth material under her fingertips. She shifted food around her plate. "Have you met many actresses?"

"A few."

Giles would probably have bedded them. How could anyone resist him? "Of course."

Giles' face held an odd expression, and then he scoffed. "Those who tread the boards are very passionate about their craft and pleasing their patrons."

"Do they please you?" Lilly asked, and Giles laughed, the deep chuckle that vibrated up from her bare toes. "Actresses, I mean."

He pressed her fork back into her hand. "Are you going to eat that food, or let it go cold?"

"Oh, forgive me. I like hearing you talk, Giles." Lilly pushed another small bite between her lips and forced herself to swallow.

"You didn't answer my question, though."

He grinned and poured himself another glass of wine. "And I was not going to either."

"Why not?" Lilly persisted, enjoying watching him squirm.

Giles' free hand squeezed the bridge of his nose, and then he shook his head. "How was your lamb?"

"Delicious, thank you. And yours?"

"Perfection. You should have another bite."

Lilly obliged and when she glanced at Giles again, he was trying hard not to laugh.

Lilly scowled. "That was not nice, Giles. If you don't want to talk to me, you don't have to keep suggesting I shove food in my mouth." Her fork fell with an unladylike clatter and she pushed her plate away.

"I'm not trying to silence you entirely. I'm simply trying to avoid the subject of my love life. It's not an appropriate conversation to have during dinner."

"Why can't I discuss them with you? I have no one else to ask what gentlemen like."

Giles leaned across the table and clasped her hand in his. "Actresses are not held in great esteem in society. Most ladies would not mention them at all."

"I'm not most women."

"Believe me, I appreciate just how special you are." When Giles released her hand to touch her face, Lilly snuggled into his warm palm, content to let the matter drop. For now.

———◆———

Lilly stood in the weak sunlight and rustled her skirts about her legs. It was such a delight to be properly dressed again and able to see the world. Even though the day was cloudy, it was a better day than she had thought to have.

Giles had made it better.

He had suggested she meet him after luncheon for a stroll around the grounds, but she was only to walk as far as the small pond and wait there for him.

Lilly grimaced at the water and kept a few feet away. Atticus, however, walked through the shallow depths, chasing tadpoles. She had once liked to watch them, too, but no longer. Water was too dangerous and she did not swim. She had enough trouble bathing and loathed water sliding over her face.

Footsteps crunched on the gravel behind her and she turned. Giles. He had spent the entire day with her yesterday, and dined in her room last night. He'd not left her side long enough for her to change into a proper gown.

They had talked until very late, but he had still soothed her back and shoulders, claiming he'd sleep better knowing she was comfortable. Last night her nightgown had remained on and his hands had only brushed her skin at her neck and feet.

It still had the same effect on her though. She rested more comfortably, but Lilly knew his actions had aroused both of them. When they had danced, she had seen the dark linen tenting over Giles' groin. Knowing him as well as she did, she had not been afraid. She was embarrassed to admit that she was pleased. His obvious state disproved her fears that she was not unappealing.

Watching Giles approach, her heart gave a little flutter and her toes curled in her borrowed slippers. He could stop her heart again at any moment, yet she would still do anything to remain near him. She liked him. She liked her friend very much.

Briefly, she wondered what she would do when Giles' healing touch was not available. Would she curl back into a bottle of laudanum and wither away? She did not want that.

Lilly wanted a normal life, but she was under no illusions that what she shared here with Giles was in any way normal.

Giles' smile widened as he reached her, and he offered his arm for her to take. The heat of him, the scent of his body, wove around her and made her feel safe. For all of his threats, she secretly thought Giles Wexham was very good for her. Beside him, she was happy for the first time in perhaps forever.

————◆————

Giles swallowed hard as the smile on Lilly's face changed. He knew that look and it did not bode well for him. Lilly was falling in love with him, and he was powerless to stop her slide.

His usual tactic would be to cool things between them before moving on to another lover. But his previous attempt had been an utter disaster and the repercussions of yesterday troubled him still. Lilly needed a friend and she had foolishly chosen him to be that friend. Her one and only. Normally, the idea would terrify him, but this was Lilly. Despite her innocence, or because of it, he liked spending time in her company.

Giles didn't know what was going to happen when her father returned to Cottingstone. Dear God, he had forgotten all about her father's plans. How foolish. He could have written to Lord Winter to let him know she was better, if the baron had bothered to trust him with a forwarding address.

Giles struggled with his doubts for a moment and then shrugged, unsure of what to make of his prickling dread. With Lilly tripping along beside him, so trusting and pure, he couldn't share his worries with her. He and Lilly were becoming too close.

He wove them around the now cleared garden, along the cobblestone path and out toward the orchard, but his mind tumbled with questions.

"Ah, I see why there is such an array of fruit with every meal. You are heartily spoiled for choice, Giles."

"The gardens were my mother's obsession, and I'm lucky they have managed to be spared damage from my neglect. Some of the trees are very old. Cook would pack up and leave without their bounty."

"She'd never leave you. From what I can tell, Cook, along with everyone else dotes on you."

Giles laughed and tugged Lilly closer. "Cook has had a willing victim for her creations for a long time."

He and Lilly seemed to talk all the time, about anything and everything. It was a strange occurrence for Giles. Usually conversation came second when he was with a woman. But Lilly had a lively curiosity about Cottingstone and asked her questions in such a way that nearly embarrassed him. She was so damn earnest about it all and he was deeply flattered by her interest.

That did not mean he had accepted his annoying attraction to her. At the oddest of times, he found himself responding in a way best reserved for the bedroom, or at least a private corner. She had the unique ability to make him hard just by smelling a rose in bloom, as she did now.

He looked away from Lilly's face in a vain attempt at control, but who was he kidding? He had not had a moment of true control since the first time he had glimpsed her haunting a dimly lit bedchamber of Huntley House.

All of his daydreams and fantasies revolved around the little ghost beside him. He still thought of her that way, too. Lilly was his own private specter, invading his dreams and his life in the most disruptive way possible.

In his short interval at Cottingstone, he had not responded in any positive way to the invitations sent to him from the ladies of his acquaintance. When he went back to London, he would have a blank appointment book before him. A clean slate with no romantic entanglements.

He had no pressing need to return and no desire to take a mistress.

Mistresses were exhausting.

Unlike Lilly.

When Lord Winter returned, Giles would not go directly back to London. He feared it might take some time to purge his thoughts of a ghost of a girl in a white, virginal nightgown.

The sound of water interrupted Giles' thoughts and he lifted his head, surprised at their location. He had not meant to bring Lilly this far from the house, and especially not here to the creek crossing.

Certainly not to the place where she'd almost died.

A quick glance at Lilly confirmed her anxiety. She stared ahead, holding her lower lip between her teeth. Giles ruthlessly held back the urge to comfort her. A kiss or two might just be the right sort of distraction and her bottom lip looked so lush and soft that he was mightily tempted to break his own rule about getting involved with virgins.

"Do you know that when my parents were newly married and disagreed over a great many trifling matters, but afterward always played silly games to make up? If they were outside, my father would bring mother here, pretend to be a monster and demanded a kiss for every step taken across the bridge."

Lilly stopped at the foot of the bridge and her frown grew. "I hadn't heard that but, then again, I don't remember your parents well."

That was a shame. His parents had liked Lilly. "I understand that in the first year of their marriage, my mother barely made it to the other side before he flung her over his shoulder and carried her back to the house. It sounds romantic, doesn't it? For some reason, that story embarrasses my sister, Katarina. I cannot understand why."

Giles looked down at Lilly, hoping his lighthearted confidence had distracted her enough. He much preferred that earlier look of hers. A frightened Lilly pained his heart. Lilly's frown faded and her lips quirked, but she didn't speak.

"I always think that story shows how much intelligence exists in the Wexham line, don't you?"

Lilly rolled her eyes. "Oh, obviously, and how fond they are of a healthy dose of self-flattery too."

"My father always said it was better to conduct any battles in bed rather than out of it." Chuckling, Giles took her hand. She still didn't look completely at ease. Rules were meant to be broken. "Do you want to play the game?"

"Giles," Lilly groaned, but he tugged her toward the bridge anyway.

"This is where you have to make the decision to cross and ask to pay with a kiss. Go on, ask away."

A look of consternation graced Lilly's face, as if she thought he was barking mad.

"Giles. Giles. How much to pass?" Giles had lightened his voice to mimic a woman's, but then deepened it to continue. "Just one little kiss, my sweet lady. Then you say, 'Oh, very well,' and I say, 'I never kiss and tell.'"

On his last word, Giles dropped his head and brushed his lips across Lilly's before he changed his mind. It was a brief kiss, chaste in fact. And he wanted another.

He tugged her forward a step and growled, "Who goes there?"

Lilly choked out a laugh at his silliness.

And it *was* silly. Giles struggled to remember the last time he had played a game and thought it possibly might have been with his mother when he was very young. Lilly, it seemed, had the unique ability to bring out the strangest behavior in him.

"Giles. Giles. How much to pass?" she asked, giggling.

To which he made the correct reply, making his voice even deeper than before. Lilly shook with laughter that simply had to stop. Giles kissed her, properly this time.

At first awkward, then growing with a surety that shook him to his boots, Giles cradled Lilly's delicate skull in his hands, holding her lips to his. Kisses had never been part of his repertoire, but he found he couldn't stop. Lilly's hands fluttered between them then settled against his chest. When they slid upwards, he dragged her close and started walking.

Giles kissed her every step of the way, walking backward over the bridge until they reached the highest point. Knowing Lilly as he did, he guessed she would have no idea that they had moved. He had never met a woman who focused on him with such single-mindedness.

When her back hit the wall of the bridge, Giles let her lips go and moved to kiss her cheek, her neck, tasting until he just had to return to her lips just one more time.

Lilly's lips parted, and his world changed.

Why the devil had he ever deprived himself of kisses? Kissing lips was a new pleasure to him, like a fine glass of wine but far more intoxicating. Or, perhaps, it was just kissing Lilly.

Her body arched off the wall and into his chest. He stroked his tongue over her plump bottom lip, tickled along the inside of her mouth and touched her teeth just behind.

Angling his head, he stroked his tongue across hers, once, twice, lost in the taste of her mouth. She tasted like honey, and that was one of life's greatest pleasures, too. He knew quite a few things he could do with honey that involved sex and eating, all at once. One day he would show Lilly.

That one thought made him stop kissing her. He had gotten carried away again. Pressing his lips to the side of her face, Giles stared off into the distance, breathing hard. Good God, he was planning more than a quick romp between the sheets.

That thought frightened him soft. Did he want to be the one to continue Lilly's bedroom adventures? Forever?

His body screamed a resounding yes.

Giles did not like possessiveness, and he was appalled to think that he could be the one to cling.

Lilly's hands untangled from his hair and she relaxed in his arms, but Giles made no move to release her. He couldn't. He was too overwhelmed by the image of making love to one woman for the rest of his life.

"That was cheating," Lilly scolded.

Giles smiled. He liked the way she talked to him, clear and un-jaded. She did not rely on coy remarks at the expense of expressing a real opinion. He liked that very much. Very few women did that around him.

"It is too late to be angry with me now anyway. You are already where I want you."

Reluctantly, Giles released her and moved to stand at her side, no longer blocking her view. Lilly took in a sharp breath. Sliding behind her, he pulled her against him and she leaned back into his embrace. In fact, she appeared to be attempting to push him back away from the edge.

He squeezed her close and his pulse jumped erratically at the contact. Anyone would think he was an untried boy at his body's antics. "It's all right. I won't ask you to show off and climb the wall again."

"Of course I won't climb the wall. I am afraid of heights, silly. Can we go down now?" she asked urgently, turning in his arms, her face pinched with anxiety.

Her innocent movement rubbed against his groin and he shuddered. Yes, he had regressed to a green boy. If he ever got inside her, he would probably come on the first thrust.

"It is understandable. You had a nasty fall, after all. These things can get better if you are prepared to face them, I understand." Although that opinion might have related to remounting a horse that had thrown you, he decided it could have some merit in this situation too.

"I have always been afraid of heights, Giles. I remember I once became stuck up a tree. I can't quite recall why I was up in the branches now, but Pinkerton had to carry me down. Poor man was as hysterical as I."

"Who is Pinkerton?"

"He's Papa's valet. At least, I think he is still his valet. I have not seen him for some time. I remember now, my kitten was stuck in a high branch. Ooh."

Lilly slithered through his lax grip and hurried off the bridge.

As he trailed after, he had time to consider her words. Boys would go to ridiculous lengths to overcome a fear, even risk injury to prove that they were not afraid of something. If a girl was afraid of heights, would she be willing to do the same?

For some reason, he doubted Lilly had been that type of young girl. Lord Winter had said, after all, that his daughter was an angel. If Lilly had not climbed the bridge, then how did she come to fall in the water that day?

A prickle of unease stirred as Giles remembered something Lord Winter had mentioned on the first night of his stay. Drunk at the time, the man had worried that too many accidents occurred around Lilly.

Without a male child to inherit, the estate—minus Lilly's dowry—would pass out of the family, and to the next male relation. Giles wondered who Lord Winter's heir was, and what he thought of Lilly's up-until-now fragile existence.

Lord Winter's family was too staid to allow a woman more than a modest dowry. But unease nagged at Giles, and he wondered if their long-forgotten betrothal agreement was here or at his London residence. There might be details of the Winters' finances in the document.

Ah, hell. What was he doing?

Did he really believe anyone had tried to harm this woman? Unfortunately, he feared someone had. Giles was supposed to use discretion and keep Lilly's presence a secret. The nurses kept leaving, and Lilly had overindulged in an opium-based medicinal. Then there were the injuries she sustained in the fall from the bridge, a feat that may very well have not been accomplished by a young girl, an angel, who was afraid of heights. Had someone tried to make the angel fly?

He needed to see that document again.

Lilly called to him and stopped his speculation. The light in her eyes reminded him that kissing her might not have been such a good idea. Yes, he had gotten her along the bridge, but he had created another problem. One he might have trouble denying.

He wanted to kiss her again. She had lips meant for it, and her mouth tasted like honey. He shuddered to think what she would taste like elsewhere.

That thought undid him. Giles fought the urge to grab her

and sink to the green grass. He wanted to slide her skirts up between them and brush his cock over her blonde curls. He longed to sink his length into her soft depths and pleasure them both blind.

Giles decided he really should stop trying to talk himself out of seducing her. It made him realize that there were far too many opportunities to play, and far too many experiences he wanted to share. If he continued as he was, he would be begging Lilly to put him out of his misery. Lilly could make him her slave, and he probably wouldn't even protest. Hot, willing and throbbing—that was how she would conquer him.

"Do you know what I think, Giles?" Lilly's low voice teased him, her fingers brushing his sleeve.

"What is that, oh frightening ghost?"

She laughed and danced away a few steps. "I believe you want to kiss me again. Your face is quite stern."

"That could be an accurate assumption, Miss Winter." At her giggle, he added, "It is altogether possible for me to assume, in turn, that you wish to kiss me as well." He raised an eyebrow and then lunged for her, pulling her to him, pressing his lips to hers, and sweeping his tongue into her mouth.

———◆———

Across the bustling village street, a tall, well-dressed gentleman laughed as if he hadn't a care in the world. Bartholomew hated him and everyone like him. This man, this viscount, was a favored son of the ton. Oscar Ryall, Viscount Carrington, held the opinion of society in the palm of his pampered hand. He could do wrong and get away with it because of his charming smile.

Foolish bloody society. He'd bet there was a nasty skeleton or two in the viscount's closet he could exploit. He'd learned every family had something to hide. As the fair-headed man stepped into the tavern, Bartholomew toyed with the idea of exposing his secrets. For a price, anyone would talk. And then society would speak of nothing but the prattling fool's less than perfect behavior.

Still, Carrington bore watching and imitating. Society expected a certain kind of gentleman and Bartholomew had to keep up appearances until he had the title and the necessary wife. But once he'd accomplished his goal, society—at least parts of it—would learn his true colors.

"My lord, I might have some intelligence."

Bartholomew seriously doubted that statement, but he turned toward his servant. Given Brown's confident bearing, the man was obviously pleased with himself, with a rare straightening of his shoulders that Bartholomew would happily crush soon. "What news?"

"A black carriage was noticed at the crossroads recently."

"And?" God, finding one old man and worthless chit was like sucking blood from a stone.

"A boy noticed a slow-moving, plain black carriage on Thursday last, then again on Saturday. Except on Saturday, the carriage traveled at a much faster clip. Springing from the nearby crossroads as if chased by demons, the lad said."

Bartholomew rubbed his jaw. The old man only traveled fast when Lilly was elsewhere. He wouldn't risk hurting his precious angel. He looked toward the crossroad, struggling to remember the baron's associates in the area. He must have dumped her and departed. Bartholomew nearly jumped for the joy of it.

Lillian was alone.

Now he just had to work out where she was staying.

Ignoring Brown, he turned for the tavern, slipped into a far table and called for a tankard of ale. Across the room, Lord Carrington held court with the innkeeper. While the viscount waved his hands expansively and earned a laugh for his performance, Bartholomew restrained a grimace.

Pampered, sheltered, good for nothing but a bullet between his eyes. Bartholomew imagined it—vividly. Then had the devil of a time restoring his expression to show nothing but polite boredom.

He managed it as a clutch of coins changed hands and the innkeeper, all smiles and easy familiarity, led Carrington down a hall toward a private dining room.

The fraudulent smile slipped from Bartholomew's lips. Carrington was a favorite with many and invited everywhere. He had friends in high places: duke, marquess and earl. They all courted his company.

Like Lilly's former betrothed, the Earl of Daventry.

A grin split his face—startling enough in its intensity to send a tavern wench far from his table. He fought for control of his features, but elation set his being thrumming with coarse need for her blood.

Damnation, could the old fool have returned her to Northamptonshire?

Chapter Fifteen

———◆———

Fear, an overwhelmingly new emotion, choked Giles of a full breath. He strode through the long grass, anxious to reach the bridge. Lilly stood at the highest point, and something about her posture frightened him. He had to reach her.

His feet hit the gravel path and the sound turned her head. Lilly slid her hands over the worn stones and smiled at him, but he was positive something was wrong.

That was not Lilly's usual smile. There was something on her mind, and he would bet his left bollock that it was not a pleasant thought. Her gaze slipped away before Giles reached her and fell to the bubbling water. Her hands, twisting together, signaled her distress.

Giles walked straight to her side, pulled her into his arms, and pressed his lips to her brow. Scant comfort, but the only kind he could offer. Running his hands over her body as firmly as he dared, he had the unsettling feeling she could fly away, and, if she left, he would not know how to survive the parting.

Lilly raised her hands to his embracing arms and gripped him tightly, but the tension was still there. His presence had done nothing to soothe her. Giles rocked them gently, as he had done the day they danced, but after a time Lilly pulled out of his embrace. Panicked, Giles fumbled for what to do.

Since his most frequent experiences with women were diving under their skirts, Giles struggled for something to say. He longed to pull Lilly back to him, but he could not. He did not think she would let him. She had to choose to let him into her thoughts, and Giles had never dreamed he would want to know what a woman thought before.

He remained close, resting his hip against the stone wall while he waited for her to confide in him. Lilly chewed her lower lip as though mulling over a puzzle. Giles reached for her clenched hands and squeezed. She smiled hesitantly again, a little quirk of her lips that did nothing to ease his anxiety, and blew out a long breath before looking down. Her hands, trapped beneath his, did not move.

"I missed you at luncheon today," Giles whispered.

"I wasn't hungry. Please don't make a fuss about me eating again."

Polite but curiously distant. Giles wondered what he had done. "I was not aware that I had become odious about it. My apologies."

He slid his hands back and Lilly did not stop him, but continued to look at her own. Her skin showed the impression of fingers where his grip had been too tight. The moment stretched as they watched the marks fade and Lilly's fingertip traced over the memory of them.

When she did not respond, Giles dragged in a deep breath. "I did not expect to find you here again. Last time you ran off the bridge very fast. What are you thinking about?"

"Lots of things," Lilly murmured. "The longer I am here the clearer my memory becomes about the past. I find there is much I do not understand."

"Such as?" Giles waited, hoping that her deep thoughts would not involve him.

"Why do you like sex so much?"

Her question both surprised him and rendered him speechless. She kept her gaze on her hands, but he could see her teeth worrying at her bottom lip again.

"Because I find it is a pleasurable activity that I do not like to deny myself," Giles answered honestly, blowing out the breath he had held.

He loved intimate relations with women, but he wondered where her questions were leading. He was sure that was not the whole of her questioning.

"Why do you have so many different partners?"

She must be thinking of the night she found him with Sabine and Millie. A night when he'd had the rare privilege of two women in his bed. He had forgotten much of that adventure, but what he clearly recalled was his ghost, Lilly, watching.

How she had watched and especially how, at the end, Giles had held her gaze and imagined he was with her instead. That memory curled around Giles' overactive brain and tormented him. He still wished it had been Lilly beneath him, even now. But he hadn't known her then as he did now, and he couldn't erase what he'd done. "As I think I may have told you before, I enjoy a life of pleasure in London. Sex can be a lot of fun. Sometimes pleasure comes from a variety of sources."

In truth, sex had become a hollow release, the only meaning found while under Lilly's ghostly gaze.

"How many?"

"I beg your pardon, how many what?"

"How many bed partners have there been in your life, Giles?"

"Dozens," he answered without hesitation, "but I do not keep a list and I am always discreet." Glancing at her compressed lips, he amended, "Until you."

"Dozens." Lilly's voice sounded flat.

"It's not quite as bad as it sounds, Lilly," Giles murmured, desperately hoping she would believe him.

"Any woman?" Lilly murmured, but it was not a question. She thought he fucked anyone.

"I tend to stick to widows and courtesans. I find less trouble in that direction."

"You don't like complications?"

"I prefer honesty, Lilly. A courtesan must earn her way in the world, but I have never kept one as a long-term mistress. Since I despise infidelity in marriage, I am select in choosing my partners. Bedding widows and courtesans hurts no one. There are no husbands to cuckold, and I do not allow myself to forget the consequences of my actions. There are no illegitimate children bearing my likeness, ruining their mothers' positions in society. I prefer to keep matters of whom I bed and where private, and as I said before, I am discreet."

Lilly's thumb attempted to rub a dent in her hand. "You could always marry them if there was a child."

"I have no wish to marry. Those women join me in bed for a romp and nothing more. They would not wish to be stuck with my poor company for a lifetime."

Giles thought he saw a tear fall from her eye, but she turned away to look off into the woodland track.

"You lied to me, Giles." Lilly swiped at her face, but pulled herself up straight to look him in the eye. "You *have* dallied with someone's wife. I know you spent a night in Lady Cameron's bedchamber."

"You know Genevieve?" Giles asked.

"Lord and Lady Cameron were my papa's friends."

"Oh." Lord Winter had visited Genevieve briefly during their affair to offer his condolences at her husband's fate, but he left soon after, if he remembered correctly. Giles hadn't heard of Lilly's existence then either, but then again, he'd had a hysterical woman to deal with. "Then you must know all about Lord Cameron's accident."

"Accident?" Lilly shook her head. "I don't know of any accident but my own."

Irritated that he had to account for whom he bedded, and just as amazed that he wanted to, Giles cleared his throat. "A short while ago, Lord Cameron had an accident involving a serving girl and a very heavy skillet. The usual sad story. He was enamored of a new servant, and thought she should let him bed her. The blow knocked him unconscious. But when he woke, his every word, his every action, was changed. He became dangerous, Lilly. Lady Cameron feared for her children's safety and her own. She needed help to have him committed. He currently resides in Bedlam."

"How do you know this?"

"Cameron is an old acquaintance from school. I was a guest the night he tried to strangle his wife," Giles murmured. "I helped take him away."

"And you took advantage of her later?"

"Believe me, no one was taken advantage of. Lady Cameron was the one to instigate the short-lived affair. I will never comprehend what she hoped to gain by inviting me to her bed."

"That still doesn't make it right," Lilly asserted, her disgust clear.

Lady Cameron had wanted more from him than just that brief affair, but guilt had already settled into his heart. Especially when he remembered Lord Cameron's bewildered requests to see his wife after his incarceration.

Glancing at Lilly, he watched her tears fall unchecked and Giles knew he had seriously disappointed her. The past was beyond his power to correct, but what surprised him most was that he thought *his* heart was breaking too.

This was who he was. By his own choice, he had pursued every imaginable pleasure, dipped his wick wherever he could fit it. Yet right now, he wished it all undone just so Lilly would smile again. The greatest shock was that Lilly had a claim on his own happiness.

"How did I not know you were there?" Giles whispered, as if speaking low would banish the event.

"I didn't want you to see me."

Giles' gut fell out through his boots. Lilly had never hidden from him before. She had always trusted him. "Lilly, there are a great number of things in life that you do not need to understand, and a great number of things that you should not have seen. That was definitely one of them."

Her brow crinkled and he reached out a hand to smooth her skin, but she jerked away from his touch. Giles dropped his hand as she took a step away. His heart faltered in its beating and he feared it might stop.

"Are you ever going to allow yourself the comfort of a permanent companion?"

It was surprising how quickly a conversation turned from temporary bed partners to the future, but it was not an unnatural leap. Women tended to expect the fairy tale, lasting love, and Lilly was no different from the others. He hadn't desired to marry any of those women, widow or courtesan. Not one had appealed beyond the moment pleasure ended. "I hadn't planned to marry, no."

Lilly nodded sharply and her body sagged. Giles caught her and held her still while she trembled. "Let me take you back to the house."

"Not yet."

"Do you want me to stay?"

"No. I am sure you have many other things to do today. It is fine."

There it was. The word fine should be erased from the English language. Whenever a woman said that word, it was never true. Lilly had shut him out and she was well within her rights to do so.

His reputation was based on fact. She knew from firsthand experience too many of those facts. Every detail that might upset a gently bred young woman paraded before her innocent eyes.

Dismissed, Giles stalked back to the house in a foul mood. She wouldn't look at him again. He did not like being shut out. He did not like it one damn bit.

"Milord, shouldn't you have stayed with Miss Winter?" his annoying butler asked as soon as he crossed the threshold of the house.

"I do not stay where I am unwanted, Dithers. Mind your own affairs," Giles growled, and had the satisfaction of seeing his butler take a step back.

"May I ask Mrs. Osprey to attend her?" the older man asked cautiously.

Giles looked back out the doorway as Lilly dropped her head to her arms. Damn. "Send Mrs. Osprey out," he ordered and strode into his study.

Slamming the door brought no satisfaction. He threw himself into an armchair to consider his problem. He grew bored with a sexual partner far too easily. That was why he had bedded so many. Each affair started with the promise of more, but there was always something lacking.

Perhaps he should stick to what he did best. Driving a woman wild with pleasure was his greatest achievement. Friendship with Lillian Winter was driving him insane.

These last few weeks at Cottingstone were the longest interval without the relief of an experienced bed partner. Yet Lilly, sweet, innocent Lilly, kept him hard all day.

It had only occurred to him once to leave and get some attention for his problem, yet since her overindulgence of alcohol, he couldn't bear the thought of it. Only she could sate him, but that wasn't going to happen. He would need something to distract him when they parted company again, perhaps an orgy of sex to cleanse away these disturbing feelings of possessiveness.

"Excuse me, milord," Dithers interrupted from the doorway.

Giles turned his head. "What is it?"

Dithers danced in the doorway. "I thought you would like to know that Miss Winter has returned to her room."

"Thank you, Dithers." He turned away to stare at the smiling portrait of his mother. If ever there was a woman who could forgive him his sins, then the late Lady Daventry might be the only one.

"There is another matter you should be aware of, milord. Miss Winter has requested to dine in her chambers this evening. Alone," the butler added apologetically. "I am told she intends an early night." Dithers approached his desk and placed a pile of correspondence on the corner.

"Of course. I will eat in here. Send me a fresh bottle of brandy with the meal." Giles slumped and planned for his return to London. He was not looking forward to the trip.

"Milord, is there anything I can help you with?"

"Go away, Dithers."

Filled with churning restlessness, Giles walked to the window and stood staring out at the beautiful grounds. But he did not see them. His friendship with Lilly couldn't be over. He—

Giles clutched at his chest. The thought of leaving Lilly did not make him happy. He paced across the room, struggling to know what to do about her. He wanted her to forgive him. He wanted her to like him as he was, but he didn't think it likely anymore.

Upstairs was a pure-as-snow virgin. She had seen him with multiple partners. He did not blame her for hiding away from him. He had believed she might have been falling in love with him before today's questions, but the shock of their frank talk would no doubt kill any tender feelings she might have for him. He thumped the chair as he passed it.

He would not push to see Lilly tonight, and Giles was already on edge at the thought of spending the night alone. He wanted to be with Lilly so badly he couldn't be still.

The house was quiet, the night as black as pitch, but Lilly couldn't sleep for missing Giles. It was sometime after three in the morning. The big clock downstairs had chimed the hour a short while ago, keeping vigil with her swirling thoughts.

She didn't know what to do. She didn't know what to think. Lilly also didn't know whether to believe Giles about Lord and Lady Cameron.

Rolling over for the hundredth time, Lilly thumped the pillow, hoping to entice it to send her to sleep. The thumping didn't help.

Nothing seemed to when she had a problem she couldn't find an answer to.

In the darkness of her room, Lilly thought of Giles. His care, his affection, and the precious gift of his conversation. He gained nothing by lying to her. In fact, he should be deliriously happy that Lilly had turned away from him voluntarily. Yet earlier, Mrs. Osprey had confided that he hadn't eaten any dinner and was drinking steadily.

Mrs. Osprey, it seemed, had a fanciful idea that Giles was courting her. She'd claimed that they were intended for each other and a rosy future of love, and largely hinted at children rushing about Cottingstone was soon to follow.

The housekeeper was wrong about that. Giles didn't want anything beyond the thrill of pleasure. He certainly didn't want a wife or children in his future.

All that remained was the possibility of taking a place as his temporary bed partner. Yet despite Lilly's desire for Giles, it didn't mean she should surrender to these intense feelings. It didn't help her accept a place among the hundreds of women who'd come before.

All of those lovers had names, some of which she knew. That thought made her insides burn with jealousy and fear. There was no way that Lilly could measure up to the scores of experienced women in Giles' past. She simply wouldn't rank.

Lilly sat up and her movements disturbed Atticus. The wolfhound had borne with her agitation all night, but now slunk from the bed and headed to the closed door. Muttering an apology, she cracked the door for him and he hurried off into the dark house.

Lilly went too, creeping along the hall until she found Giles' door. It wasn't locked and it opened quietly so she could slip inside.

She needn't have bothered being quiet. Giles was snoring in his clothes, spread sideways on his bed, and the sickly scent of brandy assaulted her when she got close.

She gagged and took a step back. Mrs. Osprey hadn't lied about the drinking.

Giles rolled, arm reaching out toward her in sleep. Her insides clenched tight. She wanted him—even in this state.

Shaking her head, Lilly retraced her steps and returned to the privacy of her room. Giles did desire her and he'd kissed her.

Did that mean she held a special place in his heart?

There was only one way to find out—if she was brave enough to take a risk to ask for what she really needed from him.

Chapter Sixteen

———◆———

How long had it been since Lilly had tried to sneak anywhere undetected? If she wasn't so nervous, so fraught with doubt about taking this step, she might have tried to figure it out. But she was inches away from Giles' study door.

He was in there—she knew it. She could hear him speaking, clipped orders in a tone unlike any she'd heard before. He practically snarled about the absence of his brandy decanter.

The butler rushed from the room, startling Lilly so badly by his fast approach that she jumped back a step. Dithers captured her arm and held her upright. "My apologies, Miss Winter," he whispered, casting a harried look to the room behind.

"I'm quite all right, Dithers."

He smiled and released her, hovering close a moment as if thinking she might faint yet. "I am so very pleased to hear it." He glanced at the study door, pursed his lips, and then turned back to Lilly. "May I ask an impertinent question? I, on behalf of the household staff, would be interested to know if you might be dining with the master this evening. Purely in the interests of providing efficient service, of course."

Oh, he was just as bad as the housekeeper—another matchmaker full of fanciful notions. And another to be disappointed when the inevitable conclusion to her visit arrived. Did he blame her for his master's bad mood?

Not trusting herself to speak, she nodded. The butler relaxed, a broad smile crossing his features before he stifled the expression.

Without another word, he bowed and hurried off towards the servants' stairs. Lilly waited until the house grew quiet again to be sure she wouldn't be seen, then she eased close to the opening, ignoring the ache of her neck, to peek around the frame.

Giles stood at the window, his back to the door. She gazed upon his broad-shouldered profile to her heart's content. His hair was as messy as always, but his clothes were neat. For a change, he did not look as if he had just risen from some woman's bed.

He hadn't been in hers and she had missed him last night, missed his company perhaps more than his hands. This morning, when she'd woken sandy-eyed and melancholy, she had known she didn't want to keep a safe distance from him.

Despite the differences in their experience, he never laughed at her. In fact, he appeared determined to educate her about the world. Yet she still had a great many doubts.

Giles enjoyed sex. She had always supposed he did. The intense expression he wore reassured her that it was in pleasure when he moaned. That look on his face at the end, wild and unrestrained, told her just how much he wanted it. But the sheer number of women he had taken to his bed and the variety he was used to were still daunting.

Giles raked his fingers through his hair, agitation clear in every movement.

Knowing he could turn and find her spying on him at any moment, she drew herself up straight and stepped over the threshold. "Good morning."

Giles spun at the sound of her voice. As it usually did, Lilly's heart beat double time as their gazes locked. He watched her for a long moment and, instead of feeling anxious, Lilly gained strength.

He appeared nervous. More nervous than she, in fact.

He fidgeted with his cuffs and waistcoat, smoothing out unwrinkled garments when there was no need. When Giles dragged in a deep breath and let it out slowly, Lilly took a step forward. His eyes flicked from her head to her toes, but came back to hold her gaze.

Emboldened by his silence, by the slight lift of his lips towards a smile, Lilly moved to stand before him. As much as she tried, she couldn't hold his gaze. Such intense inspections unnerved her. She looked outside without seeing. Heat suffused her cheeks and she guessed she would look as pink as a blushing bride on her wedding day.

But there would be no wedding, no happily ever after to this tale. Lilly would have what little of Giles Wexham was hers to take and be glad for a small slice of happiness.

———— • ————

Giles could not credit that he had missed Lilly so much. However, he was uncertain how to proceed. That Lilly was here now, standing two feet away and looking lovelier in blue muslin than he'd dreamed, surprised him.

If he were honest, her presence relieved him, too.

Giles had spent last night and today in a bundle of confused thoughts and feelings. Uppermost in his mind was if it might be possible for Lilly to overlook his past scandalous behavior and remain his friend.

If she could dare to come into his company alone again, after what they had spoken of yesterday, Giles at least had a chance to regain some lost ground. How far she was prepared to go worried him, because he desperately wanted her friendship back.

"Good morning." He wanted to call her Lilly again, but he was unsure of himself.

She raised her eyes to his. "The grounds look very pretty today." The whites of her eyes were dull and she appeared exhausted. Had she endured as troubling a night as he?

"Yes, the workers did an excellent job to repair my neglect. I hired on two additional gardeners to come in each week. Dithers is pleased with me, not that he will show it. I think he expects I may be back in residence more often because of it."

"Will you be?" she queried with a small quirk of her head, and then raised a hand to her neck, grimacing as she did so.

"I was considering it, but it is a very quiet neighborhood. I would need to have greater company to be content here for long periods of time."

Her expression changed, another delicate blush built to cover her skin in warm color. She looked toward the garden. "There would be many families hereabouts that you could befriend, Giles."

Giles inched closer, elated that she had used his given name. "Do you know any of them?"

Her eyes dropped to the floor. "I am not completely certain which part of England I am currently in. How would I know?"

Giles looked at the top of Lilly's head a long time before speaking again. She did not know her current location? How stupid of him to assume she knew everything about his estate. "We are in Northamptonshire."

"Ah."

Giles slipped his knuckle beneath her chin to raise her face. "Do you remember where that is?"

"Not exactly," Lilly admitted, then worried at her lip as if the response embarrassed her. "My education largely ended when I was hurt."

He clasped her hand, led her to a book of maps open on a lectern by the far wall, and pointed out her location, then that of London. Lilly ran her fingertip over the lines and then crisscrossed the map's surface, pausing on names that must have been familiar.

When her finger found Exeter, Lilly sighed. Dumas, her family estate, lay south of Exeter. A very long way from Cottingstone Manor.

She traced the line back to Northamptonshire and looked north. She found the border of Scotland, traced across to Wales, and then dragged her fingers away.

"Did Papa say where he was going?"

"Somewhere in Wales, I believe. He did not give me any specific directions." Giles watched her nervously. They had engaged in small talk before, but it had never been this awkward. His stomach had never churned like this before. "Is your neck paining you again? You are rubbing it."

"Yes, it's just a bit stiff. I had trouble sleeping."

Lilly did not accuse him, but he knew the fault was his.

"Would you mind rubbing it for me, Giles?" Her voice sounded so hesitant that he had to smother the urge to crush her to him. Did she doubt that he wanted to help her? Foolish, foolish girl.

Giles moved behind her. He sensed Lilly's confusion when he nudged her to rest her arms against the lectern. He gently arranged her limbs so her shoulders were relaxed and set to work. Lilly breathed deeply, perfectly compliant to his wishes.

Eyes fixed on the curve of her neck, he ran his hands along her arms, shoulders and upper back. Her sigh on the first sweep of his hands was deep and satisfied. She needed him. No one had ever needed him beyond sex before. It was a heady realization.

Giles leaned in, brushed his lips against the elegant knot of hair and applied firmer pressure. She was unique, his Lilly, and he would do his best not to disappoint her again. They stayed like that for some time. Lilly softened by degrees and he smiled. He enjoyed doing this for her. It felt natural and easy to be alone with her. She played no games and made no demands.

When she was softer, he pressed his lips to her cheek. "You should go get some rest now."

Lilly pushed back from the lectern, right into him. "I suppose I should, but it is time to dine."

"You will feel better for the rest." Giles slid a hand around her waist, imagining her stretched out in her bed, waiting for him to give her relief again later that night. "Do you want me to take you to bed?" *Well, of course, Lilly shouldn't say yes to that.*

"No, I promised the staff I would dine downstairs." Lilly sighed.

Giles pressed another kiss to her hair then had a great deal of trouble keeping his lips from her skin. She tasted better than any pheasant, better than any dessert in creation. He would rather feast on her.

A knock sounded on the door and Giles quickly put a respectable distance between himself and Lilly. "Come."

His butler stepped into the room. "Dinner is ready when you desire, milord."

The butler retreated quickly, but his eyes held amusement.

Giles' lower body pulsed as Lilly licked her lips to capture the last of Cook's most decadent dessert.

"Did you like that?" Giles shifted his position in his chair.

Lilly's eyes glowed. "Oh, that was delightful. What did you call it again?"

"My father christened it Passion's Peak."

She laughed. "Giles, I don't think that could be the correct name."

Despite his discomfort, he laughed with her. "Well, I don't question Cook too closely in case she stops creating these masterpieces for me," Giles confided, sliding to the edge of his chair and standing with trepidation. He was aroused, painfully aware of every innocent movement Lilly made with her mouth or hands.

The table had hidden his state for the meal, but now that dinner was over, he needed to walk Lilly to the drawing room or study if she wished to consult the atlas again.

Lilly stood, but turned to face him. "Giles, are you in pain?"

"To a small degree, but it is nothing I can't live with." And had lived with for weeks. Lilly was driving him to the edge of his sanity.

"What is wrong with you?" Lilly's gray eyes searched his and Giles found it hard to breathe. She looked sincerely worried for his health. Precious angel—if she knew the real reason, she wouldn't look so concerned.

He tugged her toward the drawing room where he hoped no servants awaited. Luck was with him—the room was bare of servant chaperones. He closed the door behind him and locked it for good measure. "You are so very lovely, Lilly, and you must know I want you badly. "It is not easy to resist your charms, but I am trying to behave," Giles confessed with apprehension. This level of honesty was a surefire way of scaring her off again.

"Why?"

Giles laughed and the pressure in his trousers lessened. "Angel, you say the most astonishing things."

Lilly laughed with him but settled her hands on his chest. Of their own accord, his hands curled around her back and slid downwards.

"You look like you want to kiss me again," she whispered.

The blue muslin didn't hide the warmth of her derrière, or the lush curve of her hip. "True."

"Actually, I think you want to do more than kiss me." Lilly teased him, flirting. The thought was so provoking that he lost a little more control over his libido.

"True as well," Giles sighed and pressed his lips to hers lightly. "You are not making this easy for me."

"You prefer things to be easy. You don't like complications." Lilly pulled out of his embrace and walked a few steps away.

Giles followed along behind. "I...don't know what I want when it comes to you, Lilly. But I do know I don't want to upset you again."

Lilly picked up a deck of cards and handed them to him over her shoulder. The way her head turned to him, the angle of her neck beckoned, and he lowered his lips to kiss her skin.

He didn't wander farther and clutched the cards tightly in his fist to keep at least one hand under control. Lilly angled her neck and he nibbled her earlobe.

She moaned. "Will you come to me tonight?"

Giles swallowed and tried to think of a reason to refuse. He didn't want to refuse. He pressed a lingering kiss behind her ear. "I shouldn't."

"I want you to," Lilly said hesitantly.

He turned her and gave in to the urge to kiss her properly. He deepened the kiss as soon as her lips parted, teasing her tongue, invading her warmth, and drowning his senses in the rightness of her lips.

Lilly sighed when their lips parted, as if she was as consumed by passion as he. He allowed his hands to caress lower and he gripped the firm swells of her bottom possessively, feeling her smile around his kisses. As their tongues brushed and played, Lilly pushed her hands up around his neck and held him tightly.

"Teach me to play," Lilly whispered between kisses.

"Whist or something else?" Giles murmured before he caught her earlobe with his teeth.

Lilly squirmed in his arms, brushing against his groin with less innocence than he expected. "Something else."

Giles froze, pretty sure they were thinking about the same thing. "Are you sure you want that?"

"I'm sure I want *you*."

Giles pushed her away, but held her head with one hand at her nape. He dragged in several deep breaths before he spoke, readying himself to be a gentleman and back away. "Even if it's not forever?"

Lilly nodded. "Even a single night can be enough."

Giles locked every muscle in place lest he launch himself at her bodily. Blood roared in his ears, drowning out the world around them. All he could hear was Lilly's panting breaths. All he could see was her face flushed by desire. "It's too early to go to bed yet and hope to fool the servants."

"Then teach me to play whist to pass the time," Lilly suggested, appearing surprised that the most decadent pleasure-seeker in London was quaking in his boots.

How little she knew him. He felt unbalanced for the first time in a decade around a beautiful woman. He was drowning in the unfamiliar waters of a different kind of lust. Different, better, and far stronger than anything he'd known before.

And all because of Lilly, the one woman he hadn't imagined feeling anything for. She could have been his wife once. A woman he'd have bedded to do his duty to produce an heir, but little else beyond. Arranged marriages had never been about love. Tolerance, perhaps, and hoped-for affection.

What he felt for Lilly at this moment defied his considerable experience. "All right," Giles said after a pause. "But no more kisses till later."

"Whatever you want, Giles," Lilly agreed.

Giles shook his head to clear it of endless decadent possibilities.

Chapter Seventeen

———◆———

The bedchamber door shut with the softest pressure of his hand and Giles hurried to turn the key in the lock. What he intended to do was arousing, foolish, and altogether reckless. An event that could see him face her father's pistol or blade on the field of honor.

Tonight, he would share Lilly's bed for more than a quick massage. Tonight, he'd become her lover.

Lilly's eyes followed him as he came closer, her glance flickering over his body. Despite her bold appraisal, glances that skittered along his nerves and hastened his heartbeat, she hid beneath the covers. Perhaps she wasn't quite comfortable with her own suggestion to share her bed with him. If she'd changed her mind, he'd give her a chance to call a halt to this mad slide into sin. He wouldn't hold her to her invitation.

He touched the bed, letting his fingers drag across the linen as he walked around to the far side. Lilly turned to follow his movements, and that was all it took to convince Giles that he was welcome. She lay on her stomach as usual, but her shoulders and upper back were already bare.

Lilly had stripped for him, but maidenly nerves kept her buried beneath the coverlet. That image clouded his mind so much that Giles could not move for a moment. She smiled shyly and then burrowed under the covers, dropping her face into the pillow.

Careful to keep his impulses under control, Giles removed his jacket slowly, but hesitated to remove more. It wasn't that he didn't want to make love to Lilly, but the constricting clothing would slow him down. More than anything, he wanted Lilly to enjoy his touch, his attention, even at the expense of his own pleasure.

He reached for the blanket's edge, exposing her bare upper back to the air. Once he lifted the counterpane fully, enough to admit him to her bed, he found that his ability to compartmentalize caring for Lilly had vanished completely.

He slipped into bed, boots and all, tugged the covers over his hips and pressed his lips to her spine. "Good evening, Angel."

"Good evening."

Despite the situation, a smile tugged at his lips. They both sounded so dreadfully formal, but he had to speak. He had to say something to mark the moment. Unlike the other women he'd known, he couldn't relax into bed with her so easily or so quickly. He knew what he was doing would change Lilly's life forever. Losing even part of her innocence deserved his utmost respect and care.

Rising so his weight rested on one arm, he touched her ribs, sliding his fingers over her skin, pressing little kisses along her spine. He stopped thinking, kneading muscles and caressing Lilly in a wholly different manner than normal, more sensual and erotic. Touches designed to soothe as well as deliberately arouse.

Lilly shifted, a slight rock of her hips against the bedding, letting him know he was affecting her just as badly as she affected him. He let his hands wander into her hair and pulled the pins free, letting the soft locks flow across her shoulder and spill onto the pillow. He pushed the sweet-smelling tresses aside and buried his lips in her neck. God, she tasted so sweet, so good.

Remembering that Lilly had needs he had to cater to, he sat up and straddled her carefully, while silently cursing his reluctance to remove his boots. But he couldn't pause long enough to remove them. The night was passing and he didn't want himself and Lilly found together like this. He gave her the massage she sorely needed, but when he was done he kissed the back of her knee, her ankle, and captured her wriggling feet to press a kiss to the arch.

"Giles?" Lilly complained in a whisper.

He chuckled. "I thought you might like that, but it seems you are far too ticklish yet to enjoy it fully." He crawled up the bed and lay beside her, again resting his weight on one arm.

Lilly's passion-clouded eyes held his. "Do you like that?"

He shrugged. "No one has ever tried before so I cannot say for certain."

Lilly, dropped her head, thinking something through. He let her think. She might want to call the whole thing off and there was still time to keep her innocent. He could still walk away from her bed, although it would be with considerable regret.

Lilly's bare toes slipped onto the top of his boots and pressed against him. With that small encouragement, Giles kissed her back, kissed a path down her ribs, letting his breath fan across the base of spine just above her glorious derrière. He debated whether to go lower.

"What *do* you like, Giles?"

He rose to his knees, straddling her so he could use both hands. He settled them at her waist, slid them hard along her sides until he encountered the first swells of her breasts.

Lilly lifted her chest marginally, and he palmed her breasts. Glorious, soft and a perfect fit to his palms. He dropped his mouth level with her ear. "I like you."

Dragging his hands away, he let his fingertips graze her hardened nipples. She moaned, body trembling at the new sensation. Giles swirled his fingertips around the hard buds and then palmed her breasts again, squeezing and rolling her flesh to give her pleasure.

Lilly tried to turn over, but his position restricted her movement. He tweaked her nipple and she shuddered. He flexed his hips so his aroused cock pressed against the firm swell of her bottom. Even that slight friction drove him wild.

But he didn't want to rush—he wanted to please her first.

Climbing carefully over her, he fell to the mattress. Sharing a bed with Lilly was overwhelming. He sucked in deep breaths, fighting to regain control.

"Is anything wrong?"

Lilly had turned to her side and was watching him with wary

eyes.

"You are so beautiful," Giles whispered, pressing a long kiss to her shoulder. Hair tickled his nose and he pushed it away, exposing more of her skin and a full, ripe breast.

Control was overvalued. He pulled Lilly to him, took her lips in a hard kiss and slid his body under hers. Soft, warm flesh branded his skin even through the clothing he wore. Lilly kissed him back, sliding her tongue into his mouth, setting off an avalanche of desire he had to fight hard to suppress.

She lay over his body, thighs spread and the heart of her pressed tight against his erection. She rocked, whimpering in frustration as pleasure built slowly. Too slowly for her, but much too fast for him. If she continued, he wouldn't be able to wait for her pleasure to come.

He rolled her to her back, held his weight above so as not to crush her, and slid his hand downwards. As his fingers crossed her belly, she sucked her stomach in. When his fingers touched her curls, a needy moan broke free.

"Soon, Angel. Just wait."

Giles was not normally a vocal man in bed, but desire and Lilly prodded him to speak. He could not seem to help himself— just as with everything else to do with Lilly. He could blame it on being in bed with a naked woman and still being fully dressed. It was one of his least-used fantasies. To be the one to pleasure, to be the one to control what happened, was heady.

Thankfully Lilly seemed content to take things at his pace, to let him decide the position, too.

He kissed her jaw. "I have dreamed of being in bed with you for so long."

Lilly's eyes opened and the gray depths were stormy. "How long?"

Should he confess the whole? Should he tell her that every other lover paled in comparison to just this much pleasure? Giles dragged in a breath. "Since the first night I saw you in Huntley House."

Confession was good for the soul, he'd heard, and it appeared to be very good for Lilly, too. Her hot little hands cupped his face and he groaned loudly at the desire he saw reflected back at him.

Fingers traced his jaw, burned a line to his ear and then

scraped into his hair, torturing his body with gooseflesh. She curled her arm around his head and held his lips to hers. Convinced that kissing her was not to be given up, Giles gave her the kisses she demanded.

Yet he could not remain idle under such an assault, so he stoked the side of her body, feeling the end coming closer. When he brushed the bony ridge of her hip, he kept going. Caressing and kneading the globe of her bottom, he drowned in the scent of her body, the texture of her skin.

Giles broke the kiss and let his lips trail off her face, letting her body fall to the mattress in a messy heap. He kissed down her neck and into the valley between her breasts. He knew what he wanted. Giles took her nipple into his mouth the exact moment his fingers tangled in her blonde curls. He gave Lilly no time to protest. He suckled at her breast hungrily as his fingers parted her thighs and delved into her heat, reveling in her whimpers of pleasure and the sharp tugging at his hair.

"Oh, Giles."

His fingers grew wet as he parted her folds and traced to her source of greatest pleasure. Lilly jumped as he petted her nub and his cock swelled in anticipation.

Giles lifted his head. The cords of Lilly's neck stood out as she flexed, panting, aroused beyond anything she'd ever known. So damn beautiful that Giles couldn't bear to take his eyes from her flushed face. Slowing his fingers, he waited for Lilly to look at him. He could not bear for her to avoid his eyes. "Sweetheart?"

Lilly's gray eyes drowned him, her breath panted across his lips. "Now I know why you like this."

Giles swirled his fingers again and she gasped, hips rising into his touch. "Now you know."

He would not take her virginity, but there were benefits to allowing him free play. Giles would see her climax and enjoy doing so. His fingers slipped from her folds and he grasped one thigh and draped it over his so she was wide open. She would not need to hold herself still, she would be comfortable. That was all Giles cared about.

He slid his hand down her thigh and covered her mound again, kissing her lips while his fingers pressed and twirled. When her hips rose to meet his fingers again, he knew she would peak soon. She moaned and sobbed as the pinnacle neared.

"That's it. Come for me, Lilly." Giles rose over her possessively to watch her release that first time, and didn't care that he would not even receive pleasure himself. He had never cared so much about a woman's happiness before. Pleasing Lilly was all that mattered tonight.

Eyes locked, he increased the friction of his fingers, spreading her wetness until she arched again, sobbing his name as the release hit her squarely. Thighs clenched tight around his hand as she ground her body against his fist.

For a small, frail woman, her contractions went on a lot longer than he had anticipated. With his hand buried as it was, he felt every ripple of pleasure that shook her. He felt awed and proud all at once. God, she was heaven, and he wondered how he had ever thought desire existed before today.

Her thighs relaxed and he moved his fingers, only to find greater wetness than before. Lilly was dripping, and he could not help but grind his cock against her thigh. Once, twice, then a long, protracted moan burst free as he came in his trousers from just that slight friction.

Lilly clutched his head tight against hers until he slumped to the mattress, breathing hard to recover. He hadn't needed to come that much in forever.

He hadn't soiled his garments since he was a young lad in short pants, spying on the village girls washing in the stream. But Lilly had the damnedest effect on him. One he'd never encountered before. All his carefully thought out notions of pleasure had just been thrown out the window.

"Are you all right?" Lilly asked.

He lifted his head and grinned down at her. The earth shifted again and he pressed his lips to Lilly's to prevent some banal comment from spewing from his lips. Her lips clung, her fingers threading into his hair as he tucked her tight against his body.

The way she moved against him convinced him that, given enough night hours, he could pleasure her again. But the night was passing. He had no idea of the time. They both needed to sleep and he needed to make an escape before dawn found him in her bed.

Regretfully, Giles turned Lilly, tucked his arm under her head and stretched the linen and counterpane to cover them both. Lilly sighed, pressing her lips to his wrist. Setting him alight with her simple gesture. He inched his hips back so they didn't fit so snugly and pressed a kiss to her hair, waiting for his world to settle. "Time for sleep, little ghost."

Lilly grumbled.

Capturing her hand, Giles threaded their fingers together and held them against her belly, savoring the companionable warmth between them. To his surprise, Lilly pushed his hand away and turned to face him. Laying her head on his arm, she placed her hand against his cheek. Lilly's short nails scratched at his stubble once then grew still, breath turning even and deep.

Astounded by her sudden sleep, he listened to the sound of her breathing. He'd never remembered past lovers' sleeping habits, but he would always remember this moment, sharing Lilly's bed. A night beyond his expectations and an experience he wanted again. He only hoped that Lilly would say the same come morning.

Chapter Eighteen

Apparently, Lilly could consider herself just as wanton as half of the women in London. That was her first thought upon waking. When she rolled over and found her room devoid of Giles' warm body, sadness trickled through her. Of course he would not stay. The man was built for dalliance and nothing further. But still, she missed him already.

Her second thought was less condemning and had more to do with his fingers on her skin. Oh, the things that man could do with his hands was incredible. Giles could make any woman relax with him. Not that she had ever feared him exactly, but she had known just how impossible it would be to form a tender for him and share his bed.

His skill at easing her injuries notwithstanding, he was wickedly insistent in his single-minded pursuit of pleasure. He made her throb. He made her want more.

Lilly stretched. Crisp sheets tangled around her legs as she tried to hold on to the memory of Giles' lips and fingers on her body.

Her third thought was to wonder if he would want to share her bed again. Now that he'd had his wicked way with her, more or less, would he lay beside her tonight if she asked?

Considering how focused and tender he had been, she hoped he would. He combined the best of his healing hands with scandalous touches that inflamed her senses. And he had also aroused himself.

To her shame, Lilly could take no credit for his pleasure. She had not known how to touch him. When he had groaned into her neck from the slight friction against her leg, she had been embarrassed that she had not shown him more attention.

Lilly would ask him what to do next time. If there was a next time. She bit her lip. Given what she knew now, she couldn't blame him for liking intimate relations so much. What they had shared had been intense. They had enjoyed great intimacy together.

Lilly pushed her arms beneath her and moved into a sitting position. Her body was still bare and her breasts rose high over the linens, surprising her with a thrill of cool air across her nipples. She had never slept naked before and as she wriggled against the thick cotton sheets, she decided she liked it.

Giles slept naked.

A blush crept up her cheeks. She'd sobbed Giles' name when her passion peaked. Her world had gone dark and starry as his fingers pushed her over an edge she'd never expected to exist.

At the foot of the bed lay Lilly's nightgown, ready to slip over her head for modesty's sake. She reached for it, dragging the familiar material up the bed and then struggling into the loose garment. As she pulled her hair free and over her breast, she smiled.

Giles was so thoughtful, so determined to look after her needs, though if anyone suspected Lilly and Giles were lovers that might change.

Lilly snuggled beneath the blankets again, quite prepared to lose herself in the memory of making love with Giles, but the door creaked open and a white-capped head squeezed through the gap. "Good morning, Miss Winter. I'm sorry if I've woken you too soon."

Lilly stretched. "I was dozing. How are you today, Mrs. Osprey?"

The housekeeper advanced in her usual rush, flicked open the drapes, and jiggled the window to let in the fresh air of morning. "Oh, nothing to complain of." She checked the flowers, the hearth, and her night table, then fussed with the sheets around Lilly's waist, tugging them up high. "Are you ready for your breakfast?"

"That would be lovely."

Mrs. Osprey fluttered out the door but returned a short time later with a large, heavily laden tray. It might be her imagination, but the breakfast trays appeared to be getting fuller with every meal. Lilly picked her way through what she liked best, ignoring the suspicion that Giles monitored her eating habits even after telling him not to.

While Lilly finished her breakfast, Mrs. Osprey flittered in and out of the room, selecting clothing from Katarina's bedchamber—dark blue muslin today–and organizing her bath. It was embarrassing just how much time Mrs. Osprey spent with her. Wouldn't her duties as housekeeper be suffering?

Heavier treads signaled the arrival of the male servants with bath water. Snuggling under the linens, Lilly watched the fascinating interaction between Mrs. Osprey and the butler. Today, they both kept sneaking peeks at each other. Lilly hid her smile at how comical they appeared as one twisted away before the other caught them staring.

When Dithers was around, Mrs. Osprey became even ditherier. The absurdity was not lost on Lilly. As a result, Dithers took a firm hand with the staff—even though those matters were the housekeeper's responsibility. When the bath was prepared to Dithers' exacting standards, he bowed to her and excused himself, nodding to Mrs. Osprey as if reminding her of her task.

Usually the housekeeper ignored him, but today Mrs. Osprey blew out a heavy breath and dropped every appearance of forgetfulness. "I know what to do, you devil," she complained just loud enough for Lilly to hear.

Puzzled, but unwilling to get involved, Lilly slid out of bed and hastened to bathe. Behind her, Mrs. Osprey stripped the bed in record time, wadded up the sheets, snatched her nightgown from the floor, then placed them at the door for laundering.

Lilly was surprised. They had only replaced the bedding with fresh sheets yesterday. They didn't need to spoil her to this extent.

Mrs. Osprey helped her dress. The blue muslin wasn't as pretty as yesterday's gown, but at least it wasn't another nightgown confining her to the house.

"There, all finished." Mrs. Osprey stepped back and eyed her handiwork. Turning her head this way and that, Lilly admired the pretty arrangement of her hair against the darker-toned gown. The contrast was striking. Mrs. Osprey had real talent.

"Thank you, Mrs. Osprey. You've spoiled me for my normal life."

The housekeeper grinned. "Nonsense, my lamb, anyone who can make his lordship smile as you do deserves so much more than this."

Blushing, Lilly grasped for a safer topic. "I did not think I would require clean linens as yet. I don't wish to burden the servants with unnecessary tasks. Surely they could have waited another day."

Mrs. Osprey frowned. "Ordinarily they could have, but the sheets are best dealt with directly. Now that we know your timing, we'll be better prepared for next month if you're still here then. Perhaps you should rest indoors today. The earl's mamma was always lying about at this time. Can't say I blame her for taking the opportunity. Some women do take it harder than others, and Lady Daventry was a delicate sort like you, if you can remember."

Lilly did not understand why Mrs. Osprey thought she was any frailer today than yesterday or the day before that. She could admit that her long illness gave other people the impression that she was weak, but she knew herself to be improving a little more each day.

"I remember Lady Daventry. She was kind but frail, wasn't she?" Lilly had always assumed that a strong wind could blow her over if she ever ventured out of doors, but she didn't wish to speak ill of the dead.

"That she was, and a sweeter, kinder mistress you could never hope to find. You remind me of her."

Lilly couldn't hold back a smile. It was a greater compliment than Mrs. Osprey could know. "Mrs. Osprey, I wonder if you could tell me. When did Lady Daventry die? I don't think I ever heard of it, and I am hesitant to ask the earl for fear of upsetting him."

Mrs. Osprey frowned. "That's probably for the best. Her death hit him hard. It was after your accident, but less than a year after her husband passed. Lord Daventry, the elder, took a fall from his horse and died a week or so later from a nasty infection. Perhaps two years after your accident."

"Oh, I didn't know that either."

"The mistress did not take his death well, and one way or another managed to follow him not long after. The children were devastated. His lordship tried so hard to cheer his mother, but she slipped away from him." Mrs. Osprey tucked a stray wisp of Lilly's hair behind her ear. "'Tis why the master banned laudanum from the manor. He thinks she doctored herself to death. I expect that's why he's so concerned about you. You are both fragile women."

Mrs. Osprey bobbed her head and hurried off with the linens, leaving Lilly with her heart pounding. Mrs. Osprey's news explained quite a bit about Giles' behavior.

Thirty minutes later, Lilly shook and huddled on the corner of the chaise. She had just used the chamber pot, and found to her shock that she was bleeding.

Lilly was frightened. Terrified. If this was what happened after the pleasure of Giles' touch, she was appalled. She had no idea that the pleasures of the body could result in such an injury. Would she die now that she had finally managed to thwart all the nasty voices and begun to live again?

Lilly just did not know how long it would take, so she curled up on her side and prayed. She prayed to die quickly this time.

———— ✦ ————

"So this is where you hide each summer."

Giles looked up and found Lord Carrington hovering at his door. Giles tossed his cravat at his valet and crossed the room. "Carrington, when the devil did you get here? I didn't hear the carriage." He pulled the younger man into a rough hug.

"I rode here this morning from the village. My carriage broke down late last night, so I foolishly thought to borrow a nag from the innkeeper rather than wait."

"Good God, I fear I know the one you were loaned and I'm now doubly surprised to see you. Have you no sense?"

"Apparently not."

Giles turned back to his valet and let the man fuss with his attire. "Glad to see you survived. That horse, if it's the one I fear, has thrown more able horsemen inside a mile of the village than I can count."

"That does explain why the innkeeper didn't seem too concerned about when the beast would return. He said he'd be seeing it soon. The foolish thing shied at every startled bird or rabbit." Carrington leaned against the wall. "Thanks for inviting me."

"Quite all right. I'm happy to offer a brief reprieve from your family. I'm sure your mother's been watching every wedding for the last few years and taking notes."

"Too true, too true. She has a book." Carrington blew out a harsh breath. "Why the hell did I decide to marry?"

Giles held the younger man's gaze, surprised he'd uttered the question Giles had been trying to keep from asking for the past few months. "From what I understand, you had little enough choice but to do so or risk the loss of your honor."

Carrington scrubbed his hand through his hair. When he started pacing, the usual sign the viscount was disturbed, Giles decided not to pursue the discussion. Talking wouldn't help. "I was about to go down for breakfast. Have you eaten?"

Carrington stopped. "No." He turned and met Giles' gaze. "You know, I'm surprised you're not possessed of a fuller figure. Is your answer for every crisis eating?"

"You forget I live an active life. A man must eat to feed his passions."

Carrington burst out laughing, and Giles was happy his comment had distracted the younger man from his troubles.

"Active is one way to describe your life. But with all the rest you supposedly get when in Northamptonshire, I would have thought you'd not continue to eat quite so well." Carrington grinned. "In fact, I must compliment you. You appear in remarkably better spirits for a man whose self-imposed celibacy has become a well-known annual event. I'd say you were happy."

Giles laid his hand on the doorknob. Was the bubbling feeling of contentment he'd woken with so transparent to others? It couldn't be. "Carrington, let's go down to breakfast."

He left the room and, after a moment, heard Carrington's

rushed footsteps following. For a change, the younger man held his tongue until they were left alone in the breakfast room. But Carrington's gaze pinned him in place. "Have you a woman here?"

Giles breathed deep. Here was his moment to inform Carrington of Lilly's unchaperoned presence, yet he hesitated. After last night's passionate encounter, he didn't know how to describe what existed between him and Lilly. Lovers sounded far too coarse.

"You have, haven't you?" Carrington offered. "I'll head back to London. You should have mentioned you planned to have company you would prefer your last lover not hear about. Lady Montgomery sent her regards, by the way."

"You mean she tried to seduce you?" Sabine Montgomery had shown her leg to more than one of his close friends and, to her mortification, she'd been rebuffed every time.

"I did not take up her generous offer. You've known all along how things stand with me."

Giles sighed and set aside his napkin. "That I do. How is Aggie bearing up?"

Carrington paced again. "I don't know. She won't speak to me."

"Can you blame her? What woman in her right mind could be happy the man she loves has been forced to offer for another?"

Carrington threw his lanky body into a chair and dropped his head into his hands. "I know. I wasn't paying enough attention."

Giles watched him, pitying the circumstances that had changed Carrington's charmed existence. His was a situation most men feared. "My betrothed is here."

The minute the words left his lips, Giles knew he'd just created more problems. As a rule, he didn't like to lie, but his first thought was to spare Lilly's reputation.

Carrington's head snapped up but, for a change, the talkative man remained silent.

The lie thickened his tongue until Giles had to clear his throat. "That is to say, my former betrothed, Lillian Winters, a near invalid, is residing upstairs. Without chaperone."

Truth was better.

Carrington looked at the floor, and then his shoulders shook. Concerned, Giles moved to his side and laid a hand upon him.

The minute he touched Carrington, his shakes became laughter. Giles scowled, far from amused by his friend's reaction.

The other man stood and moved about the room, wiping at the corner of his eyes as his laughter continued in an unstoppable rush. Resigned, Giles waited for him to calm, but he did not think the situation warranted such an outpouring of emotion.

Eventually, Carrington met his gaze. The other man blinked, realizing perhaps that Giles didn't think the situation was in any way funny. Lilly deserved better respect than this, and he was glad she still lay abed. Carrington returned to his chair and sat down.

"No wonder you look so happy. You've taken the girl to bed." Carrington nodded, assuming Giles' silence was confirmation. "Given my recent difficulties, I think you should tell me everything that has happened since you left London. It might be possible to save you yet."

"Save me?"

"But of course. The first thing you should do is return to London. Given Lady Montgomery's nature, I'm sure you could prevail upon her to provide you with a plausible alibi that would negate any claim by the chit. Of course, I'll be only too happy to do the same."

"I don't need to be saved," Giles growled. He'd not lie outright about Lilly's presence in his home. He'd known there'd be consequences of her being left here, and he'd tried to point them out to her thick-headed father. But after last night, marriage to Lilly held an unexpected appeal. She was a passionate woman and very undemanding. They could deal well together, but there was no need to rush into any decision. He would cross that bridge when he faced it. For the time being, Carrington would hold his tongue and, when Baron Winter returned, Giles would see if his attraction to Lilly waned. "I wouldn't be happy to leave Lilly."

Chapter Nineteen

---◆---

The discussion with Lord Carrington had taken hours and, in the end, Giles had not been able to convince his friend that Lilly wouldn't trick him into marriage. She simply wasn't so calculating.

They had parted company when it seemed likely they could come to blows over Carrington's disparaging remarks, and his friend had taken off on a country walk to cool his head. Just in case he got lost, Giles had asked for one of the grooms to follow discreetly. Carrington might navigate society with barely a thought, but he'd become lost within five minutes in the country if he were truly alone.

The door creaked and Giles prepared to deal with his friend in a more rational frame of mind. However, it was not Carrington at all but his housekeeper.

"Beg pardon for disturbing you, but I wish to speak with you about Miss Winter. She returned an untouched luncheon tray and has let a whole pot of tea grow cold without tasting a drop. She won't say why."

"Do you mean to say she's not eaten since breakfast?" Giles demanded, irritated by the news.

Mrs. Osprey nodded, shifting her weight from foot to foot on the other side of his desk.

"Is she ill, madam?"

"Oh, no, sir. Not ill. Well, not perhaps, as you might

understand matters. No, not ill at all," Mrs. Osprey assured him, but he still did not understand what the problem could be.

Watching her wring her hands in tongue-tied agitation, Giles placed both hands on the desk and rose to his feet. "Dithers!"

At his shout, Mrs. Osprey went pale. "Oh, I could not. I just could not."

The butler could help him deal with this vexing creature. He usually knew how. Giles held a hand out to stop the flow of words while he waited.

"Dithers, finally," Giles cried as the door burst open. "See if you can get some sense out of this woman, will you? Apparently, I need to know something about Miss Winter, but Mrs. Osprey cannot bring herself to tell me. At least not in a manner that I might understand clearly, if you catch my meaning."

Dithers' expression stated he did not understand anything at all, but he moved toward Mrs. Osprey. When Mrs. Osprey met his gaze, her eyes firmed at once and she swiveled to face Giles, appearing right-minded for the first time since his return to Northamptonshire.

"It is a private matter, my lord."

Giles could see Dithers taken aback by her sharp tone. Mrs. Osprey appeared to be a woman in complete control of her mind. A nagging suspicion formed. It was not only men who played games to get what they want.

Crafty woman! She'd played helpless to keep Dithers near.

Giles waved the man away. "Dithers, you are dismissed."

Mrs. Osprey hid a smile and Giles gestured toward the garden door. She stepped through with firm steps and walked ahead of him to a spot where they could not be overheard.

Giles folded his arms across his chest. "Now, what the devil is going on?"

Mrs. Osprey clasped her hands together. "My Lord, I understand it if you'd prefer not to be involved directly with the young lady, but Miss Winter's behavior today gives me great concern."

Giles' heart dropped to his toes, but he managed to strangle out a convincingly neutral, "Oh."

"When I was with her earlier this morning, and I know this is of no concern to gentlemen, but I did notice that her woman's time was upon her. At least that is what I believed then. When I left her, she seemed cheerful, but luncheon came and went and she ate nothing. She stayed on the chaise, and has not moved. When I took tea upstairs just now, she was still there and had a look about her I did not like. She does not confide in me, my lord, but I believe her to be in some sort of shock. Do you think something may have happened to her during the night? Perhaps, something sinister that could have overset her nerves?"

Giles stood rooted to the spot. Nothing sinister had happened to her other than sharing bed space with him. Nothing to account for the bleeding anyway. And Giles had not entered her. Not even with the tip of a finger. He had managed to keep his head and remained on the outside of Lilly's body through the entire glorious event.

No, it must be as Mrs. Osprey had first assumed, her woman's time was upon her and she was upset about it. He had not left her bed until the early morning light had first illuminated her room. He had slept all night in Lilly's bed, even keeping his boots on his feet.

Right now, though, he had a problem. Mrs. Osprey assumed, as he had wanted her to assume, that he had no serious interest. He had thought she might have been hiding from him out of shyness, or perhaps from Lord Carrington, and he wanted to smack his head into a very hard tree for not thinking to check on her earlier.

He should have treated her very differently after last night, and he needed to go see her now. Was it possible she came downstairs, heard his and Carrington's discussion, and hadn't cared for what was said about her? Neither he nor Carrington had remembered to keep their voices particularly low.

"You will need to speak to the girl, I suspect." Mrs. Osprey rocked on the balls of her feet. "I don't know how she will feel about it all, but perhaps you could talk to her in private. I can wait outside in the hall, or at the edge of the room."

Bless Mrs. Osprey. He did not even have to suggest behaving improperly. Perhaps she still could read his mind as he had once thought. "Yes, I suppose a private discussion would be best and prove less embarrassing all around. Thank you for suggesting it, Osprey. I will be there directly."

"Oh, that is so good of you, my lord."

He looked about him and spotted a pretty flower in a nearby bed. A flower might lift Lilly's spirits. Once Mrs. Osprey turned her back, Giles pinched it off the bush and tucked it into an inner pocket before he followed her inside.

There was no response to Giles' quiet knock on Lilly's door but he entered anyway. Instead of finding her propped up in bed, under the covers as usual, Lilly lay curled on her side on the chaise. Giles kicked the door closed, keeping Mrs. Osprey out, and drank in her subtle and very distinctive scent.

Arousal tightened his trousers and he fought it. Her face had a pinched look about it that troubled him a great deal. When he crossed the room and bent over the chaise, she did not move. He opened her hand and twirled the flower across her palm, but didn't get a pleased grin in return.

He clasped her hand tight, pressing the flower between their palms, and noticed how clammy she was.

"Lilly, darling, whatever is the matter?" Giles reflected wryly that he asked her that a great deal.

"I'm dying, Giles."

"Dying!" he exclaimed. "I don't think so, my girl. You will feel better in a day or so."

"A day or so? Will it take that long? I don't think I can bear this."

"Well, in my experience, most women find these first few days unpleasant, but I have never heard of anyone dying from it," he assured her, rubbing his thumb across the back of hers, pleased by her increasing color.

"Are you telling me that all women go through this? That pleasure produces this weakness?"

"Weakness? What the devil are you talking about?" Giles settled to his knees. "Your monthly courses have nothing to do with pleasure, my darling. They have to do with producing children."

She looked at him in horror and an abhorrent idea took hold.

"Did no one ever explain women's matters to you?"

She shook her head very quickly.

Giles clenched her hands tight. "Poor darling, what a wretched morning you must have had. I would berate your father for this, if I did not think he would shoot me for knowing such personal details about you."

"Children?"

"Ah, I see I am going to take this from the very beginning. I promise you are not dying. Here, let me see if I can explain this. Just remember that my point of view is from the man's side of things and a woman could explain it better." He deliberately chose not to say her own mother, but she should have been the one to educate the girl long before the accident.

An hour later, he summoned Mrs. Osprey to fetch tea and arranged for Lilly to dine with him and Carrington so the necessary introductions could be made. Her color grew better. A lot better. His explanations had caused a lot of blushing on her part, and a fair amount of tension on his.

They had told her nothing. Everything she knew about women came from him. First from watching him bed others, and the rest from today's frank talk.

"And I'll bleed every month."

Giles pulled her against his shoulder. "Until the time your body grows too old to bear children." He kissed the top of her head, imagining her holding an infant in her arms. He slammed the door shut on that kind of thinking.

In all the years of her illness, she had not been aware of her own monthly flux. Perhaps this was the first time Lilly had ever been lucid enough to recognize it. It was also possible that it had been completely absent, too. He would dearly like to know the answer, but satisfying his curiosity would end in a meeting with a smoking pistol.

"You must think me a complete imbecile, Giles. I am so sorry Papa brought me here to trouble you."

"I am not sorry at all. You are very sweet and delightfully innocent, Lilly. Better to blunder with me than someone else. Better to hear the truth from a friend, I think." Giles squeezed again and she wrapped her arms around his waist, gripping him tightly without provoking a feeling of suffocation other women had. Yes, they were good friends indeed. She needed someone on her side. Eventually Carrington would see she expected nothing more than that.

If Giles had whispered that she had two heads instead of one, Lilly would have an explanation for the cross looks Lord Carrington directed at her across the well-set mahogany. Odd to say, but she was uncomfortable with the most charming man in London. She didn't care for him. He didn't look the least bit friendly.

"Just how long will you be staying in Northamptonshire, Miss Winter?"

She glanced at Giles' impassive expression before answering to the viscount. Given the belligerent stare Carrington offered in return, she put her fork down, quite losing her interest in food. "Until my father returns. As I believe I mentioned already, I don't know when that will be."

Carrington turned to Giles and quirked an eyebrow. He said nothing, but some form of private communication passed between them. Lilly couldn't determine initially what a raised eyebrow might mean. But, as the silent exchange lengthened, she had a horrible feeling that look was about her and her unchaperoned state.

"Winter will return for his daughter in due course, Carrington. Never fear."

The viscount snorted at Giles' words, and she realized that the viscount did, in fact, think she had plans to entrap the earl in another betrothal. Shocked, she turned to Giles again, but his only response was to nudge her leg under the table.

Giles took a sip of his wine, rolling the taste in his mouth, as always. "Did you receive the same curtly worded invitation to Warwickshire for Christmas as I did, Carrington?"

"Yes," Carrington replied, settling back in his chair with ease. "Ettington's letter arrived last week. Mother has one as well."

"Will you be attending?"

Carrington pursed his lips. "That will depend, of course, on when my intended becomes my wife, but I fear I may distress the new marchioness if I fail to put in an appearance. Pixie seems a managing sort. She'd not like her plans thwarted."

"Yes, I wouldn't want Pixie irritated myself. Ettington would take me to task for disappointing his new wife."

Carrington glanced Lilly's way. "Will you be attending, Miss Winter?"

"No." Lilly pressed her napkin to her mouth, and then placed it over her half-full plate. "My father has little to do with the marquess. A marquess is quite beyond my father's circle of acquaintances."

Hearing the men plan future entertainments in her presence to which she would never be invited accounted for the bite to her remark. Giles had a great life, he had many friends beyond this peaceful estate. A life filled with excitement, a large circle of acquaintances willing to laugh at his jokes. In comparison to Giles', Lilly's Christmas would be bleak.

Giles cleared his throat. "Where will you be for the Christmas season, Lilly?"

When she glanced at Giles, she could see a deep frown across his brow. She managed a half smile. "Wherever my father chooses to spend it? I believe last Christmas was spent in London."

The most charming man in London wore a puzzled expression. "You believe?" Carrington laughed. "Don't you remember?"

What must it be like to be as popular as Lord Carrington? Never questioned, always accepted. Lilly couldn't imagine that kind of life. "No, my lord. I do not." Lilly rose to her feet. "If you gentlemen would excuse me, I would like to retire and allow you both to enjoy your evening. Good night to you."

Both men stood as she left the room, Atticus trailing at her side.

"You blinkered idiot, Carrington," Giles whispered furiously behind her. "Must you distrust everyone?"

Lilly didn't stay to listen to anything else.

She hadn't chosen to come here and her attempt to make a good impression on one of Giles' closest friends had failed quite spectacularly.

Footsteps echoed loudly in the hall.

"Lilly, wait."

Giles caught up her arm and dragged her against his side. "Darling, Lilly, I apologize for Carrington." Lilly stiffened. "He doesn't know you and sees deceit in every female. He thinks to save me from enduring a similar fate as his own."

A second set of footsteps echoed in the hall and Carrington

came into view. His face held an odd expression. If Lilly had to bet, he was worried. She pulled her arm from Giles' grip and stepped back.

"Carrington. Wait for me in the drawing room." Giles raked his fingers through his hair as the younger man departed. "I had hoped you two might have become better acquainted, but I don't think I want knives flinging across the table."

When she could no longer hear his friend's steps, Giles gathered her in his arms. "I'm so sorry he touched on a sensitive subject. Christmas must have been lonely for you."

Lilly shrugged. Christmas might be lonely, but it was just a single day in the empty life ahead of her. "You are hardly to blame for the past."

"I know I'm not to blame, but I do regret I never stirred myself to confirm the words your mother uttered."

Pulling away from his embrace proved difficult. It seemed he was far less worried about the risk of scandal than he should be. Carrington could come back at any moment. "You were free, Giles. Why would you have bothered to discover what became of me?"

"Lilly, if I had realized that you existed in such pain, I would like to think I could have made your life far more comfortable than it has been. I could have made you as well as you are now."

Lilly stared at him. He was serious. He would have done everything in his power to see that she didn't suffer. Too bad she'd had to go through all her suffering in order to learn that the Earl of Daventry would have made an admirable husband, if fate had chosen a different life for her.

Chapter Twenty

———— ◆ ————

Taking breakfast in Lilly's bedchamber was the perfect way to start the day as far as Giles was concerned. Since the discontinuation of the medicine, Lilly's appetite had returned to what he considered healthy for a woman her size. He had not once considered the appetite of his past lovers as a requirement for his own happiness, but in this case, it seemed it was.

"Won't Lord Carrington expect to see you this morning?"

"It's too early to consider killing Carrington."

Lilly's face wore a sweet, worried frown. But after yet more sarcastic questioning last night, Giles feared he might strangle his friend if he started up again. He would let the viscount cool his heels a while before they spoke again.

"I don't understand why he should dislike me so. I don't resemble his intended in the slightest." Lilly pursed her lips and blew across her hot chocolate before taking a delicate sip.

Aroused by the sight, Giles shifted in his chair. "Carrington will come around in time. He's considered very charming."

Lilly scrunched up her nose. "Yes. So I've heard. I cannot give credence to the rumors though after meeting him." A wry smile tugged her lips. "You once said I bring out the worst in you. Apparently that applies to other men as well."

Giles laughed. "As long as you don't rush to accept other men with my particular skills as easily as you accept me, I can live with that." He let his eyes stray, sliding over her skin the way he wished to touch her, and was rewarded with a blush.

Lilly peered past him, looking at the door. "The line of gentlemen begging for my company is gone, my lord. Your unexaggerated reputation must have shamed them all into giving up their desperate pursuit."

He grinned. Breakfast and Lilly. He'd grown to love spending all his mornings with her.

Giles froze with his fork partway to his mouth, a little surprised that he wanted to spend every moment of every day with the woman he should have married.

The panicked feeling he'd experienced on first learning of her existence had fled some time ago. He did not miss other women, crave peace or wish to have her leave his estate anymore.

He forked his food into his mouth, thinking hard. He did not dislike the bachelor existence, but there were times, such as these weeks, when he enjoyed not being alone. Admittedly, there was a constant stream of servants entering and leaving Lilly's bedchamber, giving their association a thin veneer of respectability. Very thin, actually.

His relationship with Lilly had grown far more complicated than any past affair ever had. Giles usually liked to keep things simple and this friendship they shared was anything but.

"What are your plans for the day?"

Lilly's question hung heavy in the air between them. By the way her hands twisted, she expected him to entertain Carrington and leave her to her own devices. He'd rather be with her, but he also wanted Carrington to get to know and trust Lilly.

"Originally, I had thought to ride around the property and check on the tenant farmers, but with the rain—"

"Oh, I didn't think of them. Do you have many to visit?"

"A few. They are so incredibly hard to get away from."

Lilly sighed. "Despite your grumble, you sound fond of them."

Giles grinned. "They have known me all my life and have no respect for the importance of my title. I shall be besieged by the wives and pressed to sample their cooking. The daughters will blush, stammer, and stare, and the sons will attempt to memorize everything about my person in a pitiful bid to emulate my poor self."

"Oh, dear. Poor Giles."

Giles threw his hands in the air. "At last, someone who understands the demands they make."

Lilly laughed and pushed her plate aside.

Dithers rushed to take it away, but his eyes gestured to the door. Carrington loitered outside, leaning against the hall wall as he listened to their conversation.

When Carrington's brow lifted accusingly, Giles shook his head and glanced at Lilly. But he found her staring off into the rain with a wistful expression on her face, unaware that they were being observed.

Giles touched her hand to draw her attention. "I shall go when the weather is better."

Lilly's lips lifted into a happy smile.

Sometimes Giles forgot how much time she spent indoors. Being confined, when she had only just managed to get back out of doors, must be maddening.

"I can't imagine how horrible it would be to ride around, soaked to the skin, and be so far from the ground too."

"You never learned to ride?"

"Oh, I learned. A future countess must ride," Lilly mimicked, and then scrunched up her nose. "Thank heavens that nonsense is over. My mother had me tied to my horse once because I was too obvious in my attempts to avoid the lessons. You know my fear of heights. The only pleasant thing I can thank my accident for was an end to the torture of riding lessons."

Despite what she revealed, Lilly gazed at him with a small smile playing across her mouth. Even though Carrington lingered at the doorway, Giles was tempted to drag Lilly into his lap and comfort her. Of course, there were bound to be kisses involved if they touched, and then Carrington would learn the truth about who was corrupting whom here.

Giles stood. "I had better go find Carrington. We will be in my study when you are ready to face another interrogation."

Lilly pulled a face, lips twisting into a very kissable shape. "In a little while."

Giles hurried out before he did something foolish. Carrington waited until they reached the staircase before he grabbed Giles arm and pushed him into the wall. "Breakfasting together? After everything we discussed yesterday. You're asking for trouble."

Giles shook off Carrington's grip. His friend's comment about his state of mind was surprisingly accurate. He did not know what had come over him. He was chasing after Lilly like a lovestruck boy.

Lust-struck, he corrected. This was not love.

He felt an attraction to her. An overwhelming one, most certainly. One glimpse at his trousers at any time of the day could confirm his condition, but it was certainly not love. It could not be.

They were friends, and she was incredibly lonely. "You should pay attention to your own affairs."

Carrington didn't comment so Giles stalked down to his study, already missing the uncomplicated conversation with Lilly. They maintained an uncomfortable silence, each developing an interest that didn't require them to speak to each other. But after a while, he noticed Carrington fiddling with a note in his hand. "What is that you have there?"

Carrington grimaced. "The marriage contract. I had hoped to show you and see if you could find a way out of it."

Giles sighed. "As far as I'm aware, there is nothing you can do without being sued for breach of promise. Why didn't you speak up earlier?"

"When her father found us together, I couldn't prove I hadn't just bedded her." Carrington shifted uncomfortably. "I was a trifle rumpled already after being with..."

Giles scowled to cut off what most likely was going to come out of his mouth next. Giles had already made some assumptions about that night. "Don't tell me. I don't want to hear it."

"So," Carrington began, "when will you be returning to London? You've been here much longer than you initially planned."

Giles glanced up at the ceiling toward where Lilly resided. He wouldn't go until her future was set to his satisfaction. Exactly what that entailed, he didn't want to speculate on just yet. But he honestly didn't look forward to the day when Lilly and he parted ways.

Footsteps approached, saving him from tendering an answer. Lilly poked her head around the door. "Am I disturbing you?"

"Always, but please come in."

Carrington scoffed, but Lilly braved his poor welcome and paced about the room. Giles watched her for a moment, lingering on the curve of her cheek and the stray wisps of soft hair that would tickle his nose later that night. Sensing the heat of arousal tightening his trousers again, he dropped his eyes to the paper Carrington still held. "Give me that."

Carrington tossed the parchment across the desk and Giles settled in to read. Couched in near-illegible scrawl was a fairly short betrothal document. He stumbled over a small section of poorly formed words. "Who wrote this?"

"Her father," Carrington replied after coming around the desk to peer over his shoulder.

"Worst bloody penmanship in history, I should think. What the hell does that say?"

Carrington took the page and peered at the smudged text. "I cannot make it out."

"Neither can I. Lilly, would you have a look at this please and see if you can read it?"

Lilly moved toward them, but her expression conveyed reluctance. Did she think Carrington might snarl if she uncovered bad news? He held the paper out to her.

As she crossed to the window, Giles watched the sway of her skirts. Just a few more days and he could delve beneath them. It was a pity patience had never been a particularly noticeable element of his character. He was wound as tight as a violin string.

"It's badly smudged," Lilly pronounced, turning the page over to examine the reverse side. "I can only just make it out but there appears to be a stipulation that you reside at a certain address. What is the document?"

"My betrothal document. How could you tell what was underneath?"

Lilly shrugged. "I've had a lot of idle hours to occupy. Quill nibs can leave impressions on the other side. I used to try to read old letters in reverse to pass the time." She handed the page back. "Did you really accept the condition that you reside in your father-in-law's home for the duration of the marriage?"

"What?" Carrington scrambled to the window and Lilly patiently pointed out the letters.

"Is she right?" Giles crossed the room and, while Carrington was distracted, looped an arm about Lilly's waist. He squeezed and had the pleasure of seeing a proper smile cross her face.

"She is." Carrington slumped against the window frame. "All I can hope for now is an act of God, or for Lady Penelope to call the whole thing off to save us both an unhappy future. I don't like my chances."

Lilly sighed. "I don't like your chances either. The Thorpe's are evil. It shouldn't surprise anyone that my mother likes them very much."

"Your letters, milord."

Dithers placed them on his desk, and a thick letter in the pile stood out. Recognizing the heavy perfume in the air, he grabbed it first.

Laced with possessive tones, Sabine was demanding his return to London. Giles stared at it a long moment then tore it in half.

"I take it that wasn't good news?" Carrington asked, lifting his nose from his brandy long enough to peer across the room with an unsteady gaze.

"Sabine."

"Persistent?"

"Suffocating."

Carrington sat forward. "I may have been wrong about your Lilly."

About time, and a great relief. At least a truce of sorts had developed between Lilly and Carrington over lunch, but Giles had worried that might have been only because of the viscount's distraction over the swindle of his betrothal.

Giles blew out a breath. "Of course you're wrong."

"I should have been more concerned for *her* because you seemed very likely to leap the luncheon table and devour her. Almost couldn't finish my meal. No offense to Cook, of course."

"I think—"

The sound of horse and carriages on the drive ended whatever Giles was going to say. He was at the front window in a heartbeat—and saw with horror that Lord Winter had returned.

Lilly. He smacked his fist into the window frame and turned for the door, trying not to think about the future.

Lilly's time alone with him was over.

He slowed before he exited the house, his butler and Carrington close on his heels, as another thought slammed home. Most of his satisfaction came from the uncomplicated companionship they had shared. He had been happy. Dear Lord, that was certainly finished now.

On the steps, Giles was annoyed to see that Lord Winter had brought another guest with him, Mr. Bartholomew Barrette. A cousin of Lilly's, if Giles remembered correctly. Seclusion at Cottingstone was turning into a regular house party. His mother had held the last one, and that was the sad occasion of Lilly's injury and there'd never been another.

"Lord Winter, what a pleasure to see you, sir," he said. Since the old man had asked him to keep his travels plans to himself, he decided to keep the charade in play until Lord Winter informed him otherwise. At least Giles had the forethought to prepare Carrington. He'd already explained that Lord Winter had particular requested Lilly's presence remain secret. "You should have sent word of your impending arrival."

Lord Winter looked harassed, and Giles found himself measuring the interloper. The cousin stood a little under Carrington's lanky height, but possessed none of his style. The man was a peacock of the worst sort.

"Good to see you, Daventry, and very glad to catch you at home. Do you mind if I stay a day or two? I have an overpowering need to devour some of your exceptional brandy before I return to London." He glanced sideways. "My nephew, Mr. Bartholomew Barrette."

"Mr. Barrette."

"Daventry."

Simple and straight to the point. At least the man didn't simper, as he had the last time they met.

Carrington pushed himself forward. "I'm afraid you will have to share the brandy, sir. Viscount Carrington, if you remember me."

The baron looked startled at his friend's identity, but he recovered swiftly and, after a brief hesitation, he shook Carrington's outstretched hand.

Giles laughed to cover the awkward greeting. "I do have a good drop stashed here, and certainly enough to share around. Please come in and let your body catch up to the carriage."

"I'd be grateful. But I must get back to Lilly in London soon. She's expecting me."

Carrington coughed as they ascended the front steps and caught Giles' eye. Giles dipped his head. Yes, they were going to pretend Lilly wasn't here. Mr. Barrette was to be left in the dark about Lilly, but how long would that be possible when she was wandering about the manor in near fine form?

He had a quick word to Dithers about the situation and asked him to convey to Lilly that she should wait upstairs until he could speak with her father.

Giles pushed away his anxiety and hurried after his guests, desperate to have them ensconced in the drawing room as quick as may be. At the offer of brandy, Giles could swear that Barrette looked satisfied. Perhaps he liked to indulge as much as his uncle did. But when offered brandy, Barrette was very quick to refuse. His only use, it seemed, was topping off his uncle's glass.

As Winter divulged his plans for Lilly's confinement, Giles knew something was very wrong with the baron. He distinctly remembered Winter mentioning a trip into Wales—not Scotland.

"The situation in Scotland will be perfect for my daughter's fragile state," Lord Winter promised everyone. "Lilly will enjoy the feminine companionship of Mrs. Harris and her daughter instead of my dull attendance. The quiet of the small village will appeal to her."

"When will you take her there?" Barrette's question sounded like a polite inquiry, but Giles could see he hung on Lord Winter's every word.

"Soon, soon." Winter chuckled, a sound that rang false to Giles. "Lord Daventry must be visited with first."

"Of course. A few days' relaxation, and then a period in Town to sample London's delights should see you right for the long trip. It's just the thing," Giles agreed.

Winter rubbed his hands together and picked up his glass again. "Just the thing, indeed."

Privately, Giles thought they were laying it on a bit thick, but

Barrette looked to be lapping up all the little details. He could see the other man counting out the days. Lord Winter would be lucky to get away from him at this rate. They'd made the next weeks sound like too much of an adventure.

An hour after dinner, Lord Winter was asleep by the fire.

Giles excused himself, leaving Carrington and Barrette to talk of London while he went in search of his butler. "What did Lilly say about remaining upstairs?"

"She didn't want to until I mentioned her cousin had arrived uninvited. She seemed in no rush to renew her acquaintance and asked to be left alone for the evening."

"She did eat, didn't she?"

"Indeed she did."

"Good." Giles bit her lip. "I don't suppose you asked the staff to hold their tongues did you?"

"If her father wishes to hide her existence then who are we to thwart him." He glanced around. "Besides, once Barrette's man started asking too many questions about the house and occupants everyone found a reason to be busy."

He returned to the library and discovered Carrington had at last turned to a book for better companionship than the other man provided in his absence. Barrette was a crashing bore, and hinted at connections that Giles doubted were real. He was not good friends with half of the ton, but he would bear watching.

Since Barrette made no move to tuck old Winter into bed, Giles supposed he'd best do the job. With Carrington's help, they negotiated the drunken baron up the stairs and to his bedchamber and handed him off to his waiting valet. "Give us a hand with the old boy, will you Pinkerton?"

Barrette, claiming to be headed for bed too, remained paused at the door, a speculative look gracing his face as the baron was manhandled under the covers.

Since Pinkerton appeared efficient and capable of handling the loose-limbed baron, Giles left him to it and bade Barrette a good night before retiring to his room, claiming he kept country hours.

———— ◆ ————

Not long after the clock struck two, the bed dipped. Giles surged upright, found Lilly's face with his hands and kissed her. God, he had missed her this evening. When he eventually let her come up for air, he was painfully aroused. He had her in his room and on his bed. Oh, the things he wanted to do with this woman.

"Is Papa going to banish me to Scotland?"

His desire didn't abate entirely with her question. "Were you spying on us tonight? That is a dangerous practice, darling." Giles flicked her hair back behind her shoulders and pressed his lips to the skin below her ear.

Lilly squirmed. "You did not answer my question, Giles. Stop distracting me. Is it true he is sending me away?"

In the dark, he could lie, but he preferred not to. "Not Scotland—a place in Wales. He went to investigate the possibility of settling you there. I don't know why he speaks as he does in front of Barrette. But the separation will not happen now, Lilly. I wanted to talk to you about that. You are so much better. Your pain is far less and I have noticed a gratifying improvement in your health. I am sure he will not send you away once he sees the improvement himself."

"Did you know of his plans before? When he left me here?"

"He did mention them," Giles admitted. "He was very upset by the possibility, but he thought it was for the best. The doctors had admitted defeat and he just wanted your comfort assured." Giles ran his hand down her nightgown-clad arm. "Remember, you were very ill when you first came, Lilly."

"What am I going to do, Giles?"

"Show him you have improved," he told her, firm in his belief that it was the best course. The only course. "But I am a little puzzled why he told your cousin you were in London."

"Papa said that?"

"He did, but he did not explain why he lied to Mr. Barrette. Carrington and I played along but I don't know how long we can hide you."

"You cannot. I apologize that my father put you in an awkward position. It was very wrong of him." She sighed. "I've been trying to decide how to explain my sudden improvement. I will not tell him the truth."

Giles framed her face. The average chit would have landed

him in the muck without a backward glance. It just went to prove how far above the average London miss Lilly was. "We will say that the fresh air, food and comforts of a quiet country house have gradually restored your health. We could attribute the massages to Mrs. Osprey."

"But Papa would try to take Mrs. Osprey with us when we leave. And if she will not come, as I'm sure she won't, he would try to find some other person to fill that role. How could I let a stranger touch me as you do?"

She was right. That could be a problem, and not just for her. Discussing Lilly leaving Cottingstone, and him, unnerved Giles to an alarming degree.

She sounded so stricken that Giles pulled her into his arms and pressed light kisses over her face and lips. But his panic never left.

Chapter Twenty-One

———◆———

"Good morning, Papa."

Those three little words cut through the clatter of silver on fine porcelain like a rampaging bull in a china shop.

Giles was astonished to see her downstairs so early and delighted too. They had talked last night about how they would discuss her recovery, but he had thought the moment would have been private with just her father present.

Lord Winter sat in stunned silence while Lilly glided the remaining distance into the room to stand beside his chair. Only Giles and Carrington remembered to stand; their chairs sounded harsh in the quiet room. Lilly leaned in to kiss her father's cheek, and then she pulled back to look into his rapt face.

She quirked an eyebrow at her father's continued silence, then her gaze flicked to Giles in hesitant greeting.

Giles wished he could kiss her good morning and that was unnerving. His weight shifted to step forward to take her hand, but that moment gave Lord Winter a chance to blink and to breathe. Once he had done so, he achieved movement. Winter reached out a hand to his daughter's pale face and lightly rested it upon her skin. Giles noticed the slight shake of his hand as Lord Winter regained his sense and balance in his mind.

"Daughter!" Winter breathed.

"Surprised?" Lilly rubbed her cheek into his touch like a cat starving for affection. That simple gesture was enough to get the baron to his feet, and he crushed Lilly to him as a shout of laughter escaped him. "Indeed I am," he said with a hearty chuckle.

Lord Winter's laugh sounded rusty and a startled gasp drew Giles' gaze to Barrette's reaction. The man looked decidedly pale, as if he had seen a ghost. Barrette gulped, and warning bells rang in Giles' brain. What reason did Barrette have for looking so discomposed?

When he turned back to Lilly, she was wiping tears from her father's cheeks. "I didn't know it rained indoors at this time of year, Papa," Lilly laughed. "Did you have a pleasant trip?"

"Not nearly as pleasant as seeing you looking so well. What has happened?"

"I told you when I was younger that Cottingstone was magical, didn't I?" Lilly replied, still smiling brightly at him. "It still is."

"Good morning, Miss Winter," Giles greeted her formally, as if they were barely acquainted.

"Good morning, Lord Daventry," Lilly replied with excruciating politeness, but their gazes held.

Trapped by her remarkable eyes, silence lengthened between them. He was remembering Lilly stretched out in his bed last night. Warm and soft—a perfect bed partner. Was she thinking of those hours, too? He did not know what to do or say next, and when Dithers entered the room to set a place for Lilly beside her father, he was relieved for the distraction.

Lilly murmured her thanks to the butler, and Lord Winter relinquished her hands only long enough for her to seat herself comfortably before he reclaimed one again.

"Magical, indeed." Lord Winter glanced between them, strumming his thumb across the back of Lilly's hand. Giles hoped Lord Winter wasn't wondering how well acquainted they'd become. He didn't have a good answer prepared yet.

Giles busied himself with pouring Lilly's tea, adding milk and sugar, as well as acquiring a plate of food for her. He supposed he should not have heaped it as high as he did, but he got carried away remembering Lilly in his bed last night and forgot to stop.

When Giles sat down again and glanced her way, Lilly tapped her plate edge to let him know she wasn't amused by the amount of food. He buried his smile behind a mouthful of egg and let the conversation waft over him.

It was a good thing Giles had managed to return Lilly to her room last night undetected. Her return to her cold bedchamber occurred on the cusp of sunrise coloring the sky a deep purple. He had entertained a woman in his bed last night and had not made love to, nor caressed her to any great degree. That was unheard of for him. His holiday was becoming one of vast surprises.

When their talk had begun to spin in circles about what to do today, Giles had silenced her with a lengthy kiss and tucked her beneath the blankets with him, spooning her back into his front.

It was as if they had lain together for years.

He had drifted to sleep in a cloud of light perfume and long white-blonde hair. Lilly had fallen asleep quickly and had not stirred until nearing daybreak.

To his amusement, she had not wanted to leave his bed this morning. In the end, Giles had lifted the grumbling woman and carried her to his door. She hinted he was developing a mean streak. He thought, perhaps, it was the tattered remnants of a conscience.

"Shall we take a stroll, daughter?" Lord Winter enquired. "There is much we should speak of."

"Of course. The gardens are lovely."

Barrette excused himself and he left the room.

Giles tried to contain his anxiety as the pair walked outside.

Carrington appeared at his shoulder. "Are you certain she will hold her tongue?"

"Yes."

"You know, that Barrette fellow gives me an odd feeling. I couldn't swear under oath, but I don't think he likes your Lilly. Do you mind if I keep an eye on him?"

Since Giles' main concern was what Lord Winter planned to do with Lilly, he kept his eyes on the pair outside. "I'd appreciate that."

Carrington clapped a hand to his shoulder. "Try not to show you're so interested in the girl. You are usually more discreet than this."

"Everything with Lilly is different."

"I can see that plainly. If you're not careful, Lord Winter will see it too." Carrington exited the room.

Lord Winter expressed his delight over the miracle of Lilly's recovery in a physical way, stopping often to stare at her, reaching out to touch her cheek, and even once walking with his arm around her shoulders while Atticus trotted alongside.

Giles wanted to do that, and his chest ached at the lost opportunity. They looked comfortable, but Lord Winter kept Lilly out of doors too long for his liking. With a quiet word to Mrs. Osprey, Giles had Lilly's wrap brought to him. A presumption on his part, of course, but a wise precaution given the nip in the air.

"Join us inside for luncheon, Lord Winter. My cook is overjoyed at having so many mouths to feed," Giles asked, settling the wrap about Lilly's shoulders and giving her shoulder a brief squeeze.

"Of course. Forgive me, Daventry. When one day you have the opportunity to walk around with your daughter on your arm, you will understand my possessiveness."

Giles coughed and Lilly looked away from him quickly. They gained the terrace and strolled toward the dining room doors.

"Lilly and I were just discussing a return to London. I know it might seem something of a rush, but have proposed that we return to see if any young gentleman catches her eye. She does not seem convinced of her appeal, but I think she will do very well in Town. Don't you?"

Giles' hand gripped the door handle tight as he opened it. "A return to London seems a good decision but are you sure you shouldn't give her more time to adjust to her improved health?" He did not enjoy the image of Lilly surrounded by young men. They would swarm after her like bees.

"No time like the present I always say," Lord Winter stated brightly.

Giles ground his teeth. Impotence wasn't an enjoyable situation to be in. "I suppose it will be up to Lilly to choose."

"We can return to London and lease a townhouse at the best address," Lord Winter continued, without giving Lilly a chance to respond. "I shall be very proud to launch Lilly on society."

Giles' jaw dropped. Lord Winter's plans for Lilly's future were very different from his plans of yesterday. The man seemed determined to be rid of her as quickly as possible. But why? It irritated Giles unbearably that Lilly didn't meet his eyes while her father outlined his plans for her life and gave her no say.

Dump her in the country, or a quick marriage to the first man that offers. The poor woman's head must be spinning. But Lilly continued to smile her way through lunch, and became reacquainted with her cousin little by little. Barrette seemed over his shock of the morning, and appeared very keen to be friendly with Lilly.

Giles did not like that.

Carrington exchanged a long look with him and his frowns seemed to coincide with Giles' worried thoughts.

While Barrette played at the pianoforte for their entertainment that afternoon, Giles watched Lilly and Lord Winter from the sidelines. Barrette kept up his smiles for Lilly and the baron eyed the pair with something like speculation in his gaze. Giles decided it had better not be happy speculation.

While Barrette's face lit with animation as he played a vigorous tune, and Lord Winter's beat the chair's armrest, Lilly's remained still and stiff. If he had to guess, and Giles was getting very good at reading Lilly, she was tired. But of course, she wasn't going to speak of it in company and be thought weak.

Giles had Dithers announce dinner an hour earlier than usual. Lilly shot him a grateful look. In honor of the guests, the servants had exceeded his instructions on the dishes. That unfortunately meant a longer attendance at the table. By the end of the meal, Lilly was sagging. Giles wanted to say something, to offer Lilly a chance to escape, but how could he?

Lord Winter kept a viselike grip on her arm as they left the table and had barely let her out of his sight all day. It had been a very long day for her. Usually she reclined on the chaise in both the morning and the afternoon. Today she had been on her feet for most of it.

As Giles followed her into the drawing room, he concluded that it was damned inconvenient to be so attuned to another's suffering and not be able to do anything about it. He couldn't take much more without speaking out.

———— • ————

Pain began to slide behind Lilly's smile, and she dug her fingertips into the chair padding beside her. Lord, she was tired. If not for Papa and her cousin, she would have pleaded fatigue long ago.

But she was a Winter, and a Winter did not show weakness in the presence of the enemy.

Oh yes, she remembered Barrette's mean ways now. All too well. He was a favorite with Mama. At ten, Barty had convinced Mama to give him a puppy. Lilly's. Brackus had been a sweet-natured hunting dog before Barty had gotten his hands on him. The child Brackus later mauled had lost a hand.

Lilly eyed Barty critically. He seemed like a frivolous sort of fellow on first glance without too much going on in his head. Handsome and dressed in fine satin. Lilly had not recognized him at first. It was not until later, at luncheon, when one of the words he uttered reverberated strangely.

As Lilly watched him playing the piano, she had made the connection to her past. She was horrified that Barty was keeping company with her father now. That was not a good thing. Not a good thing at all. Mama had forbidden her to mention what she referred to as "groundless accusations" against Papa's heir, and she'd held her tongue many times up until her accident. Afterward, she had not had the opportunity to tell, even without Mama's prohibition.

She wished she could talk to Giles. Lilly had no idea how much she'd depended on hearing his thoughts until she had lost the ability to speak to him. All the plans Papa had mentioned at dinner made her head hurt. It was either that or the noisy piano playing. Music had never interested her.

Mama had adored Barty for his skill at the instrument, and she had displayed him to her guests whenever he was in residence. Lilly, always banished to the farthest reaches of the house when they had guests, didn't mind being away from Barty. But that meant he was closer to Papa.

Lilly had never coveted the responsibility of the estate, but Barty was strange about it all. Her years of illness away from Dumas had left her ambivalent about her childhood home. She wondered if Barty would believe her this time.

Mama had taken Barty under her wing, teaching him about

Dumas at around the time Lilly lost her puppy to him. Perhaps Mama hoped to ingratiate herself, since she would be dependent on him for life's little extra luxuries.

Papa's talk of her marrying must also be in preparation for that day, too. If she was well, she had better have a husband to protect her from Barty, she thought grimly. Barty had always resented her existence, although today she found him strangely pleasant. Perhaps he had changed his opinion of her over the years.

Perhaps snakes had learned to blunt their fangs, too. He would bear watching.

A low growl reverberated through the room as Atticus stalked toward them with a menacing posture. Lilly was surprised. The dog had been so mild in his manner until now.

"Atticus." Giles spoke sharply, but the dog did not heed him.

Atticus growled at Papa and Barty, and that was not to be allowed. "Atticus, come." Lilly spoke low like her father had taught, and the dog came to her outstretched hand.

She leaned forward and whispered a command directly into the dog's ear. He quivered, but complied, pressing against her leg and turning slightly so he faced outward toward the men.

Embarrassed that the dog showed such a marked preference for a woman instead of his master, she chewed her lip. The wolfhound was a powerful dog. She knew firsthand that his teeth were very sharp. Too sharp to make mistakes with.

———◆———

Giles was blessed with a vast experience at prowling manor houses undetected. It just did not seem to work in his own home. When Lilly had finally retired just ahead of her father and Barrette, he had been relieved. A few hours later, he walked the hall, only to stumble into Mr. Barrette doing the same.

"Daventry? I knew you couldn't possibly keep country hours as Lord Winter does. I was just on my way to find a nightcap. Care to join me?"

Given the way he phrased it, Giles had little choice. Together they descended to his study and acquired glasses of port. They spoke little, but Giles did notice the man's restlessness.

"I have the devil of a time sleeping in a new setting. I always require a little extra something to help me nod off. What about you?"

Giles laughed. "Oh, I can usually sleep anywhere, and frequently do."

"I imagine the ladies around here lap up the attention. They must be starved of good company until you return with guests," he murmured.

"What are you implying?" Giles set his drink aside. "Importune any woman under my roof and we shall have a less than pleasant conversation. Is that understood?"

Barrette appeared surprised. Apparently, he thought he knew Giles' reputation. But Giles would never touch a woman whose very livelihood rested within his power.

He also realized that his reaction was just a touch too insistent. He had included Lilly in his warning without meaning to.

"Of course, of course. Simply testing the waters."

"Drink as much as you wish. I'm for bed. Good night."

As Giles ascended the staircase, warnings danced upon his skin. Society knew of his insatiable appetite for pleasure. If he wasn't more careful with his temper, Barrette might become curious about exactly how Lilly had recovered so quickly.

Barrette followed him up the stairs at a distance, watching as Giles strode past Lilly's doorway and slipped into his bedchamber. Just to be sure there were no misunderstandings, Giles allowed the lock to turn loudly for good measure.

Lilly was not in his bed, and he slumped back against the door in disappointment. She was under his skin in a most uncomfortable way, and he was not sure he wanted to remove her. Surely this restless desire was just thwarted lust.

Beyond his door, he heard a low growl as Atticus marked a trespasser near his territory—territory that included Lilly's bedchamber. Barrette must be walking past, but he was certainly at the wrong end of the hall if he was near Lilly's bedchamber door.

Giles considered peeking out to check, but he discarded the notion. There was no guarantee Atticus would allow him to enter

Lilly's room without raising a great deal of noise either, given the dog's prickly mood tonight.

Outside, thunder boomed in the distance, and he crossed the airless room to the window to lean out and breathe in the night. A storm was coming up fast and furious. Storms were always good cover for a midnight rendezvous. He glanced left to judge the distance and available handholds to Lilly's room. There were very few, and he had to concede that even *he* could not cross the distance to Lilly's window without breaking his neck in the attempt.

Better to attempt to see her before breakfast.

He would have to be sneakier than ever before and he was going to need some accomplices if he failed tomorrow. That meant he would have to enlist the aid of the servants. Most particularly, Dithers and Mrs. Osprey.

It might force the pair to speak to each other again. In general, he did not interfere with the personal goings-on of his staff, but after observing Barrette watching Lilly all day, he needed them on his side. And Lilly's.

Chapter Twenty-Two

Giles stood in the damp kitchen garden watching Dithers and Mrs. Osprey approach him from opposite directions. He had been out here walking the rainy paths for some time, working out some frustrations, and he surmised they sensed his agitation already.

His morning had not gone according to plan. The first thing that bothered him was that his valet, Worth, was doing a poor job. He seemed distracted and had ruined nine neckcloths before Giles was presentable enough for company.

That delay did not help Giles catch Lilly alone for even a moment. She was already sitting at the breakfast table with her father and the obsequious cousin. Barrette loitered around her. And he seemed to be trying to direct Lord Winter. First he suggested a country ride, but since it was raining, Lord Winter did not consider it. And, as Giles also pointed out, his stables housed carriage animals, not horses suited for riding.

Then Barrette proposed a walk, but the wet grounds were unsuitable for Lilly to trudge. Winter abandoned that idea, too. Giles had been pleased she would not risk becoming chilled.

Dithers did not stand close to Mrs. Osprey when they reached him. "You sent for us, milord."

He could sense anger from Dithers and, judging by the stubborn set of her face, Mrs. Osprey knew exactly what she was doing. Had Dithers hinted that Mrs. Osprey was losing her mind?

This was not the face of a woman with failing understanding. They had both been duped. Giles would have laughed aloud if he did not think that Dithers would quit. The man's pride had been sorely battered.

"What do you think of our houseguests?"

The butler shot one last disgusted look at Mrs. Osprey before answering. "Well, Lord Winter has recovered from the shock quickly. It's good he is going to bring her out in London soon, don't you think? His staff is excited for her."

He looked as if he'd continue, but then he pressed his lips together over another tidbit of information.

"Dithers, I do not have time for evasions." Giles wanted to return to the house as quickly as he could. "Just tell me the rest."

"I'd not like to be held accountable for bringing grief between friends."

"Out with it."

Dithers stood straight. "I noticed Lord Carrington has been spending much time with Mr. Barrette. Given his disapproval of Miss Winter, I thought you should know."

"With my consent, Dithers." Giles pinched the bridge of his nose. "I cannot watch over Miss Winter and the cousin at the same time."

"But given the viscount's opinions of Miss Winter, milord, I—"

Giles barked a laugh. Damn that woman. She had all his staff looking out for her best interests. "Don't worry about Carrington. Miss Winter is well on her way to winning him over. She could make a dead man smile."

Dithers appeared affronted by his comment, and Giles held back a grin. When Lilly left, would she take his butler too? It seemed a distinct possibility.

"Listen, I need to return to my guests soon, but I would like to ask you to keep your eyes open and report back to me if there is anything that disturbs you."

Mrs. Osprey cleared her throat. "Disturbs us? About what, my lord?" Dithers scowled at Mrs. Osprey and the little woman had the good sense to drop her eyes.

"About Lilly, of course. Keep an eye on her. I don't know why but I have a bad feeling about Mr. Barrette." He turned to leave.

"Before you go, milord, Lord Winter's servants have finally noticed the absence of the nurse."

"Christ, I had forgotten all about that woman." Giles shook his head. That was going to be an awkward conversation too. "Oh, and by the way, I don't care what your problems are, but settle your differences and do your jobs, unless you prefer to see others promoted to take over your positions."

Giles strode off for the house without waiting to see the reaction to his threat. Dithers was an idiot and Mrs. Osprey had played him, and continued to play him, for a fool. That woman might have run rings around the aging rogue before, but the cat was out of the bag now. He wondered what Dithers would do. He should probably run, but then Giles would have to endure the training of one of the younger footmen into the role of butler. That was all the trouble he needed this week.

Luncheon was followed with another musical performance, and while Barrette was distracted by his playing, Giles studied both Lord Winter and Lilly. Lilly sat back into her chair with a posture that was not quite correct. A scandalous lapse in London, but a necessary posture today. Since Giles had not managed to visit Lilly last night, he imagined she was in pain.

Tonight, he would get into her room and help her. But how she was going to cope with the trip to London for her triumphant launch on society, without his hands on her at the end of each day, escaped him.

But Lord Winter appeared happy. That was such a new outlook for the older man that Giles could not decide if it boded good or ill. Lord Winter frequently held his daughter's hand and, when they were not watching, Barrette glanced at their entwined fingers with an unreadable expression. Giles was sure, however, that it was not delight.

When Barrette took his leave of them, they could talk freely again and Lord Winter was quick with his questions. "What has become of the nurse I left in charge of Lilly?" Lord Winter asked. "Lilly mentioned she disappeared one night."

Giles scrubbed his face before he answered. He could tell the truth and would prefer to do so, but Lilly—sweet, innocent

Lilly—could be damaged by it. He would be careful how much he revealed. "She left us the night of your departure. We found not a trace of her the next day."

He could tell Lord Winter that he suspected the nurse might have made Lilly ill but he had no real proof only suspicions..

Lord Winter nodded. "I did not think she would be with us long, but I had hoped she would await my return. None of them seem to stay. However, it appears that you have exceptional servants to rehabilitate my daughter so quickly, when years of consultations and examination have failed us. Would you do me the honor of pointing out the servant responsible so I can reward her? My daughter's recovery is due in no small part by her efforts, and the stubbornness of a Winter's willpower." He leaned forward conspiratorially. "I might steal the woman from you."

"Of course." He refused to correct the man of his wrong assumptions. It would have to be Mrs. Osprey who took the credit. He could not claim it himself when to do so would make Lilly's father look at her with disapproval.

"Wherever did you acquire the gowns my daughter wears? If there is a bill to pay, I would like to hear of it now, if you please." Lord Winter reached out a finger and touched the trail of gown strewn beside his daughter's leg.

Giles laughed in surprise. He had forgotten about the clothes. "My sister maintains a substantial wardrobe here still. Shocking, is it not? Katarina is addicted to fashion, but will probably never wear half of them. Perhaps you could approach *her* with the request for the bill, but perhaps not. Katarina is a bit of a shrew, after all. Lilly was deemed a similar size and I have allowed her access to my sister's possessions. She could not continue to wander the house in her nightgown."

Winter stilled, and then his jaw clenched tight as Giles realized just how bad that sounded. It sounded as if Giles had seen Lilly in her nightgown more than once, which was true, but Lord Winter did not need to know the full details. He would have to be more careful how he phrased these matters relating to Lilly.

Winter gave him a strange look. "Cottingstone is as lovely as I remember. You've had work done since I left."

While Giles spoke of his improvements, Lord Winter stirred

three lumps of sugar into Lilly's teacup. Since Lilly only liked one, Giles swapped his untouched cup with hers.

"Thank you, Giles."

When Giles sat down again, the baron was glancing between him and Lilly, a frown restoring his face to its usual expression. Giles held his gaze. The man should have predicted he'd at least speak to his daughter while he was off in Wales. He shouldn't be surprised he knew how she liked her tea either. There was nothing scandalous about knowing that.

Lilly fidgeted.

Come to think of it, why hadn't Winter simply asked these questions of Lilly already? Did the baron not believe her explanations? Lilly was unusually pale, even for her, and while he could not guarantee it, he was pretty certain Lilly had something on her mind.

Giles caught her eye. "How do you think Cottingstone compare's to your ancestral home?"

Her frown grew. "Cottingstone is—"

"Cottingstone is a lovely, rustic setting, but it cannot compare to the splendor of Dumas," Barrette assured them from the doorway. "I have been reacquainting myself with the house and grounds but I must say it could use Lady Winter's superior touch. She will be greatly relieved to have my cousin under her wing again."

Giles had not heard Barrette in the hall, and he wondered just how long he had been there. Lilly didn't want to return to Dumas. She had been very insistent on that point just a few days ago. "I did not realize that you had visited Cottingstone before."

Lord Carrington swept into the room and circled behind Barrette to take a chair a little to the side of the group. His expression appeared puzzled.

"I have always been invited everywhere," he promised.

Giles had to think. Barrette had not been at Cottingstone during the time Giles had held the title. He would never have invited this toady anywhere in the past or in the future.

He also couldn't bear to let the quip about his home being rustic pass without comment. "Cottingstone is the least of my concerns in England, Barrette. Like many progressive men, I find great pleasure in pursuing investment in other areas that offer a higher return."

Had he thought that because Giles was not a substantial landowner that he was not wealthy in other ways? Did he think that the lack of servants and ostentation was an indication of economy? It was an exercise in achieving a peaceful, responsibility-free existence. There were many ways to acquire wealth, after all.

Barrette clenched his jaw. "As am I."

Giles thought that an exaggeration. If Barrette had funds to spare, he wouldn't be hanging around his uncle and trespassing where he wasn't invited.

Barrette settled himself in a vacant chair with a cup of tea and appeared inclined to brood so Giles left him to stew in his own juices.

Lord Winter reached for his daughter's hand suddenly and squeezed. His action to reassure Lilly confirmed that Lord Winter was not entirely comfortable around her cousin either, though why he did not get rid of the leech escaped Giles.

Dinner was unbearable. Giles could clearly see the internal strength Lilly used to support a happy demeanor all through the meal, but wondered at her stubborn avoidance of rest. He wanted to say something, but given the way Lord Winter hovered, he didn't dare.

After dinner, Barrette suggested a game of cards, and when Winter started to refuse on Lilly's behalf, Lilly stopped him. "I would be happy to play, Papa. I know a little of the games people play."

Barrette grinned.

It was fortunate Lilly was a fast learner. But they had never played for money—not once. They'd never gambled. He doubted the game would end well or in her favor unless he helped her along.

When the stack of coins landed on the table before her, Lilly looked at them, puzzled, and then her gaze darted to Giles. She held his gaze for a long moment. Giles nodded an encouragement, and settled on a chair facing the table with a clear view of the proceedings. She knew how to play, but not how to bet. He hoped Lilly would understand his signals well enough to put up even a brief resistance.

"You will have to forgive me if I am a little rusty. It has been quite a while since I've felt well enough for games," Lilly murmured.

"Of course. I always make allowances for you, my dear." Contempt dripped from Barrette's tongue and Giles wondered if Lord Winter could hear it too.

"That is so very kind of you." Lilly's lips pulled into a small smile. "Barty."

Barrette's jaw clenched at the nickname, and he swiftly dealt cards then settled into his chair, exuding confidence. Giles sat forward a little. This was not going to be a friendly match after all, and he was pleased that Lilly would stand up to her cousin.

Through a series of finger taps on his bent knee, he counted out the greatest number of coins to bet. At times she followed him, and others she did not. Giles could not see her cards, so it was not necessarily cheating. At least, not to his mind.

Barrette's brow glistened with a light sheen of perspiration. There was not a lot of cash involved with the bets, and Giles wondered at his display. Was his anxiety an accurate representation of his hand or was anger he was trying to contain? Giles was betting on the former.

He started when the sound of glass striking glass broke his focus. Carrington and Lord Winter had moved away to replenish their glasses. With the tension of the game, he had forgotten anyone else was in the room.

Winter sank down on the cushion beside him to watch the game to completion. He nudged his arm. "An excellent match, don't you think?"

Given the way Lilly avoided Giles' gaze, he had a feeling she had overheard her father. Giles hoped Lord Winter meant the card game, and not a potential match between Lilly and his heir. The thought revolted him.

Carrington laughed when Giles remained silent. "Yes, it seemed a fair match in the end. Mr. Barrette wins."

Lilly made her excuses and retired.

As the library door closed behind Lilly's back, she found herself surrounded by servants. Dithers and Mrs. Osprey were waiting, worried expressions clouding their features. Mrs. Osprey slipped an arm around her waist and Dithers held out his arm. She was grateful for their support. Her back and legs ached like fire. It took an eternity to reach the halfway point up the stairs.

"If you will forgive me, miss, this will be faster."

Dithers swung her up into his arms and carried her the remaining distance to her bedchamber. Just before she crossed the threshold, she heard a deep chuckle behind them.

"Better not let Daventry catch you doing that, man."

Dithers turned his head slightly. "My wishes exactly, Lord Carrington. Excuse us."

"You have bewitched an entire household, Miss Winter," Carrington said as he followed them as far as her doorway. "I hope you do not play with my friend's affections insincerely."

Lilly glanced at him, pain spearing down her legs and robbing her of patience. "I play at nothing, my lord. Life is too short for insincerity. You should know that better than anyone. Now get out. I must rest."

Mrs. Osprey helped her to bed and she heard Dithers step out into the hall.

"That gent is so suspicious of everyone."

"Ignore him." At the moment, Lilly didn't care a whit for Lord Carrington. All she cared about was getting off her feet.

Mrs. Osprey huffed. "He's been watching you too often for my comfort. He may be betrothed and all, but he's got no right to be so watchful of you."

Lilly shrugged and the gesture caused more pain. "He is only looking out for his friend, Mrs. Osprey. Don't let him trouble you."

Lilly crawled into bed and stretched out. Her body complained heartily and she closed her eyes so Mrs. Osprey wouldn't see just how bad it was.

One of the maids rattled into the room, bringing a supper for Mrs. Osprey, by the sound of it. The housekeeper sighed just a little. She sounded sad, and Lilly wished she were well enough to ask what troubled her.

But there was no escaping the agony. She needed Giles

tonight more than ever. She missed him. Once Papa had his wish, she would return to London and descend into a pain-filled existence once more.

Her eyes filled with tears as she understood just how much she had grown to depend on him. Decadent, impulsive pleasure-seeker that he was. She hadn't meant to fall for him too but she had. He had made her love him for his gentle ways and determination that she take better care of herself. She had not considered any other way to live in so long.

A light pressure on her cheek wiped away her tears and the cloud of cinnamon-sweet scent that always cloaked Mrs. Osprey surrounded her. She liked Mrs. Osprey. She liked this house and its servants. She did not want to be made to leave.

A sob escaped her, and she turned her head away to cry. She did not want to leave Giles either, but she'd always known this interlude couldn't last. She was far too much trouble for a rogue to bother with past the moment of amusement.

"The master will set you to rights soon," Mrs. Osprey whispered. "I know what he's become to you and I am glad for you and for him. He will not let you suffer through another night of pain when he knows how to take it away forever. Trust in him and all will be well, you'll see."

Bless Mrs. Osprey her romantic heart, but he would not have a chance. Lilly would be gone from Cottingstone in a matter of days. Once Papa made his mind up there was no stopping him having his way.

Bartholomew hugged the shadows and watched Lord Daventry's servants scurry about. Although he thought his present location was beneath him, he had to determine who best would suit his purpose. The kitchen thrummed with activity, but he caught sight of a buxom country maid with a head of dull brown hair, and hoped she would be the one.

This time he would do the deed himself. He'd not let some transient servant destroy his future with her fickle attention to detail. But first he needed accurate information and a way to reach Lilly undetected.

He could see a breakfast tray waiting to be filled as the cook scurried back and forth, piling the plates high and fiddling with the little flower arrangement. She called to the maid he had his eye on and, when she picked up the tray, Bartholomew backed away, preceding the girl up the servants' steps until he was well beyond the stairs.

The timing was perfect, the upper hall empty. Lords Daventry, Carrington, and Bartholomew's uncle were still talking together below. He snatched a curio from the hall table, pocketed it, and then withdrew his knife from his boot. The blade glowed in the morning sunlight, dancing shadows upon the wall.

He sliced his skin.

Blood welled from the shallow cut and he leaned against the wall, near a table, and arranged his body untidily.

Footsteps clattered up the steps and hurried along the hall toward him. The maid glanced at the hand he cradled. "Oh my word, are you hurt, Mr. Barrette?"

"Quickly, fetch a towel from my chamber."

The maid slid the tray onto the table beside him and raced for his room.

Servants were indeed a stupid breed. He tugged the cork from the bottle and added drops of laudanum to every dish of his cousin's food.

Holding in a chuckle, he tucked the bottle into his inner jacket pocket and accosted the maid in his bedchamber. "You can forget the cloth. I've got you where I want you now."

The maid spun and made a show of refusing his advances. She tried to dart past him, and he let her think she had a chance. But he still extracted a kiss and groped her breasts before he let her escape the room.

The door crashed shut behind her, and he placed a hand over his mouth to cover a laugh. The foolish chit wouldn't speak of his advances and, if he were lucky, he'd have her clutching at his arms tonight while his cousin struggled for her life.

Bartholomew whistled a merry tune, removed the trinket from his pocket, and examined it in better light. Old, but given its quaint appearance, the duck was potentially worth trading for a tumble along the road. He crossed to his trunk, lifting out a handful of linen to reveal his hidden treasures.

The duck fit snugly beside a pair of candlesticks, and he secured the compartment, placing his linens over it carefully. He didn't want any helpful servant thinking he needed them to straighten things for him but their help would serve him in other ways soon enough.

Chapter Twenty-Three

———◆———

If yesterday had started bleakly with rain, today was worse. The weather had settled into a gloomy shroud over the countryside as if sad at the prospect of losing Lillian Winter from the district. She had not come down for breakfast today, and Giles had not seen Mrs. Osprey to ask questions. What annoyed Giles most was that he had not managed to go to Lilly's room last night either.

As he left his chamber to try again, he had spied Barrette pacing down the length of the hall, and had to head for his study as if he had forgotten something. Perhaps the man simply could not sleep as he claimed. Giles hoped he was misjudging, but every night he came across Barty prowling the halls, as Lilly liked to call him, his unease grew.

Winter planned to leave soon.

Giles looked out the window at the weeping sky, and then closed his eyes. He knew what he had to do to help Lilly feel better. But given the cousin's behavior, it would be a very public assistance. Did he have the right to barrel through her door and take over her care completely?

Yesterday, Giles had seen Lilly's suffering, and the distress of doing nothing had pained him. What must Lilly feel like today? Did she even want him to become more involved?

Carrington cleared his throat. "Stop frowning."

"Could *you*?"

His friend leaned against the window. "I imagine not. She needed help to climb the stairs last night."

Fury gripped him. "Did you follow Lilly after you left us?"

"Calm down. Calm down," Carrington whispered, glancing toward the door. "I wanted to be sure she made it safely to her bedchamber. She was listing to starboard like a ship in a gale. But the butler and housekeeper had her right and tight."

He gripped Carrington's arm. "Stay away from Lilly."

"My friend, she told me that very same thing, and right smartly indeed. She has a remarkable temper for such a little chit."

"My ghost."

The scrape of boot on marble alerted them to company. Lord Winter crossed the room and headed directly for the liquor tray. Giles snorted. Lilly deserved better than a father who ran for a bottle at the first sign of trouble.

"Your woman is with Lillian, Daventry, but I don't see she is doing her any good." Lord Winter's words dripped with bitter accusation. "Any number of nurses have done just the same and with no improvement. Why isn't she better anymore?"

Giles turned back to the window to grind his teeth. Of course there was no improvement without him. Mrs. Osprey had no idea what he had been doing with his nights. However, he was spared the need for an evasive reply because Barrette, of course, had followed close behind Lord Winter.

He suppressed a growl. The only way he could help Lillian was if everyone would leave them alone. If Lillian was his responsibility he could see her any time he liked.

But to avoid causing her reputation harm they'd have to wed.

He pinched the bridge of his nose. Lillian Wexham, Lady Daventry. Her name sounded perfect next to his and always had. Yet everyone would say a rogue was all wrong for someone as innocent as Lilly.

When she did not make it downstairs for dinner either, Giles realized his time for vacillation was gone. He spent the early part of the meal watching a smug little smile flit across Barrette's face, only to disappear into a grave expression. He appeared happy that Lilly was unwell again, and was doing his best to hide it.

Giles wiped his mouth with his napkin. "Carrington, would you keep my guests entertained? I have just recalled a task that requires my attention. I shall rejoin you before the dessert course."

Carrington waved him away. "Excellent. That means I can have seconds of your cook's famous braised duck without fighting you for it. This visit, I am going to pester her into giving me the recipe for my own cook to try."

"Ha. You can make the attempt, but she guards that book with her life."

Giles left the room and hurried up the stairs. He tapped on Lilly's bedchamber door, and after a brief word, Mrs. Osprey let him in. "She is so much worse, my lord."

Lilly said his name when he touched her skin, and then fell silent. He raised her hand to his lips but, judging by the heavy weight of her limb, she didn't realize he was there.

"Mrs. Osprey, I do believe I could kill someone."

"Oh, no, my lord, you mustn't. What would happen to Miss Winter then?"

"Yes. What indeed?" He glanced at Osprey. "She seems drugged to me?"

The housekeeper swallowed. "To me too, but I cannot account for how it could have happened."

He pulled back the covers and slipped his arms beneath her body to lift her against his chest.

"What can I do, my lord?"

Giles nodded to the door. "You can help me compromise Miss Winter. Get that door open, but keep the dog inside this room. Then hurry along to mine. Now. And be very quiet in the hall and make sure no one sees you."

With Lilly lying boneless against his chest, he slipped into the hall and watched Mrs. Osprey convince his wolfhound to stay. The poor thing appeared bereft. "Make sure to throw in a bone later. We don't want him howling all night."

Mrs. Osprey rushed up the hall before him and held his door open wide. "You're doing the right thing, my lord. Miss Winter was so sad last night. She missed you."

He'd missed her, too. He tucked Lilly into his bed. "Stay here. Keep the door locked, and only let myself or Dithers come in. No exceptions. And no disagreements tonight. You can torture my butler tomorrow."

Mrs. Osprey bit her lip over a smile.

"Wicked woman."

All in all, Giles was only absent for perhaps ten minutes, and neither Barrette nor Lord Winter appeared interested in what he'd been doing upon his return. Carrington, however, threw him a questioning glance, but kept up a steady stream of confidences that only enhanced his reputation as a chatterbox. Lord Winter got steadily foxed.

As before, Barrette did not offer to help put the old man to bed, and Giles supposed he should get accustomed to the activity. Was Winter always three sheets to the wind with drink? It was surprising he'd not lost track of Lilly more often if that were the case.

At his bedchamber door, Giles hesitated a moment tapping. Osprey flung the door open and he pushed the heavy wood closed with his back and leaned upon it. Everything was in readiness.

"She hasn't stirred," Osprey told him.

Giles nodded. "As I expected. You are dismissed, Mrs. Osprey. Stay away from this room tomorrow until I call for you."

"But—"

He met her gaze, and she had the good sense to blush before hurrying from the room. Giles hardly needed a spinster's help to compromise Lilly.

He strode across the room and lifted the lid on the light supper Dithers must have sent up while Giles had been entertaining his guests. The food looked good and should not spoil before daybreak. He lit a cigar, placed it on an ashtray, and then poured a glass of brandy. He set both beside the bed, along with a clean chamber pot.

Lilly lay insensible to her surroundings. He removed his jacket, cravat, and waistcoat, and then rolled up his sleeves. Her face was ashen, her lips pale blue, but her pulse was good. Yet she did not stir when he moved her arm.

The fact that Lilly was under the effects of laudanum could only mean one of his guests had brought the poison into the house and dosed her food somehow.

Giles opened the bedroom window wide, letting a cool blast

of air enter the room. He struggled to raise Lilly to a sitting position. Her head lolled, and he juggled her so she rested against his shoulder. He waved the cigar under her nose a time or two until he got a twitch of reaction, and then set it into the porcelain bowl in her lap. The smoke curled toward her face.

"Lilly. Little ghost, wake up."

She grumbled as if she heard him, but the potion clouded her mind still. He had no choice but to force her to drink the brandy.

She choked, and then gasped, swallowing the liquid and smoke in equal parts. Moments later, she vomited into the porcelain bowl, over and over until his stomach hurt from the sound of it.

When she was done, her face pink and sweat-shined, he laid her down and removed the bowl and brandy to the window, throwing both far out into the night. Giles stripped Lilly of her nightgown and dropped her into a tub of cold bathwater, remembering to support her with his arms so she didn't drown. Lilly gasped.

"Forgive me, but you must wake." Giles drizzled water over her face. "You see what happens when I leave you alone for a day or two. You make me do the meanest things, my darling."

He was careful not to wet her long hair too thoroughly, and rubbed her arms and legs, hoping to burn off the poison. He hoped this worked. He couldn't bear to wait out days to see her smile again.

When her teeth started to chatter and her arms covered with gooseflesh, he lifted her from the water to hold her close. Even though she soaked his front right through, it was a small price to pay for the unhappy sounds she started to make.

"Walk, Lilly, and then I promise nothing but pleasure forever."

Gulping over his choice of words, Giles marched her around the room naked until she was using more of her own strength for the task.

"Why are you making me walk? Let me rest," Lilly grumbled.

Giles brushed at his eyes. "Because I have to, Ghost. Bear with me a little longer."

When Lilly attempted to pull away, Giles picked her up in his arms and laid her out on the lengths of towel waiting to dry her.

"She should have definitely added tyrant."

Giles laughed softly, picturing what his mother might make of his activities tonight. She would not be happy with his choices but he believed she would understand he only meant to help. "If you insist, we'll add tyrant tomorrow."

Down the hall, Atticus barked out a warning, but Giles would not go to the door and see who was stumbling about. His stout bedchamber door was locked tight against intruders. However, to be sure they were not interrupted, Giles blew out the candles and relied on firelight to return to Lilly.

When she was dry, he tucked her into his bed, then moved around the room, straightening things and closing the bedroom window. He picked his way across the space in darkness before removing the rest of his clothes. Giles slipped into bed beside Lilly and drew her against his skin.

Lilly sighed against his bare chest and ran her hands over his body, lighting fires she had no right to encourage, given her current state. But her breathing settled into a normal, deep rhythm, and he did his best to fall asleep too.

———◆———

Lilly woke to find her body trapped under something heavy. She breathed deep, and drew in Giles' scent so close to her. His arm draped over her chest and his hand covered her breast. When she shifted a little, so did he. He rolled and pulled her tight against his hot skin.

It took Lilly a moment to get over the shock of skin-on-skin contact. Giles burned. Lilly swallowed nervously, then wished for a drink to be rid of the horrible taste in her mouth. Swallowing again didn't help, so she lifted Giles' heavy arm, attempting to escape him.

"What do you want, Lilly?" he murmured.

"Water. I have a terrible taste in my mouth, but I am capable of getting it, you know."

"It's either the laudanum, or the brandy I made you drink. Let me look after you. You know I enjoy it." Giles kissed the side of her face and moved out from behind her. Glass clinked in the dark.

The bed creaked when he returned, and he felt for her face, clumsily offering the glass for her to drink from. She downed the lot and handed it back.

Glass rattled against wood, then Giles crawled back under the blankets. When he had them arranged comfortably again, he kissed Lilly's shoulder before falling back asleep. His light snore made her laugh because it tickled her neck so strangely.

While Giles slept, Lilly lay awake and wondered how she had come to be in this room. Yesterday was another blur, just as if she had taken the medicine for her pains. Had she been tricked into consuming laudanum again? Giles had said she had. But she didn't remember accepting the potion. As she puzzled over what had contained the brew, she twirled her fingers around the swirls of hair on Giles' forearms.

The arm around her tightened, then stroked down her torso. She had woken Giles with her restlessness. Heat shifted behind her, and she became aware of a hot spot on her bottom.

"Can't you sleep?" Giles whispered as his lips pressed against her neck, along her shoulder and back again.

"No. I was attempting to remember yesterday."

"Don't worry. I'm not going to let anything happen to you again, darling. From now on, you stay with me," Giles promised.

Lilly grinned. Staying with Giles was a nice fantasy.

Giles' hand stopped its random wandering and soothed her stiff muscles. Lilly rolled over without any prompting and Giles set to work on her back. Oh, Giles was so good at this. When he had turned her senses to putty, Lilly turned over to stop him by pulling him down for kisses. He sank his full weight against her and she eased her legs apart to accommodate his lower body.

Heat scalded her skin. A strip of her inner thigh burned. Giles moved his hips while they kissed and slid along her skin. When he changed position so his body lay beside hers, she tried not to be disappointed. *How wicked am I to want more?*

Very wicked.

When Giles ran his hand over her skin, Lilly explored him in return.

Chest hair was such a revelation. The hairs seemed long and soft, so she played at smoothing them, only to encounter a male nipple. When Lilly's fingers brushed the peak again, Giles let out a groan. Lilly giggled.

"Wicked temptress."

Lilly kissed his cheek. "You only have yourself to blame."

He rewarded her impertinent reply by returning the favor. Lilly arched at the sensation of his pinching fingers, and then his lips settled on the tip and suckled.

This was not like the last time she'd shared his bed. Giles was less reserved, more demanding in the way his hands skimmed her curves. He tortured her with his lips and tongue. She purred when he swapped to her other breast and used his fingers to tease the wet nipple he'd just left.

She shifted her legs restlessly on the linens until Giles trapped one of hers with one of his, wedging her legs apart just when she had started to hum at the junction of her thighs. He abandoned her nipple and his breath caressed her skin. His fingers slid to her belly in twisting patterns until they rested on the top of her curls.

If only he would just move a little lower, she thought, squirming up the bed toward those clever fingers. He did not move them, but caught her lips again and kissed her like a starving man. Perhaps he was just that. Lilly was certain that he had no lover here at Cottingstone. She had seen no sign of one. Until Papa came, they had been together most nights.

Muscles flexed and twisted beneath her hands as she explored Giles thoroughly. She stroked his chest, down toward his belly button, following the line of hair. Giles' mouth lifted from hers. He shifted his hips and deposited his erection right into her hand.

As he kissed her, Lilly got over the surprise. She made a hesitant stroke over his soft skin. Giles groaned his encouragement. His teasing fingers slid into her curls then pushed into her cleft, driving her mad.

As Lilly learned how to pleasure him, he stroked her until she gasped. She tightened her grip on his length and moved in time with his own fingers.

"That's it, my darling. Just like that."

She stroked him until he groaned again and he teased until she whimpered.

Giles pressed his head to Lilly's. "Together?"

Lilly's world exploded and hot liquid splattered over her belly. She struggled to catch her breath, but Giles soothed her until their breaths held steady again.

Giles' lips brushed her cheek. "My god, you'll be the death of me."

She could not remember ever hearing Giles speak to his lovers after sex before. But knowing she had the power to change him made her smile.

Chapter Twenty-Four

———◆———

Lilly opened her eyes in the dimly lit room and was instantly awake. The sheets were tight against her neck and she wriggled out from under them, content and wonderfully relaxed.

She was still in Giles' bed, and when she turned her head, she could see that he was sleeping beside her, tangled in the edges of the blankets, his torso half bared to her eyes. His face was beneath a pillow and she looked her fill of the smooth lines of his chest and the light ginger hair that covered the parts of his chest she could see.

She wanted to touch him.

Last night had been so amazingly tender and as she thought about holding the length of him in her hand again, a throb began between her legs. She loved touching him.

Looking about the room, she spied a covered tray near the fire and a still-full bathtub. She could remember parts of yesterday. Unpleasant parts. She remembered casting up her accounts now and wrinkled her nose in embarrassment.

Poor Giles. She was a burden to him. Not one of his other lovers would have caused him this much trouble.

Lilly paused and thought about being counted among Giles' many lovers, and decided she did not like to be included with them. If he had not entered her body, did that still make her one of his lovers? She thought so. She loved what he did to her. He made her body sing as she had never thought possible.

Feeling the urgent need for the convenience, she carefully extracted herself from the soft sheets. Giles grumbled, but she managed to ease out of bed without waking him to stand on wobbly legs. Unfortunately, Lilly did not know where a chamber pot might be. She looked around and spied a doorway, but no screened corner to the room. Lilly decided to investigate the doorway and found Giles' dressing room.

Row upon row of clothing graced one wall of a fair-sized room, and a low screen covered a far corner. She headed there first and happily found what she needed.

When she was comfortable again, she examined Giles' clothing, trailing her fingers along the sleeves of expensive jackets in silk, wool, and brocade. There were rows of somber waistcoats, and quite a few gaudy ones she hoped Giles did not actually wear. The sight would be hideous.

Gleaming Hessians and evening slippers marched together in a neat row and she marveled at the luxury of having so many clothes to choose from. Her own wardrobe consisted of unflattering nightgowns and a heavy cloak. All the clothes she had worn in the past weeks had been borrowed from the forbidding Katarina.

Lilly prowled around Giles' private rooms, fascinated by the small curios she found. The distinctly masculine chamber was filled to overflowing with items of a kind she had never noticed before. Little girls, for instance, should have nothing to do with pipes.

Giles' collection graced one small curio cabinet attached to the wall. Some of them were ornate and some were very crude and old. She wondered why there were spaces, and then she remembered the half-finished butterfly collection in the nursery from years ago. Did Giles never finish a collection?

She moved to the tray and uncovered a meal of bread, fruit, and cheese. She picked up a bread roll and took a bite, strolling around the room and peeking at everything Giles owned.

He had several nice landscape paintings and Lilly liked the look of them. She knew nothing about art or important painters, but she liked what she saw as these places looked peaceful.

She found Giles' discarded clothes strewn over one chair and, noticing her skin had chilled, she slipped on his shirt. It fell below her knees, swamping her in linen. Holding the bread roll between her teeth, she fought to get her hands free. She tried rolling the sleeves up and out of the way but made a messy job of it. Obviously, she was not meant to escape their soft clutches.

She read the spines of Giles' small collection of books. *Udulpho*, *The Monk*, and *Dangers Through Life*. Lilly had never heard of them and wondered what they might be about.

There was one small book set to the side. She picked it up and opened the cover.

A gasp escaped her as she recognized her own handwriting. It was *her* book. The one she had started before the accident and forgotten. She stroked her finger over her writing in fondness. She had always kept a journal up until her accident.

Mama had disapproved of many things Lilly had enjoyed doing, often taking her pleasures away as a means to get her way.

Lilly held the book close to her chest, suddenly light-headed. Needing to sit down, she sank into a window seat thick with cushions. She pulled her knees up to her chest and wrapped her arms about them.

Mama was not safe to be around. Regardless of what Barty suggested, she would never agree to go back to Dumas. She would refuse. She would run away and find somewhere else to live.

Lilly flipped the book open, reading over the words of her younger self, whose only pleasure in life was pleasing her papa. It seemed such a long time ago and now she was older she'd begun to doubt whether he really had her best interests at heart. She did not agree with his suggestion that she marry. It wouldn't be fair to the man.

"Now there is a sight to wake up to."

Lilly looked up to find Giles propped on his elbow watching, a devilish smile playing over his lips. His eyes dipped and he tilted his head to the side as he viewed her legs flashing him beneath the shirt she wore.

"Good morning." She leaned her head back on the wall and smiled at him, stretching her legs out, suddenly restless under the heat of his gaze. Giles tossed the covers, swung his legs out, and got to his feet. He was completely bare and utterly perfect.

Lilly gulped at the sight of his lean, muscled body. How could he walk so confidently toward her when her hands had begun to shake in earnest at the sight of his blue eyes? The unveiling of the rest of him fairly took her breath away.

She tried not to stare, but failed abysmally. She examined everything about him and found nothing lacking.

When Giles reached her, he stood still, allowing her a closer inspection of his anatomy. Then he leaned down to press a light kiss to Lilly's lips. The kiss changed when she touched his thigh, moving from gentle greeting to flaming passion in a single heartbeat. Giles remained bent over her as their tongues tangled, but his hands caressed her neck and shoulders, making her body flush and tremble with need for him. He clasped Lilly's waist and drew her to her knees, then pressed their bodies together.

Lilly tangled her fingers into his tousled hair and held their lips together, lost in the wonder of his kisses and unwilling to stop. His hands slid down her back to cup her bottom and he pressed his stiff length against her belly.

She wanted to explore him in the light, to let her fingers slip across his skin and learn why he was so different. When she ran her fingers down his neck and shoulders, covered his silky chest hair and found his nipples again, he groaned out her name. She brushed her thumbs over the hard peaks and he chuckled before picking her up to carry her back to bed.

"More pleasure for you, my wicked ghost?"

"Yes please, Giles."

Giles kept her close as he crawled over the messy sheets and deposited her against the pillows. His gentleness still surprised her. He teased his shirt from her shoulders and bared her breasts. This morning, he only gave them cursory attention, and she dug her fingers into his scalp when he went to leave them.

"My, my, I think I have created a monster. You're very demanding this morning," Giles chuckled, but he did not return to them.

"I don't know any other way to be," she replied, wriggling as his lips pressed against her belly. She knew she was greedy. In her limited experience of pleasure, his focused attentions were a drug to her starved senses.

"Never fear, I like it very much."

Giles licked her stomach then moved lower. With horrified fascination, she realized where he was headed. At his first light touch, her hips bucked upwards into his face and he dug his tongue deeper. Yet it was not close enough. He spread her legs, pushing at her knees insistently.

Giles' hot breath fanned over her thighs and her exposed flesh as he pressed his lips to her skin, flicking his tongue against her. Lilly moaned at the warmth of his mouth, but shrieked when his tongue returned to that small spot of intense pleasure and flicked it with light, soft strokes. Fearing for her sanity, she threaded her fingers into his hair and held on as he tongued her cleft.

When he sucked, Lilly labored to breathe. He shifted and settled in to wrench yet more tremors from her. This was by far more intense than what they had done before. If this was not making love, Lilly feared she'd not survive that event.

Another sensation, pressure lower down from where Giles kissed, distracted her. She wriggled her hips. When Giles raised his face from tormenting her, she could see his fist curled next to her entrance, and feel the slide of his finger enter her body. He looked down and worked his finger into her gently then lowered his mouth to suck her hard.

Sensations built rapidly and when he pressed deeper inside her, fist pressed against skin, the waves of release rocked her body.

"Giles, Giles, Giles."

It took a while, but when Lilly opened her eyes, she found him lain out beside her. She blushed, but he just grinned wickedly, and then kissed her.

As his erection rubbed against her body, reminding Lilly that he remained unsatisfied, she rolled closer. She wouldn't lie idle in his arms again. That wasn't at all fair. When their lips parted, Lilly pushed Giles to the mattress and looked him over. Giles flexed and pushed his hips out to her and she could not help but smile.

She let her fingers walk over his skin lightly, and he shuddered from the touch. She swept her hand over his flat stomach and he sucked in a breath, showing her the bones of his hips in more detail. Her hand slipped down into his hair and her fingers closed around his shaft.

Giles gasped and pushed his hips into her hand, showing her how anxious he was for more. The first stroke up his length fascinated her. Giles guided her to increase the pace of her stroking, and when he took his hand away, she saw a small drop of moisture at the tip. Lilly leaned forward to lick it up with her tongue.

He tasted salty, and when she licked her lips again, she finally noticed the way Giles' breath labored. Still looking down, she wondered if she should do what other lovers had done for him. She shrugged away her nervousness to press a kiss to his head. The groan that wrenched from Giles' lungs rattled the bed. She pressed another kiss to him, then flicked her tongue out and swirled it around the smooth head.

Five fingers dug into her upper back. She licked her way down his length and back up, feeling the ridges of his shaft, the baby-fine softness of his skin over the hard, hot core beneath.

When Lilly reached the head, she hesitated then opened her mouth to take him in.

"Mother of God," Giles muttered, and fought to get away from her.

Lilly wrapped her hand around his base, pried him upwards, then took him in her mouth again. Deeper. She thought to cover her teeth, slid him back out and in a time or two, wetting his skin further. Giles swept her hair over her shoulders and rose up to watch.

The wet slurping noises excited her as much as she thought they did him. She wet her lips again and experimented on how far he could go inside her mouth. When she found a comfortable depth, he moved her head in an up-and-down motion and she understood that what she could do with her hand, she could do with her mouth.

She closed around his shaft and Giles groaned. His fingers rubbed her spine and down to her bottom. She shifted so she knelt more comfortably and increased the pace of her movements and the strength of her jaw.

"Dear God, you have a talent for this, but if you don't lift your head, Ghost, you're going to get quite a mouthful," Giles growled.

But she wanted everything he could give. His breath became frantic. He arched to fill her mouth and warmth gushed over her tongue, forcing Lilly to swallow quickly.

———◆———

"Do you know that you hog the blankets?" Giles asked a while later as he massaged a particularly tender spot into submission.

"Sorry. I did not realize."

Giles pressed a kiss to her spine. "I'll have to learn to be more aggressive in my sleep if I want to stay warm."

"Ah, in a little while you won't have to worry." Lilly smiled despite her sadness. She was determined to enjoy everything that Giles Wexham had to offer. Including the bad part of saying goodbye.

"What if I want to worry? I like taking care of you, Ghost."

Lilly stilled, wondering what he was suggesting. It wouldn't be marriage. It couldn't be. "Then I think you should lie back down until the sensation passes."

"If you married me, you could be very comfortable."

"I'm comfortable now," Lilly squeaked.

"But this interlude cannot last, darling." He brushed his hands more lightly over her skin as he was finished. Lilly was afraid to turn over. Giles must be drunk. Sober, he wouldn't contemplate such a change in his life. "That is not a very good reason."

"Marriage to me would protect you, and give you every comfort you might desire. If you haven't noticed, we are very compatible in bed."

"I could be comfortable in Wales, too. I have considered Papa's original plan and have decided it has some merit. If I live my life carefully, and rest often, there is no reason a country house wouldn't be acceptable."

"Did you change your mind about letting someone else touch you?" Giles didn't sound happy and, reluctantly, Lilly rolled over. His jaw was clenched into a stubborn line Lilly wasn't familiar with.

"No," Lilly confessed. "No one else will ever touch me as you do."

That seemed to appease him for a moment. "I've compromise you, Lilly. I've already done it many times since you came to stay, but by now the whole staff knows where you spent last night. They will send him here. It is only a matter of time before your father comes knocking on that door."

Lilly hadn't counted on that. She had assumed Giles had been as discreet as before. "Are you sure you want to do this, Giles?"

"It's the only way I can look after you."

Giles rolled off the bed and strode to his dressing room. He must be unhappy she had resisted his plan, simply because he wasn't ready for their affair to end. She was a bit stunned that he thought to marry her to keep her in his bed, though.

Giles had told her that he would not marry, and she had believed him. Lilly had accepted that condition. She had allowed him to tempt her in order to satisfy her own growing curiosity, but had no belief that anything further would come after the pleasure she expected.

But yesterday Giles had stolen her, deposited Lilly in his own room, locking them in while she recovered. What had come after in his bed had been wonderful. He did appear to care for her. Perhaps it would be enough to keep him by her side at least for a little while. Lilly doubted she had the ability to keep him satisfied for long, though.

When she slipped into the dressing room, she found him partially dressed, so she ran her hands across his bare back, marveling at the hard muscles under his skin, and slipped her fingers down toward his backside.

"Are you trying to tempt me back to bed?"

"Is that a possibility?" Lilly grinned. She would miss their scandalous conversations too.

"I could promise it was. But we will have company soon, and I would prefer to be at least partially dressed for the occasion of asking your father for your hand in marriage."

Lilly glanced down at her forgotten nakedness. "I would prefer that, myself."

"But you look so lovely, just as you are," Giles teased, glancing her over with appreciation and lust brightening his eyes. "If you open that wardrobe door, you will find Mrs. Osprey provided some fresh clothing for you. You are going to have to at least agree to a betrothal, you know. There is no other way."

Frustrated, Lilly turned her back. But Giles captured her in his arms and kissed her neck. She gasped and forgot all about dressing and marriage in favor of feeling pleasure again.

Chapter Twenty-Five

———◆———

Giles tapped the paper beside Lilly's plate and she picked it up. Her eyes widened as she reached the end of the long document. "You never signed. Why?"

"Shocking lapse on my part, isn't it?" He shrugged off her question. He didn't remember why he hadn't but given Lilly wasn't expected to survive her fall he supposed at the time it hardly seemed important. "It suits our purposes today very well.

Footsteps thundered down the hall toward them, then Giles' bedchamber door burst open.

"Damn you, Daventry." Lord Winter rushed inside and appeared to be frothing at the mouth.

Despite having the best intentions of marrying Lilly, Giles stepped back from him. "Now, sir, there is no need to get into a lather. Would you care for some breakfast?"

Winter appeared to shake himself and glanced at the unmade bed that was clearly well used. His jaw tightened, and his hand curled into a fist.

He and Lilly were both fully dressed and, aside from the unmade bed, looked at first glance to be perfectly respectable. Except for the fact that neither of them were married to the other. Yet.

Giles had used seduction to get Lilly to agree to marry him. He'd pinned her against the wardrobe doors and withheld her release for so long that she'd screamed out her acceptance. He'd enjoyed tormenting her like that. Hearing her sob his name when she came had made his remaining irritation with her resistance disappear altogether.

What could be wrong with being married to him? He was attentive in bed, not to mention very restrained. This morning he could have taken her virginity easily, and had considered it repeatedly, but something held him back. To his considerable shock, he found he wanted to wait until they were respectably married.

All his adult life, Giles had lived his life on the edge of respectability, but there appeared to be one thing he held sacred. He would not risk creating a life in Lilly's body without a ring on her finger, and a permanent change to her name.

"What gives you the right, sir, to take advantage of my daughter in such a way? She's no mean trollop to swagger after like a jaded lothario! She deserved better treatment than this, and she will have it before the week is through. We are not without means, you degenerate scoundrel. You may be above me in rank, but we are not without friends. Did you think to dabble with her and then discard her for greener fields? Guess again, Daventry! I will see that the deed is done properly."

"The deed has already been done," Giles assured him, then ducked a blow. He had not meant his words to be taken quite that way. He trapped the older man's swinging hands, pinned his arms behind his back, and turned him to face his daughter.

"Lilly, if you please, the paper. Show your father what I was referring to."

Lilly looked white with fright and she shakily held the document up to her father's gaze.

When Lord Winter sagged, Giles carefully released him, prepared for the next swinging fist. He had certainly made an impression on his future father-in-law. Oh well, at least he would not be expected to call him Papa.

"You never signed to end the agreement." Winter took the paper and it shook in his grip. "You are still betrothed to Lilly?"

Giles glanced at Lilly and winked. "So it would seem."

On the whole, Giles was actually happy that he would marry Lilly. Since the chemistry between them in bed was thrilling, and he did like her out of it too, he thought they had a chance to be happy.

He was not used to feeling this good. Three trysts this morning had not sated his ardor for her touches. Good God, the woman had taken him into her mouth with such hunger and generosity that his cock stirred a little even now.

The next time he had her would be after they were married, and he could finally enter that sweet, frail body that belied such a fierce passion for life. He doubted he would ever tire of her. He knew she did not believe him capable of monogamy, but the depths of their combined passions were barely tapped. He felt closer to her than any other. He couldn't imagine wishing to stray.

Lilly was passionate, uninhibited, and the most giving woman he had ever taken to bed. He hoped he did not pass out when they did make love.

There it was again, he chided himself. He'd called it making love. He could not abide to use the word fuck when thinking about Lilly. Winter was right. She did deserve better treatment.

He walked around Winter and pulled Lilly up from her chair and into his arms. She was shaking badly from the violence her father had exhibited, completely unprepared for such raw emotional displays. He kissed the top of her head and settled her into the window seat, pouring her another cup of tea just the way she liked. She took it and when Giles turned back, he found Winter gazing at him in astonishment.

"I thought you barely knew each other."

Giles shrugged off the question, grabbed another chair for Lord Winter, then sat to finish his breakfast. When the stunned man joined him at the table, Giles looked him in the eye and let some of his own anger show.

"You left her with only the mean attentions of an incompetent nurse who drugged and deserted her the first night. What would you have had me do? Ignore her? Allow her to suffer needlessly? She's endured more than her fair share of misery, but fortunately has recovered and now is mostly pain free. I followed your instructions and contacted no one. Not even you, since I did not have your direction, if you remember."

"What do you mean, mostly pain free? I thought you said she

was cured," Winter asserted.

"Nothing of the sort was spoken in this house. If you can bear to consider the matter, you can see when she is in pain. Like the stubborn Winter she is, she does her best to keep that knowledge wedged firmly behind clenched teeth," Giles informed him, disgusted at explaining such an integral part of Lilly's character to her own father. Did the man truly not know her?

Lord Winter rubbed a hand across his face.

"Papa." Lilly fidgeted. "Am I truly betrothed to Giles still?"

"It makes no difference now. You will be married before the month is out."

Giles discarded his teacup.

Rapid steps approached the open bedroom door. He stood, clasped Lilly's cold fingers in his just as Barrette burst into the room, red faced and puffing mightily.

"What is the meaning of this?" The foppish demeanor had been discarded for hissing outrage. The man acted nothing like the amiable gent he had pretended to be just yesterday.

"Congratulate us. Your cousin has agreed to marry me. Again." Giles pressed a lingering kiss to Lilly's trembling fingers. He glanced at the clock as it struck the hour. It was exactly thirty minutes since Lilly had last screamed his name. The thought of it made him smile, and he wondered when he could get her alone.

As if reading his thoughts, Lilly blushed a deep shade of red. He turned to find Barrette glowering at his uncle.

"Are you three sheets to the wind? There can be no wedding!" Barrette's gaze fell on Giles. "You have obviously coerced the baron into agreeing to this travesty of a marriage. Lillian isn't fit to be a wife. You are just on the hunt for funds."

Winter surged to his feet. "Now see here—"

Barrette sneered. "No, you see here, you old fool!"

Lord Winter bristled. "How dare you? Lord Daventry will marry my daughter, as has always been the case. Just remember, it isn't unheard of for a man to challenge his relation to a duel for an insult. Do not tempt me."

Giles dropped Lilly's hand and stood beside the baron. "I believe that shall be my honor, my lord. He just insulted my future wife."

A successful duel would teach Barrette a lesson, but if Winter failed and died, Barrette would have control over Lilly's future. They had to be married.

Barrette shook with rage. "After everything I've done for you, Uncle, you'd consider dueling over that pathetic creature? She probably arranged the whole affair just to live in the center of another scandal."

"Be gone," both Giles and Lilly's father growled in unison.

The little weasel held his ground. "You forget, sir, that I reached this destination in your company. I'll leave when you do and not a moment before."

Giles had had enough. He reached past the baron and grabbed hold of Barrette's arm. He hauled the lightweight to his bedchamber door and threw him towards Lord Carrington's grinning visage. "Dump him in the village to await the stage."

"With pleasure, my friend."

Carrington grasped Barrette's arm and hauled the spluttering man down the hall and hopefully out of the house.

Giles found Lilly standing, but her hands twisted with agitation. He moved around behind her and rubbed into tense muscles again.

"That's how you did it, isn't it?" Lord Winter exclaimed, watching Giles automatically soothing Lilly's neck and shoulders that had clenched again in worry. "It never occurred to me, or any of those medical men."

"It was an accident."

"A damned lucky one at that!" Lord Winter approached them. "How often?"

"Every day."

"Since when?"

Giles considered the embarrassment Lilly would suffer if he answered honestly, and judged she would probably blush bright red. He could not answer.

"Since the day after you left me, Papa."

Lord Winter groped for his chair and sank into it, gulping loudly. "That long."

Giles eyed him for a moment then bent to Lilly's ear. He drew in a deep lungful of her scent to get him through the next few hours. "Why don't you go and rest to give your father some time to get used to the notion. Ring for Mrs. Osprey as soon as you get to your bedchamber."

She didn't automatically go, but gave her derrière a gentle pat out of sight of her father, and she took his suggestion to leave.

Lilly didn't need to hear any more.

"You do care for my daughter, don't you, Daventry?"

Giles paused to consider how he felt about Lilly. He hadn't tried to put that into words. They were friends and lovers, but Giles didn't think Lord Winter would be happy to hear it phrased that way. "She has been uppermost in my mind for some time now, sir. I will take good care of her."

Winter did not seem completely happy, but let it pass and began to discuss the wedding and marriage settlement. He informed Giles that Lilly's dowry remained unchanged. Giles had paid little attention to the amount but the mention of the size now surprised him. "Are you certain that's right?"

"It is what your father and I agreed."

Giles hurried to read through the former betrothal document to confirm that statement.

There it was in very clear letters. Lilly had a dowry of sixty thousand pounds.

Giles sat down as the shock set in. He'd had no idea Lilly would have been the most eligible bride on the marriage mart for all these years if only she'd been well.

He glanced toward the door as Mr. Barrette's reaction to the happy news of their marriage played over in his mind again. With funds of that size up for grabs, he wondered how far Lord Winter's heir might go to stop any marriage Lilly might want to make.

———◆———

"And I'm telling you it is."

Lilly jumped at the sound of Giles' voice raised in anger. When she'd come downstairs, she'd discovered that Giles and her papa were ensconced in his study. By the sound of it they were not getting along. She leaned closer to the door, trying to better hear her father's reply.

"The money is not open for discussion."

Debates over finances always caused strife between men but a dowry was a sign of a girl's worth, and a source of pride for her family. At least that was what her papa had always claimed.

"Her dowry does not need to be that large. I've already told you of my concerns," Giles insisted. "You risk crippling your estate and putting Lilly in..."

"Ahem."

Lilly spun to find Lord Carrington a few paces away. He appeared amused by her eavesdropping. "I wasn't—"

Carrington smiled. "Of course you were, but no matter. I shan't tell on you."

"Thank you."

"I must say, meeting you has proven exciting. And throwing your cousin from the house this morning was a spot of fun. Detestable fellow—tried to convince me you planned it all."

"I—"

Carrington held out his arm. "No one could make my friend behave in such a way if he was not completely committed to the outcome he has now. I offer an apology for doubting your motives. Shall we have tea in the drawing room?"

Lilly glanced up at Lord Carrington and frowned. She didn't know whether to trust such a reversal in his demeanor as a true overture of friendship or not. He was attempting to charm her.

She took his arm rather than speaking because there was a maid near to act as chaperone who followed them into tea.

"I cannot wait to see the ruckus this marriage will cause amongst the ton."

"You mean among Giles' paramours?"

Carrington coughed. "I was referring to society at large, not his past associations."

Lilly frowned. "You needn't pretend that he is one step away from sainthood. I am aware of some aspects in his life most women in my position would not be. I don't expect he will change."

"Past aspects." Carrington shook his head. "Do you know much about his family?"

"A little."

"The Wexham's are an oddity in society. Always have been, too. They don't marry until they must, and once they do, they pledge constancy to their wives. Decidedly unpopular stance to take in this day and age. I used to tease Daventry about it when I was young."

"You disapprove?"

Carrington shrugged. "My friends have all made love matches, not matches designed for dynastic greatness. As far as I can see, they remain besotted with their choices of wives, and their connections and dowries, or lack of, held little sway in the decisions. I didn't understand the appeal before I became engaged."

"And do you understand now?"

Carrington nodded and turned his face to the window. In profile, she could see why most women liked the look of him. He was handsome, could hold a compelling conversation, but he was nothing like Giles Wexham. Could Giles pledge eternity to one woman?

"What does Carrington understand?"

Watching Giles stalk across the room set her heart to pounding again. He dropped to the cushion beside her, leaned over, cupped one hand about her face, and kissed her soundly.

Lilly pushed him away. "Please."

She glanced around, but her father hadn't followed Giles and Carrington had stepped out of the room taking the maid with him.

"Suddenly shy?" Giles dipped his head and his lips caressed her ear. Gooseflesh rose along her skin in waves. "You were not so restrained last night."

Lilly licked her lips, struggling not to think about sharing Giles' bed. Her body hummed in anticipation. "Papa sounded angry earlier. I don't want to upset him."

He caught her earlobe in his teeth, and she vibrated with pleasure. He let go and kissed the skin behind her ear. "Your father and I have come to an understanding at last."

Lilly set her hand upon Giles' arm, intending to push him away, but her fingers curled around his limb and pulled him closer. "And that was?"

Giles' breath was harsh. "I get to marry you as quickly as I can arrange it. If I thought you could bear a trip to the border, we would be on our way already."

Lilly frowned. That had not been what they had been arguing about.

"Is it safe to return?" Carrington asked, a plaintive whine in his tone.

She sat up straight and fought a blush. "Please do."

Carrington settled himself in an opposite chair, long legs crossing until he had just the right pose. "The two of you will be besieged with invitations once the announcements are made."

"I'm sure Giles will enjoy the attention."

Giles settled his arm around her shoulders and squeezed. "We will both enjoy the outings until you grow weary and then we will go home together. I can have no reason to attend balls without you by my side."

Lilly bit her lip, appalled that he would give up so much so quickly. She feared it would be a decision he would regret all too soon.

Chapter Twenty-Six

---◆---

It wasn't entirely necessary to marry simply because you'd foolishly fallen in love. Lilly squinted into the early morning light, admiring, with half her mind, the garden wreathed in thick tendrils of swirling fog. It had been a long time since she had seen a morning such as this, and she hurried to lose herself in the swirling white wisps.

The gravel path crunched beneath her slippered feet and made her wish for sturdier boots. Unfortunately, nothing like that resided in Katarina's wardrobe.

She pulled Katarina's heaviest shawl tight around her chest as the damp air stroked her face and lungs. Fog was one of her favorite things. In the pearly whiteness, she made out the dark shape of the central pond and wondered what the little fishes would think about her situation.

She was afraid.

Of marrying Giles, of leaving her father, of the eventual return of pain when Giles grew bored with caring for a fragile woman.

Her thoughts swirled round and round, going nowhere, like those poor creatures in the pond. They had done that from the moment she'd woken.

She loved him, but that did not mean he had to marry a broken woman. Now that she knew what was required to keep the pain at bay, Giles had no real need to marry her and limit his enjoyment of life.

Lilly would never ride a horse. She doubted that her weakened body would allow it. She would never travel far. The stress of even a short carriage ride had always produced the strongest pains. She could not even dance very much. Her body was just not strong enough to allow her to engage in much beyond a simple walk, followed by a generous amount of time wallowing on a well-padded surface.

She would make him a very poor wife and companion, indeed which was why she feared he'd soon come to regret his rash offer of marriage.

Giles was a very physical man, and not just in bed. He was always moving. Lilly could make love to him, produce his heir, but the thought of childbirth—even of carrying the child—gave her a great fear. She had a memory of someone once saying she would not be woman enough to produce a child. She rather thought they might be right.

Without Giles, her life would still be shrouded in misery. But now she knew she could plan for the future. She could not imagine having another man's hands on her skin. But she thought she could bear the touch of a woman.

If she engaged the services of a kindly female companion Lilly could explain what to do for her pains.

As she rounded the pond, she remembered the small stone bench on a side path and headed in that direction.

As she neared the bench, a gray shape resolved into her papa's form. He was sitting forward with his hands on his knees, staring down at the ground. He must have heard her, for he looked up sharply then let out a deep sigh. He seemed so relieved to see her that she obediently leaned down to kiss his cheek, and then sat beside him.

"Good morning, daughter. I am glad to see you up and about so early. Lord Daventry appears to have looked after you very well last night." His compliment made her blush and she didn't know how to reply.

"Lilly, there is no need to be embarrassed with me. The fault is all mine. Lord Daventry has quite a reputation with the ladies, and it was remiss of me to have left you alone with him. I hoped that you would be comfortable here. Not that he... Not that you would..."

"You mean you did not think he would be interested in a broken woman."

"I did not say that," he said quickly.

"But it is the truth, Papa, whether you wish it or not." Lilly sighed. She preferred to live her life in reality, not fantasy. Marrying Giles was pure fantasy.

"Well, that is neither here nor there. He has compromised you and done the decent thing by offering to marry you again. He has accepted there are consequences to his actions, and that is the end of it."

"There can be no consequences when a particular event has not taken place, Papa." Lilly would have him know the truth before it was too late.

"Not taken place? But...you have shared his bed. Surely...he...you...?" He trailed off.

"Shared a bed, certainly, Papa. But the rest, he has not." Lilly looked forward at the swirling fog and hid a grimace. She was lying by leaving out what sharing a bed with Giles had entailed. If there was any way to save Giles from this marriage she had to do it now. "It is true he has made me well but I will not allow Giles to give up his life to take care of me." She still had a chance of making her own choices if her father could be convinced it was the right thing to do for everyone. "What did you see in Wales, Papa? Was the estate acceptable?"

"How do you know about that?"

The surprise in his voice convinced her to go on. "The night of your return, I listened outside the dining room and heard you tell Giles about the nice old lady and spinster daughter in Scotland. I asked Giles about it later that night. He told me the truth, Papa. He does not lie to me as you do."

Lilly watched her father gulp down his guilt and understood his dilemma. If he admitted to the plan, he would be admitting to being tired of caring for her. After all these years, she would be tired too.

She patted his hand. "It is all right. I am very grateful for the time you have spared for me these past years. It cannot have been an easy task, and I know you must have given up a great deal of your freedom to care for me and keep mother away. The far estate is a good choice. Can I take a companion with me, do you think? I should like that better than a nurse. Tell me about the place I will go to live."

Her father raised his hands to his face, but she did not turn to see whether he wiped away tears. Parting would be painful enough when the time came to head west.

In halting words, he told her about the house and grounds. Since there was also a small village nearby, she might even make friends and have visitors.

Lilly did not ask if he would be one of them. Why else would he choose a place so far away if he wished to be free of her?

"Now, I want to know what you spoke to Giles about earlier in his study. He would not tell me."

"We did not want to worry you."

"Papa, I am worried *now*. What could possibly make a man like Daventry shout?"

"Giles is a better man than I gave him credit for," he chided.

"Papa, you are blind to his faults. He is a man most suitable and happy to seduce any woman. How can you be happy to have such a notorious skirt-chaser in your family? You cannot be keen on this alliance."

"As a matter of fact, I have no issues with you marrying Lord Daventry. He does care for you. He told me that yesterday, and I believed him. You will be marrying Lord Daventry, Lillian. Just as soon as the matter can be arranged."

"No, I will not." She stood and looked down at her father. "You cannot make me say the words or sign the register. I am going to Wales as you've already begun to plan. What did you discuss with him?"

He shook his head. "You do not need know the details."

Lilly turned toward the house, furious for the first time in many years, and left without saying a goodbye of any kind.

She ignored Carrington's enquiries as she passed him on her way to her bedchamber. The stout door would keep those foolish men from her sight. She just might be tempted to whack some sense into their defective brains. She may not be worldly, but she wasn't stupid. What they discussed was very much her business.

"She did not mean that," Lord Winter promised Giles as he stepped out of the fog.

"Yes, she did." Giles chuckled. "And I deserve a great deal more of your daughter's anger beyond this outburst. She appears to have a terrible temper. Is that a family trait I need to prepare for? Perhaps I should acquire a suit of armor from somewhere. Maybe Ettington has had enough of that ghastly suit in his front hall."

Lord Winter winced. "I have not seen her lose her temper in years. Not since her mother gave away her puppy."

Giles blinked. "I beg your pardon?"

"It was years ago. When Barrette was younger, he came to our estate while his parents traveled abroad. He took an instant liking to the young pup my daughter had acquired from the stables. Since my wife lived in horror of dogs but liked to indulge our nephew, she handed him over. Lillian did not take it well."

"I do not blame her. That seems a particularly cruel thing to do to a child."

"Yes, well, my wife was unable to bear more than one child. She had wanted a son quite desperately. She took her frustrations out on our daughter."

"That is no excuse," Giles argued as he glanced around. "Lady Winter seems usually cold."

The baron shook his head. "Are you out here to spy on me, Daventry, or is there something I can do for you?"

Unfortunately, Lord Winter's problems were Giles' problems now.

"I was watching over Lilly. You know I have suspicions concerning her accident and the other odd occurrences all add up to a worrying conclusion. It is a situation I cannot ignore, especially when I have just learned Barrette has not left the area. Since a foggy day can hide many an act of tomfoolery, perhaps you had better come back inside."

Lord Winter stood and glanced around quickly. "You fear for me too?"

"Let us say that you're a little too close to that bridge for my liking. Come back inside and we will play a hand of cards."

Giles had no wish to loiter outside on a day where there was no chance to see if Barrette crept up on them. The hair on the back of his neck stood on end as it was. He hustled his soon-to-be father-in-law towards the house as fast as he could.

"Would you know if Barrette can shoot with any degree of accuracy?" Giles asked as they crossed the threshold into the drawing room and locked the door behind them.

"No. Barrette is a terrible shot. I am always surprised to see him out in the country. I don't believe he cares for any place other than Dumas or London."

"Of course he is here. You are here, and I understand he has become something of a shadow. I was thinking about the nursemaid you brought with you earlier. The one who disappeared in the night as soon as you departed. Did Barrette know her?"

"I don't recall?" Winter frowned. "Wait. Yes. They have exchanged a few words now I think about it further. Barrette has always been keen on the ladies."

"Yes, I noticed that here too which might explain how Lilly came to be drugged with laudanum again." Giles shook his head; unable to believe any of his staff would knowingly agree to anything that would harm Lilly. "I wonder if he somehow gained access to her trays of food."

"You are convinced he means to harm her?"

"How can you not suspect him?" Giles shook his head. "I believe Lilly's accident was no accident at all. An angel would always behave herself. Do you know she is afraid of heights?"

"Well, of course she is, and who could blame her?"

"She was afraid of heights before the accident, Winter. Lilly would never have climbed that bridge on her own," Giles assured him.

Lord Winter's face paled. "How the devil did you get that out of her? We never could discover how she fell. She was too ill to answer questions, and then later she *wouldn't* answer."

"She may not want to remember. I took her to the bridge myself a few days after her recovery, and she told me of an incident with a kitten, an apple tree, and your valet. She said she had been hysterical even then."

"You are right, come to think of it. Lilly was as white as a ghost. We all thought she'd climbed that bridge."

"We? Would that be you and Barrette, perhaps?"

Lord Winter passed a shaking hand over his brow. "He was a kind boy before his father's passing."

"Things change—people die," Giles reminded him, even more certain to be on guard for Lilly's sake. He did not know how far Barrette might be prepared to go to achieve his misguided goal of saving the estate from the loss of Lilly's ridiculous dowry. At least Winter had compromised on the amount, but it would be better to be prepared.

"Did you teach my daughter to play cards?"

"I simply refreshed her memory. She learns fast." Giles glanced at Lord Winter's clenched fist and sighed. Oh, his previous life was irritating. He was well known to favor table stakes when gambling privately with women, and quite often clothing was gambled away too. But everything he had done with Lilly had been fresh and very different from his usual antics. It was not Lord Winter's fault if he anticipated the absolute worst of him.

"You taught her to gamble to trick her into your bed," Lord Winter fumed.

"I taught her to play cards. Not to gamble," Giles corrected. The least he could do was tell the truth about that. "Lilly placed her bets with some help from my signals."

"So Lillian was correct when she said that she was not bedded?"

"She said that, did she? Silly widgeon. Winter, I hate to bring up such a delicate subject, but I promise you I have compromised your daughter most thoroughly. It is taking all my fortitude to restrain myself until our marriage, but she won't make it past the first ten minutes with what's left of her virginity intact when the happy day arrives." Giles chuckled, anticipation making him giddy. He would be very happy to keep her trapped in his bed for the first six months of marriage.

Lord Winter pressed his lips together tight, but said nothing further as they passed the afternoon playing cards. Giles supposed he should not be quite so blunt about the matter of bedding Lilly, but Winter appeared to take it quite well. Giles found it a relief to be able to be himself with his future father.

They ate dinner without Lilly. Winter watched for her, but Lilly did not come or send a note. Giles wasn't worried. He would see her when he went to bed. He was looking forward to holding her in his arms again.

Giles walked into his bedchamber at close to midnight and stripped off his clothes in the dark. He hardened in anticipation of running his hands over Lilly's curves as his fingers touched the sheets. She was filling out, and the sight of her ribs no longer pained him by their sharpness. He climbed into bed, eager, but found only cold sheets and emptiness. Damn that woman. Lilly was going to be the death of him.

Giles jumped back out of bed, pulled on his shirt and trousers, and strode out the door towards Lilly's room. He turned the handle but found she'd locked the door. He knocked, but heard no sounds within. Not even the dog. Silly widgeon. She forgot he could use the housekeeper's key.

He hurried down the hall and found the servants' stairs leading to the exit closest to Mrs. Osprey's office. Once he woke the housekeeper and took the set from the sleepy woman's fingers, Giles turned back to the stairs, but something stopped him. He dragged in another breath and froze.

Smoke.

Chapter Twenty-Seven

———— ◆ ————

Atticus' whine woke Lilly from a troubled sleep and she sat up, disoriented in the dark. She did not know what time it was, but thought it must be very late. Atticus barked at her then scratched at the door urgently.

That was what must have woken her. The dog must want to go outside.

She slipped from the bed, tired and unhappy to be awake. Her sleep had been filled with images of falling and cold, hard water rising up to meet her. She shuddered and wished the dream would never return.

She hurried around the bed in the darkness to the dog, patting his head as she reached him. "Sorry, boy. I didn't mean to lock you in."

He was such a well-trained hound, but she must have locked him in too early. Her bad mood the day before was no excuse for neglecting the beast. She liked him too much to be cruel. Lilly flicked the lock, turned the knob to pull the door open—and drew in a lungful of thick smoke.

She coughed and pushed the door closed with both hands.

A warning bell rang out.

"Dear God, the manor is on fire!" Lilly staggered back from the door, coughing and wiping her stinging eyes. Confused, she crashed into a side table and tumbled a vase to the floor. Glass shattered. Her feet were bare.

When she could see again, she judged where she was in relation to the break and worked out which way to go to avoid cutting herself. She stepped carefully, sliding her bare feet along the floor until she found herself far away from the glass.

Atticus whined at the door, but she ignored his complaints. They needed to get out, but she would need more than a nightgown on her back and bare feet.

Lilly hurried to her wardrobe, threw a dark gown over the top of her nightgown, grabbed the only pair of slippers she had and jammed them on her feet. She wished she had something thicker, but Katarina purchased only beautiful things, not practical ones.

Grabbing up a length of towel, Lilly soaked it in water from the jug, then wrapped the wet cloth around her neck, effectively tying down her long hair. Lilly grabbed a second length of cloth and wet that too. She could cover the dog's snout as well if he would allow it. She couldn't risk losing him to the smoke.

With shoes now protecting her feet, she rushed across the room to the door and draped the wet cloth over the dog's snout. Atticus tried to back away, but she commanded him to obey while she tied it loosely behind his ears.

With one last look about the room, Lilly curled her fingers in the wolfhound's collar and told him to get out. If she held on tight, he might be able to lead her outside more quickly than if she tried to find her way blind. She did not imagine it would be easy to pass through the house as it burned, but she trusted the dog to do his best for both of them.

Lilly opened the door slowly and smoke poured through the crack, rising upwards to the roof. Atticus rushed forward and she stumbled after him.

She could not see much of anything and she could barely breathe. When she looked down, Lilly saw that the smoke was thinner closer to the floor. But bending down was difficult for her; her skirts twisted about her legs and hampered her every step.

At the top of the stairs, she stumbled heavily into the railing and gasped in pain, sucking up too much smoke when her wet cloth became detached. She coughed and struggled to find her feet again. Lilly gripped the railing with one hand and inched downwards, Atticus pulling relentlessly on her arm.

On the first landing, she stumbled again and went down hard, losing her grip on the dog. She felt a touch on her hand and he whimpered as he fretted over her fall.

Lilly pulled herself up, but pain lanced down her back. As much as Lilly hurt, she could not count on anyone coming to help. She had to save herself. Sweat broke out over her face as she inched down the last flight carefully.

She could not see the main door, but a faint breeze made the smoke swirl.

She reached out with one hand and her fingertips brushed a wall. Lilly followed the wall, found the door then searched for the lock.

Atticus pressed at her side.

The lock finally opened with a snap and she pulled on the handle, gasping in the fresh air that streamed into her face. They had escaped. Atticus had already bolted for the front drive, shaking his head to remove the cloth and barking at her to hurry. He raced back to Lilly and nipped at her skirts to pull her with him.

Lilly stumbled across the front drive and found the little patch of grass surrounding another ornamental pond. She collapsed to the grass, groaning as the hard ground slammed more pain into her, then coughing until she thought her lungs might burst. Atticus abandoned her to gulp down pond water.

When she lifted her head, smoke billowed from the back of the moonlit house. When she could find her feet again, she would go looking for the others, but the grass was so cool and soft that she lay there while she got her breath back.

Right now, she could not dream of getting to her feet again. She would be no help to anyone in her condition and would only be in the way. She dragged herself to a sitting position, groaning against the pain, and held her head while the stars behind her eyes faded.

When she could see again, she reached for the rag at her neck and pulled it off, squinting at it in the faint moonlight as she searched to find a clean patch to wipe over her face. She must look like a chimney sweep.

"That dog deserves a ball between its eyes for the trouble he's caused me."

Lilly spun on the ground to locate that voice and heard metal click on metal.

———◆———

"Oh, its only you," Lilly said, but then her eyes focused on his hand holding the pistol aimed at her heart.

Fortune smiled upon Bartholomew at last. He had Lillian alone in the dark of night, and all to himself, no less. He giggled then pressed his lips together. They had to be silent, lest someone hear them. As it was, he was sure they had little time enough before that scoundrel Daventry came looking for his whore.

It was true. She had shared his bed and done things with him that ought to be reserved for her husband. Her betrayal cut him to the core, and he shifted the pistol in his hand, debating how he might kill her.

There was a nice pond of water behind her back to drown her in after smashing her skull upon the marble. Anyone who found her later might imagine she did it herself. He glanced around and then tucked the pistol in the back of his breeches. He would enjoy watching her face as she drew her last breath.

That would provide far better enjoyment than the last time. Last time he had rushed, and not stayed to ensure the deed was done. His cousin would not be alone this time. He would stay until her end came.

"What are you doing here again, Barty?"

Her gaze flickered around the garden and back to him. Even though she was impure, touched by that swine, Lord Daventry, Bartholomew still desired her for himself. "You have always been my favorite cousin. How could I bear to leave you be?"

Lillian shifted to her knees, and he decided he liked her in that pose. She looked weak and pitiful. He could approach her, grasp her neck and squeeze until she took her last breath. The thought was appealing, so he stepped toward her.

The dog moved to her side and watched him.

He paused. The dog was a complication. To dispatch the beast with little fuss, he would need to use the pistol. But the noise would surely attract the notice of others unless they moved farther away.

"On your feet."

The bitch licked her lips. "Why?"

He could always count on Lillian to be difficult. Her response pleased him. He would distrust her more if she suddenly became compliant and willing. He wanted her to fight, to battle with him to make his victory all the sweeter.

"Let me give you a choice. Either you get to your feet, or I shoot the dog. I know how you love to dote on the poor creatures. You can count on me to ensure that his end is agonizingly slow. Perhaps I could shoot one of his feet off first, or perhaps his tail. Do you wonder how he would feel about it?"

Lillian whimpered. Pleasure raced down his spine. He'd had no idea that killing her in person would bring him so much joy. He'd forgotten so much of his earlier attempt. He'd been too young to appreciate the moment. He pulled the pistol from his pocket and took aim at the dog.

As he expected, Lillian surged to her feet.

"Now walk."

"Where are we going?"

Bartholomew pressed a hand to his forehead. "Don't ruin this for me by babbling now. I much preferred it when you were insensible."

"Papa taught me to speak my mind."

"Your father is a foolish man. He would have done better to have listened to his wife and smothered you where you lay all those years ago." At Lilly's gasp, Bartholomew stepped closer. "She could have succeeded, too, if he wasn't so weak! Your hands looked so pretty as you scratched at the pillow."

"Lillian, where are you?" Lord Winter called.

Lilly opened her mouth to reply, but Bartholomew shook his pistol. "Say one word and he dies now."

Bartholomew backed into the shadows. He skirted his uncle and, when he reached Lillian, Bartholomew swung the pistol hard at his uncle's head.

The baron slumped to the ground and did not move again.

"You said you wouldn't hurt him," Lillian cried out.

"I said I wouldn't kill him first." Bartholomew grinned. Now he had two things he wanted, and all in one night. Lillian on her knees, and his uncle one step closer to death.

He could be master of Dumas before the night was through if he did this right.

———◆———

Giles rushed up the stairs, opening every door he came to. Outside, servants ran back and forth from the well and stream, carrying anything that could hold water. He searched inside the house, checking how far the fire had spread and looking for signs of Lilly. So far the worst of it seemed to be merely a great deal of smoke. He hurried to Lilly's bedchamber door and pushed it open.

No sign of her. Although he was relieved she was out of danger, he worried at how the smoke might have affected her. He moved along to check Carrington's door and found it locked.

When he knocked, he heard Carrington cry out. Using the housekeeper's keys, he fumbled to open the lock only to be bowled over by Carrington.

Giles hit the ground hard.

"Sorry about that." Carrington pulled him to his feet. "Damn door was stuck. I was just debating jumping out the window."

"Not stuck, locked," Giles managed to gasp out.

Carrington ducked back into his room, returning with a pistol in his hand. "Better to be careful then. Where's your Lilly?"

A pane of glass broke below them, and he turned his friend toward the stairs. "I haven't found her yet. Get yourself outside and look for her. I'll check the rest of this floor in case she became lost in the smoke."

"Be careful."

Giles pushed him on his way and checked the rest of the floor. The rooms were all empty. He re-closed the doors as he went and headed down the stairs into thick, swirling smoke. He checked along the edges of each step, making sure no one had been overlooked. Giles was gasping horribly by the time he reached the front door, but he was confident that everyone was safe.

Outside, the air was blessedly cool and clear. He dragged the fresh night scents deep into his lungs. The cooler air irritated his throat, and he coughed until his lungs hurt. A grunt opened his eyes and he looked about him.

Across the drive, Lord Winter lay beside the pond. Poor man must be done in. But at least he'd found Lilly. She and Atticus were huddled around the older man—and it wasn't until the dog started growling that he realized they were not alone.

Barrette stood over them.

Atticus edged between Lilly and Barrette, teeth bared and snarling. The dog was enraged.

Giles ran toward them as fast as he could. Just as he neared, the dog gave his presence away by turning toward the sound of his approach. He suddenly found himself facing a dueling pistol.

The last time he had seen this man, he'd desired to have a dueling pistol near. He wished he had one now. His aim would be pretty good, given his motivation tonight.

"Stay back," Barrette warned.

Lilly wrapped her arms around her father. Covered in soot from head to toe, her white hair dull in the limited light, Lilly thankfully did not look hurt.

Giles took two steps back as the sound of more footsteps could be heard coming up behind him. The pistol swung to Lilly, and then back to him.

"Put the gun down, Barrette," Giles ordered, using false bravado to intimidate the man.

Barrette curled his lips into a sneer. "This has nothing to do with you. I suggest you go take care of your own affairs."

"Lilly *is* my affair. I'll not leave her."

Barrette laughed. "Then I shall have to make sure I do a better job of helping her leave *you*." He waved the pistol at Lilly. "Get back on your feet, wench."

Giles held his breath as she complied. He was afraid for her. Terrified to lose her. But he had no gun or weapon on him to fight with. He'd have to be cunning—and damned fast about it. He could attempt to tackle Barrette, but the gun might just go off and hit one of them.

"I'm not going anywhere with you again," Lilly began. "I'll not be a fool like last time. Put the gun down. What can you hope to gain from this?"

"Dumas, you idiot."

"I've never wanted Dumas!"

Barrette growled. "You still don't understand. The interest from your dowry sustains Dumas. The estate will be as crippled as you."

Lilly looked at Giles. She sought confirmation in his gaze and he let his head nod infinitesimally. The loss of her original dowry would do what Barrette feared, and leave the property in dire straights. But Giles had negotiated, settling for a lower sum. "The amount has changed. There will be no danger to the estate now."

"I need it all," Barrette insisted.

More footsteps sounded behind him, and Giles spread his arms wide to warn them back. "You cannot hope to harm Lilly and get away with it. There are too many witnesses now."

Barrette pointed the pistol at him instead. "She was supposed to die. But if you want something done, you just have to do it yourself. It should have worked the first time!" Barrette complained, adjusting his grip on the weapon.

"The first time was when you threw her off the bridge, wasn't it?" Giles asked conversationally, unsure where he was going to go with this, but anxious to draw out the exchange.

"Damned dog. Should have known she would have spoiled the brute." He waved the gun towards Atticus, and Atticus growled until Lilly laid a restraining hand on him. "She quite ruined that hunting dog of mine before I got him. Had to starve and beat the beast before he would behave like a proper dog." Barrette laughed, a cruel smile tugging his lips upward.

Lilly scowled, her tiny fists clenched.

All he needed was for her to fly into a temper over a long-dead dog to provoke Barrette into doing something foolish. Like shoot the pistol at her.

Winter chose that moment to groan, and his eyes fluttered open. But he did not see the situation before him. Barrette waved the pistol erratically, and Giles prayed the weapon would not fire accidentally.

"Just lay there, old man, and die! You should have brought her to me when you wanted to be rid of her. I would have done the deed myself. Did you know the cork-brain was planning on packing you off to some pissing little estate in the wilds of Scotland?" Barrette hissed. "A waste of effort I must say. All that was needed was a shovel and a ditch full of dirt. No one would have missed you. They all think you're dead anyway thanks to your mother."

Lilly flinched and clutched her father's hand. "I know what Papa planned, Barty. It is not news," she told her cousin in a strong voice.

Giles inched closer to Lilly. Barrette swung the pistol back to him, and he lost the ground he had gained.

"You don't want to do this, Barrette. Consider what the consequences will be. There's a dozen or more people on this estate, and every single one is watching you."

"She promised it would be all mine. She never lies. A cripple doesn't deserve to be a Winter!"

Barrette renewed his grip on the pistol and aimed at Lilly.

Giles threw himself forward as a pistol shot rang out. He landed hard on top of Barrette.

When he rolled off the man but Barrette lay still, eyes wide, a gaping hole oozing blood from his forehead.

Lord Carrington strode forward, pistol in hand, and nudged the fallen man with his foot.

Chapter Twenty-Eight

Giles should have thanked his friend immediately, but he was too anxious to hold Lilly. He lifted her to her feet, and then kissed the breath out of her.

The sheer terror of the past moments could only be assuaged by the joy of holding her close against his chest, feeling her warmth in his arms. He did not turn away from the spectators. He did not pretend to feel anything but the utter relief of the moment.

Lilly was safe and whole, still here with him. If she had died, Giles did not know what he would have done. Those moments when the pistol barrel was aimed at her chest had almost stopped his heart.

Giles pulled back and breathed deeply, allowing Lilly to do the same. He rested his head against hers and their breath mingled hot between them. He held her up off the ground and Lilly wiggled her legs slightly, rocking them both. "You're safe. You are safe now."

He twisted so Lilly would not have to see her cousin's body removed or see the pain cross Carrington's features as the truth of his actions slowly registered. The servants, perhaps noticing Carrington's stricken expression, rallied around him and led him to the house.

Giles pressed his lips to Lilly's again, gently this time. He tenderly swiped the tip of his tongue across her lower lip, tasting the warm sweetness of her mouth and the gentle response she gave him. Her hand lay against the side of his face and her fingers traced the edge of his ear.

He loved this little bundle of trouble, and the relief of finding the one person he adored above all others sent him a little wild.

"Ahem."

Giles lifted his head to find his butler waiting.

"The fire is under control," the butler croaked. "A few of the neighboring families heard the warning bell and arrived in time to see what transpired. They wish to speak with you, and with Lord Winter."

Giles quickly glanced around, discovered his future-father-in-law had moved to the front steps of the house and appeared to be guzzling spirits again.

"The viscount is badly shaken, milord. You should speak to him soon."

"I will come directly." Giles smiled down at Lilly. "We have guests. I suppose I shall have to behave now."

Here at Cottingstone, they had lived in a fantasy where no one could see what they did. It had allowed Giles to get to know Lilly better and fall in love with her. He did not want to force her into a marriage with him if she hated the idea, but he would have to be far more circumspect now.

After dropping Lilly to her feet, he held out his arm for her to take. After the first few paces, he noticed a limp to her step. Giles slowed so his butler moved past them. "Are you hurt?"

"I fell down the stairs," she told him. Her prompt response was a nice change from having to pry answers out of her.

"Should you be walking at all? Where exactly does it hurt?"

Lilly tugged on his arm and Giles lowered his head closer to her lips so she could whisper her answer. His eyebrows shot up, and she giggled at his reaction.

"Something to look forward to tending. How delicious."

Lilly might have blushed at his remark, but he could not tell in the dark.

Dithers waited at the steps and prevented their progress. "The smoke is still very strong throughout the house, milord. There could still be embers burning beneath the rubble of the study. Perhaps the stable would be more comfortable and safer for Miss

Winter tonight. At least the air would be fresher. She could be quite comfortable in your traveling carriage."

"No thank you. No carriages." Lilly shuddered. "Some hay in the stables will be good enough."

Giles took a pair of blankets and a lantern from Dithers, then led Lilly toward a clean corner of hay. He swiftly made as soft a bed as he could and lifted her onto it, then draped her with the second blanket.

"Not comfortable enough by far, but it will have to do for one night. Mrs. Osprey is already settling in nearby to keep you company, and I will send your father along in a little while."

He brushed a few long strands of hair back from her face and pressed a quick kiss to her cheek. She was safe now. There was no longer any threat to her from Barrette.

Lilly clutched his arm. "Will the manor recover?"

"She might be a little scorched on one side, but I am assured the damage can be repaired easily enough. Barrette seemed intent on driving everyone from the house, not burning Cottingstone to the ground. The worst of it was out long before I found you, but I need to ensure the embers are all dug out. I am so sorry you have to sleep out here. Stay warm. If you need anything, ask Mrs. Osprey."

"I'm sorry."

Giles frowned. "For what?"

"For my cousin. Tell Carrington I'm sorry too, but grateful for his intervention," Lilly murmured. "You be careful, too, Giles."

A thrill raced through him. No one had concerned themselves over his safety in a long time. Maybe in a few hours Lilly might come to reconsider her desire to live in Wales. If that was what she truly wanted he would have no choice but to let her go. He swallowed past the lump in his throat and whispered, "I will," before he left.

———•———

Giles worked his way through the damaged part of the house with a few staff and Carrington, removing debris and extinguishing any glowing embers that still burned. His neighbors were long gone and he planned to catch a few hours' sleep somewhere soon.

"Thank you for your assistance tonight," Giles said, seizing a moment when they were free of the servants' company to speak to Carrington who'd grown uncharacteristically quiet in the last hour.

Carrington shrugged and continued shoveling.

"She means the world to me and I can never repay you for what you did to save her."

Carrington shifted another pile of debris to a barrow for removal. "I knew that," Carrington said, words whispered in a sad rasp of sound. "You love her and would have died for her tonight."

"I do love her." It surprised Giles how little those words frightened him. Lilly might have understandable misgivings about marriage to him, but he would promise his fidelity before all of society if she asked him to. "I always will."

"Can I get you anything, milord?" Dithers stood in the doorway, not quite as prim and straight as usual.

"Dithers, what the devil are you doing still here? Hasn't Mrs. Osprey tucked you into bed yet?"

"I managed to escape her fussing," Dithers assured him with a smug smile.

"Why the hell did you do that? You had an opportunity there, old boy. Can't believe you passed up the chance. Get off to bed," Giles ordered. "Preferably hers."

"Sir!" Dithers sounded so shocked that Giles could finally laugh.

"You have been immersed in the country for too long, Dithers. I think you've lost your touch. Hurry off to the stables and kiss the woman good night before I sack you both for stupidity."

Dithers drew himself up, spun on his heel, and left without a word.

Carrington dropped his shovel and leaned against the wall for support. "You're matchmaking the servants now?"

"They did it to me," Giles protested and Carrington started to laugh. Giles let him, watching the tension begin to leave his friend at last. "I have every right to strike back at them, don't I?"

———— ◆ ————

The fire damage was not as bad as Lilly had feared. The room where the fire had started did not have a chamber directly above it and she could see no lasting damage to the structure of the house, except for the glimpse of blue sky through the missing roof.

The men did not appear worried that the house might collapse, so she let her anxiety fade. A thick layer of ash coated everything else, however, and Cottingstone was in need of a very good cleaning to bring Giles' home to order again. The men poked around the fire-damaged room, pulling down parts of the wall badly scorched by flames, and churned up more dust in the process. Lilly stepped into the hall and observed from a distance.

Mrs. Osprey approached, eyes fixed on the distant room.

"What is it, Mrs. Osprey?"

"I was wondering what the master would like tackled first, Miss. But I dare not interrupt him. Do you think you could ask for me? I don't want to be a nuisance."

Giles was inspecting the damage to the far wall and Lilly decided to be useful for a change. "Perhaps you could start by airing and cleaning the bedchambers. Lord Daventry looks set to collapse at any moment. I don't know if he has slept since the fire. And they will want to bathe later."

"Yes, my lady."

"After the bed chambers, the dining room should be next. The gentlemen will be hungry."

Mrs. Osprey hurried off to do her bidding.

Lilly's back ached. She would need to lie down soon, but the couch she usually rested upon had burned to ashes. That meant she would have to tackle the stairs soon and return to her room.

She kept her eyes on Giles and his head lifted and his gaze met hers. Lilly blushed, wondering if Giles had heard her ordering his servants about. He should at least be angry about the damage her family had caused him. But no, here he was, giving her a cheeky grin, as if he was not just gesturing to charred timbers a moment ago. She did not understand his calmness today. His study was a mess, or what was left of it was.

Lilly headed for the stairs and a much-needed rest. She got as far as the bottom step before Giles caught up with her. "Are you off to lie down?"

She nodded and he lifted her into his arms, flowed up the long flight of stairs without any jarring, then set Lilly lightly on her feet. She waited for his kiss and was surprised when he stepped away.

"Enjoy your rest, Ghost."

He left her standing with her mouth hanging open. She waited for him to come back and kiss her but he continued down the stairs with a cheery wave. He gave her a courtly bow from the base of the stairs before disappearing from view.

Why now of all times did he have to be proper? Such behavior was all wrong for him. At every turn, Giles broke the rules. It amused him to misbehave, she thought. A proper Giles, obeying the dictates of good society, was out of her experience.

Uneasy, she rubbed her hands up and down her arms. Now the danger had passed there was no need to marry Giles. She was still innocent, and if she went to live in Wales he would be free to pursue his normal life of balls and dalliance.

If she did not marry him she'd have a lifetime without his touch.

Dithers and Mrs. Osprey were arguing farther along the corridor. Dithers' voice sounded dreadful, and Mrs. Osprey kept reminding him that he should be resting rather than telling everyone what to do.

Lilly had to agree with her, Dithers would only cause more damage by speaking. They were such an odd pair. Him so tall and handsome, her so plain. Yet there were times when she caught Dithers watching after Mrs. Osprey strangely, and more than once she suspected something more was brewing beneath the surface.

"Is there a problem, Mrs. Osprey?"

"Yes. Dithers refuses to close his mouth long enough to let his throat heal. I am quite capable of organizing the cleaning of this house. It is my job, after all." She glared at him, but his jaw clenched.

"Dithers, are you stopping Mrs. Osprey from doing her job? Are you attempting to have her replaced?"

Dithers glanced at Lilly in horror.

She arched her brow and stepped closer to him. "That is what it sounds like to me. Perhaps you should listen to what she suggests for once."

Dithers' jaw clenched before he bowed and stalked off. Clearly, he did not appreciate Lilly's support of the housekeeper.

Mrs. Osprey bit her lip, watching until Dithers disappeared from view. "Can I help you, my lady?"

"Why do you keep calling me that? I've not married his lordship yet."

Mrs. Osprey smiled ruefully. "Just trying to get you used to the idea."

Lilly snorted, a very unladylike sound. "I need to rest, but the downstairs chaise was burned. Are any of the upper rooms prepared yet?"

"The only room ready so far is the master's bedchamber. You can rest there until your room is properly aired."

Lilly squeezed the housekeeper's hand and turned to check the corridor. Since it was empty, she slipped inside Giles' room and crawled onto his soft bed.

Giles did not wake her. Mrs. Osprey did.

The magistrate had come and wanted to talk to all the witnesses to the shooting. When Lilly glanced around, she could see no sign that Giles had returned to his room at all. Her stomach fluttered to think he might be avoiding her.

Lilly returned to her own room, and Mrs. Osprey helped her bathe away the grime and change into a fresh gown. She could still smell the scent of smoke beneath her usual perfume and wondered how long the smell would linger.

"Osprey?"

"Yes, my lady?" The little woman seated herself on a chair nearby.

Lilly frowned. "What are you going to do about Dithers?"

Mrs. Osprey blinked and did not say a word.

"Would you care to hear a suggestion?"

When the housekeeper nodded, Lilly leaned in close. "He is a good man. After dinner tonight, why don't you go find him and talk? I'm sure if you give him the slightest encouragement, he will find a way to take advantage of it."

"He doesn't think of me that way, Miss Winter. He doesn't even realize I'm around unless I bungle something."

"Oh, I think you will find that he notices much more than

that," Lilly laughed. "He watches you. Now you only have to catch him."

"What if I can't?" Mrs. Osprey whispered. "I don't think I could bear the shame."

"Then he doesn't deserve you," Lilly told her firmly as she stood, ready for her meeting with the magistrate at last.

Lilly's interview did not take long, since she was the last to be spoken to. Her father sat beside her and held her hand throughout, as she recounted her experiences of last night and spoke of events that had happened so long ago.

The magistrate frowned through it all, but concluded that Lord Carrington had acted correctly to save their lives from a madman. He closed his notebook, hailed Lord Carrington as the hero, and hurried off to arrange the burial.

———◆———

Lilly slipped into the library and pushed the door closed behind her. Giles had formally asked for an interview too and she was so nervous her hands were damp with stress. Given that she'd been anxious since Dithers had delivered the invitation on his little silver tray, eyes sparkling with glee, she should be used to the sensation.

After hours of waiting to speak to Giles alone, she was particularly nervous.

Pain lanced down her back as she stepped farther into the room. Pain was good. It distracted her from the choice that was in Giles' best interests.

He would be better off without her slowing him down. He was full of energy and had great passion. He deserved more for his future, more than a fragile woman for a wife.

Lilly sank onto the chaise, fiddling with the ribbon of her borrowed gown.

"I am going to have to make a decision soon." Lilly glanced up to find Giles leaning against the door. "It is much too important a matter to put off."

Lilly inched forward on the chaise. "About what?"

"What color do you think should my study be repainted?" He

grinned.

"I beg your pardon?"

"I thought perhaps you might have a favorite color. I should like to paint my study to suit your taste." He crossed the room to sit opposite Lilly while she tried to gather her wits. That question wasn't even close to what she expected them to talk about.

"I don't understand. I thought..." She let her words trail off.

"You thought I was going to ask you to marry me properly, didn't you?"

Heat flooded her face.

He shook his head, and her mortification grew. "I already know what your answer will be. I overheard your discussion with your father in the garden yesterday. You wish to live in Wales rather than marry me and I can understand why you would," he said softly. "I'd probably make a terribly improper husband."

Lilly stared at him. He was upset with her and trying hard to hide it. She looked down at her gown to hide her dismay at having the power to hurt him.

"What is your favorite color, Ghost?"

"Primrose," she answered, bewildered by his insistence on knowing the color.

"Thank you. Now, about Atticus. I anticipate he will not be happy to be separated from you. He seems to be more your dog than mine. He never listens to me half as well," Giles frowned. "He should be wherever you are."

Lilly recoiled in shock. "I cannot take your dog."

"Of course you will. You don't want to leave him behind and have him suffering. The poor beast will never understand why he cannot be with the one he loves, will he?" Giles tilted his head and Lilly squirmed as his gaze pierced her calm. "He cannot go to parties and pretend he is happy. He cannot eat a meal alone and understand why it has to be that way. I know I have erred beyond forgiveness, Lilly, but I should not like to see him suffer, too."

"What are you talking about?"

"I can understand that you want nothing further to do with me." When she went to protest, he shushed her with his outstretched hand and stood to look down at her, eyes dull with pain. "I refuse to trap you into marriage too so this is farewell."

Lilly blinked rapidly. He drew closer and her pulse raced.

Giles leaned down. "A kiss to last me a lifetime, Lilly. I won't ever kiss another soul. I can promise you that for all eternity." He pressed a kiss to her lips then moved away. His blue eyes were swimming with unshed tears. "I love you."

The words fell over her skin like rain, and she closed her eyes as unbearable wonder filled her with hope.

She wiped furiously at her eyes to look for him, but she was all alone in the library.

Giles had only asked her here to say goodbye in private. So he could kiss her one last time and then go.

She buried her face in her hands and sobbed, unable to bear the loss of such a good friend. He planned never to see her again. She was sure of it.

He loved her.

Lilly had never known before what hearing those words would do to her resolve. It crumbled to dust.

She'd been so foolish. She'd been afraid she'd be the only one of them in love.

Lilly stood and hurried for the door. She stifled a cry of pain as her body refused to behave with the speed her heart insisted it must.

He'd given her the damned dog too. She brushed her hands over her face to be rid of the tears. The idiot loved her and would still let her go.

A laugh escaped her. He was as much a fool as she. What a perfect pair they made.

Lilly moved as fast as she could to the door—and barreled straight into the butler.

Dithers caught her elbow to keep her upright. "Be careful, my lady, you could do yourself an injury. That would be most disagreeable to all the staff of Cottingstone."

Lilly gripped the rail for the climb. "Well, if I do, I will be in the right place to be fixed, won't I?"

"Can I speed your ascent, Miss Winter?"

"No thank you, Dithers. Why don't you go chase Mrs. Osprey around her office? I think she heads there at this time on most nights," Lilly confided and started up, grimacing as pain speared down her legs. She ignored it.

"I was aware of that," Dithers replied carefully.

She glanced down at him in consternation. "And you have never taken advantage of her seclusion before? Shame on you, Dithers. I'd heard you were a rogue."

"Reformed, as all men in love should be. However, I will remain until you reach the top at least."

"If you must, Dithers, but you are wasting valuable time," she warned him.

When she reached the top stair, she heard his rapid footsteps fade away.

Chapter Twenty-Nine

———————◆———————

"You are a fool, Giles."

He sat by the window looking out at the night, holding Lilly's old diary loosely in his hands. "You should not be here, Lilly," he warned her, his voice grim.

Lilly moved toward him. "What if I want to be?"

"That, of course, would require a wedding ceremony you don't want."

Lilly clutched the skirts of her borrowed gown in her sweaty palms and asked the fatal question. "What if I changed my mind?"

Giles spun around to face her and Lilly saw the glitter of tears on his cheeks. Lilly crossed the room to him and cupped his face between her hands. Such a dear, wicked, and sinful face. One she loved so very much. "You deserve more than a broken thing like me but I cannot live without you."

He gaped at her a long time but then wet his lips. "And you deserve better than a degenerate for a husband."

Lilly shook his head from side to side and smiled. "You are not a degenerate. You're wonderful. I love you."

He smiled as she denied his faults, but then scowled fiercely. "You are not broken. I have never known a stronger woman than you," Giles said, firmly clasping her hips.

"People will think you took pity on me or that I tricked you into marriage. Whenever you leave me, they will say I was too needy. They will say that I drove you away with my demands."

"I like that you need me, Lilly. I want you to." Giles turned his face and pressed a kiss to the palm of her hand, letting his lips caress her as she liked him to. "I won't ever leave you. You were going to leave me for the delights of a small village in Wales, remember?"

"I guess that makes me foolish too." She brushed her fingers through his hair. "So what do we do now? We were betrothed once. The way I understand matters of marriage when the couple is wildly in love, someone needs to go down on bended knee. I warn you that if you expect me to do it, you might have to help me to my feet again afterward."

"It will be my pleasure to do the truly hazardous tasks in this marriage," Giles promised.

Lilly grinned. "So?"

Giles sank to his knees and clasped both Lilly's hands in his. "Marry me, Lilly. Stay with me and share my life. Let me give you every pleasure I can, and some we invent together."

When Lilly nodded, Giles swept her into his arms and carried her to his bed.

"Stay with me from now on. I have the worst trouble sleeping without you beside me, darling."

Lilly laughed. "Do you know I have the same difficulty?"

"A perfect match then."

She kissed him into silence and tangled her fingers in his hair, holding him close to express how much she desired him. How could she have given him up?

Giles broke the kiss, rolled her over, and then went to work on the buttons of her gown. As each patch of flesh became exposed, Giles dug his fingers deep into Lilly's muscles, alternating with his lips until she was breathless with want. He touched her skin lavishly and made her crave him in ways she did not believe possible.

As Lilly melted into the mattress, she prayed that this time Giles would not be a gentleman. That he would not be proper. She liked the wicked man as he had always been. She knew exactly what she was getting herself into. A lifetime of pleasure at his hands.

She helped raise herself, and her gown and chemise were stripped from her in a moment. His fingers pushed under her stockings and he massaged her out of them with long, languid strokes, pausing to rub the arch of her foot and out to her toes.

Lips pressed to her foot and she flexed in response.

This was what she wanted from him. This drugging pleasure bound by trust, warmth, and friendship.

From there, he kissed up the back of her leg, kissing every inch of her skin until he reached the source of her most recent pain.

"You'll have a bruise," he told her before pressing his lips gently to the tender spot. She shuddered as pleasure washed over her.

Reaching behind her back, she struggled to touch any part of him she could find. He pressed his lips into the crease of her thigh, and her hips arched upwards to meet him.

He kissed her back, buried his lips into her neck, and suckled hard. Cloth scraped against her bottom and she wriggled into Giles. He settled beside her and pulled the pins from her hair, smoothing out the strands along her back and tickling her skin with the ends.

Lilly shuddered and turned over. "How much longer are you going to make me wait before you steal my virtue?"

———•———

"Tonight," he promised.

Lilly move on top of Giles and he was utterly breathless at the look in her eye. She was every bit as aroused as he. Dear God, the shudder that went through her when he had kissed her bottom defied description. As she attacked his clothing, he let himself be lulled by her movements, attempting to regain some control. As her lips settled on his neck, he started counting the number of plain women he had danced with in the past.

When his shirt was gone, he had moved on to the number of grim-looking men in parliament. That certainly cooled him. But when she had his trousers at his knees and took him in her hand, he lost all the benefits of those disturbing images. He rolled her over to her back and removed her hand from his cock. "If you kept that up, I will leave you disappointed," he warned.

The bounce of her breasts distracted him, and he took a hard nipple into his mouth and drew on it, shaping her breasts with his hands. He switched to her other breast and ran his tongue around the nipple as she pressed her chest upwards. He took in the hard peak with less finesse than he liked. Her painful grip on his hair assured him she welcomed his rougher play.

He raised himself to kiss her again, watching her as they rubbed together, seeing her gray eyes glowing in the candlelight. He kissed down the length of her body, settled between her bent knees and ran his hand over her thigh, upward into her blonde curls. He liked that she did not flinch from his close scrutiny, because he found himself fascinated by her pale curls and the pink lips beneath.

As his fingertips teased and parted her lower lips, they became slick with her moisture and his pulse raced, hungry for her around him. He lowered his mouth and tasted her, careful to keep his cock from touching anything. He did not want to come on the sheets tonight.

A low moan from her told him that she would be ready when the time came. Giles removed his mouth and pushed a finger inside her, pressing until his knuckles touched her springy curls and could go no farther. Lilly's back arched and she thrashed upon the bed as he worked inside her, feeling the soft passage tighten around his finger.

When he thought her ready, he added another, pushing in slowly, preparing her as much as he could. He wanted as little pain for her as possible.

Lilly gasped at the thicker intrusion and, as her juices coated his fingers, he sped up his movements. The sounds her body made were unbearable, and so erotic his legs started to quake.

When her hips were rising to meet his thrusts, he removed his fingers and rose to his knees to look down upon her. Her eyes were wild. She was breathing in rough pants, breasts jiggling deliciously in the candlelight. He wanted to slow things down, and tried to let her calm a bit before he went further, fearful that his entry was going to hurt if he rushed.

But when she gripped his hips, he had no choice but to obey her silent command. He fitted himself to her entrance, keeping his body weight from crushing her, and pressed in all the way, unable to stop until he was fully embedded within her.

Lilly shuddered violently and screamed out a release so great he thought her father would have heard her at the other end of the house.

Giles held perfectly still, counting sheep, mucky stables, and slimy green frogs as he resisted the urge to pump within her immediately. He could not believe she'd come that fast. The heat of her, the thrilling scream, and her clutching fingers had pushed his own arousal up a notch further than he needed right now.

He waited for her thighs to relax their hold on his hips, her hands to give up some of his flesh and slide down his sides before he dared move. He watched her face, flushed and sweat-stained, and felt extraordinarily proud. This woman's passion matched his. He'd never be able to leave her alone.

Lilly opened her eyes slowly, and smiled such a welcome that he could not help but thrust. Dear God, she destroyed him without trying. Her eyes misted with happiness and he kissed her, fully in control of their lovemaking at last.

Lilly glanced down to where they joined and her eyes widened. He pushed in to her limit and heard a little pant of air leave her lungs as his possession stirred her senses.

He loved that she was so fearless. She had been watching him for so long, but it was better to be with her like this at last. She was his, now and forever, and he belonged to her too.

A primal need rose to possess her completely.

As he thrust and withdrew, he checked for signs of pain on her face, but he could sense no discomfort from their joining or pain from her position.

Thrilling to every stroke, hearing every sound, drowning in the thick scent of arousal, Giles knew he had at last found what was missing from his life. Chills raced down his sweat-damp back as he held his body above Lilly, and he found a rhythm he could maintain until he lost himself to the pleasure.

When Lilly's hips rose to meet his thrusts, Giles sped his movements to give her more pleasure. Her breaths changed to gasps, and he grinned because she was with him again. Her legs wrapped high around his back, her feet brushed his bottom, and he could not hold back.

With excruciating care, he lowered himself onto her.

Lilly's hands gripped his sides and her nails bit deep, telling him without words that she was close to another release.

"I love you Lilly," he whispered, then repeated it over and over into her ear.

They cried out in unison.

Giles cuddled Lilly close for as long as he felt she could bear his weight and then lifted up.

Lilly's eyes were closed, and a small smile played around her mouth, so he assumed all was well with her. He gripped her hips and rolled them, keeping her close, laying her over him while remaining buried inside.

As he landed on his back, he slid her hair out of the way when it would have smothered him and pressed her head to his chest. He found his way under the counterpane, covered their sweat-damp bodies from the threat of getting chilled, and wrapped his arms tight around her, vowing never to let her go.

———◆———

Lilly stirred and flexed under the sheets as the sun rose, a discontented grumble emerging from her lips. Giles twirled a pale lock around his finger and waited patiently for her to wake fully. He'd never felt so satisfied and content.

Although his mind raced with plans for his future with Lilly, Giles closed his eyes again. He could not rush Lilly. The pace of his life had to slow to accommodate her needs and comfort from now on.

When she moved against him, he cracked his lids open wide enough to see what she was doing. She shifted again, drawing her knees together, curling onto her side. It had become a habit to keep watch over his little ghost, and now he could do it for the rest of his lifetime.

Giles turned toward her. She always appeared so so happy in her sleep.

Lilly's eyes fluttered open, and after a moment, a grin twisted her lips. She brushed her finger over his bottom lip and he twitched away. Lilly did it twice more, until he captured her fingertip and sucked it deep into his mouth. Her eyes widened, her lips parted to drag in a deep breath.

"I take it you want to wake me," Giles murmured when he released her finger. "Wretched woman. A man about to marry needs all the rest he can get. He needs to keep up his strength to meet the demands of his adorable wife."

Lilly's smile touched that part of him long dormant. His heart, his soul, the very essence of his existence depended on that smile. Giles tucked her against his chest, her back to his front, keeping her clever little fingers trapped beneath his. With his lips, he worshiped her neck as he rubbed his thickening cock into her soft bottom, making her moan in delight and him press harder still.

He captured her breast and would have continued onwards to further pleasures if his eyes were not drawn to the opening door, and the very unwelcome face peering inside his room.

Lord Winter.

The door crashed open to reveal a houseful of servants behind him, along with Lord Carrington, all smiling insanely as he attempted to make love to his future wife.

Lilly squeaked and attempted to hide. Giles flipped the covers up over her head. "Can we be of assistance?"

Carrington covered his face as if ashamed and turned away laughing.

"No escape at all now, daughter. You will be wed within the month, or sooner if a special license can be obtained." Lord Winter bellowed loud enough to make all the servants flinch at his fate, but not Giles. He'd always known he could only marry a woman he adored.

He peeked under the covers and met Lilly's cheeky smile. He loved Lilly with all his heart. She was the center of his world. "You will never hear me complain. Lilly was the one who compromised *me* and I demand she make an honest man of me."

Lilly nodded and suddenly pulled him under the sheets with her and proceeded to kiss him witless despite the audience still gathered at the door.

———— ◆ ————

IF YOU ENJOYED BROKEN DON'T MISS THE
NEXT DISTINGUISHED ROGUE

Charity

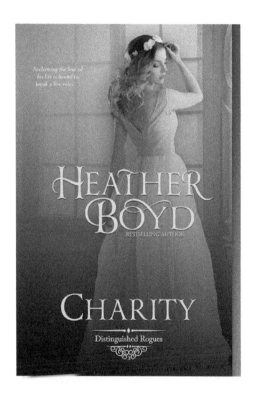

In the third instalment of the Distinguished Rogues series,
a desperate rogue will break every rule to reclaim the love of his life
before its too late.

Chapter One

Autumn, 1813
London

"The child is asleep now, Miss Birkenstock. You should put her into bed."

The nurse's curt voice dragged Agatha from her rebellious thoughts of running away to a simpler world where people kept their promises.

Wearily, she opened her eyes. "Yes, I believe you are right, Mrs. Bates."

She looked upon tiny Betty Smith lying peacefully in her arms at long last, and her heart fluttered. No matter how tightly the babe clutched Agatha's fingertip, or how much she longed to stay, she couldn't remain at the Grafton Street Orphanage overnight to oversee the child's care. The trustees would never stand for it. Nor would her grandfather.

Slowly, Agatha rose to her feet. The babe in her arms startled at the movement and Agatha pressed a kiss to her cheek. "Hush, sweetheart, all is well."

Betty grumbled and, instead of giving the sleeping infant up to the nurse's outstretched arms, Agatha carried the child to bed, tucked her snug into the linens, and then placed her favorite rag doll beside her. The nurse clucked her tongue in disapproval at the toy.

Agatha fingered the little girl's pale curls and smiled that Betty rested easily. "Please send word if her night should be disturbed again, Mrs. Bates. I will be here early tomorrow morning to visit with her."

"As you wish, miss."

No matter how harmless the words, the old nurse's tone

hinted she'd rather Agatha be gone from the orphanage, never to interfere with her charges again. Well, that wasn't going to happen. Not a chance of it.

After smoothing her hand over the child's pale curls one last time, Agatha straightened to look about the chamber. Six narrow beds hugged the imperfect walls of the chilly room, each containing a peeking set of eyes belonging to a child in need of warmth and kindness. She'd love to drag each of them from the covers, smother them with affection, and stay until they were all sound asleep. If she could take them from this depressing place and home with her tonight, she would be perfectly happy.

But her grandfather and the board of trustees wouldn't allow that either.

Agatha paced the length of the room, doing her best to ignore the cheerless severity of the chamber. The children's bodies under the frayed covers didn't so much as twitch. A fear of Nurse Bates' displeasure kept them still as statues, she was sure. Such strict adherence to rules saddened her. These children needed the freedom to run about on cool, green grass, to smile and be silly instead of being expected to appear perpetually grateful for the bed space they occupied.

She would promise them everything would be well, if she didn't harbor a kernel of doubt that she could live up to her own promises. The sting of disappointment was the hardest emotion to conquer. She would promise them no more than she could vouchsafe: her time, her affection, and a game of cricket in the tiny, rear walled garden if the weather allowed.

Even though the children showed no sign that they were awake, she made a point of checking each one to be sure they would be warm enough for the coming night. As Agatha reached the end of the room where the drafts were at their worst, the nurse cleared her throat. Nurse Bates always appeared anxious for her to leave, but Agatha refused to hurry. She checked the remaining children and left the room when she was ready.

Her maid waited in the front hall, hands clenched over Agatha's cloak. Nell rushed forward. "It be a frightful night outside, Miss Birkenstock. The fog is thicker than pea soup."

Since Nell was such a fanciful creature, often prone to exaggerate the mildest of events into the worst possible calamity,

Agatha disregarded her words. She donned her cloak, secured her reticule about her wrist, and then turned for the door. "It's just a bit of fog, Nell. It hardly signifies. Come along."

The butler opened the door for them and then stepped back. Pea soup, indeed. Agatha couldn't see the street clearly from the top step. Her confidence slipping a little, she hurried down the stairs and turned right into the mist. The orphanage door closed with a heavy thud.

Rushed, light footsteps behind her confirmed that Nell was but one pace away. "People get lost in the London fog, miss," Nell whispered.

"That shall not happen to us. I know my way home perfectly well."

Nevertheless, Agatha clutched her cloak tightly about her and kept her eyes fixed on her path. She followed the high front fences along Grafton Street, ignoring the disturbing way nearby houses appeared out of the thick fog only to disappear from view a moment later. It was eerie and quiet and, with Nell crowding her left shoulder, Agatha's heart raced in a foolish rhythm.

The maid's nervousness tainted Agatha's mood. She turned left at the corner of Dover Street, chiding herself that she knew this route like the back of her own hand. The landmarks between the orphanage and home were distinctive. If she paid the proper attention, instead of panicking as Nell appeared to be, they'd be home as quick as if walking about on a clear, sunny day.

As she approached the next corner, Agatha's gaze drifted to the left. A faint glow burned from the windows of a tall townhouse, signifying that some amusement might be underway within.

A deep sadness gripped her. Could she hear laughter from Lady Carrington's house? She slowed her steps. With the thick fog muting all sound but their breathing, it was impossible to tell with any certainty where the laughter came from. Perhaps there was a dinner party in progress. After all, Lady Carrington was very fond of entertaining, and she had her son's position in society to maintain. The viscountess must be so happy that Oscar had secured such an advantageous match with an earl's daughter.

The hot sting of jealously burned through her body. She pushed the sensation down, leaving only her teeth to unclench.

Perfect Lady Penelope. Wealthy and titled Lady Penelope. Desirable attributes for the image-conscious viscount.

The front door of Lady Carrington's townhouse opened. Dark shapes—a man and woman, judging by their attire—descended the steps and clambered into a waiting carriage. Agatha expelled a sharp breath. She should not be interested in the goings-on of the Carrington family. She was far removed from their business now.

Determined to forget them, she started off again, but her eyes strayed to the departing grand carriage, and she wondered who it had contained.

Agatha stumbled off the pavement onto the Hay Hill crossing and pulled up sharply. Her steps had propelled her faster than she'd thought. Woolgathering on a foggy night was foolish in the extreme. She needed to keep her wits about her in order to avoid becoming turned around.

Nell clutched at her arm. "Are we lost?"

"No, of course not. I just stumbled."

The maid yanked her fingers from Agatha's upper arm. Agatha hadn't meant to snap, but agonizing over past mistakes was a futile endeavor that no amount of tears or self-recriminations could fix. She was angry at her own foolish gullibility, not the maid.

With that thought firmly in mind, Agatha turned right and hurried along the deserted street, pleased to be almost halfway home. She turned right again and peered into the mist, looking for the next cross street on her left. The comfort of Berkeley Square should be very close.

More Regency Romance from Heather Boyd...

Saints and Sinners Series

Book 1: The Duke and I
Book 2: A Gentleman's Vow
Book 3: An Earl of Her Own

Rebel Hearts Series

Book 1: The Wedding Affair
Book 2: An Affair of Honor
Book 3: The Christmas Affair
Book 4: An Affair so Right

The Wild Randalls Series

Book 1: Engaging the Enemy
Book 2: Forsaking the Prize
Book 3: Guarding the Spoils
Book 4: Hunting the Hero

Miss Mayhem Series

Book 1: Miss Watson's First Scandal
Book 2: Miss George's Second Chance
Book 3: Miss Radley's Third Dare
Book 4: Miss Merton's Last Hope

And many more...

About Heather Boyd

———◆———

Determined to escape the Aussie sun on a scorching camping holiday, Heather picked up a pen and notebook from a corner store and started writing her very first novel—Chills. Years later, she is the author of over thirty sexy regency historical romances. Addicted to all things tech (never again will Heather write a novel longhand) and fascinated by English society of the early 1800's, Heather spends her days getting her characters in and out of trouble and into bed together (if they make it that far). She lives on the edge of beautiful Lake Macquarie, Australia with her trio of mischievous rogues (husband and two sons) along with one rescued cat whose only interest in her career is that it provides him with food on demand and a new puppy that is proving a big distraction.

You can find details of her work and writing at
www.Heather-Boyd.com